THE SUMMER
MAN

BY

S.D. PERRY

THE SUMMER MAN

47N⬤RTH

Published by 47North
P.O. Box 400818
Las Vegas, NV 89140

ISBN-13: 9781611099164
ISBN-10: 1611099161
Library of Congress Control Number: 2012951474

For Private "Slippy" Eddie of the Heroes

and those who named him. And for Yama,

Lord of Death, a.k.a. Crunchy Face.

CHAPTER

1

Amanda was stoned out of her mind the night everything started to change. So high, in fact, that the sounds of the party around her, the voices and laughter, all sort of blended together into a big, echoey stew, punctuated by the beat of bass-heavy music coming from another room and by the old movie playing not far from where she sat. David Lynch, she thought. Something with Laura Dern, anyway.

The way everyone kept moving around didn't help define matters; from her position, leaning against the wall next to the bathroom, the shapes of the other partygoers were vague, dark blurs, people shuffling themselves to watch the film, to pass a pipe, to leave the room or enter it. Half the people there seemed to be wearing black. At least half.

"Me too," she said, looking down at her skirt, noting how pale her skin looked through one of the carefully cultivated rips. Man, she was white. She was one of those people who didn't tan, anyway, just turned red, and too much sun gave her a headache. She wore sunblock all the time, put it on after every shower. Which meant she was white, white, white. Kind of fat, too. The tear in her skirt revealed a tiny white island, rising from a black abyss. She seriously needed a new diet.

Devon, sitting next to her on the floor, was saying something. Amanda blinked, focused on his wide, seemingly sober gaze. Ha. As if he hadn't finished off most of a six-pack by now. At least.

"What?" she asked. "Did you say something?" Her voice seemed to be going through a tunnel, echoing away as she spoke. Cool. Weird.

"That's what I asked you," Devon said. "You said something."

"When?"

"A minute ago," he said, then shook his head slightly. "Never mind. You're out of it. High as a fucking kite."

Amanda hesitated, digesting the information, then grinned. It was kind of embarrassing to be caught out unable to function, but it was only Devon, he of the perfect skin and just-so hair and the charming overbite, which he hated. She couldn't count the number of times she'd seen him puking in the bushes, beer being his usual drug of choice. He said pot made him paranoid. She thought it just made him think too much…which, if she were him, she'd probably want to avoid, too. He was smart and funny and he had friends, but being gay in high school—he wasn't technically "out," but it was pretty obvious, even to a bunch of backwoods hicks like their alleged peers—was a suckfest, no doubt. He got hassled all the time.

"I am not; fuck off," she said. Too loud. A couple of the movie-watchers glanced over at her, then turned back to the film. Onscreen, someone was punching someone else. Blood splattered.

Devon was smiling, too. He drained his beer, then set it aside. "I do believe I will. There's more beer here, somewhere. And I need a smoke. I think Keith's back from the store; I'll see if he got ours. I'll be back in a few, OK?"

Amanda nodded, slightly amazed at how he was able to talk in complete sentences, to express whole thoughts. There was a beginning, middle, and end to his plan, and he hadn't forgotten any of it as it came out of his mouth. Impressive.

I want a smoke, she said, but only thought it, which was just as well. Devon was already gone, rising in one fluid motion, disappearing around the corner into the darkened room.

A dilemma, then. Cigarettes were outside only; Pam Roth's parents were out of town for three more days, but Pam insisted that they'd be able to tell if anyone had smoked inside. Pot didn't count; incense covered that up pretty well, and the actual smoke-to-air ratio wasn't so bad, but cigarettes were a different deal. So, out back with the dog crap and the cold, cold night, where the other addicted souls huddled together, blowing stinky smoke at the moon. Making their clothes reek. Making their lungs black.

Sounded fucking *awesome*. Amanda started to get up, then remembered that Devon was coming back to get her—wasn't he? Or was he going to have a smoke first? She tried to remember...he had been unclear. They were both out of cigarettes, but Keith had made a run to the Qwik-Mart at the bottom of the hill for like seven different brands, some soda, candy, possibly even beer— if Clark Emory was working, he'd sell to Keith—carrying a scrawled list and a fat handful of crumpled bills. Missy had probably gone with him. Keith and Missy were practically married... and if they were back, there was a hard pack of Camel filters and a grape soda waiting for her, beer and barfy Winstons for Devon. No way that fag would come back for her before catching a smoke first; she was on her own.

God, grape soda and a cigarette. She ached for them suddenly, and she decided she would brave her stoned legs, find her coat—it was almost the middle of June (school out for one whole day now, hoo-fuckin'-rah!) but the nights were still way too cold to go without—and head out back, see if Devon had—

Somebody started to scream. Amanda froze, and the terrible, high-pitched shriek filled her ears, filled the room, went on and on like the end of the world. It was loud—or it *seemed* loud, but it was in her head, too, deafening, but she could still hear talking, heard someone laugh a few feet away from her. She looked at the TV, saw that the movie was still playing—and then a movie began to play out in her mind, like a vivid memory or dream. It overtook the room, the party, carrying her inside herself.

What the fuck?

There was a girl, running, screaming, and behind her a dark shape, a man in dark clothes; his hands were empty, but he was so much bigger than her, faster, and he grabbed her, caught her sleeve, and then pulled her close. The girl screamed again and he shook her, hard, and now Amanda could see her face—

That's Lisa Meyer, what the fuck—

It was dark, and there were trees; they were outside somewhere, and Lisa stopped screaming because the man's hands were on her throat now. She was making horrible choking sounds, her hands fluttering up, pulling uselessly at the thick fingers around her throat. Her eyes were bulging, her face red, drool running over her lower lip as the attacker squeezed and squeezed. He was breathing hard, fast, like he was excited, and as Amanda watched he leaned forward almost casually and bit Lisa's face, high on her cheek.

Blood poured from the bite. Lisa's entire body flailed and shook, but he was holding tight; her hands fluttered uselessly, and the attacker grinned, his teeth red, and Amanda saw that she knew who he was, it was the fucking *shop* teacher for fuck's sake, Mr. Billings was killing Lisa Meyer; she was sagging now, and he was chewing on her fucking *face*—

Amanda screamed. She screamed, and for a few seconds it was the only sound in the room as the dark shapes around her fell silent, as someone snapped off the movie. Then there were hands on her, excited voices, someone telling her to calm down, someone else telling her to shut the fuck up. Somebody touched her spiky hair, and then the lights came on, a painful shock of light that illuminated the shabby carpet, the off-white walls, a dozen familiar faces looming over her, teenage and afraid and curious and surprised.

"'Manda?"

Devon, pushing through, crouching at her side. She started to cry then, too terrified to care that she was sobbing in front of everyone, that she was being a total freak. Devon put his arm around her, and she smelled smoke, smelled the product in his hair, and she cried harder into his itchy sweater.

"It's OK, sweetie," Devon cooed, patting her back. "Breathe, OK? Breathe."

People were talking. "What happened?"

"Is she dosed? 'Cause if it's that shit that Mark Jacobsen got from Seattle, it's supposed to be bad shit, and I heard—"

"Is that Amanda Young?"

"Jesus, that scared the *shit* out of me—"

Amanda closed her eyes, clutched Devon tightly. She wanted them to shut up; she wanted to be home in bed in her flannel night-shirt, warm and safe and sleepy. She wanted a fucking cigarette.

"What happened?" Devon asked, his voice low and close to her ear.

Amanda gasped a hitching breath. "I saw—I swear to God, I saw Lisa Meyer getting killed, I saw Mr. Billings killing Lisa fucking *Meyer*!"

She tried to say it softly but it was too difficult; her straining lungs pushed it out with force. A number of frowns now, the people closest—Doug and Sean from drama, Sean's little sister, Ally—drawing back slightly.

"What?"

"What did she say?"

Devon pulled back to look at her. "OK, that's cool," he said, his voice smooth and relaxed, pitched to carry. "Not a fuckin' show, people. She's cool. Back off, OK?"

He smiled at her as those gathered around started to move off. "You're OK," he said, more softly. "Let's go have a smoke, just hang out for a few minutes…reefer madness, right? You're fine now. No big deal, we'll just hang out."

Amanda managed to stop crying, though her voice was still catching, the fear and panic close. "No, I'm not high…listen, I saw…I'm…I mean, I am, but—"

"Relax," Devon said. "Whatever it was, you're fine. It's all good. Oh, and Keith brought our smokes, they're in the kitchen. Why don't we go get them, get you an apple or something, and head out back?"

He grinned, lowering his voice slightly. "Come on, we can make plans for the big picnic. You know Justin Anders got tapped to sing the anthem this year? What a fuckin' joke. We could show up with air horns, maybe, blast 'em when he hits the high note. What do you think?"

She'd seen him do this before, at Chris Lahey's house last December, when Doug had taken acid and gotten all freaked-out about his uncle being dead. Doug's uncle had been carjacked the year before in Seattle. Devon had been all Mr. Rogers smooth, as relaxing as a warm bath, and had talked Doug out of a hysterical fit and into a lengthy philosophical conversation about the sociological impact of the Butthole Surfers. Watching him do his routine now, trying to take care of her, gave her something to focus on. She took a deep breath, blew it out.

"I got high, OK, but it's not like that," she said. Other than a general brain fuzziness, she now felt quite sober. "Devon, I *saw* something…"

She looked into his eyes, his familiar, cool, gray eyes, determined to make him see how serious she was, how not-crazy. He was her closest friend; he had to see that much—

"Is she OK?"

Pam Roth stood behind Devon, arms crossed tightly. She looked worried.

Devon stood up. "She's fine."

"Because if she's freaking out, she should maybe go home," Pam said, her voice a near whisper. "I mean, no offense, but if my parents even find out I had people over, I'm so totally fucked."

Amanda pulled herself to her feet, put on a smile. It was a dismal one, she could tell, but it was the best she could do.

"I'm good," she said. A flat-out lie, but she wasn't about to get her ass thrown out, either. Whatever had happened to her, she knew that going home wasn't an option. It was her mother's night off; she'd be parked on the couch and looking to engage. "I'm sorry."

The lame smile worked, somewhat. Pam's frown faded, and the few others still standing close by started to wander away. The television was turned back on, the movie started up again.

"What happened, anyway?" Pam asked.

I had a vision, Amanda thought, and though nothing like that had ever happened to her—it was strictly for movies or TV or bad thriller novels—she thought it was true, and knew also that if she talked about it, she'd be branded a total psycho. Worse than already being the only real retro-goth in a metalhead high school. Port Isley was a small town, and word traveled fast.

So what? You and Devon'll be out of here by the end of the summer, God willing, the second he turns eighteen. Fuck the townies.

So what was she knew better. And maybe she had fallen asleep, a little…

"I dozed off, is all," she said. "Got high and then fell asleep, with that movie on…"

She nodded toward the screen, where some guy in makeup was lip-synching a Roy Orbison tune. She thought she sounded convincing, and Pam was nodding. Amanda relaxed a little further, forcing the thoughts of Lisa and Mr. Billings away, far away.

Her excuse made sense, actually. It made a lot more sense than what had seemed so real only a few moments before—

Lisa Meyer stepped out from behind Pam, wearing a puzzled smile.

"Hey," she said. "Someone said you were talking about me?"

Amanda stared at her, entirely dumbstruck, though a part of her mind was already filling it in for her.

Premonition, like ESP or something—

Her rational self shouted it down. It had *seemed* real; oh, totally real, but she must have fallen asleep and dreamed it. Must have, because psychics weren't legit, everyone knew that, at least people who weren't dumb as rocks. At best they talked themselves into believing they had some kind of special power, but mostly they were money-grubbing shitheels, psychics, palm readers, astrology, all that shit.

Lisa was still waiting. She was a senior—or had been; she'd gotten her diploma at Friday's ceremony—and was pretty OK. Not popular, exactly, but not bottom of the barrel, either. Her family was a hair above poor through the winter, lower-middle class in the summer, same as most of Port Isley; Lisa's dad was an accountant or something; her mother worked in the bookstore on Water Street. She was just a girl, some random girl who Amanda had seen being murdered by Ed Billings, the shop teacher at their high school. Mr. Billings also coached girls' basketball. And Lisa was on the team, Amanda remembered…

Don't try to make connections. It was a dream.

She smiled at Lisa, the smile better now, almost real. "It was nothing. I was asleep."

Ally Fergus, Sean's little sister, was standing close by. "Not nothing," she supplied helpfully. "She said she saw you get killed by Mr. Billings. Screamed like her tits were on fire, too. What, you didn't hear her?"

Lisa wasn't smiling anymore. She looked from Ally back to Amanda, her expression unreadable. "Are you serious?"

Devon scowled at Ally. "Fuck off, brat."

"*You* fuck off," Ally mumbled, but melted away a moment later. Amanda tried her smile again on Lisa.

"I got too high or something," she started. "Had a nightmare is all. Really, it's—"

"That's fucked," Lisa said, her voice tight. Her face was flushed, and Amanda realized that mild, pleasant Lisa, whom she'd grown up with, known for most of her young life, and never known to have a harsh word for anyone, was totally pissed off. "Why don't you keep your little dramas to yourself from now on, OK? No one wants to hear your shit."

"Jesus, Lis, you on the rag or something?" Devon asked. His voice was mild with surprise. "Calm down. She said—"

"I heard what she said, and it's…it's *bullshit*," Lisa snapped. "Like usual. Just stay away from me, all right?"

She turned and stalked off, leaving Amanda and Devon staring after her, Amanda feeling like she'd been kicked in the stomach. They'd never been friends, but she'd always considered Lisa to be kind of a neutral personality, not an enemy, certainly. The people watching dropped their gazes, turned away, tried to act like they hadn't been entirely engrossed in the exchange.

"Psycho cunt," Devon said loudly. A couple of people laughed. "Come on, let's get some air."

Amanda allowed herself to be pulled toward the back door, her head spinning, stumbling over an extended foot as someone turned the lights out again as the party returned to itself. Everything had happened so fast, she didn't know what to make of it, of anything.

The air outside wasn't as cold as she'd expected, summer coming on fast, and as Devon handed her a smoke, one of his barfy Winstons, she had a sudden flash of understanding, a thought that was complete in its clarity.

He's here, she thought, and because she didn't know what that meant, didn't know how she knew or who *he* was or pretty much anything at all, it seemed, she began to cry.

CHAPTER

2

Lisa waited a few steps down the trail, in the dark. Coach usually parked at the head of the trail—there were no streetlights where Eleanor dead-ended—and she went to his car, but tonight, she wanted to walk and talk, not to do it, not have sex.

Thinking of sex with him gave her a chill, sweet and heavy and terrible, too, her heart suddenly picking up speed. He was married and more than twice her age, and she knew what people would think if they knew, but it felt so good, so wrong and wild and good…

He says I'm beautiful; he says I'm his beautiful girl.

She clamped down on the thought. It was over. It had to be over now. He had been getting…strange. It had been a mistake, telling him that she loved him. She hadn't meant to, but two weeks ago he'd said he loved her, and she'd had to say *something*, she couldn't just leave him hanging. And then he'd started talking about the two of them running away together, and she had nodded and agreed because she didn't want him to feel bad, but she had to tell him; she couldn't let him keep thinking what he was thinking.

Lisa crossed her arms against the chill, wishing she had somewhere to sit, hoping it wouldn't go too badly, that he wouldn't be too upset. She knew it was going to hurt him and was afraid he might cry or even yell at her. He'd never yelled at her before—not since they'd started doing it—but he'd raised his voice to the team more than once, like when they were playing Port Angeles and gone into halftime down by seven…Coach definitely had a temper, but he wasn't crazy; he wouldn't yell if they were outside where anyone could hear them…

That made her think of Amanda Young, what she'd said at Pam's party. Lisa's lip curled. Total bullshit. Coach would never hurt her, never, and Amanda was a bitch for calling that shit out right in front of everybody, practically. That was not cool. Nobody knew anything; they'd been careful, there was no public connection between her and Coach, and Amanda's dramatic bullshit scene had created one.

All the more reason to do this now.

She saw the glow of approaching headlights a block down, heard the familiar purr of the Volvo's engine. He could have walked, he lived close enough, but he almost always drove if he could, so they'd have a dry, clean place to lie down. Not tonight, though, not unless it was to say good-bye, one final time together…

That sweet, heavy chill tried to overtake her again, but she was suddenly nervous, because there was his car, it was time, she was going to tell him, tell Coach—

Ed! His name is Ed!

—that she didn't want to be with him anymore.

She took a deep breath, straightened her shoulders as the lights splashed over the dead end's turnout, trying to make herself ready. Walk and talk. It would all turn out OK.

><

Miranda Greene-Moreland breezed into the newspaper office early Monday morning with a beaming smile and open arms, followed a beat later by her husband. James Greene-Moreland was lugging a large cardboard box—presumably containing the picnic leaflets—and he set it on Bob's desk with an audible sigh of relief.

"Robert!" Miranda said, and Bob stood, allowing himself to be embraced, his cheek smacked. As usual, Miranda reeked of lavender oil. Her outfit today was a long, blousy floral affair over an ankle-length skirt, belted with a wide macramé sash that she had undoubtedly made herself.

"Please, Miranda, it's Bob," Bob said, knowing she'd ignore him. She always did. "We've brought the flyers," Miranda said. "They turned out *beautifully*. James, show Robert the flyer."

James hurried to comply, handing over one of the leaflets, a half page of tan paper—what Miranda would undoubtedly call "ocher"—that was adorned with a pretty good sketch of the lighthouse to one side. COME ONE AND ALL, the flyer proclaimed, and beneath that:

PORT ISLEY'S ANNUAL EMBRACE OF THE SUMMER SOLSTICE
FINE FOOD, GOOD COMPANY, DIVERSIONS OF EVERY KIND

At the bottom, in smaller print, were the specifics—June 21, eleven a.m. to eleven p.m., Stanton's Point Park at the lighthouse.

'Embrace of the Summer Solstice'? What the hell was wrong with 'picnic'?

"Isn't it *perfect*?" Miranda said, not really a question so much as an exclamation. "Simple, clear, and concise, but inviting, too—the font is Copperplate Gothic Light. James actually suggested Times New Roman, but the Copperplate is so much more refined, don't you think?"

"I like the lighthouse," Bob said.

"I *know*," Miranda said, presumably in agreement. "It's by Darrin Everret. He's new this year, came to us all the way from Massachusetts. All his landscapes are simply *amazing*. He did a piece on one of the trails in Kehoe Park? You can just *smell* the trees, it's so real."

"Well, I can't thank you enough for picking the flyers up," Bob said, hoping to deter her from launching into a fresh spiel of uninspired adjectives. Once she started talking about the retreat's new "prodigies," he'd be doomed to a good half hour of *amazing*.

"Or designing them," he added, before she could remind him. "They're very nice. Um, eloquent."

"They are, aren't they?" Miranda gushed. "Now, they'll be going out in this week's edition, is that right?"

As if she didn't know. "That's the plan," Bob said. The *Port Isley Press*—managed, operated, and edited by the silver-haired Bob "Robert" Sayers—came out every other Wednesday. Since the picnic was on the coming Saturday, having it go out two weeks from now didn't make a whole lot of sense.

"Wonderful," she said. Miranda had crowned herself Isley's unofficial PR personality at some point and had decided their annual picnic wasn't trumpeted nearly loudly enough, to her taste. She'd actually lobbied for the job, presenting her case at one of the council's quarterly meetings, offering to foot the cost of advertising herself. The council's response had been a big shrug, which had pretty much mirrored Bob's regard for the issue, thus leaving Ms. Miranda Greene-Moreland in charge of the yearly picnic flyer.

Summer solstice embrace flyer, actually, Bob thought. *Good Lord.*

Miranda filled Bob in on the news from the retreat—officially the Greene-Moreland Artisans' Community—as James fussed with the flyers. There were several new artists, twelve in all, making it a full seventeen residents for the summer. Bob nodded at what she said, the quicker to relieve himself of her presence. He didn't dislike Miranda, exactly, or her henpecked husband—she was like a force of nature, to be endured rather than judged, and her husband was as close to a cardboard cutout as a person could get—but

Bob had work to do. Deadline to get the issue to the printer's over in Port Angeles wasn't until six, but while his pieces were finished, he had yet to edit what his "reporters" had turned in. This week, there was still the high school English teacher's monthly book review to get to, plus a few final tidbits from this year's journalism class. He hadn't looked at Nancy's stuff, either. There was also one of Dick Calvin's gardening columns. Dick didn't understand what punctuation was for; his pieces always took time.

Which Nancy was going to do, Bob thought, stealing a glance at the clock by the door. *Where the hell is she, anyway?* He didn't particularly give a crap about punctuality, but Nancy was almost always in on Mondays by eight, eight thirty at the latest. It was after nine already.

"All done," James said, smiling. He held an armful of bundled flyers.

Nodding at him, Miranda wrapped up her gently wandering rant about the spiritual rewards of art, how much more satisfying those were than the monetary, and leaned in to kiss Bob's cheek once more.

"It's been wonderful, as always," she said. "Now, you'll be at the picnic, of course."

"Of course," Bob said. Everyone would be. There were connections to be made, affairs to rekindle, summer faces to be air-kissed. It usually had a better turnout than the Fourth, when half of Isley would be out on boats, watching Port Angeles's firework show. Or getting drunk at a backyard barbecue.

Behind Miranda, the door to the office opened. Nancy Biggs, his sole part-time employee, walked in. Her expression was dark, almost grim, but when she saw that the Greene-Morelands were in the office, she smiled widely. Bob could barely tell it was fake.

Miranda didn't bother with the hug-kiss for Nancy—Ms. Greene-Moreland only seemed to deem it appropriate with men—but she did go through the flyer presentation again. Nancy responded appropriately, briefly oohing over the lighthouse drawing…but then went out of her way to apologize to Bob for being late, which was when he knew that something was up. Nancy cared as much about being on time as he did.

Miranda took the hint and sailed out of the office after another round of see-you-at-the-picnics, James at a close heel. The second the door closed, Nancy dropped the smile.

"They found a body at Kehoe Park," she said.

"What? When? Who did?" Even in his surprise, he had to appreciate Nancy's decision to hurry the Greene-Morelands off before speaking; if she'd dropped that particular bomb with Miranda in earshot, they'd have had to suffer her for another hour.

"A body," Nancy said. "This morning, by the trail the kids use to get to school."

"A kid found the body?"

She shook her head. "School's out now, remember? Since Friday. A jogger, I think. A teenager."

"The jogger was, or the victim?"

"Was what?"

Bob clenched his teeth and tried to remember that Nancy tended to rattle easily. "Nancy, who was killed?"

If she noticed his agitation, her face didn't show it. She simply seemed anxious. "A teenage girl, is what I heard. This morning. I got up just before eight, and there were already deputies there."

It took the county sheriff's people almost an hour to get to Port Isley, their upscale little town on the northwest tip of the Olympic Peninsula. Someone had called it in early. Assuming that the chief had called the county after securing the scene, the body had been found—or reported, at least—no later than six thirty.

"By your apartment?" he asked. Nancy lived in one of the nicer complexes west of the park, on the back of the hill.

"Yeah. Well, that little dead end half a block away, where the trail starts. And there was another state car at the main entrance, on Eleanor. I swung by on my way in."

"Any idea who was killed?"

Nancy shook her head. "Annie was there, but she said she couldn't talk. She said she'd try to call later, once Vincent says OK."

Annie Thomas was their "in" at the police office, part of Chief Vincent's summer patrol. Stan Vincent employed about twenty full-time officers between June and September, plus any number of part-timers. In the off-season, there were only ten, and Vincent still sometimes closed the office on Sunday afternoons, routing everything through cell phones. Port Isley wasn't exactly abuzz with crime.

"She's who told me it was a girl. She also said...she said it was a mess," Nancy added, her voice lowering as though they weren't alone. "That it was most definitely homicide."

"Who found her? The body, I mean?" Bob was surprised to find that he felt a bit flustered himself. He'd been a reporter for almost forty years, interned on a paper right out of high school, and though he'd never worked a crime beat, he'd seen a few murder scenes in his time. Since coming to Port Isley, though? Not a homicide town. He'd lived there nine years and thought he could count the number on one hand.

"Maybe Nora Dickerson? She was there, in her sweats. Or Poppy Peters, he walks in the park most mornings. Could have been one of the summer people, though."

Bob nodded, looked at the clock. He should wait for Annie to call, or put in a call himself to Stan Vincent; the guy was uptight but usually fair...it was still pretty early, though...

Fuck it. Bob walked to the door, grabbed his coat off the hook. "I'm going up there," he said. "Can you man the office? Take a look at Dick's column, check over the book review?"

"I can, but…I thought I could go with you," she said. "I mean, this is a real story, isn't it?"

A real story. And right at the kickoff of tourist season. He'd be hearing from Dan Turner within the hour, probably chockfull of phrases like "let's handle this carefully" and "we don't want to start a panic." There was no way the council would trust Bob to go solo on this, not without at least trying to help spin it…and considering that the *Press* only ran because of a healthy town subsidy, courtesy of the mayor's office, *and* half the ads in his little rag came from council members or relatives thereof, he'd have no choice but to play ball. Even a decade ago, the very thought would have raised his ethical hackles. These days…these days, deciding not to run some nasty little detail in order to spare someone—a neighbor or friend, likely—pain or embarrassment didn't strike him as all that terrible.

A murder, though.

"Yeah," he said. "Looks like it. But we've got to get this week to bed, and you're better on layout than I am. A lot better."

Nancy looked pained.

"But I was already up there…doesn't that make it my story?" she asked.

Bob shrugged into his coat. "In comic books, maybe," he said. "Don't worry, you can write up Deputy Annie's interview, do all the follow-up. I just want to see what's going on."

He reminded her to clear a spot on the front page—he'd written an op-ed on classic film that could hold until a future issue; that would give them enough space with a little juggling— and promised to pick up coffee on the way back, which earned him an actual smile. Then he was on his way, stepping out of the small building that housed the *Press* and Wiseman's Insurance and into a brilliantly bright day, the sky cloudless, the wind from the bay sharp and numbing this close to the water. He considered walking—Kehoe Park was maybe fifteen minutes from the office—but it was almost straight up the hill, too. And there was the paper to consider. He didn't want to be out long; Nancy couldn't be expected to do everything...

Could be you're just getting old, Bob, he told himself as he settled into his battered, aging pickup. *Don't want to walk when you could drive.*

Well, no shit, he thought, and cranked the heater before starting up the hill.

✥

As soon as the police let her go, Nora went home, ticking off a to-do list as she jogged the half mile from the park. She'd want to call Curt, first, obviously, shower...Then she'd hit the Klatch, to tell Jen.

She'll shit, Nora thought, feeling an anticipatory guilty glee, *she'll just* shit.

It was funny. Jen had just been talking about personal safety, hadn't she? Like her and Curt, Jen and Alex had migrated to Port Isley from a larger city—Seattle for Curt and Nora, LA for Jen and Alex. Jen ran Coffee Klatch, a charming little cafe just off Main, and the two would meet up most mornings for lattes. Two—or three?—days ago, they'd been talking about how strange it was, not to live somewhere you had to worry about people breaking into your car, and then Jen had said that with the summer people coming, she and Alex had been talking about getting a dog, for protection. There were a number of drifters who inevitably blew through each year. What little crime there was in Isley always seemed to be a summer thing. Never mind that both couples had been summer people to Isley for a handful of years before; now that they were "natives," the annual tourists were to be despised, just the tiniest bit. And really, there *were* always a few strange men wandering around each summer.

She winced and drew a deep breath as she turned up her drive. It had been terrible, less than halfway through her run and then just stumbling across her like that, one pale hand practically right on the path, the rest of her crumpled in a little runoff trench that skirted that part of the trail. The state of her clothes, the rips and the stains...

...her face...

Nora stopped at the attached garage and leaned in to stretch her hamstrings, breathing deeply. She hoped she wouldn't end up with some sort of posttraumatic disorder from what she'd seen, but she could already imagine picturing that poor girl every time she closed her eyes.

It had taken Chief Vincent and two of his people less than fifteen minutes to get there. Nora had been impressed by Chief Vincent's thoroughness, using a video camera, blocking the paths, just like the true-crime-type shows she occasionally caught on cable, only with the dull parts left in—the waiting, the bland conversations among those who waited. Funny how reality could be so much less dramatic than television.

I saw plenty enough drama, she thought, visualizing the girl's face as she grabbed one ankle, lifting her heel up to her butt, stretching her quads. Mutilated, no other word for it, and Nora was pretty sure she'd seen bite marks. The girl had apparently been a local, Lisa something. When one of the officers had seen her, he'd said it was Lisa something before Vincent had shushed him. Meyer? Myron?

Nora shook her head and went inside, kicking her shoes off in the kitchen. She took a shower first, then called Curt. He needed several assurances that she was well enough to let him stay at work and actually brought up the whole getting a gun thing again. She decided to go to the Klatch, but after she'd dressed and started up the SUV, she felt compelled to drive by the park on her way. And when she slowed to a stop behind the parked ambulance— its lights dead, the attendants standing by for a cigarette as they waited for the police to finish whatever they were doing—she felt further compelled to get out for a moment, to stand with the dozen other watchers. Nora didn't recognize most of the watching group—summer people, mostly, although Sadie Truman was there. Sadie nodded and smiled at her but was too immersed in conversation with some overdressed summer woman to come over. When a hand touched her shoulder, Nora jumped.

Then smiled. It was Bob Sayers, one of the more interesting local characters…he ran the town paper and was a popular dinner guest with the better educated of Port Isley's population. Bob had worked for the *Seattle Post-Intelligencer* for decades as a reporter, before retiring to Isley.

Bob smiled back. "Sorry," he said.

"That's OK," she said. "I'm not usually so jumpy."

Bob tilted his head toward the park and the gathered cops. "Understandable, considering. I heard there's been a murder."

Nora nodded. "A local girl. Right on the main trail."

Bob lowered his voice, leaning in slightly. His breath was warm and inoffensive. "You saw it?"

"On or off the record?" she asked, smiling again.

Bob grinned. He was handsome, in a paternal sort of way— silver hair, warm eyes, good crow's feet—though a little too old for her to seriously flirt with. Besides which, she and Curt weren't that bored with each other. Not yet, anyway.

"Absolutely on," he said. "But if I quote you, you don't have to be Nora Dickerson. You could be 'a female jogger,' if you'd rather. Or just 'local citizen.'"

Nora kept smiling, but hesitated anyway. No one had *told* her not to speak with the press, but it seemed obvious, what with the victim's family notification and all. Did they already know? Surely by now.

Nora nodded. "Yes, I saw her. I—I found her, I guess. I called the police, anyway."

Bob's expression turned solemn. "That must have been scary. Were you out jogging?"

"Yes. And yes, it was," she said. "I was just a couple miles in, too. I hit the trail, probably around six thirty, and I was just past this dip in the path, maybe two hundred meters in, and there she was."

She grimaced. "Just lying there in this little runoff next to one of the trees, faceup, one hand practically right out on the path. Her eyes were open, but it was obvious that she was dead, that she wasn't *seeing* anything, you know…"

Was she babbling? She stopped talking. Bob nodded. She had the impression that he was listening very carefully.

"I heard it was bad," he said. His tone was gentle.

"It was definitely unpleasant," she said. "There was…there was a lot of damage."

"Did you recognize her?"

"No, but one of the deputies said that it was Lisa. Lisa Meyer, I think. Definitely Lisa something."

Bob opened his mouth to say something, then closed it, gazing over her shoulder. Nora turned, saw that there was a flurry of motion among the assembled police. Several of them, the police chief included, were hurrying to their cars. Vincent shouted a few orders to those remaining behind before climbing into his 4x4. His face was decidedly flushed. The state cars turned on their flashing lights, and all of them—three cars but at least seven people, in all—sped away from the park, barely slowing at the cross street as they took off toward downtown, east, up and over the hill.

"What's going on?" Nora asked, not really expecting an answer.

"My guess, they've found another body," Bob said mildly, but when she turned to look at him, she saw that his expression wasn't mild at all. He looked grim, which was very much how Nora was feeling as she considered the idea.

Perhaps she'd been too hasty to reject the whole gun thing, after all.

>‹

Although she woke up and got dressed immediately—she always did when Peter was over—Amanda ate breakfast, four cold Pop Tarts and instant coffee with assloads of sugar, in bed, and was reading when her mother tapped on her door. Pink Floyd played quietly on her ancient stereo. She liked *Dark Side* in the morning. Mellow.

"'Manda, your friend Devon is here."

Amanda ignored the vague sarcasm, frowning at the clock on her nightstand as she stood up, book still in hand. It wasn't noon yet. "Yeah, OK."

Devon had mentioned that he would be coming by, but not until later, like three. Peter had usually cleared out by then—he worked part-time at the docks, some kind of boat maintenance thing, also did some construction work when it was available— and Devon tried to avoid him as much as possible. Well, and Amanda's mother, too; she used to be nicer to him, but since hooking up with Peter, she'd picked up some of his general bigotry. In Peter's book, fags were for bashing, or at least making fun of. He was a total shithead.

Amanda turned off the music and stepped out of her room, closing the door behind her. She scooped up her high-tops on the way to the apartment's front door; Devon would be waiting outside. Peter and her mother were sitting on the couch, watching TV, Peter in jeans and a ratty Motorhead T-shirt, her mother still in her bathrobe. There were a number of beer cans on the coffee table by their feet, though most were undoubtedly empties from the night before. Grace Young wouldn't really get going till later.

"Where're you going?" her mother asked, barely glancing away from the television, although there was a commercial on. She lit a cigarette, flicking her cheap lighter with chipped-polish nails.

"I don't know. Down to the Klatch, probably." Amanda tied her shoes leaning against the front door, wishing she had more time to get ready. She hadn't been wearing makeup lately, and her hair was short enough that she didn't really need to fuck with it, but she should've brushed her teeth. She didn't want Devon to have to wait too long, though, and there was no way he'd come inside.

"Have you seen my bag? The flowered one?"

Peter snorted loudly. "Maybe your boyfriend has it. Bet he looks pretty with a flowered bag."

Her mother didn't laugh, but she *did* smile. Disgusting.

"Hilarious," Amanda muttered. She wanted to say about ten other things, to both of them, but didn't. Devon was waiting, and picking a fight with the motherfucker and motherfuckee would only prolong her stay. Peter snorted again but didn't say anything else.

"When'll you be home?" her mother asked. "'Cause I wanted you to go to the store later; we're out of some stuff. Bread. And chips."

"I'll call," Amanda said. Her bag was crumpled under her coat, propped against the stereo shelf. She grabbed both and opened the door, saw Devon standing next to Peter's pickup, smoking. When he saw her, saw her watching, he tapped his ashes on the rusting hood in a dramatic overhand gesture. Amanda smiled.

"When?" Her mother's voice, hoarse from years of chain-smoking, was rising in volume and pitch. Not a good sign. "When are you going to call? You say that, but then you never do, and I don't know where you are half the time, so when?"

"By four, OK?" Amanda started to step out.

"Hey!"

Amanda gritted her teeth, turned back to look at her. At them.

Her mother's worn but still pretty face was caught in a shaft of sunlight from the open door, the light making her squint. Smoke swirled through the light, a warm rush of air spinning in from outside. "Be careful, baby."

For a half second, Amanda felt the nearly perpetual knot in her stomach spasm tighter, a random burst of sadness and anger and guilt, along with too many other feelings to sort through. Her mother was barely a parent most days and drank too much when she wasn't at work to be even halfway reasonable. Amanda had mostly accepted it; it wasn't like she had a choice. She'd be out in a few months, anyway, away from her mom and whatever new dickwad she dragged home every year or two. It was that rare moment when Grace expressed concern—sober concern, anyway—that still got to her, that made her feel really deep-down shitty.

"Yeah, don't you two go picking up any sailors," Peter added.

Grace mock-slapped his shoulder, turning away from the door. "Peter!"

Nice. Amanda slid out before anything else could be said. Peter sucked. He wasn't as bad as last year's model; Ted had

been a total dirtbag—he'd been "in between jobs" for the entire
six months he'd been around, and dumb as a stick, besides—
but Peter was a bigot and, she suspected, a total letch. He'd
never actively hit on her, but the few times they'd been alone
together, even for like five minutes, he always tried to strike
up conversations about her love life. She wasn't an idiot. It was
sick.

"What, you didn't feel like coming in, hanging out with
Peter?" she asked, hopping off the front step.

Devon dropped his smoke and ground it out with his toe.
He didn't answer but looked searchingly into her face. His hair,
usually so carefully and subtly spiked, looked kind of flat. Like he
hadn't checked the mirror before he'd left home.

He still wasn't talking, either.

"What?" she asked. "What's up?"

"I tried to call like an hour ago," he said. "Peter answered, so
I hung up."

"OK," she said. No news there. "So, what's going on?"

Devon continued to stare at her. It was starting to get weird.

"What the fuck, Devon?" she snapped.

"That thing at Pam's, that—that dream or whatever."

Amanda nodded but didn't say anything, her heart thud-
thudding in her ears. Time seemed to slow. She already knew
what he was going to tell her, from the confusion and appraisal in
his expression. She'd had a vision, and she knew it had been real;
of course it had come true.

"Cops found Lisa this morning, in Kehoe Park," he said. He
nodded vaguely behind the complex; Amanda turned to look, in
spite of the fact that there was nothing to see. Amanda and her
mother lived seven blocks from the park's west entrance, three
over and four away; from where she stood, she could only see a
few waving, crooked treetops over the apartment's rooftop.

"And then they found Ed Billings at his house, dead," he continued. "And his wife. Darva, her name was Darva. He killed her, then killed himself."

Amanda turned back, stared. "You're shitting me," she said, her voice far away, except she knew he wasn't. It was just something to say.

Devon shook his head. "I don't know who found Lisa, but Tiny Tina found the Billingses. She went over to have coffee or something with Darva, and there they were. She ran out screaming, made a big scene."

"How'd you hear?" she asked, though she didn't really care. Again, it was just something to say, to make the conversation happen. She felt numb and kind of stupid.

"Carrie called to tell Sid. I guess Carrie's mother gave Tiny some water or something while they waited for the cops to show. And while they were waiting, one of *her* friends called to tell her about Lisa."

Sid was Devon's uncle and legal guardian, Carrie Watson his girlfriend. Carrie and her mother lived near the Billingses, as did Tiny Tina Yeltsin, the ancient town librarian. Tina was actually fairly average in size, but Amanda and Devon had privately dubbed her "Tiny," based on her very small and wrinkled mouth, which looked remarkably like an anus when she pursed it at loud library guests, and anyone with "teen" in their age. It was one of their billion private jokes.

Amanda glanced back at the apartment and thought about what a huge drag it would be if Peter decided to leave early.

"Let's get out of here," she said. "Get some coffee."

They started walking, Devon being uncharacteristically silent as they headed downtown. Fine by her. Usually he wouldn't shut up, and she still felt numb, unable to process. They'd talked it out at the party on Saturday night, like, two hours of chain-smoking in Pam's backyard, and Devon had insisted that she have a drink, and she'd had, like, four, and they'd both decided she'd fallen asleep, after all. She'd spent most of yesterday working to enforce the decision in her stupid, hungover brain, and had managed to make herself believe it by last night.

Wasted time, she thought.

From the apartment they walked the flat and meandering blacktop of Fessenden until they hit Bayside, passing a trailer park and a couple of more complexes on the way. They slogged up the hill, both of them slowing as the incline steepened. Bayside Drive, Isley's northernmost street, ran from the back of town— the downslope away from the bay, where most of the less-than-well-to-do folks parked their families—all the way to Main, and though it was a well-traveled road, it was still woodsy near the top of the hill. The shoulderless road was flanked by wide stands of evergreens, their tops twisted or broken; Isley suffered more than its fair share of windstorms. The sun was almost directly overhead, bright but not too hot; the sweep off the bay usually kept the temperature fairly moderate during the summer, at least on the upslope.

Just after the crest of the hill, two blocks after they'd started down, they reached Devlin Street. Devlin ran from Bayside along the eastern boundary of Kehoe Park, eventually becoming Eleanor, a small, dead-end bit of street at the park's southeast corner, where the middle school used to be. People occasionally parked there at night to make out or fuck; it was a dark spot.

As they crossed Devlin, Amanda slowed and glanced down, saw a scattered handful of people at its curve several blocks away, where the trees began and Devlin turned into Eleanor. She could also see a county cop car parked there, pulled off to one side, and what looked like a news van, probably from the local station affiliate in Port Angeles.

"Do you want to—did you want to go down there?" Devon asked.

"Fuck, no," Amanda said. "Why? Do you?"

"No," he said. "I just thought—I mean, you saw it, right?" He sounded excited, but a little wavery, too, his voice taut and high. "You said you saw Mr. B kill Lisa Meyer. You told me he was—that he was eating her face. You *saw* it."

Amanda suddenly felt almost violently ill, her mouth flooding with watery spit. She dropped her bag and turned toward the ditch that ran alongside Bayside's north side. There were more trees after the ditch and no houses past them, just a high, rusty fence that blocked a steeply angled drop to the water, two hundred feet below. She only made it to the bottom of the ditch—which, thank God, was muddy but not full of water—before she threw up her meager breakfast in a single, throat-wrenching *glurt*. She spit several times, leaning over the brownish puddle of chewed-up food, then stood up, looking back at Devon. He held her bag clutched to his stomach, his expression almost ridiculously concerned.

"I'm OK," she said, not really sure if she was. Her voice sounded thick and hollow. She spat a few more times, then climbed back up to the pavement, her high-tops squishing in the soft dirt. "Tell me I've got breath mints in there."

Devon rummaged through her bag and came up with a tin of Altoids. Thank God for small fucking favors. She chewed several as they crossed to the south side of the street, walked to where the sidewalk began, and sat on the curb. Both of them lit up, the smoke rasping down Amanda's grated throat, the mints making it taste like menthol. The entire puking experience finally made the world real again; she'd started to think, coming out of whatever lockdown she'd been in for the last fifteen minutes. She thought over the plots of at least a half dozen B movies that dealt with her very situation, trying to avoid the scariest ones.

"So what do you think?" Devon asked finally. He didn't clarify; he didn't need to.

She exhaled heavily. "I don't know. I mean, I had, like, a vision, right? Saw the future?"

Devon nodded.

"If I'd said something…"

"Don't even," Devon said. "You didn't make it happen."

"But if I'd done something to change things, she wouldn't have died." She thought about Mr. B and added, "None of them would have."

"Right, and if you had a time machine, you could go back and try to fix everything, but then something would happen that would make you see that it was fate, and you never could have stopped it anyway," Devon said. "That's an old *Twilight Zone*, I think. You feeling bad now does exactly shit. You know that, right?"

She sighed. "Yeah, I guess. But I still feel bad."

"Fair enough," he said, "though you're totally wrong. But guilt aside, don't you think—I mean, *do* you think you're psychic or something? Did you have, like, some traumatic event lately, or an injury…?"

She looked at him, her best you're-shitting-me face. "Yeah. You remember last week, when I got hit on the head with that big rock?"

"Fuck off," he said. "I'm just wondering if maybe something triggered it. There's always a trigger, right?"

She nodded, conceding the point. Presuming her experience was following movie logic, anyway.

"OK, so has anything like this ever happened before?" he asked. "I mean, obviously not like *this*, but some other ESP thing?"

Amanda didn't dismiss it right off, though she would have before Pam's party. She started to tell him no, then remembered something her mother had said a few times.

"I guess—when I was little, I used to say things about how people were feeling," she said, deciding it sounded dumb even as it came out. "Never mind, that's stupid."

"No, what do you mean? Seriously?"

He *looked* serious, and she felt a rush of real affection for him. They'd been fast friends since eighth grade, when he'd come to Port Isley to live with his uncle after his parents had split and his mother had had some kind of nervous breakdown. He actually had a few friends—girls, mostly, since the hickdicks were too homophobic to be caught hanging out with him, although there were a handful of California-transplant faux punks who didn't care…Devon was witty and likeable; he did pretty well in spite of his rather obvious orientation—but he was pretty much the only person she talked to at all. About anything real, anyway.

They were both due to graduate in a year, but he'd turn eighteen in October, and they had plans to run away to Seattle together as soon as they could, away from tiny, snooty Port Isley. Between them, they just needed to earn enough to put down first and last on a place, get real jobs and GEDs, get out of this shithole of a town…

Maybe I could take up reading palms or something, she thought. It wasn't funny.

"My mother said that when I was just learning how to talk, I'd tell her things about her friends," she said. "Like ask why someone was sad, or say that someone was angry. She said that she'd always find out later that I was right."

Devon dragged off his smoke, exhaling as he spoke. "Well, that sounds psychic to me. Or, whatsa…*empathic*, anyway."

She shrugged. "I guess," she said. "But that was, like, what, fifteen years ago."

"Have you—has there been anything since the party?"

Which had been Saturday night, and it was only Monday. "No," she said. "Just—"

He's here.

In the backyard, right after.

Devon had an eyebrow raised. She shrugged. It was probably too vague to mean anything, but maybe he'd have some insight. She wanted all the help she could get.

"No," she said. "At the party, though, when we went outside to smoke? I had this feeling—or thought, or something—that someone was…here."

"Here, like here-at-Pam's?"

"I don't know," she said. "I just thought, 'He's here.' Like, literally, that's what I thought, that's all I thought."

"Here in Isley, you think?"

"Dude, no fuckin' clue. Maybe."

They sat and smoked for a moment. She felt like she should *do* something, take some action, but she wasn't sure what or how. Maybe she should call the cops, tell them…tell them what, exactly? That she knew Ed Billings had killed Lisa Meyer? Duh. If they didn't know it already, they'd figure it out in like three seconds, from blood and fiber evidence. She watched *CSI.* Even considering the TV bullshit factor, it was a wonder anyone tried to get away with murder anymore, and she seriously doubted that Mr. B had tried to clean up *after* he murdered Lisa but *before* he killed his wife and himself; he was crazy, obviously, but that seemed downright retarded. The cops wouldn't need her input. The realization was a relief.

Of course, someone else might call the cops, someone from the party. It was unlikely that Stan Vincent would bother to follow up on something like that, but she supposed it was possible. The idea of being interrogated by the man wasn't appealing, but it wasn't like she had done anything wrong. Besides smoking pot, anyway, and she couldn't see any need to mention that.

Thank God school is out. She wasn't actively disliked at Isley High—at three hundred students, seventh through twelfth, the student body was too small for there to be actual outcasts. It was too inbred, everyone having grown up together; even the problem kids, special ed or whatever, had brothers and sisters. New kids still got hassled—she had unpleasant memories of it from when she and her mom had moved here, when she was nine—but they were generally accepted into the fold within a year or two. She had been. Still, a lot of people thought she was weird, because of how she dressed and her musical tastes and her tendency toward general morbidity. Even with school out, word would get around that she'd "seen" Lisa killed before the fact; just not as quickly.

Yeah, it will, she thought. *The picnic.* Fuck. Everyone went to the annual picnic, which was on Saturday. Maybe she should skip it this year…

"Were they having an affair?" Devon asked abruptly. "Lisa and Mr. B?"

"Probably," she said. "I mean, considering how she acted at Pam's, and then this."

"You don't know for sure?" he asked. "I mean, when you saw him kill her, you didn't get like…I don't know, a sense that they were…doing it?"

"I told you what I saw," she said. "It was like watching a movie. No voice-over."

He nodded. "What about the someone being here thing? Was that like a movie?"

"No, that was like—" She thought about it, tried to think of a way to express it. "Like just knowing something. Like a secret that someone tells you, or how you feel about someone. Does that make sense? It was almost like it related to me, kind of."

"Not like some absolute fact," he said. "More…subjective."

"Right," she said. "That's totally it."

"I'm fucking brilliant," Devon said. "That's why the chicks all dig me."

Amanda smiled, for about the first time since leaving the apartment. "Fag," she said.

"Fat gothy lesbo whore," he said promptly.

"I'm not a lesbian," she said, and they both laughed. A strained laughter, maybe, but better than nothing.

They butted their smokes and started back down the hill, Devon letting the matter drop for the moment, telling her instead about his latest chat with gguy7. Gguy7 (gay guy, seven inches, Devon had gleefully informed her a few weeks back) was pushing for a meeting, which Devon was dodging. It was one thing to have an Internet love interest—a type-n-jack, in Devon-speak—another entirely to actually hook up. "Besides," Devon said, and not for the first time since "meeting" gguy7 online last month, "that picture might be from twenty years ago; he's probably a total troll now. It might not even be him."

He was babbling a little, trying to make things normal, and Amanda nodded along, still thinking about what she'd seen at Pam's party. She was absolutely sure that there were some vast implications to it all, that there were things she needed to figure out, decisions to be made, but nothing was occurring to her; she had no ideas.

Well, I won't smoke pot anymore, she decided, and promised herself to give it up, at least for a few weeks. *No pot, no visions, right?*

Right.

CHAPTER

3

Since he'd arranged his workweek to run Tuesday through Saturday, John Hanover slept in on Mondays. Sometimes late. It was one of the nicest things about setting one's own hours, as far as he was concerned; besides the concession to his ability to be a total slacker, it also gave Candice a chance to catch up on office work, hassling with the insurance companies and the like.

This particular Monday was no exception; he'd stayed up until two in the morning, half-watching trashy cable shows—a semiexploitive documentary on the history of circus geeks had been the winner—while he caught up on some of his own paperwork. He'd slept until almost eleven, which was truly obscene and wonderful. A leisurely breakfast, a long shower, and it was almost one before he was dressed and presentable. Not that he had anywhere he needed to be presented; he would run by the office, pick up some groceries, maybe stop at Patisserie or the Klatch for a coffee. In all, a perfect Monday, or at least the best he could manage on his own.

He winced inwardly as he jingled his car keys in his pocket, walking toward the back door. The internal jabs had grown sporadic, but they still popped up every now and then. It was inevitable; divorce wasn't an antidote to pain, after all. It had been official for more than six months, and while he knew it had been the right decision, in the end, that didn't make it a happy one.

Someone knocked on the front door, the sharp tap echoing through the kitchen…John glanced at his watch, headed back to the front of the house. A package, maybe, or one of the kids selling lawn maintenance. He knew a few of his neighbors, but not well enough for there to be just-dropping-bys.

A glance through the side window revealed Annie Thomas, in uniform. John opened the door, trying on a smile. Annie was a law student most of the year but worked as a noncommissioned police officer during Port Isley's tourist season. He only knew her slightly. She and Lauren had been friendly.

"Hello, Officer," he said, and was relieved that her answering smile looked real enough. She also seemed—different. Formal. Perhaps it was the uniform. The last time he'd seen her had been…before New Year's, anyway. At Le Poisson, which he still treated himself to every few weeks. She'd been wearing a dress then, something dark and flattering. She'd had a dinner date.

"John," she said, "I'm sorry to bother you, but I'm running a canvass. Is it all right if I ask you a few questions?"

"Sure, of course," he said, stepping back from the door. He realized he was wearing his coat and felt a need to explain, to assure her that he wasn't too busy. "I was going to run some errands, but they can wait. Come in."

"You probably noticed all the commotion earlier," she said, not moving.

"Actually, I was…" He automatically ran through a couple of reasonable excuses, before remembering that Annie almost certainly didn't care. More leftover Lauren angst, apparently. His ex-wife had always seemed slightly disgusted with his desire to sleep past eight.

"It's my day to sleep in," he admitted, smiling a little.

"There was an incident in the park, early this morning," she said, not smiling back at him. "Probably late last night. I'm wondering if you heard anything, or saw anyone around…?"

"What kind of incident?" he asked.

Annie hesitated, studying his eyes briefly as she decided whether it was appropriate to tell him.

"Homicide," she said finally. "A jogger found a body this morning, near the park's west entrance."

"Oh my God," he muttered.

"I know it's unlikely that you heard anything," she continued. "It looks like the, ah, victim was killed there, but the chief wants us to cover everyone living on the border, just in case."

"Sure," he said. He lived on the park's eastern edge, twenty-plus acres of trees between his house and the apparent site. "I don't remember hearing anything...I was up late, too. Wind in the trees, but nothing out of the ordinary. Can I ask—who was killed?"

Again, that brief, scrutinizing gaze. Her own eyes were a mild, bright brown, quite pretty, actually; he'd never noticed before.

"I suppose you'll hear about it soon enough," she said. "Actually, I'm surprised you haven't already. A teenage girl was strangled. A local."

"That's awful," he said.

She nodded. "Yeah. Listen, do you know your new neighbor? The car's there, but they're not answering the door..."

She tilted her head toward the house next to his, a gray bungalow that had recently been rented out, perhaps a week ago. John only knew it was occupied at all from the consistently stationary Bimmer in the drive and the lights at night; he had yet to see the man, woman, or family that had moved in.

"No, I don't," he said. "It's a rental, though." He paused, frowned. "You don't think that there's any possibility—"

Annie answered with a shake of her head before he finished asking if there might be a killer next door. "Just covering the area. Anyway, if you remember anything, give us a call, all right?"

"Absolutely," he said.

She stayed where she was, clearly wanting to say something else. When she spoke again, her voice was pitched lower than before.

"Listen, unofficially, can I ask you if you've ever had Ed Billings as a patient? I know you can't answer if he was, but it would save us a records warrant if you could rule it out for us…"

"Technically, I can't answer either way," he said, noting the "was," wondering if that meant what he thought. "You know that."

She moved slightly closer to him, her expression very flat. "Yeah, I do. But let me be clear—it looks like one of our high school teachers killed one of his students, then went home and choked his wife to death before shooting himself. You're the town shrink. It's going to come up, and if you can just tell me whether it would be worth our time to get a judge's order for your records, I'd personally appreciate it very much."

John blinked, caught off guard as much by her manner as by the news. He didn't know her that well, but she'd never struck him as particularly assertive. It seemed the uniform did make a difference.

"OK," he said slowly. "I think it's safe for me to say that it would be a waste of time to bother a judge, but I'm not the only therapist in—"

"You didn't treat him," she said.

He sighed. "I didn't treat him," he said, because it seemed that nothing short of that would do. Annie was a law student; she knew better than to even broach the subject…but then, he knew better than to answer, and here he was spelling it out.

"Thank you," she said, and finally smiled again. She had a very nice smile, warm and slightly crooked. As with her eyes, it seemed like he was just noticing for the first time.

Not so married anymore, am I?

John quashed the thought, surprised that he'd even had it. He wasn't looking for a romantic relationship of any kind. He nodded, summoned another smile. "Sure," he said.

There was an awkward pause, and for the barest of seconds, he thought that he could see a different kind of scrutiny in her eyes, an appraising one that matched the sudden flush of red across her cheeks...but then it was gone, and she was only Annie Thomas again, a vague acquaintance to his ex-wife, a police officer on a rather unpleasant duty. She thanked him for his time and left.

John closed the door, stepped to the flanking window, and watched her through the blinds as she walked past the mostly empty lot across the street, back toward State. Her head was up, one hand on her belt; she looked good, lean, and efficient. She cast a lingering glance at the rental next door, slowing a moment, then walked on. Her car, a mud-splashed SUV with a police decal on the side, was parked near the corner, across from Dick Calvin's tidy blue house.

When she got in her car, he started to turn away and caught a glimpse of movement from the house next door to his. A flicker of the deep-red curtain that had been strung behind the picture window...which he hadn't seen open since it went up, now that he came to think of it. The slight motion could have been his imagination, or a cat or something—he'd have noticed a dog, probably—but he thought it was his new neighbor. Watching Annie walk away, as he had been.

John stayed at the window another moment. The rental and his home were separated by a wide strip of lawn and both driveways, maybe fifty feet total. He'd actually been inside the gray house once; Lauren had befriended the couple that had lived there four, five summers ago, Jim and Melody...Saunders? Sanders?

There had been a few chance meetings and a single mediocre dinner party to remember them by. He vaguely recalled the layout of the house, remembered that the pork roast had been horribly overcooked. Walking back across the lawn in the summer dark, Lauren had commented that it was good to know there was no possibility that they'd contacted trichinosis, and he'd laughed hard enough to make his face ache. She could be so funny, so random...he'd loved that about her...

Oh, stop.

John turned away from the window, decided that maybe it was his imagination after all...and if it wasn't, so what? Maybe his new neighbor had been napping, or just didn't feel like answering the door. Hell, maybe he—or she—was a terrorist on the lam; didn't really matter, in the grand scheme of his own life. He wasn't sure if that made him a realist or just self-absorbed. A question for another day.

He headed for the back of the house, again jingling his keys, surprised to find his thoughts wandering back to Annie Thomas's eyes and sideways smile. It seemed he was adjusting to life after divorce after all, like it or not.

CHAPTER

4

"Mom! *Mom!*"

Sarah Reed winced at Tommy's enthusiastic shout from the kitchen, then remembered that the Oswalts were still out. And Karen wasn't back from the store yet. Sarah knew her sister loved Tommy as much as she did, but Karen had a business to run and Tommy hadn't quite gotten the hang of not screaming every time he came through the door.

"In here, baby," she called back, gently. From the dining room, right next to the kitchen. Whispering distance, practically. With two running steps, her son was standing in front of her, his cheeks flushed, his eyes bright.

"Guess what?"

"Remember what I told you about shouting? Where's Jeff?" Jeff Halliway was two years older than Tommy and lived a block over.

"He went home," he said. "But guess what happened?"

Sarah's smile pinched a little. "Listen. I can see that you're excited about something, but Aunt Karen's house is a business, remember? There are people who pay to stay here, and they might not like to hear you yelling. OK?"

Tommy nodded along, waiting for her to finish. The second she did, he blurted it out. "A bunch of people got killed. A lady in the park, and then the guy who did it killed himself and his wife. With an *ax.*"

Sarah felt her jaw clenching, forced it to relax. She shouldn't be surprised…Karen had been on the phone half the morning with assorted gossip-hound locals, getting the lowdown; it stood to reason that word got around in kid-land almost as quickly.

"Where'd you hear this?" she asked.

"Friend of Jeff's," he said promptly. "Uh, Mike. He and some other kids came up to us and said that this guy, he teaches at the high school? He went insane and murdered one of his students, and then his wife. He chopped them up into pieces. And then he killed *himself*, with a three fifty-seven."

Delivered with the unadulterated excitement that only a twelve-year-old boy could muster for something so tragic. She briefly considered telling him that an ax hadn't been involved, but decided against it…strangulation wasn't all that much less horrifying, and while she generally tried to be honest with him, she didn't feel the need to be *that* honest; he was only twelve, after all. Sarah pulled out one of the dining room chairs and sat, keeping her tone even and mild.

"That sounds kind of scary," she said.

"Yeah," he said, although if he was frightened, he hid it quite well. "The cops are all over the place. We saw two state police cars on the way home. *And* a news van."

Sarah nodded. "Sometimes people do crazy things," she said. "That's why I'm always so cautious about where you are and who you're with."

"Yeah," he said, barely humoring her. "So, can we go to the park? They're already taking the crime scene tape down, and Jeff says he knows exactly where they found the body. He says there's probably still blood on the ground. He says maybe…maybe like guts or something, too."

Wonderful. Jeff Halliway, tour guide to the macabre. Sarah hesitated, trying to give the appearance that she was considering his proposal, then shook her head. "I don't think that's a very good idea," she said.

"Why? I won't be alone. And the guy who did it is dead, right? So it's safe."

Sarah hesitated again, searching for the right answer. Was there one? It was perfectly natural for him to be curious and even enthused about a grisly death; most kids his age weren't overly burdened by empathy or an awareness of actual suffering. Really, she was a little surprised that he was actually asking for permission, but they'd only been in Port Isley for a few weeks, and he'd stuck pretty close to her since they arrived. She'd been delighted that he'd made friends with Jeff so quickly. Prematurely delighted, maybe.

"I'm sure it *is* safe," she said. "But it's—when someone dies, honey, it makes people sad. Remember when Grandma died? I was really sad, and so were you. Do you think it would have been OK if there were people who went to the nursing home to look around where she died, to see if they could find—to see where she died? Just for fun?"

He didn't answer. She could actually see him struggling to tell himself that it would have been fine, so that he could, in turn, convince her that an excursion to the murder site was acceptable, but he was a bright boy, and sweet-natured; she doubted he'd be able to rationalize it.

"It's normal to be curious," she said, "but it's just not very nice to, to poke around in other people's business when something so awful has happened…does that make sense?"

"Yeah," he said, and though he looked disappointed, he also seemed resigned to it. "I'm gonna go tell Jeff I can't make it."

"Live or Memorex?" she asked, smiling, and he gave her a look, which she tried not to take personally. Hard to believe a twelve-year-old could muster such an adult eye-rolling.

"That's so *dated*," he said, turning to head up the stairs. "Then I'm going to play awhile, OK?"

"OK. Karen'll be back pretty soon, and we'll get on dinner. I'll let you know when it's ready."

She was already talking to his back. She watched his spindly boy-legs and sloppy sneakers retreat up the stairs, loving him deeply. He had his moments—days, even—when he could be a real pain, but mostly he was a good boy, a wonderful boy. She'd been lucky. He'd be leaving to see his dad over the Fourth, stay a few days after, and though he'd only be away for a week in all, she thought she'd miss him terribly. The week at Christmas had been tough enough.

She heard Karen coming up the back steps to the kitchen and went to help, although her sister was only carrying two bags. Sarah took one of them, a pleasant whiff of warm bread coming from a smaller paper bag inside.

"Hopefully fresh fish tonight, but we've got roast chicken and bread as a backup," Karen said, setting her bag on the counter.

"You really think William Oswalt is going to bring home a big one?" Sarah asked. Oswalt was a retired banker who'd obviously enjoyed a lot of deep-fried meals; he weighed three hundred pounds if he was an ounce.

"Actually, I'm counting on Helen," Karen said. "That woman looks like she could wrestle bear; sea bass aren't gonna be a problem. Where's Tommy?"

"One guess," Sarah said. She pulled out the bag of rolls and unloaded a carton of half-and-half and a jar of pesto.

"Let's see...*Warcraft*?" Karen asked.

"Shocked, aren't you?"

Karen smiled. "He plays a lot."

Her tone was perfectly innocent. Sarah glanced at her older sister, looking for any hint of judgment in her expression, but it was as bare as her voice had been. Sarah sighed inwardly and went back to unloading groceries. Tommy loved *World of Warcraft*, Dungeons and Dragons for the computer as far as she could tell, and though she didn't mind him playing—once they'd established some serious Internet ground rules, obviously—she had her concerns. She felt like she had a good relationship with her son, believed that he was honest with her about the things that were important in his life…but he was growing up, too, growing away. As much as she appreciated the inevitability of the process, she worried about him. It had been a hard year, and he played his game every day, sometimes for hours. She wanted him to be happy, but the game added another whole subset to the ongoing list of parental worries. She checked on him, she asked about the people he chatted with, she watched him play sometimes, asking questions about the game so she'd have some credibility when they talked about it (she'd been able to rejoice with him when he'd reached the fifty-eighth level, so he could go to Outland; the things she'd never thought she'd know before raising a kid). Then she worried about being too smothering—Tommy could recite the house rules by heart, and while she knew the divorce had been hard for him, he hadn't rebelled much beyond the aw-Mom stage. Just as often, though, she feared that she wasn't being parental enough. Even the *possibility* of a smart-ass comment from Karen had her defenses fired up, and she wanted so badly to stay on good terms with her sister, to make it a nice summer for all of them…

"You think he plays too much?" she asked, unable to help it.

Karen paused, a celery bunch in hand. "I guess I'd worry about it if he didn't know how to interact with real people, but he's fine. Better than fine. He's a great kid."

Sarah nodded and smiled. "Yeah. He is, isn't he? I thought with the divorce…I'm just glad he's doing so well."

"You and Jack did it right," Karen said. "You kept him in the loop, you made it clear that it wasn't his fault, you don't talk shit about each other in front of him—well. You know."

Sarah nodded again but didn't answer. Karen was right, Jack had done well by their son, and while that went a long way toward making things better between them, it didn't make up for Vanessa. For falling in love with her. For what *that* had done to Tommy, to all of them. That part of it still hurt, a lot.

"He's a total asshole, though," Karen added, and Sarah smiled.

"I won't fight you on that," she said, keeping her voice low, though it was highly unlikely that Tommy could hear them. The way she saw it, when Tommy got older, he would make up his own mind about what kind of man his father was; he didn't need to hear it from her. The half dozen self-help divorce books she'd read had all insisted on this.

"William and Helen aren't supposed to be back until sixish," Karen said, "and the Gosmans won't be here till Wednesday, so we don't have to make up the west bedroom yet...want a drink? I've been working on my sidecar."

Sarah made a face. "Uck. Do we still have any of that Pinot from last night?"

Karen grinned. "Only a half case of it, in the basement. Didn't I mention? It's the house red this summer."

"I'll be in AA by the time September rolls around," Sarah said.

Karen's smile faded slightly and was replaced by a softer, warmer look. "You don't have to leave, you know. The schools here are decent. And Seattle isn't so far away. Tommy could see his dad regularly enough—"

Sarah interrupted. "I know."

"There are going to be at least two openings at the grade school by Christmas, with Wes Martin retiring and that English teacher getting married—"

"I know," Sarah said again. "And I haven't ruled it out. But I just got us settled in Bellevue—"

"—in a two-bedroom *apartment*, which is just sitting there right now, anyway—"

"—*and* I've got a job waiting for me, and it's a lot closer to Jack. I want Tommy to see him as much as he wants."

Karen seemed about to say something else, then shrugged. "It's your decision, of course. But think about it. Not just for you, either. I like having you around, OK? You and Tommy both. It's—it gets lonely here in the winter."

Karen's husband, a much older man whom she'd loved quite deeply, had died almost three years before. Heart attack. The couple had opened the bed-and-breakfast together—affectionately called Big Blue for its paint job—apparently in lieu of having children. Sarah had never understood the attraction between them—Byron had been nice enough but somewhat controlling and close to their father's age—but she knew that Karen missed him awfully.

"I promise I'll think about it," Sarah said, sincerely. She couldn't really see herself living in Port Isley, but she didn't want Karen to feel blown off, either. "Now, you said something about wine?"

"No, *you* said something about wine," Karen said. "I'm having a sidecar."

"Glah," Sarah said. They were both smiling. Karen headed for the basement, just off the kitchen, and Sarah finished putting the groceries away, listening to her sister's light steps tapping down the stairs. It was good to see Karen, to spend some real time with her, and Port Isley was a nice little town. Tommy had already made a friend—Jeff Halliway was older but he seemed like an all right kid, and he was also a fellow *Warcraft* player, which apparently made them blood brothers of some kind—and there were parks and woods for him to explore, hikes and picnics to look forward to as the summer progressed. And she was on a real vacation for the first time in what seemed like years; no summer school for a change, no pickup classes or certification tests to study for, and an aide who'd already volunteered to go in early to set up the room and be available for questions from parents. Except for a short trip back to Bellevue in late August for the orientation, there was nothing she had to do until September, time stretching out in front of her as it had when she was a child, when summer lasted forever, when autumn was a distant dream.

"Life is good," she said to herself, feeling that it might actually be true, for a while. She got a wineglass out of the cabinet by the stove and waited for Karen to come back up, happy to be where she was.

➤❮

That darned front page. Front page, and he told me he'd play it down. Gosh darn*it.*

Dan Turner sat at his desk, fuming, waiting for Marcie to get Bob Sayers on the line. The *Press*'s editor was in hiding, no doubt; there was no answer at his office, and if he was at home, he wasn't picking up.

Probably still out delivering the goshdarned thing, Turner thought, staring down at his own fresh copy, the headline screaming like a barn fire. TRAGEDY STRIKES PORT ISLEY, probably sixty-point type, top of the darned front page.

The copy itself wasn't as bad as it might have been; there was that, at least—no sensational details, nothing but the bare facts. Not that it wasn't bad enough; Ed Billings had murdered Lisa Meyer, then his wife, then himself. The article didn't actually spell out that Ed and the girl had been intimate, but only because

Sayers didn't know about it yet, or hadn't when he'd jammed in the last-minute front page. The evidence had been overwhelming, according to Stan Vincent. The cops had found compromising pictures of the Meyer girl at Billings's house, tucked away in Ed's desk, plus a handful of love letters and, of course, the suicide note itself. "She said she loved me." Short and sweet, entirely pathetic, and actually spattered with a few drops of Ed's blood. Or his wife's. Or Lisa's. It didn't matter. What mattered was that it was the very start of the season, three-quarters of their summer people were already in town, and Bob had promised to keep it soft, he'd darn well *promised.*

He'd be pottering around, tying flies or cabinet-making or some such thing if it wasn't for us. Turner's lips curled. The *Press* only ran because the town subsidized it, and the town meant the council. Sayers didn't appreciate what he had. And Dan was sure that he drank.

"Mr. Turner?" Marcie's reedy voice piped through the intercom, irritatingly unflappable. "Rick Truman is on line two."

"Shoot," Turner muttered, then leaned across his desk to stab at the intercom button, his not inconsiderable gut hindering him slightly. "What about Sayers?"

"Not yet. I'll keep trying."

He picked up the receiver, muscled a smile into his voice, and gave a silent prayer for strength. "Rick, how are you?" he said, though he was sure he already knew. If there was anything Rick liked more than complaining about his wife, it was throwing his weight around the council. Dan was the acting head councilman; he was hometown, and to win the spot you had to be hometown, but that meant nada in reality; the reality was, Rick Truman was Ricky-effing-Rich and what he said, went.

Let he who is without sin, Dan reminded himself. It seemed like he had to do that a lot lately.

"I thought you said Bob was handled," Rick said. The anger was barely disguised, his voice high and tense. "Isn't that what you said? 'I handled him, Rick'? 'Cause that's how I remember it."

Dan fought a sudden urge to throw the phone. "I don't know what you mean," he said, barely a twinge of guilt for the lie. "Are you talking about the paper?"

"What do you think I'm talking about, Danny-boy? Aren't *you* looking at the fucking thing? See those words, up above my ad, the ones that talk about the fucking crazy people who live here? On the front page of the annual goddamn welcome-to-Isley issue?"

"I see them, Rick," Dan said, wincing from the language. "And I told Sayers to go easy, but he had to say *something*. I mean, it is news, right?"

"On the front page? Are you shitting me?" Rick was so mad he almost spluttered. Dan got a brief, highly detailed mental picture of Donald Duck dressed as a drill sergeant. He could actually see the spittle flying from his beak, the olive cap, the clenched feather fists. It wasn't funny and did nothing to ease a dawning headache; Rick was all nestled in to chew him a new one, and Dan was probably going to have to let him.

Sadie Truman's parents had been loaded, and had left everything to her when they'd passed in an auto accident a decade earlier; Rick had invested her inheritance wisely, and as a result, they were easily the wealthiest couple in the port. Besides Le Poisson, the Trumans owned a popular specialty foods shop, plus an apartment building, plus a number of as-yet-empty lots in and around the area, just waiting to grow new businesses and expensive housing. If Dan ever wanted a piece of anything—which he did, of course, being a silent partner in his brother-in-law's construction outfit—he'd be wisest to find something to bite and let Rick go at it.

"He got a good quote from Peters," Dan tried, but Rick headed him off.

"The day that the slurred words of Poppy fuckin' Peters mean shit to anyone with half a brain is the day I willingly fuck my wife," Rick said.

"Most of the summer people—"

"Most of the summer people have met our cartoon mayor, and you know it," Rick said. "Poppy's a joke. Where's *my* quote, Danny-boy? Fuck, where's *yours*?"

"Poppy sounded fine," Dan said, unable to keep a snap out of his voice. He was tired of being cursed at, and he hated, *hated* being called Danny-boy. "He said it's resolved, he said the cops are just wrapping things up, he said not to worry. That's all that needs to be said. I'm sorry, all right? Bob messed up. What the heck am I supposed to do? I'm not his babysitter."

There was a long pause. Dan closed his eyes and waited.

"First fucking welcome-to-Isley issue," Rick said, his voice still heated—but not at Dan anymore. "Can you believe it? What the fuck was he thinking?"

Dan felt himself relax a fraction. "I know," he said.

"Thank God he didn't get any of that shit about Ed fucking that girl," Rick added. "Christ, what a balls-up."

"I hear that," Dan said, wincing again—Rick was a real potty mouth—but after listening to Rick have a bird, as his wife liked to say, he didn't feel so bad about the whole fiasco. The deaths were terrible—Lucy had spent the last two days telling him that God was smiting the wicked, declaring it almost contentedly over poached eggs and dry toast—and the timing impeccably bad, but at least Rick was having a really rotten day. He silently chastised himself for the un-Christian thought, but couldn't actually make himself feel bad about it.

Rick blew off the last of his steam, and they agreed that Sayers needed a reminder of his place in the world—and then Dan was let go, free. He hung up the phone with barely any headache at all, a bit surprised that he'd stood up for himself...and after a moment's consideration, slightly worried. Rick never forgot anything. If Lange's Construction lost a contract because of something Dan had said, Scott would shoot him for a yellow dog. His wife's brother could be a real donkey for holding grudges.

We'll burn that bridge when we come to it, he thought, hoping that he hadn't just torched it himself. And since Marcie still couldn't track down Port Isley's elusive editor, Dan closed up his desk and went out for breakfast at Elson's, deciding that the business of the day could wait awhile.

CHAPTER

5

Amanda Young woke up from the worst nightmare of her life very early on Saturday morning, the day of Port Isley's annual town picnic. Gasping, clutching at her sheets, she was sure she had screamed—but the apartment was still, not a sound anywhere but the watery tick of the refrigerator in the next room and her own fluttering heart. If she'd screamed, no one had heard.

"Jesus," she whispered, rubbed at her eyes, and found they were wet. She'd cried in the dream, early on, and again at the end. When she'd seen what had happened to that woman. God.

Nightmare, that's all, that's all. It was a knee-jerk thought, and it didn't ring true. The dream still made sense, in a creepy, surreal way, as though sleep reality had leaked through the veil, into her conscious mind. Generally she made it back to real life as soon as she woke up, but every now and then it took a bit longer. She hated that feeling, that lingering, a sense that real life had become subject to the laws of the dream universe, where unexplained things were common knowledge and time was all fucked up; days passed in a blink, seconds stretched to hours. She felt that now, staring around at the edges and shapes of her small room, what little she could see by the parking lot light that filtered through the ancient, dusty curtain. She could still vividly feel the fear, the sadness…it had all seemed *normal*, even inevitable, and it still did.

Because it wasn't a dream. Not all of it, at least. And you know it.

"Jesus," she said again, drawing in a deep, shaking breath as she fumbled for her bedside lamp. The light crashed on, making her blink, the hyperbright banality of her room a welcome and wonderful sight. The click of the switch seemed overly loud, the light overly harsh, but it was otherwise safe and sane. Her cheap digital clock glowed a quarter after three, what seemed to her the absolute dead of night.

She'd dreamed that she'd been away for a time and had returned to the apartment tired, ready to sleep. As she'd walked through the living room, she'd seen some small, dark shape moving, something, out of the corner of her eye, but hadn't paid attention, eager to get to bed. The carpeting, a sad, dull-blue shag that ran the length of the apartment, had been teeming with lice, with bugs, with what appeared to be tiny snakes or worms, but that hadn't seemed weird; she'd made a note of it, is all, and gone to bed. She'd slept, and woken to streaks of sunshine laying across her bed. She was wearing her mother's warm, ragged terry robe, although she couldn't remember borrowing it or putting it on, and she'd headed out of her room, down the short hall, thinking that the carpet must have been cleaned, there were no bugs, no tiny snakes or worms—and she'd seen her mother lying on the floor of the living room, dressed in a thin nightgown. Her face was turned away, and Amanda approached her slowly, pulling the robe tight, starting to feel a terrible dread.

Her mother wasn't asleep, or dead; she was staring at the far wall, a distant, dreamy smile on her face, her eyes open and unblinking. A sleek rat sat next to her face, cleaning its whiskers with tiny, skeletal paws, its dark fur greasy and thick, and the dread was spinning up into something worse, something bigger; her mother *hated* rats—

Grace Young sat up abruptly, holding her arms out to her daughter. "Give us a kiss, baby," she said, and Amanda felt an incredible darkness wash through her. Terror, but also an aching recognition that her mother was lost to her, now and forever. She covered her eyes and started to cry, because she knew that she would have to kiss her mother, she had to, and it would be the death of her...and when she dropped her shaking fingers a beat later, she was in the dark, outside at night. Not alone, though.

There were trees, and what looked like part of a building—Amanda thought vaguely that it was the restroom block up at the fairgrounds—and very little light but enough to see. From nearby, a couple of hundred yards behind her, maybe, she heard music and people, a background thing. She could smell the sea and trees and wood smoke—and in a clearing not twenty feet in front of her, two, three dark figures were bent over a fourth, down on the ground and draped in shadow. The fourth was on her back on the ground, struggling.

I was dreaming about my mother, she thought, confused.

"Hold her!" Low but perfectly audible, a shouted whisper from one of the group.

"Fuck, she's *strong*—"

"Shut the fuck up! Do it!"

She knew that voice, that angry, whispered shout. It was Brian Glover, linebacker for the Isley High Cougars and the biggest asshole in the universe. And two of the Dicks, his toadies, probably Todd and Ryan. The three of them had been on probation together since beating the crap out of an eighth-grader last fall. The kid had been hospitalized, and they hung tight. It was obvious what they were about to do, what they had already begun, and Amanda felt sick. She was dreaming, but this wasn't hers, this hadn't existed in her mind before. It was as alien as her vision of Lisa Meyer had been, like having someone else's memory, their nightmare.

The woman was mostly silent as she fought, either because one of them had a hand over her mouth or because she was saving her breath for the struggle, Amanda couldn't see—but one of the boys pulled his arm back and hit her, hard, and after that the struggle was mostly over. Amanda saw one of the boys stand up, heard a zipper, heard a laugh—not an evil chuckle but a happy, drunken laugh. They were enjoying themselves; she could feel it, like the frenetic, joyful energy of a party. That was when Amanda started to cry again, because although she opened her mouth wide and screamed as loud as she could, there was no sound. She could hear people, was close enough to them that she saw by the light their revelry cast, but she was a ghost, ineffectual, a voyeur and nothing more. She had kissed her mother after all, and had not survived, and it was the saddest thing she'd ever known. With her new reality just taking hold, she drew in another breath to scream, to force the sound into the world—and woke up.

She scruffed at her hair and made a small sound of aggravation and despair. The frustration she felt was huge. She wanted to reject the dream, of course; it was crazy and...well, crazy. Fucking psycho nutbag, but it had also been like the vision she'd had about Lisa Meyer and Mr. Billings. The one that had turned out to be true, that had kept her sticking close to the apartment for the last week. The rape dream had come with the feeling of personal knowledge, of awareness of fact as it related to her—subjective, like Devon had said. Whatever she had experienced before, this was the same.

Brian Glover and the Dicks—Devon had bestowed the title on the local bully asshead and his pals years before, and the name had stuck, like a band name—they were going to rape someone at the fairgrounds. In the dark.

What about the rest of it? The part about her mother, that had to be some kind of regular dream thing, symbolic, or whatever. She didn't want to turn into her mother. Peter was probably the rat, who fucking knew. What Amanda knew, what she believed, was that the rape was going to happen.

"Town picnic," she muttered, sitting up straighter in bed. The big annual picnic was today at the fairgrounds. Everyone went. They did lunch, a big, usually lame-ass show in the afternoon—high school band, a presentation from the drama fags, some acoustic hippie from the artist colony—and then dinner. And drinks, big-time; the Trumans usually sponsored a couple/five kegs, although they only gave out drink tickets to the summer people and their own snotty clientele; everyone else got ridiculously overcharged. Anyone in town with a good or service to sell showed up to schmooze…and for the disaffected youth of the small community, it was a chance to meet new blood, to seek out others of their own kind. To create some summer memories, stories that could be retold throughout the long, boring winter. The picnic ran until eleven, wrapping with a moldy-oldie rock show. Well after dark.

Shit. She had to tell someone; she had to do *something*. She looked at the clock again. She couldn't call anyone, not now. Except for Devon, she couldn't think of anyone *to* call. And waking up her mother…even if Grace wasn't dead-to-the-world drunk—which was extremely unlikely—what could she do about anything? Believe her daughter? Call the cops? Provide comfort? Fat fucking chance times three.

Amanda had been thinking that she'd bag the picnic this year, after what had happened at Pam's house. A couple of the kids who'd been there had tried to reach her—Ally Fergus had called twice—but she'd dodged the calls, determined to avoid the whole thing. Even Devon had mostly dropped it; there was nothing else to say, nothing to figure out, and once the initial shock had worn off, she hadn't been able to come to any conclusions about anything. She'd foreseen a death, and that person had died, and after most of a dull, reality-based week in her mother's crappy apartment, she'd kind of given up on revelation.

Plus, Brooks might show. Her ex-boyfriend. Her only real boyfriend. Brooks lived in Port Angeles. They'd met at last year's picnic and dated for almost five months before she'd realized he was pretty much a moron. Plenty of good reasons to skip the picnic this year.

But that woman...

She would go. She and Devon would figure out something, some way to tell somebody...they'd stop it from happening.

Amanda eased back against the pillow and took a few deep breaths. OK. OK, she was going to do something. They could tell Chief Vincent that Brian stole something, or assaulted somebody. The truth was obviously not an option, but—

—*but yeah, it is*, she thought. There had been witnesses to her freak-out at the party. She didn't particularly relish the thought of trying to explain what had happened—or how seeing the future was even possible, since she had exactly no clue—but they'd have to take her seriously if she could prove she'd done it before. Wouldn't they? Or was that hopelessly naive?

It wouldn't come to that. She'd think of something, or Devon would. They *had* to.

Amanda closed her eyes to think, sure she wouldn't sleep again, and spent a solid fifteen minutes coming up with plans and discarding them before drifting off again. She slept deeply and without dreams until late in the morning, until people were already gathering at the fairgrounds for the town picnic.

CHAPTER

6

Inconsiderate bitch, Rick thought, looking at his watch again. Again, because Sadie was late, almost certainly fluttering around with the fucking details, even after he'd told her ten times—at least—that the details weren't a big deal. It was a picnic. No one gave a shit if the crackers on the salmon trays went above or below the fish; no one gave a shit if the mint leaf arrangement on the potato salad made a flower or not. Well, OK, considering their target audience, maybe they would, but that wasn't the point. The point was they were going to care a fuckload more if the food wasn't there. They'd care enough to wander over to the other side, *faggots, they'll go right over there to those cocksuckers' goddamn tapas buffet and fill up, and we're fucked for the summer.* And, as an afterthought, *bitch.*

All the town's eateries were selling food for minimal fees— even with the council footing a hefty portion of the bill, they had to charge something or every white-trash family in three counties would be lining up—but Poisson had stocked up for full lunch and dinner crowds. They had crates of fine food ready to go in the walk-in at the restaurant to impress the summer people into buying their wine and high-fiber organic scones at the shop, into choosing Le Poisson for the season. Both of the head chefs and all the Trumans' deli prep workers had been at it for the better part of a week, and now all anyone would remember was Elson's foray into Spanish appetizers, because Sadie was fucking *late.*

Rick was at the top of the service drive, near the line of cars that were stacking up on Bayside to park in the fairground lots. Teenage town boys weaved in and out of the line, took money from drivers, and pointed to the open tracts of packed dirt to the east or south. There were a lot of SUVs and more than a few hybrids, summer cars ferried over for the season, but Rick barely saw them. He watched the turn for their truck, for the first delivery, which should have been unpacked and set out an hour ago. Josh was back at the table now, watching the ice melt and making excuses.

He thought about calling again, even reached for his cell, but he'd already left two messages on Sadie's voice mail in addition to the half dozen unanswered texts. She wasn't at the restaurant, and he didn't want to call the shop; he'd already totally bitched out Randy, who'd simply had the misfortune to answer the kitchen phone. *She just left*, he'd said, but it had already been more than twenty-five minutes, it was a five-minute drive, and where the fuck *was* she?

Fuck it. He unpocketed the cell and stabbed the redial. Beeping. Nothing. He punched another button and fumed through her bland and tiresome message. God, she was wound tight. Even her *voice*, that tense, nasal pitch, as if the horrible strain of trying to sound like a friendly, easygoing person was strangling her.

"You've reached Sadie Parris-Truman, co-owner of Le Poisson and Truman's Specialty Edibles. I'm unable to take your call right now, but if you leave your name, number, and the time you called, I'll get back to you as soon as possible. Thank you."

Beep. "Sadie, where are you?" He took a deep breath, tried to control his tone a little better. With things the way they were on the Eleanor development deal and the ordering expansion coming up, he couldn't afford to lose her goodwill.

"Sweetheart, I know how you like to get caught up in the arrangements, but people are already heading in, and I really wanted to have everything set up in advance." He forced a laugh into his voice. "You know how I get. If you get this, hurry up, OK?"

He cut the call, cursing under his breath. Bitch. Fucking inconsiderate uptight rich bitch.

Rich. That one little word canceled out the rest of them. He couldn't afford to leave her, and if she left him he'd be royally screwed. The latter was a possibility, he sometimes thought; their marriage was a dry and stale affair, and he didn't doubt that she was bored...but she was comfortable enough, and he meant to keep it that way. He worked hard, he took care of the business end of things, he had a place in the small town's political arena, just like her Daddy'd had, God rest his rotten soul. No fucking around, either; Port Isley was too small, and he was too busy, anyway. He had no overtly bad habits and was known to provide occasional servicing in the bedroom, with a smile. If she'd take her ridiculous head out of her own narcissistic ass for a single minute and take a real good look, she'd realize he didn't even like her, let alone love her—but as that never, ever happened, their marriage was essentially sound.

He was about two heartbeats from turning around, heading back to the service lot to get the pickup and go to Poisson himself, when he saw their van join the line of cars.

There was her pinched face behind the wheel, and when she saw him, she gave a cheery wave, as if she was right on time. He raised his hand in turn, deciding for the millionth time that he would leave as soon as the suit settled on the Eleanor deal. That money would be his, all of it. Then he'd hire the best divorce attorney alive and see what he could do about getting a few other things put in his name.

The cars crept forward, and then she was turning into the drive, crunching to a stop so that he could climb in.

"It looks like those murders didn't dampen anyone's appetite," she said brightly.

"No, everyone came," he said, aware that he sounded strained, unable to help it. "Early, too."

"Honey, I'm so sorry about the time," she said. She smiled at him again, the van idling. "But wait till you see the prosciutto. Remember how I was telling you I didn't like the arrangement, that it wasn't just perfect? I stopped at the shop and had Katie redo the melon. It came out—"

"Just *drive*," he snapped, the relief of saying it immediately overshadowed by the need to backpedal. He smiled, exhaled heavily.

"I love you, honey, but you're late. Didn't you get my messages? We've got to get set up."

"Of course," she said, and the chill in her tone, in her look as the van lurched forward, told him he'd better step it up.

"I'm sorry if I snapped at you, sweetheart," he said, reaching over to pat her bony knee. "I'm sure everything looks beautiful. You know how I get."

She nodded sullenly, not answering, her concentration fixed on the narrow drive as it wound toward the service ahead, the van inching forward.

"I just want everyone to see what you've done," he added. "This is a showcase for your talents, Dee—"

"That's right, it is," she said, her voice cool. As if deciding where to put the radish roses was some kind of skill.

"But I've worked hard, too," he said. He hated the slightly hurt sound in his voice, almost as much as he hated having to dance this fucking dance every time she got her feathers ruffled. "You're the spark, honey, the artist, but someone has to crunch the numbers, make sure things are on time, and that's me. And I hate it when we run late, you *know* that."

He watched her struggle with her naturally sour disposition for another half second, then nod, not so sullen this time.

Good enough. He patted her leg again, then motioned toward one of the few open spaces as they pulled into the service lot, a good two hundred yards from the fairground walkway. All the other spots were taken, delivery vans and a few small school buses already crammed into place for the day. His own pickup was front and center, right at the curtain of trees that bordered the fairgrounds' northern edge, where the food was being set up; he'd get Josh to come out, help him change places with the van. Rick had been among the first to arrive, for all the good it had done them.

She parked, then turned a thin smile his way. "Do you mind if I go see what Elson's brought? You can handle the unloading, can't you?"

He smiled back at her. *No problem, honeybunch. You mingle, I'll do the shit work.* "Sure. Just stop by our table on the way, ask Josh to come give me a hand."

"Sure thing." She gave him an obligatory peck on the cheek and handed him the keys before climbing out, smoothing a new and particularly unflattering linen dress over her skinny hips as she walked toward the trees. She was built like a stick figure. He watched her a moment, watched her reach the small path that led to the fairgrounds proper, and wondered what his life would be like without her.

A hell of a lot better, he thought. It wasn't that he hated her, or even wished her ill—he just wanted her to drop off the face of the earth so he didn't have to see her, ever again. Her narrow, mirthless face; her barren, skeletal body; her stupid, boring, debutante wannabe background—everything about the woman was tiresome. If he could hang on a little longer, a year at most…the Eleanor Street project, the old middle school site, was going to be big. Assuming the contract workers ever got what they wanted from the condo company, the buildings would go up, and he was a primary investor. Not Sadie.

A year. One year. He'd spent nineteen of them with her already; waiting through another wasn't going to kill him.

Sighing, he got out of the van and started to unload the food.

><

John had three appointments on Saturday morning, all regular clients, all struggling to make their lives better. Tanya had slept with her ex again and was feeling crappy about it—but she had finally taken some responsibility for her actions, admitting that she'd made the mistake. For five months, the sex had just "happened," and he was glad to see her making some progress. His ten o'clock, Marianne, an incest survivor, had gone through a whole session without making any self-effacing comments, a first for her. And while Dale was still having a hard time with his anger, he'd been surprisingly calm for a change; John's small incitements hadn't set him off. A good morning, in all, and John was free by one o'clock and hungry for food he didn't have to make himself. He headed home to change, then took the Blazer up to the fairgrounds, lucking into a just-opening spot close in, only a few rows from the main trail in the east lot. Both lots were packed, and as he locked up and headed for the trail, he could hear the crowd through the trees, faint music and laughter and raised voices. Elson's was doing the barbecue this year, and he could smell smoke from the fire pit on the light breeze, something meaty. Le Poisson had done the roasting last year, salmon and sausages spitted around the pit, plus an excellent crab boil.

He and Lauren had enjoyed the food, if not each other's company. That had been one of their last public appearances together, actually right near the end…

He felt a sudden stab of real heartache, remembering that time—the days of polite distance, sporadically interspersed with long and dismal conversations about what she wanted. Turned out, she'd wanted not to be married. They'd been together for eight years; he'd expected to be with her for the rest of his life.

He felt his throat lock up, his eyes sting—and for the first time in months, he really missed her. He shouldn't be here, he decided abruptly, he should just go home. He could spend the afternoon puttering around the house, watch TV, maybe take a nap.

He hesitated near the last line of cars, frowning. Other than the standard array of maladaptive reactions when Lauren left— sleep issues, a depressive mood episode, some off-and-on body aches—he hadn't suffered any real adjustment troubles once the final decision had been made. It was a little strange, the sudden re-edged sharpness he was feeling…though that was how emotions worked sometimes. God knew he'd said as much often enough to his clients. Still, it felt…unexpected, somehow.

"Hey, Doc!"

He saw Bob Sayers standing near the trail entrance, smiling widely. John smiled in turn, suddenly very glad to see him. Bob had been an acquaintance before the divorce but had become a friend since. Almost immediately since, actually; John had happened across the older reporter a few days before Christmas the year before, about half an hour after he'd signed the final papers and dropped them in the mail. They'd both stopped at the gas station, were pumping their own in the cold, bitter sunlight, bundled against the icy wind, and when Bob had asked his friendly how's-things, John had blurted out the inelegant truth—that his divorce was final, and he therefore felt like a big pile of dog shit. Bob had raised his eyebrows, his gaze mild and warm, and offered to bring over a pizza and a bottle of really good whiskey, anytime, so they could chat about it. That very night, as it had turned out, and the dinner and multiple nightcaps had been more enjoyable than John could have expected. One or the other of them had made a point of getting in touch every few weeks after that. Sometimes they went out for a drink, usually they just shot the shit for a few over the phone, but their conversations had proved a welcome break from the loneliness. For both of them, John thought. Bob didn't talk much about his personal life, but he'd let a few things slip about a long-deceased wife, a relationship he still mourned, however gently.

"Are you leaving?" John asked, as he got closer.

Bob grinned. "Just taking a breather. Seems like everyone wants to talk about the Billings thing."

John nodded. He'd read the story, even caught the news clip on the local affiliate, and three of his clients had brought it up in the last few days. "Lot of dumb questions?"

"Nope. Lot of people wanting to tell me what I left out," Bob said. "Billings and the teenager were having an affair. They were in love, he was stalking her, she was pregnant, he was on drugs, his wife liked to watch."

He lowered his voice melodramatically. "There were videos. Apparently still on the Net, if you can believe it."

"I can't," John said.

Bob shook his head. "Buncha gorehounds. I'm as curious as the next, don't get me wrong, but a lot of our friends and neighbors seem to want to wallow in it, if you know what I mean. Isley, you know?"

"Yeah, I do," John said. Port Isley wasn't all that big, and not all that exciting, either. A bit of gossip about the artists' colony or some scandalous affair would be passed around for weeks in various circles, squeezed for every detail. A double murder–suicide would be making all the rounds well into next winter. He assumed that most small towns were the same... although that assumption was based on fiction, he realized, more than on experience. He'd lived in Seattle most of his life. *The Last Picture Show*, a high school production of *Bus Stop*, pretty much anything by Faulkner—his concept of small-town community was what he'd been fed. He'd been in Port Isley for six years, and while he did have clients who liked to gossip, he'd had just as many of those when he'd practiced in the city. The only difference was now he usually knew who they were gossiping about.

Bob swept his arm back toward the picnic—"Shall we?"—and John nodded. Whatever emotional tic had hit him, it had passed, and he was still hungry. They started walking the short trail and passed a fashionably dressed young couple with two small children, heading back to the lots. The woman carried a young boy, perhaps a year and a half old, on one hip; the father had a six-month-old—a girl, by the profusion of pink she wore—in a chest carrier. Both children were crying, red-faced, and snotty and vaguely adorable in spite of it; the parents seemed entirely exhausted. John had wanted kids pretty early on, but Lauren had wanted to wait. She'd been working on her master's a few classes at a time, general sociology. They'd fought about it, more than once. Considering how things had turned out, it seemed that she'd had the right idea.

"The best one I heard was that the whole thing was foretold," Bob said.

John refocused. "What? The murders?"

Bob nodded. An elderly woman walked past them, also headed for the east lot, wearing an expensive lightweight pantsuit.

Summer folk. She glanced at Bob's shapeless shorts and golf shirt and looked away with a sniff. Bob didn't appear to notice.

"Heard it from more than one source, too," he said. "The night before, some teenager at a party told the other kids that Ed Billings was going to kill that girl."

They reached the turn in the trail and stepped around the last stand of trees. Much of the fairground opened up in front of them, vast and green and crowded. There were hundreds of people—brightly dressed families, couples, groups of teenagers. They milled about or sat on blankets or at tables eating off paper plates. At the far side of the grounds John could see concession tables and the large fire pit, presumably manned by one or both of Elson's co-owners/chefs; they were too far away to tell. Mick was one of his clients. A hundred-plus conversations, laughter, and shrieks from a band of little kids racing by all competed for air, which was pleasantly warm. Nice.

"You believe it?" John asked. He thought he might get a beer first, even if it meant having to chat with Rick Truman for a few moments, which it likely did. John made a serious effort not to try to categorize people, clients or no, but he suspected an array of unspecified personality disorders in Rick's case; he was passive-aggressive and obsessive in turns. On the other hand, he always ordered top-notch microbrew...

He had expected an immediate *no* to his question. Registering Bob's silence, he turned, smiling, expecting a punch line. Bob had slowed, his expression thoughtful.

"You really think someone prophesied the murders?" John asked.

Bob finally smiled back at him. "No, not really. But stranger things have happened. Remind me to tell you sometime about my brother." John nodded, keeping his own thoughts on the subject to himself. In his line of work—for anyone's line of work, really—it

didn't pay to scoff at another's beliefs. Not everyone had the training he did, understood how the subconscious could create a convincing reality from barely perceived details, give the seer a sense
that he or she knew the unknowable—when, in fact, they were only
picking up on things that their conscious mind hadn't registered.
Combine that with a universally felt desire to believe in something
greater than oneself—God, family, love, government conspiracies,
or extraterrestrial life, real or unreal…everyone had their *greater-
than* of choice, and belief in psychic phenomena wasn't particularly uncommon. Telling that to someone who believed, though,
that was beyond patronizing, and while he knew what he knew, he
wasn't in the habit of being an ass.

They walked slowly toward the food tables, stopping several
times to chat with other locals. Bob got most of the wave-overs;
he was well liked and well known. John got a few friendly hellos.
He saw several of his clients around and about and was careful to
let them acknowledge him first, mindful of their privacy.

"John!"

He turned, smiled. Karen Haley stood up from a rumpled
plaid blanket on the ground where another woman and a young
boy were sitting. She waved him over, and seeing that Bob had
been waylaid by one of his cronies, John headed in her direction.

She looked good, fit and smiling. Karen had suffered terribly
after the death of her husband three, four years before. Guiding
her through it, watching her slowly regain herself through
months of therapy, had been professionally and personally quite
rewarding for him; she was a strong, capable woman, a bit blunt
at times but a pleasure to work with.

They hugged briefly, exchanged pleasantries, agreed that it
had been too long, and then Karen was introducing her sister
and nephew. The other woman stood and leaned in to shake his
hand. Her own was slender and warm.

"This is Sarah, Sarah Reed," Karen said. "And my brilliant nephew, Tommy."

"Jeez," Tommy muttered, but smiled agreeably. He looked about eleven or twelve. Sarah, John remembered, was four or five years younger than Karen, perhaps late thirties. His age. She was a teacher, married, lived in Seattle. Karen had spoken of her fondly.

"Sarah, this is John Hanover. Dr. John?"

"Oh, right," Sarah said, her smile deepening. "Karen's had good things to say about you."

"It's nice to meet you," he said. "Are you here for the summer?"

"Yep. Got a job to get back to in September," she said. He noticed how blue her eyes were; she had tiny fine lines just starting to etch at the corners, accenting them. When she brushed an errant dark-blonde strand of hair out of her eyes, he saw she wasn't wearing a wedding ring.

"Not if I can talk her out of it," Karen said. "I finally got her here, I want to keep her around for a while. Well, and my nephew, of course. He's the brains of this operation. He's been working on the inn's web page for us."

Tommy managed to shrug without moving his shoulders, a kind of eye flick and smirk, but John could see that a smile lurked there as well.

John nodded at him. "Impressive. Mac or PC?"

Tommy grinned. "Mac by choice, PC by necessity."

They all laughed. Tommy asked if he could go get a Coke. His mother gave him a few bills and he mumbled a rote "nicetameetcha" before disappearing. He seemed like a nice kid. Bright. John hadn't spent a lot of time around children, but he found he generally liked them.

"Susan, you should totally hook up with John," Karen said abruptly.

Susan raised her eyebrows. "What?"

"You said you were looking for a good therapist since the divorce," Karen said, matter-of-factly. "You should call John."

Blunt as ever. There was a brief silence, John trying to think of something to say, but Sarah managed to smooth it over.

"Thanks, Kare," she said, sarcastically but with no real bite. "Way to make me feel totally awkward. Is your gynecologist around?"

John laughed, deciding he liked her. And those extraordinary eyes...it was the second time in a week that he'd noticed a woman's eyes, he realized. Or cared whether she was married.

And only a few minutes after you were ready to go home, depressed over Lauren. Aren't we the bipolar bear?

Bipolar bear. His girlfriend in med school used to call him that. Katherine. She'd been the great love of his life before Lauren...

He shook himself mentally, dragging himself back to the present. Karen suggested that he join them for dinner sometime, and he went through the brief internal dance of whether to explain that it wasn't likely to happen; even if it had been more than two years since their last appointment, what the APA guidelines recommended, he didn't feel comfortable socializing with former clients. If one of them ever needed his services again, it could be problematic...not to mention, the client-doctor roles weren't easily sidestepped, which caused its own set of issues. Luckily, she seemed to pick up on his hesitation, adding a cheery, "or maybe we'll just run into each other around town." John nodded, glad that she was as perceptive as he remembered. He said his good-bye and smiled at both women, his gaze meeting Sarah's and lingering a split second longer than he meant. She seemed to flush ever so slightly, quite prettily, although perhaps it was just the sun.

He headed back to where Bob was now standing alone, waiting for him, thinking that maybe he was due for a check-in with his therapist.

Maybe you just need to get laid, he thought, and tried to make it fit, but the thought wasn't very funny, even in his head.

"Sorry about that," Bob said, as they started walking toward the tables again. "Henry Dawes wants to drag me out on his boat again next week. I keep trying to get out of it; he likes to be on the water by sunrise, but he won't let up and—hey, there she is."

Bob nodded toward a couple standing in the shade of a narrow tree stand not far away, a pale teenage girl in black with short, choppy dyed-black hair and a tall, slender young man in a tight T-shirt. They were smoking, and both had the alternative look; the girl wore a ripped skirt and heavy boots, and the boy's short hair was carefully mussed with product. He recognized the boy as Devon Shupe. The high school counselor had asked his advice two years before about dealing with an openly gay student and hadn't been particularly careful about keeping the name to herself. Devon had been pointed out to him since then, by someone or another. Being gay, even flamboyantly so, didn't come with the stigma it once did, but Port Isley wasn't all that liberal. Not in winter, anyway.

"There who is?" John asked.

"The psychic," Bob said. "Rita Fergus pointed her out. Said her daughter swore up and down that she—Amanda, I believe— told people that Lisa Meyer would be killed by Ed Billings."

"Huh," John said. The girl seemed tense, her shoulders up, her arms folded. As he watched, she dragged deeply off her cigarette and said something to her friend, smoke leaking from the corners of her mouth. "You going to talk to her?"

"No. I imagine some of her friends—or enemies, more likely—are playing a joke on her. I doubt she even knows. And

I'd kind of like to get through the rest of my day without being scoffed at by a punk-rock girl."

The girl looked up then, and right at John. Her face was soft and round and surprisingly innocent. Pretty, really. She stared at him for a minute, then reached up with her free hand and carefully scratched under her eye, using just her middle finger. John looked away, almost smiling, trying to remember if he'd been so hostile at her age. It seemed likely.

"So, beer first or food?" Bob asked, as they reached the small crowd that was breaking into lines, heading for hors d'oeuvres or grilled sea bass or microbrew.

"Beer," John said, emphatically. It suddenly seemed like the perfect answer to his strangely wandering thoughts. Pure escapism in a top-quality IPA, and he absolutely refused to feel guilty about it. "And I'm buying."

><

Sadie Truman ate a water cracker topped with smoked salmon, delicately licking her lips and smiling in Josh's direction. It had been a busy day, but he was in between customers for the moment, the lunch rush mostly past, the restocking caught up. The beautiful Josh was packing ice around the perishables, but he caught the smile. He glanced around, saw that Rick was talking up some summer people, and smiled back at her, a hint of a leer in the expression. It had been six whole days since they'd had a minute together, with Rick barging around, sticking his nose into every corner, getting things ready for the picnic, and she missed him—missed "it"—terribly. What Josh could do with his hands, once she'd shown him how...

Rick's boisterous fake laugh assaulted her ears, dragging her away from a particularly pleasant thought. She looked over at him, at his grinning, chunky face, and felt a chill of disgust. He was a wizard at managing their portfolio, seemed to know exactly what to invest in and when, and she had no doubt that without him, her restaurant dreams would have remained just that. Plus, he adored her. But God, she was sick of his lame jokes and aggressive social behavior and sad bedroom antics. If he had any idea how much disdain she felt, even *looking* at him some days...

Rick was shaking hands with another summer couple, his patented hearty grin plastered firmly in place. Sadie stole another look at Josh, now serving a new gathering of summer people, at his comfortably slouchy jeans, his too-long hair curling behind his ears, imagining the tight, muscular torso hidden beneath his silly Hawaiian shirt, and felt a tingling in her belly. He was fifteen years her junior, he was relaxed and handsome and passionate, everything that Rick wasn't, and she couldn't get enough of him. Couldn't wait to get more of him, either. They only had the summer; he'd be going to graduate school in the fall, and it was unlikely he'd be back next year. There would be another Josh, of course— over Rick's intermittent protests, she always insisted on doing the summer hiring for the shop—but some years she'd been forced to settle for much less. Worse, some years, there'd been no Josh at all.

A heavy hand crashed across the back of her neck, then rubbed briefly and viciously.

"How ya holding up, sweetheart?"

Sadie smiled automatically, moved away from the pinching fingers. How had he managed to sneak up on her? "Good, I'm good. How are you?"

Rick grinned, his flushed, sweaty face too close to her own. His breath was sour. "Great. Everyone's raving about the salmon. And half the people I've talked to said last year's barbecue was better. Guess they like our sausages better than Mick and Jason's."

She tensed, waiting for the inevitable joke. He dropped his voice slightly, leaned in even closer. "Course, some people are more particular about where they get their sausage, you know what I mean?"

Sadie managed a slight smile. The co-owners of Elson's, Mick and Jason, were gay, and Rick couldn't say two words about them without adding some vaguely homophobic innuendo. It was so... so pedestrian, in this day and age. So very like Rick, to be threatened by whatever he didn't personally benefit by.

"And you were right about the melon, honey," he added. "Everything was spectacular...beautiful. Look, I'm going to go make a couple of calls; we're going to need to order more of the smoked salmon, and I've got a couple other requests for the shop, some organic stuff...can you and Josh hold things down for a few?"

As if she'd fall apart without his guiding hand, as if she didn't know how to smile and charm with the best of them. She was the one who'd grown up with money; that kind of thing was second nature for her. It was Rick who had to thrash and struggle to make contacts and kiss ass to keep them. Sadie didn't know the business specifics as well as he did, true, but she definitely knew more than he thought—and she was learning more all the time.

One of these days. It would be a nasty divorce, she was sure of that. Rick was a bully and miserly to his core, two essential facts that he'd kept well hidden until after he'd convinced her to marry him, so, so long ago. But almost everything was in her name; he'd be left with nothing. She was in no hurry to get to it—Rick worked hard and did his best by her—but the end was inevitable; their lives had been separate for so long, she doubted she'd even notice his absence, assuming she could find a good manager to take his place. And just the right Josh, of course, to attend to her other needs.

"I'm on top of it," she said, and if her smile was a bit more sardonic than it needed to be, he didn't notice. He never did.

Rick bussed her cheek and headed for the service lot, already pulling out his cell. Sadie watching him walk away, his square, heavy ass accentuated by off-the-rack khakis, and wished that he was already gone.

Perhaps it was time to whisper a few well-chosen words into Josh's tender ear. Sadie smoothed her fabulously expensive dress down her slender hips and walked his way, smiling for real.

><

They'd been at the picnic for almost an hour and still hadn't come up with a plan. Devon thought they should approach the cops—well, Chief Vincent—and tell him that they'd overheard Brian talking about raping someone...which wasn't too bad, except that talking didn't exactly qualify as a crime, and Amanda was worried that the chief would blow them off. Devon's reasoning was that Vincent would go hassle Brian a little, scare him off the idea, but she wanted something better, something more concrete. They had yet to see Brian Glover at all, and except for a rather sullen-looking Ethan Adcox, there with his family, none of the Dicks were in attendance. Ethan was only a semi-Dick, anyway. Amanda was fairly certain that her dream—her vision—had been of Brian, Todd Clay, and Ryan Thompson. Devon agreed. If anyone was gonna go pro, he said, it would be those three.

They stood in the shade, smoking, still pondering their options, talking it over. What had seemed so clear in the dead of night, her decision to save the unknown woman by any means necessary, now seemed kind of far-fetched. She wasn't Buffy, she wasn't a crime fighter or superhero, she didn't have the resources—or, she had to admit, the credibility—to make things happen. Or not happen, in this case.

"What if I tell Vincent that Brian assaulted me?" Amanda asked. "He'd at least pick him up, right?"

Devon considered it. Amanda noticed a man staring at her, some guy walking to the food lines, and discreetly flipped him off. Fucking tourists. The guy looked away, an expression of mild amusement on his face, and she realized that he looked familiar. Not a tourist, then.

Who cares? Someone is going to get hurt if you don't come up with something.

"Seems risky," Devon said finally. "I mean, if he's got an alibi, you'll look like a liar."

She sighed, pulled another cigarette out of her crumpled pack—had to love soft packs, there was always another one hiding in there—and lit it off the butt of the one still burning. She'd been chain-smoking since she'd left the apartment; her mouth tasted like crap, but she was too wired to do anything else.

"Well, technically, I *will* be lying," she said, stomping the old butt into the dirt. "But I'm thinking that by the time they figure it out, it'll be too late. I could talk to Vincent right before dark."

"Maybe. But what if…"

"What if what?"

Devon shook his head. "Nothing, it's stupid."

"Now it's going to drive me nuts. What?"

"I was just thinking…I mean, what if we tell Vincent, or whoever, and he hassles Brian…and Brian wasn't *going* to do anything, but he gets so pissed off about being accused…"

Amanda felt a knot form in her gut. "You mean, what if I actually make it happen by trying to stop it? That—that sucks, Dev. That totally fucking *sucks*."

Devon dropped his own smoke to the ground, tapping it out with the pointed toe of his wingtip. "Forget it. I told you it was stupid."

"I mean, I can't just do nothing—"

"I know, I know."

"—because if I keep my mouth shut and it happens—"

Devon sighed. "I know, all right?" They were both silent for a moment. Amanda felt entirely overwhelmed. The situation was so unreal, like she was in a movie or something, but everything was taking too long and she still felt like her normal self. Not bored shitless for a change, but otherwise just plain ol' Amanda Young. Certainly not like some fictional young psychic detective with brilliant plans and a network of talented friends and a handgun.

"Maybe we *should* talk to Pam, and Ally Fergus," Devon said. "Couple of the others." He'd already brought this up like three times. "If we can get them to back you up, *then* go talk to the sheriff—"

Amanda shook her head. "No way he'd believe us."

"He'd have to, though, if we could prove that you saw—that you saw what happened before."

"We talked about this," Amanda said. "A bunch of teenagers, most of them totally trashed on the night in question—and Pam Roth won't own up to having a party, you know that. Her parents would shit."

"Stopping a, a *rape* totally trumps Pam getting in trouble with her parents—"

"You remember when she took her dad's car last year, drove it to Port Angeles?" Amanda asked. "She had a fuckin' black eye the next day, and she was grounded for like four months."

"Still," Devon said, but he didn't sound as sure.

"We're *children*, Devon. They'll think we're full of shit; you know it. Not just the cops, either. You think Sid would believe us? Or my mom?"

Devon's uncle Sid was a good man, but he also had no imagination whatsoever. And her mother...Grace's solution to anything she couldn't handle was to get shit-faced and cry about it.

"OK, but there are other people," Devon said. "If we could get someone with some real credibility to listen to us, maybe they could talk to the cops...like what about Willie?"

Willa Tenungren, Willie T, was the art teacher at the high school. She was maybe the only teacher there who made any real effort to connect with her students, and Devon was a particular favorite of hers.

Amanda gave it a second's thought, then shook her head. "Not exactly credible." Willie liked to hang out at the artist colony in the off-season and wrote poetry books in her free time, published by Kinko's. Amanda had seen her read a couple of times; she wrote poignant odes to wilting flowers and late-summer days and dreams about flying. Someone like Chief Vincent probably thought she was a flaming hippie.

"She'd believe us, though," he said.

"Dude, her underwear's made out of hemp," she said, and in spite of the seriousness of what they were discussing—or, more likely, because of it—they both started to laugh.

The laughter had started to die down when Devon added, "When she farts, midgets get high."

Amanda choke-laughed out a lungful of smoke, grateful to Devon in spite of the near attack of dry heaves that followed. For making her laugh. For believing her. She'd called his cell as soon as she'd gotten up, told him what had happened in about a dozen words—well, except for the part about her mother and the rat, which was too weird and upsetting and somehow too personal— and he'd immediately changed his plans in order to hang out with her.

When they'd finally calmed down, Amanda felt better. Still freaked, absolutely, but not as tense, not as flat-out terrified. She looked around at the people, the warm day—it'd be hot in their shithole apartment tonight, but it was kind of nice, here, now, in the shade—and she couldn't help that the live wire she'd had in her stomach, there since Pam's party, was as exciting as it was terrifying. Something was happening, she didn't know what, and she wished wholeheartedly that this unnamed something hadn't happened to *her*, but her life was changing, had already changed. For the first time ever, she felt…she felt special, kind of, and she didn't like thinking that, was sure that made her a terrible person, but that was how she felt.

There was a guy over toward the food booths, looking their direction. He was young, their age, rail thin but tall, dressed in baggy jeans and a plain black tee. His hair was a thick, dark brown mop that hung in his eyes and stuck out over his ears. He had a wallet on a chain, the shining silver links hanging over one hip, his thumbs tucked in his front pockets. Picture of cool, a summer boy, and when their gazes met, he gave her a chin nod, that slight raise that told her she was being acknowledged. She nodded back. On any other day, she would have flirted, a smile, a shy look-away-and-back—he was a hottie, hands down, and he was checking her out, and considering her entire lack of a love life since Brooks (who wasn't at the picnic this year, thank Christ for small favors), a new boy in her reality was nothing to dismiss lightly.

Not today, though. She looked away. When she glanced back in that direction a moment later, he was gone.

"What about Bob Sayers?" Devon asked suddenly.

"Who? The *Isley Press* guy?"

Devon nodded. "Sandy's always going on about how cool he is, how he's respectful of their ideas, doesn't shoot anything down no matter how out there it is. Remember, he published that whole thing on UFOs they did last year?"

Sandra Mulvey was the editor of the school paper and a good friend of Devon's. Amanda thought she was kind of pretentious but all right otherwise. The journalism class sometimes wrote little articles for the *Press*. "Yeah, that was pretty stupid."

Devon rolled his eyes. "Not the point, dumbass. He published it, didn't he?"

"Doesn't mean he believes it," she said, but felt a faint spark of hope, anyway. She wasn't entirely conscious of the desire, but part of her wanted very badly to turn the whole matter over to a certified adult, to someone who would know what to do, who would *act*.

"But he *is* a reporter, and there's a story here, right?" Devon asked, obviously warming to the idea. "He could talk to Ally. Scott was there, too, when you—when it happened. So was Joey K, a bunch of people. I mean, worst thing, he doesn't believe us, we come up with something else."

Amanda shook her head. "Worst thing, he tells the chief that we're running around making shit up. Which would blow our shot at getting Brian arrested."

Devon met her gaze squarely, and his light, airy tone dropped a notch. He rarely used his "real" voice, only when something was important, and it carried weight.

"We have to do *something*," he said. "And if we can convince him, maybe he can help. If we—"

He stopped abruptly, looking past her. Amanda turned—and saw Brian Glover walking through the milling crowd, heading toward the restrooms, his upper lip stuck in its perpetual sneer. Amanda suddenly had to catch her breath; her heart was pounding her whole body. She'd never felt anything but disgust at the sight of him, since the day she'd first become aware of his existence, her first week of school after moving to Port Isley—the day he'd been leaning against her locker, talking to some of his dickhead buddies and she'd said, "Excuse me," because she had to get her math book, and she didn't want to be late to class, she was still new. He'd turned his mean, piggy gaze to her, the pink of his scalp shining through his eternally crappy crew cut, and grinned a sharp and shining grin. "Why, d'ya fart?" he'd shot, and his friends had laughed, and so had a bunch of other people. Since then, she'd come to know him as a moronic force of high school evil. His mom was a shivering mouse of a woman, and his dad was a mean drunk who hung out with those survivalist psychos out past the lighthouse, probably plotting to overthrow the government or something. Mostly, Brian disgusted her. What she felt now was so far beyond disgust she didn't know how to express it, how she could even contain it.

"We'll talk to Sayers," she said, and Devon nodded, reaching out to put a hand on her trembling shoulder.

CHAPTER
7

After a few minutes silently pondering the lingering remnants of the murder site—crushed vegetation, a mound of dying bouquets left by the miscellaneous bereaved, a profusion of shoe and boot prints—police chief Stan Vincent slowly continued along Kehoe Park's main trail. Sun filtered down through the high treetops, which hissed and roared with the wind off the bay; down on the thickly wooded trail, it was barely breezy, the air warm, the sound of the thrashing trees high above strangely muffled. It was a nice day, good for the picnic, which was as big and well behaved, as usual. Annie and Trent were watching things, though most of the rest of his deputies were there as picnickers; if there was a problem, it'd be contained. He'd put in an appearance already, glad-handed some of the summer people, and done his best to avoid the worst of the gossipmongers, but Dan Turner and the rest of the council would have a giant shit if he didn't show up again before dinner.

They need to feel safe, Dan had told him, trying to be encouraging and coming off like the fat, whiny, sanctimonious little prick that he was. *They need to be reassured that Port Isley is a haven, and that the man responsible for their safety is on the job.*

On the job. Vincent snorted, stepping lightly over a dip in the trail. Like those soft, manicured metrosexuals and their latte-slurping wives would give a fuck for whatever Deputy Dipshit had to say. They treated him like the hired help—unless there was trouble, of course, a parking violation or a noise complaint or, God forbid, a break-in. Then it was yessir, nosir, thank you Officer...

Vincent didn't really mind the hypocrisy, most of the time. He was the chief of police in a tourist town; part of his job was to make the summer people feel comfortable so they'd come back, spend more money. But after what Ed Billings had done to the Meyer girl, and then his wife...all anyone wanted to know since Monday morning was how the *sheriff* had handled it. And how far away were the staters, and could deputies come quickly in an emergency, and just what *was* the jurisdiction breakdown, anyway?

Why the fuck do I bother, they think I'm so incompetent? Vincent continued to walk slowly, determined to keep a lid on his temper. He'd listened to their stupid, insulting questions for almost three hours this morning before he'd managed to get away. He could understand it, of course—the tourists didn't know his background, didn't know that he wasn't some hick elected official with a badge who'd run on a smile and a solid handshake. With his experience—military background, degree in criminology, even most of a year of advanced special tactics training—he could be working anywhere. When he'd been looking for work after the thing in Denver, he'd chosen Port Isley because he'd been invited in at the top, because he'd been allowed to pick his own people, organize things the way he wanted them. Yeah, Ashley had pushed for it, too. She'd fallen in love with the little town on their first vacation there, a good three years before Lily had come along, her birth forcing the need, in Ashley's mind, to move someplace "good" for kids—but the final decision had been his. For the most part, he wasn't sorry for the change, either; he was damned good at his job. And the first big case to come through since Walter Allen beat a fellow bar drunk to death three years back, and what did everyone want to know? Where were the county guys. What did the county guys say. Or the winner, from that hatchet-faced lesbian couple renting out the white Victorian for the season, "You've turned all the evidence over to the authorities, of course."

Vincent took in a deep breath, blew it out. If he didn't hate Wes Dean so goddamn much, Sheriff Western Dean of the big-boy county office, it might not be so bad—

A noise, a rattle of bushes, and Vincent saw something move ahead, a branch to the main trail some twenty yards away—a young man was stepping through the light screen of bushes there, tall, thin, dark hair, tan corduroy jacket. He was wearing expensive new hiking boots, the kind that weren't really made for hiking—and considering how pale he was, he only could have been hiking at night, anyway. He didn't notice the cop, was about to step across the main trail to the small branch he'd been walking. He wasn't a local. Vincent knew about every face in town.

"Good afternoon," he called out, and the young man stopped, not looking at him, his gaze still focused on the path. For the briefest of instants, Vincent had an impression that the guy meant to run—and then it passed, and the man turned toward him, unsmiling.

*Something about the way he was standing, maybe, tightness in the jaw...*Vincent wasn't sure, but he dismissed the impression as he walked closer. The guy—mid-to late twenties, probably—had a straight-arrow look, the face of a well-to-do grad student. Not the running type.

The younger man stayed put, made no move to meet Vincent as he neared.

"Chief," the stranger said, his tone as neutral as his expression. "Vincent, isn't it?"

"That's right," Vincent nodded. He stopped in front of the man, put on his best PR smile, reached out his hand. "I don't believe we've had the pleasure…?"

The man hesitated a beat, then stretched out his own and shook briefly. "David Mallon," he said. "I'm here for the summer."

"Oh, yeah? Where are you staying?"

"Rental," Mallon said. "On Eleanor Street."

Eleanor was only a block and a half long, an extension of Devlin; the short street ran along the east side of Kehoe Park. For a half second, Vincent thought about mentioning the tragedy that had occurred in the park Sunday night, asking if Mallon had been bothered by the hoo-ha afterward, but quickly dismissed the thought. No point in reminding anyone of what had happened. Goddamn media had done enough of that. The last crew had split town just this morning, after a disgustingly exploitive "and now the little town bravely faces its future" piece.

"Nice day for a walk," Vincent said, still smiling, observing the summer man carefully. Vincent was privately quite proud of his readings on new people, on feeling like he knew something about them at first impression. If nothing else, people's feelings about cops usually came out right away, on their faces or in their body language, the big smile and hearty handshake of the pro-police folks, the sneery petulance or bravado of youth, the tension of a guilty conscience—but he got nothing off Mallon. Zip.

"It is," Mallon agreed. He didn't add anything, didn't ramble nervously or talk to fill space. Just waited.

"You know, there's a big picnic over at the fairgrounds today," Vincent said. "Kind of a welcoming party for our summer guests, food, music, some nice people. It goes on until late, if you feel like heading over."

Mallon nodded. "Perhaps I will. Thank you."

A man of few words, apparently. Vincent saw no reason to keep him, and he obviously didn't want to make conversation.

"Well—nice meeting you," Vincent said. "Welcome to Port Isley. And you might want to think about sticking to the main trails. Some of the smaller ones aren't cleared."

"I'll be careful," Mallon said, then smiled, ever so slightly. "I like the privacy."

Vincent was about to offer his hand once more, but Mallon apparently felt excused. He nodded politely at Vincent and then went on his way, moving along down the smaller trail.

Vincent watched him walk for a few seconds, thinking that in spite of that old saw about how everyone had a story to tell, the only remarkable thing about some people was how entirely *un*remarkable they were, and then continued on his own walk. He'd have to head back soon; Ashley was planning to bring Lily to the picnic for an early supper, and he wanted to spend a little time with his family, counteract some of the bullshit he'd been shoveling all morning, would probably still be shoveling well after dark.

He sighed, turned back toward the west exit, where his just-washed-for-summer PIPD patrol unit was parked, and started walking.

>‹

The sun was bright and shining, like the faces of the children who ran and played among the smiling picnickers. Like their little shining souls. And bright voices. Or, their faces glowed from sun and shade and, and...

The children glowed like tiny suns, their voices radiating like heat...their faces like...brightness in the shade...

"Miranda?"

Miranda blinked, her sunstruck vision slowly dimming back to the day. She squinted, shaded her eyes, and saw Patricia Carter standing there, smiling tentatively. Patricia was a promising painter who'd come to the artisans' retreat for the summer two years ago. She'd married the following spring and hadn't been back, which had vexed Miranda somewhat; she and James had subsidized Patricia's room and board, and the girl hadn't even managed to respond to last year's invitation...although she *had* sent a lovely, hand-painted seasonal card to the retreat around the holidays, Miranda recalled, which counted for good manners, at least. She'd taken a day job as a bookkeeper or some such...paralegal? Something white-collarish.

"Patricia, how are you, dear? You look wonderful." She stood, embraced the girl, then opened her arm to the other chairs. "Sit and tell me how you are."

"Oh, I can only stay a minute," Patricia said, her face set in an apologetic smile. "Mark's over fending for himself at the concessions, and—"

"You don't mind if I...?" Miranda sat down again as Patricia shook her head, mumbling her acquiescence. "I've been on my feet all day; you know how summers are. We've got seven new people in, just in the last week. We're still getting settled."

Patricia folded her arms across her chest, nodding, smiling. "Are Brenda and Steve here this year?"

Miranda felt her grin set slightly. Steve and Brenda DeLinn had been with the retreat every summer since...since she'd started the retreat, really. The second or third summer, anyway, and that meant ten years, at least. Miranda had considered them both her close friends. If they'd needed money, they could have come to her; they didn't need to lie about being busy, they didn't have to choose California over the retreat...

They were shallow and ungrateful people, she and James were in complete agreement. And not nearly so talented as they believed themselves to be. Thought they were the second coming of the Natzlers, for heaven's sake.

"No," Miranda said, as evenly as possible. "But what are you up to, dear? What's lighting up your life right now, right this very moment?"

Patricia smiled widely. "Well…Mark and I are trying to get pregnant."

"You *are*, how wonderful! I just love babies, love them. I have three nieces, you know, and all of them have children, and they're just the sweetest things."

"We're really excited," Patricia said. "Mark just got a new job. And we can afford for me to be a full-time artist for a while, so the timing is right. We're just ready, you know?"

"That's so lovely," Miranda said. "You know who we *do* have this year—Darrin Everret, from Massachusetts. You know his work?"

"Ah, no, I don't think—"

"He's still quite young, but he's going to make an impact, I can tell you. Drawings, mostly, pencil and charcoal. You—you and Mark, of course—you'll have to come to the show at the end of the summer, to see his work. It's extraordinary." She hesitated, then added, "I don't believe I saw you there last summer."

Patricia crossed her arms tighter. "We meant to come, but we had a minor emergency…"

She trailed off. Miranda smiled, waited.

"Mark's mother spent some time in the hospital. She's in Portland, so we had to be down there for a while," Patricia said finally.

Miranda pressed one hand to her chest. "Darling, I'm so sorry. How dreadful."

"Oh, it's fine. She's doing fine, now."

"Well, thank heavens," Miranda said. "And the two of you with a baby on the way. Hopefully soon. We never had children, you know. How lovely. I hope you're keeping up with your work?"

Patricia nodded. "I am, actually. I'm not as prolific as I was when I was here, though."

"It's the community spirit," Miranda said firmly. She and James spoke of it often, the productivity that was possible when so many artistic minds were creating, together. It was why they'd begun the retreat in the first place.

"Oh, I always meant to ask—did Monet ever come back?" Patricia asked.

The cats. Miranda frowned, trying to recall if Patricia had always been so tactless. "No, he never did."

"Poor Manet," Patricia said. "They were so cute together."

"Manet was gone a week into the fall," Miranda said. "We've stopped keeping cats at the retreat." Just saying it aloud made her feel grim and unhappy. Monet and Manet had been the fourth and last pair of cats they'd had since opening their community. All of them had disappeared, some within a week or two of their arrival. The summer Patricia had been there, the mystery of the disappearing cats had been a frequently covered topic at mealtimes. The most often agreed upon explanation was that the cats had all been killed by the animals in the woods that bordered the retreat. The hills just outside town stretched into federally protected coastal old-growth habitat. There were owls and foxes and wolverines, even black bears a bit farther south. It was likely reasoning, but Miranda knew better.

"It's just as well," she added, and didn't try to smile. "No reason to give those, those *crazies* anyone new to kill."

"So you really think it was them?" Patricia asked.

Miranda nodded, feeling a flush of anger. "I'm certain."

Crazies. Survivalists. They had their own compound less than a mile from the community, back in the woods. They had guns, and they ate dehydrated food and built bomb shelters and God only knew what else. When she and James had first opened their retreat, she'd made the terrible, horrid mistake of asking them to not shoot things on her property. Within a month, Francisco and Georgia were gone. She hadn't *known*, of course...and even as late as the summer Patricia had been with the community, she'd only had suspicions. Last October, though, Miranda had run into the leader of the whackos and one of his sons at the market. She'd looked up from perusing the apples—James was off at Truman's, fetching organic milk and cream cheese; the local store didn't carry either— and there he'd been, Cole Jessup and one of his spawn. Both in dirty flannel and military boots caked with mud, both with the same faded blue eyes and leathery skin, though the son—Mitchell?—had better teeth than his father. The younger Jessup had been holding a handbasket filled with jars of peanut butter and had spotted her first from near one of the checkouts. He had nudged Cole—he had a cart stacked with cases of cheap beer, of course—and the two men had grinned through a mumbled exchange, staring at her.

As she'd gone back to picking over the apples, Mitchell Jessup had clearly said, "Meow."

Terrible, terrible men. She'd complained to the police, of course, but they'd been unable to do anything beyond talk to Jessup, who'd flatly stated that if people didn't want to lose their pets, they ought not let them roam...

"Well. I'm sure they'll get what's coming to them. Anyway, I've got to—"

"Karma," Miranda nodded.

"It's wonderful to see you, but I've really got to go rescue my husband," Patricia said. "And you can count on us for the show this summer."

S.D. PERRY

"That's wonderful, dear," Miranda said, shading her eyes again as Patricia backed away. "We have our performance night coming up next month, mid-July—well, poetry, mostly, but I'm sure there will be some other—"

"We'll check the paper," Patricia called back, and hurried away, disappearing into a crowd of sundresses and shorts. Miranda saw a few of her colonists walking toward the stage area together and was about to shout them over when her husband spoke.

"Was that Patty?"

Miranda turned and saw that James had finally managed to make his way back to their designated spot. He held two paper plates, loaded with those little Spanish appetizers that Elson's had put out this year, a giant plastic cup cradled against his side.

"Patricia, dear," Miranda said. "And where have you been? I'm *parched.*"

>‹

The kids approached Bob during the Baptist church choir's enthusiastic rendition of "Nearer My God To Thee," fervently conducted by the high school music teacher. Bob was glad for the break. Enthusiastic, the singers were; talented, not so much. Besides which, Bob liked a good story, and the two teens looked like they had one to tell. The four pints he'd had since the picnic's kickoff certainly helped kindle his interest, and the cagey suggestion from the fey young man that they go "somewhere private" added a touch of the dramatic. Thinking of what he'd heard earlier in the day, about the girl's alleged psychic revelation, Bob had gladly accepted their invitation, preparing himself for either a sincere story of harassment or a wonderfully tall tale.

As he'd dared to hope, the story they started telling was a creatively exciting one. The young man introduced them both—they were Devon Shupe (pronounced "Shoo-pay") and Amanda Young, respectively—and did most of the talking, explaining what had happened and what they believed was yet to happen. In short, the girl had foreseen Lisa Meyer's death a week earlier and had experienced another vision since, of a rape that would occur that very night if nothing was done to stop it. An assault that would take place not far from where they were standing, sheltered from the crowd by the cinderblock restrooms. The girl seemed nervous. Understandably so, if she'd actually seen what she claimed.

It was their obvious sincerity that had Bob paying closer attention than he might have otherwise. By the time Devon had touched on all the high points, Bob's initial smirk had taken backseat to a genuine curiosity.

"So," Devon said, taking a deep breath. "We need help. We figure no way the cops'll believe us, and it's not like we're going to, like—kidnap Brian Glover or something."

He fell silent, glancing at Amanda, who was lighting a cigarette. She half smiled back at him, exhaling smoke as she spoke.

"That's one we didn't think of. Why don't we just kill him? We could hide the body in Peter's truck."

Devon chuckled at the obvious sarcasm, and though Bob didn't know who Peter was, he smiled politely, distantly, his mind ticking through their assertions. Out on the main concourse, the Baptist choir had gone into a rather chilling interpretation of "Down by the River."

"Back up a minute," he said, addressing Amanda directly. "You saw Billings *bite* her, is that right?"

"Yeah," Amanda said. "He started choking her, and then he just leaned forward and…and bit. Her face." The corners of her mouth turned down, her expression one of extreme distaste. "Pulled off a piece and chewed on it."

Bob looked at Devon. "Did she say that? When she, ah, started shouting?"

Devon hesitated, then shook his head. "I don't think so. She said Mr. Billings was killing Lisa Meyer, is all. She told me later, though."

"That night?" Bob asked.

Both nodded. Bob kept his polite smile on, thinking it over. It hadn't gone out in the *Press*, of course, but Annie Thomas had told him about the facial mutilation—had told him only this morning, a few hours earlier, that the ME had identified it as a bite. This supposition was solidly backed up by what they'd found in Billings's stomach. It would get around, of course, the details always did in Port Isley, but he was fairly certain that that particular nugget of unpleasantness was still unknown to the general public. Which begged the question, how did Amanda Young know about it at all, let alone prior to the attack?

No way to check it, though. She told her friend, nobody else. She'd apparently told half the party that Billings killed the girl— and Lisa Meyer had actually been there at the time, alive and well, according to his sources—but had only told Devon about the bite to her face. Bob could check the story, talk to some of the partygoers that hadn't already approached him…but that wasn't proof of anything, even if he could count on a group of unknown teenagers at a beer-and-pot party to tell him the truth. Maybe Amanda knew about the affair between the teacher and student, knew that they were about to split up or something, and had decided to make the party a little more dramatic. Maybe Billings was sleeping with Amanda too and had told her his plans. Looking at the girl's rather sweet young face, innocent in spite of the deliberately jaded air she assumed, he doubted it—but he'd been lied to before, and by people more innocent looking than her. Looks could be deceiving.

The thing about the bite, though…

"Assuming I were to believe you, what would you have me do about it?" Bob asked.

Devon looked awkwardly at the girl, then back to Bob. "You could tell the police," he said. "They'd listen to you."

Bob had to smile. "What makes you think that?"

"You're—your opinion matters," Devon said. "People would listen to someone with, um, credibility."

Spoken like a true idealist. "What would I say?" Bob asked.

Again, the look exchange. "You could tell them the truth," Devon said, and Bob could actually see a glimmer of that pitifully hopeful optimism fading, his young gaze going murky, confused. "You could check everything out, and then you'd have evidence, you could convince them to listen."

Bob looked at Amanda, saw that she already understood. It was in her face, in her tight shoulders and defensive stance.

"No way he could do it by tonight, though," she said. Took a quick drag off her cigarette. "And he can't prove that we're telling the truth."

"If he talks to some of the people who were there—"

"That's a bunch of kids talking," she said, her tone flat. "Not evidence."

"It's not going to be dark for like four hours," Devon insisted. "That's plenty of time."

Her voice was as heavily sarcastic as only a punk teenage girl's could be. "Right. Plenty of time to convince fucking Stan Vincent, Mr. Supercop, that seeing into the future is a valid means of crime prevention."

Devon was starting to look angry. "So what, we drop it? You felt guilty about Lisa, and that's before you knew this was real. How are you going to feel tomorrow morning?"

Bob watched with dawning amazement. The exchange was genuine, not an act put on for his benefit. They were both frustrated—the girl bitterly, angrily resigned, the boy desperate—and Bob believed them. Not that they weren't entirely wrong about the rape—he was willing to bet on *that*—but that they weren't lying about it. *They* believed what they were telling him.

He opened his mouth to suggest that they go over it again, ashamedly aware as he did so that he meant to look into the matter, to at least talk to a few people—and that was when the shouting started.

Unintelligible at first, loud and angry, coming from the main concourse, close by. The church choir had finished singing at some point—Bob had barely registered the relieved applause—and now the ambient noise of the assembled crowd fell away, making the shouts much clearer.

"...not gonna take no more a' this shit!" A man shouting. "You can lock him the fuck up and keep him!"

A lower voice, conciliatory in tone, pitched to carry. A woman's voice. "Sir, I'll ask you to step back—"

"The fuck I will! Look at 'im! Kid's seventeen years old! He's—don't you look at me like that, I'll slap that look off your face, boy—"

"Sir, I said—*sir!*"

That was Annie Thomas. Bob hurried out from behind the restroom block, followed closely by the two teenagers. He was already putting together the conversation with the voices, realizing what was happening as the ugly scene unfolded in front of them, less than twenty feet away.

Nathan Glover, dressed in ratty jeans and a blue work shirt, was shouting at Annie Thomas and another officer, one not in uniform—Ian Henderson, Vincent's right-hand guy. The two cops were standing close in front of a younger man, physically shielding him from the angry adult. The young man's shirtfront was covered in vomit, and from the way he was standing—barely, to Bob's trained eye—he was gloriously, toxically drunk.

Brian Glover, if I'm not mistaken.

"That's him," Devon breathed, confirming it.

Nate had apparently also had more than his fair share and seemed ready to take on the two cops to get to his son, though he wasn't a big man—average build, bit of a gut. Ian Henderson had three inches and fifty pounds on him, easy. The gathered picnickers openly gawked at the drama, a few small children still clamoring for attention in the otherwise silent circle of watchers.

The elder Glover had his chest out, was pushing toward Henderson in a showy effort to intimidate, still yelling at his son. "You can stay in there, if I got anything to say about it! You should get use' to the inside of a cell! Then wait'll you get home, boy! You just *wait!*"

"Fuck you," Brian slurred out loudly, and then Annie was pulling the staggering boy away as his father rushed Henderson, his expression just short of murderous. The deputy quickly and neatly stepped to one side, grabbed Nate's arm, and brought it up behind him, which Nate didn't realize until he was falling. Both men went down, Henderson on top. Margot Trent appeared out of the crowd, in uniform, and jumped in to help. With both officers on his back, Nate Glover spluttered uselessly into the dirt, flailing for about two seconds before he gave it up.

"*OK OK OK OK,*" he yelled, going limp, and Henderson bent down and started talking clearly, firmly into his ear as Trent pulled her cuffs from her belt.

Bob scanned the watching faces for reaction and saw frowns and open mouths, conversations slowly starting up. He looked back just in time to see Brian follow his father's example, pitching heavily to the ground. Annie immediately crouched at his side, then stood a few seconds later with a carefully blank expression that said it all—Brian had passed out drunk and was down for the count. Bob didn't see Mrs. Glover anywhere in the crowd, which suggested that further dramatics were unlikely, but there had been enough. A real episode of *Cops*, right in front of the best of the summer trade, who had already started to break up, their low voices tight with excitement and dismay. Dan Turner would crap himself.

Bob glanced at his two young storytellers, saw the twin looks of amazement, of surprise and confusion—and on Amanda's face, a dawning flush of embarrassment or shame. She looked back at Bob, then dropped her gaze, her shoulders sagging.

"I *saw* it," she said, turning to Devon again. "Swear to God, Devon."

Her friend nodded, no doubt in his eyes. "I know. I know you did."

The crowd was breaking apart, flowing into itself as its attention followed the departing cops, Nate and his son both unceremoniously dragged away. People were going back to their food and drink. Devon looked at Bob.

"It could still happen," he said.

Bob arched one brow. "You see that kid?"

"He was just drunk," Devon said, and though he tried to sound dismissive, he couldn't quite pull it off.

"Son, that boy was a hundred and ten percent shit-faced," Bob said. "If he can do anything but puke or sleep for the next ten hours, I'll be dipped. You know that, right?"

"OK, yeah—but what if it's supposed to happen next week, on the Fourth?" Devon persisted. "Or at the carnival in August?"

Bob looked back and forth between the two of them. The young man was still the epitome of earnest, but the girl wouldn't look at him for more than a second at a time, her cheeks burning.

Maybe because she'd been caught out. Still, Bob was gentle, deciding that the benefit of the doubt wouldn't cost him anything. Maybe she was just embarrassed because she looked a fool.

"What if it's next summer?" Bob said. "Or the one after? Or never? What if it was a bad dream after all?"

"It wasn't, though, it was just like before," Amanda insisted suddenly, her voice almost pleading. As though she wanted him to explain it to her.

"Maybe so," Bob said. He kept his expression serious but friendly. He liked kids, mostly, had found in himself a sense of humor for the stumblings of the young, the attitude, the styles. Not all of them, of course—God knew there were some real shitheads in the mix—but as with every generation, the vast majority of the little buggers meant well, wanted simply to grow up and have good things in their lives, love and money and family. Perhaps these two had extra issues to deal with, he certainly couldn't say, but he saw no reason to be *elderly* about it.

"When my older brother first went away to college, he had this roommate, name of Travis Thompson," Bob said, finally deciding to give voice to the story that had been in his mind for most of the day. He hadn't told it in a long time, and he hadn't expected to tell it at all, certainly not to a couple of teenagers, but it was spilling out before he could think twice. All that beer, probably.

"Thompson killed himself over Christmas break," he continued. "Not on purpose, mind you. He drank and drove, though, and he took his girlfriend and his own mother with him, driving them home from a New Year's Eve party. All three of 'em burnt up in a big crash. The thing was, I was with my brother when it happened—Rich and I were having a few beers out in my dad's garage to celebrate the New Year—and he…" Bob hesitated, not sure how to explain…he'd only meant to tell them the anecdote to be kind, to let them know that just because they were wrong, that didn't mean he thought they were crazy—but as he tried to do justice to the tale, he felt a shiver of that, that *uncanniness* he'd felt when it had happened, all those many years ago.

"Rich was telling me some story or other from school, and he went quiet. He set his beer down, and looked at his watch," Bob said. "And he'd been a little tight, you know, but he suddenly looked stone cold, and a little green, too, and he said, just as clear as could be, 'That dumbshit roomie of mine just crashed his car into a light pole off Route Two Nineteen.' "

Bob let the image go and returned his attention to his audience of two. "Knew about the mother and girlfriend, too, and had the time exactly right, though the accident happened in Colorado. A different time zone, for us. And he knew the name of the road, which he shouldn't have. He never could explain it to his own satisfaction...but he once told me it was like he just knew it, like he'd read about it somewhere. Like it was fact."

Amanda was nodding, her cheeks still red but her eyes bright with renewed interest. "Yeah, like that. I saw it first, though, but then it was just like—like knowledge."

Bob continued, his voice mild. "He never saw anything like that again. Stuff like that happens, I think. Not often, probably, but I think it does. And maybe it happened to you."

He fixed Amanda with what he hoped was a kind, paternal look. "But just because it happens sometimes, doesn't mean it happens *every* time," he said.

Devon started to protest, but Amanda, her clear gaze meeting Bob's own squarely enough, stilled him with a wave.

"No, he's right," she said, talking to Devon but still looking at Bob. Her eyes were a lovely shade, dark and greenish, and he was struck by the intelligence there, reflected in the complexities of her emotion, at least what he could read. Embarrassment and resignation, self-doubt, relief. Although there were a lot of smart people in the world, Bob had generally found that stupid abounded, deliberate as often as not; as his own father had liked to say, *some people, if they had a spare brain, it'd be lonely.* It was refreshing to see someone with something going on under the hood.

"You said—" Devon started.

"I know." Amanda cut him off.

"But if it was just like—"

"I *know*," she said. "But he's right about Brian. It's not going to be tonight, anyway. And if I was wrong about *that…*"

The unspoken rest of the thought was enough for Devon, and for Bob.

"Listen, I'm sure everything's going to be fine," Bob said, finding a smile. "If you had a real, ah, an *extrasensory* experience before—and it sounds like maybe you did—it makes sense that you'd start looking for omens every which way. Sounds like you had a hell of a nightmare, and maybe the way you felt about it, like it was a premonition, maybe that was part of the dream."

Amanda was nodding. She looked relieved most of all—which renewed Bob's feeling that she'd been telling the truth. She wanted a sane, logical answer to what had happened to her; she wanted the world to make sense.

Don't we all?

They thanked him very politely for his time, and he reassured them that it had been a pleasure; even told them that if anything else came up, to give him a call, though he doubted very much that he'd ever hear from either of them again. He watched them walk away together, pleased with himself for being of some use, still half thinking of his brother's strange insight into the death of his college roommate. If it had been anyone but Rich, Bob might have thought it some kind of distasteful joke, but his brother didn't have that kind of humor in him. Rich had died of a heart attack at the ungodly young age of fifty-nine, coming up on seven years past, but from childhood till his dying day, Richard Sayers had dismissed anything he couldn't explain as utter hogwash, from God to women's intuition. That night, though, he'd known something he shouldn't have known, that he absolutely *couldn't* have.

Weirder than fiction. Bob decided he'd done enough community work for the day, that it was time to go home and get to the serious drinking, maybe delve into his prized movie collection for an old man's wild Saturday evening; something by Hitchcock, perhaps, to continue the day's theme. He'd lost track of John Hanover somewhere along the way—last he'd seen, John had been chatting up Annie Thomas, though of course she was off arresting people now—but perhaps he'd give the good doctor a call later, invite him over to share a few whiskeys and a viewing of *Rope*...or maybe not. Like many an old bachelor—or so he assumed—Bob had grown quite fond of his own company. And much as he liked John, he also liked the idea of getting a little sloppy in front of an old movie tonight, dozing on the couch, and wearing something entirely unsociable. Drawers and socks, maybe.

He faced into the crowd, saw a half dozen people he'd rather not have to walk past—well-meaning friends and neighbors who would undoubtedly want to get his take on the to-do with Nate Glover and the local PD—and decided he'd wind around to his truck by way of the service road.

Annual Picnic a Success, he decided. Front page, probably. Bob shoved his hands in his pockets and sauntered west, writing breakers in his thoughts.

CHAPTER

8

John woke up with Annie Thomas's soft hip pressed against the small of his back. He had one of those vague, half-dreaming seconds in which he didn't know anything beyond an awareness that he wasn't alone—and then he was awake enough to remember.

Oh, he thought. He opened his eyes, saw the familiar corner of his bedroom—saw, in fact, the open box next to the closet door, the one with the quilt. Lauren's grandmother's quilt. He'd been meaning to mail it to Lauren; he'd come across it just a few weeks back, apparently forgotten in a storage bag of blankets labeled "winter" in his wife's neat hand. When he'd unfolded it, remembering Lauren wearing it wrapped across her shoulders on more than one icy winter evening, he'd teared up a little. And in spite of that still-tender spot in the general vicinity of his guts, last night, he and Annie had...

He blinked, worked not to jump to any diagnostic conclusions, part of him marveling at how quickly things had happened. Except for a few forays led by adolescent hormone rushes—which he'd mostly managed to get through by his midtwenties—he wasn't one for casual sex. It wasn't for lack of trying, back then, but he'd been an awkward youth, and by the time he'd grown into his social skills, he'd learned pretty fast that just because you *could*, that didn't mean you *should*. Sex created complications.

Behind him, Annie stirred, her supple warmth pressing closer, and John almost smiled. Hello, complication.

"Hey," she murmured, cleared her throat. Her voice was as soft as her skin.

"Hey," he said. He rolled toward her, backing away slightly at the same time so he could see her. Not sure what he would see, what to expect. He couldn't remember the last time he'd acted so impulsively, without at least having some idea of where things stood. Where *he* stood.

Her bangs were mussed, her lips slightly chapped, but in the soft light of morning, naked in his bed, she looked beautiful. He smiled at her. She was an attractive woman, and last night had been...

"Wow, huh?" she said, smiling back at him, and he relaxed into a grin.

"I was thinking the same thing," he said.

Her crooked smile was endearing. "This is going to sound dumb, but I don't usually—I mean, this is kind of a surprise."

"You're not that kind of girl," he said, meaning it as a joke, but her own smile faded.

"No, I'm really not," she said. She seemed almost puzzled, her expression matching his own feelings about what had happened between them. Glad but tentative. Uncertain.

John nodded. "I believe you," he said, sincerely. "This isn't— I'm kind of in the same boat you are."

Her smile was back. "But don't rock the boat, right?"

"If this boat's a-rockin'," he replied, and if there had been any tension between them, even for a second, it was gone.

"So, since we both never do this kind of thing, what's next?" she said. "Do we have coffee, or should I just gather up my panties and sneak home? Walk of shame, and all that."

"Coffee, definitely," he said. "In fact, I'll go make it. You stay here, I'll bring it in."

"Automatic drip?" she asked.

"French press."

"Oooh. A gentleman of taste."

He grinned, sat up, and looked around, spotted his boxers crumpled on the floor. "Obviously," he said, scooping up the drawers and pulling them on. He actually sucked in his stomach a little, amused at himself for it but not letting out his breath entirely, either. He wasn't in bad shape, but no one would ever accuse him of sporting a six-pack, either. "I mean, look at you."

"Why, Doctor, I do believe you're flirtin' with me," Annie said, mock-Southern. She fluttered her eyelashes.

John laughed, pleased with how the morning was going so far. Pleased with the whole affair, as it were. They'd struck up an interesting conversation at the picnic, about criminal psychology, of all things, but had been forced to cut it short; she'd been on duty, after all. When she'd asked if she might drop by later, to talk more—she got off at nine, she'd said—it had seemed perfectly natural to accept, and to offer dinner. The bottle of wine she'd brought along had gone quite well with the pasta he'd managed not to overcook. After dinner they'd had more wine, talked for a while about all kinds of things—her third year of law school at UW in Seattle, her work as a deputy, the sheriff's control issues. He'd mostly listened, enjoying her optimism, her wit, the sound of her laugh...and at some point, he'd actually talked about Lauren a little. Or, rather, how he'd felt about the end of their marriage, about how he'd finally realized that while he had been willing to keep trying, Lauren just didn't want to be married anymore; she hadn't wanted to do the work, or at least not with him. Annie had been understanding, had really seemed to empathize; he'd felt comfortable talking with her, relaxed. And when she'd leaned in and kissed him, he'd responded wholeheartedly. Going to bed with her had seemed inevitable by then, although he hadn't made any conscious decision about it...and the passion with which they'd tackled that particular chore had been almost embarrassingly enthusiastic. Both times.

Another warm smile exchange, and he went to make coffee, while she disappeared into the bathroom. He looked out the kitchen window as he waited for the water to boil, saw that it was going to be another sunny day. Across the street, two men were picking through the wreckage from the old school. He'd seen a lot more activity around the site since early spring; perhaps they would finally get around to clearing the lot, although John figured he'd lose at least part of his view as soon as the new development went up, whatever it was slated to be. Both men looked like construction workers, dressed in flannel and jeans—although after a bit more scrutiny, John could have sworn that one of them was Rick Truman.

He watched the two men gesture at the various piles of debris, struggling again to avoid picking apart what had happened.

He got a pair of matching mugs out of the cabinet by the fridge—mugs that he and Lauren had received as part of a set a couple of Christmases past, from her cousin or aunt, he couldn't remember...and was pleased to note that the thought didn't hold any sting, or at least not much of one. He started to analyze that—postcoital euphoria or actual personal growth, as evidenced by the spontaneous encounter and his subsequent calm?—and told himself to shut up.

Just make the coffee, John.

Annie stepped into the kitchen just as he'd finished pressing the coffee. She wore only her underwear and the light blouse she'd worn the night before, partially buttoned. He could see the curve of her breast as she approached, could clearly recall the feeling of it beneath his fingers and lips.

"Smells great," she said.

John poured. "Cream or sugar?"

She took the offered mug, inhaling deeply. "No way. This is the good stuff. I only doctor it up when it's undrinkable otherwise. What they serve at the station, or the dispenser at the university library. I go through buckets of that nondairy creamer."

John grimaced. "Gah. That stuff'll kill you."

"Don't I know it."

They each sipped, smiled. At each other, at themselves. John opened his mouth to ask her how she was feeling, then closed it again. He wasn't her doctor. If she wanted him to know, she'd tell him.

"So, are you going to take me on a real date now, or am I just a sexual plaything, to be used and tossed aside?" she asked.

"I was about to ask you that."

She blew on her cup. "Date, definitely. Though I'd be OK doing that plaything part again. You know, if you didn't hate it too much."

John laughed. "I endured. I'd like to take you on a real date, though. What's your schedule like?"

"Too busy for a real date," she said promptly, but added, "I have Tuesdays and Wednesdays off. I'm usually studying, but I can make time, I've only got the one Net class until September. Wednesday night's good—if you want to do this week."

The last held a hint of question. She was stepping carefully, perhaps feeling him out for depth of interest. There was a time in his life when he would have responded according to what he thought she wanted to hear, or what he wanted her to believe, but he liked to think he'd grown out of playing those kinds of games. Thank God. Life was much easier when you were honest.

"I do," he said. "So, Elson's or Poisson?"

Annie cocked an eyebrow. "You want to stay in town?"

He smiled and sipped his coffee. "I'm OK with people talking. Unless—we could skip over to Port Angeles, if you'd rather…"

"No, no," she said. "I'm good. Umm…Poisson, I guess. I love their bisque."

"Wednesday at…seven? We could meet there, if you like."

"I like," she said.

They smiled at each other again. John felt like a teenager, almost dopey with sudden infatuation…and with an optimism he'd not had much of, lately. That Annie might turn out to be someone special. That his life would go on, go somewhere new, and that he might have someone to share it with, at least for a time. He'd known those things, of course, but there was a vast difference between knowing and feeling. And even if it was only the dying gasp of last night's endorphin rush, it was good to feel hope again. Jesus, it was fucking great.

><

Amanda woke up from a late-afternoon nap feeling sticky and unpleasant, her brain in fugue. The apartment was hot, the box fan on her floor washing muggy air over her sweaty self, doing pretty much nothing at all. She sat up on the edge of her bed and reached for the half-empty can of warm diet soda on her nightstand. Drank. Yuck, but at least the fuzz on her tongue tasted better.

The nap had been kind of involuntary, brought on by an extreme lack of sleep. She'd stayed up too late the night before; it had been hard to get to sleep, thinking about the whole picnic thing. And then Peter and her mother had woken her up way too early, fighting, both still half-drunk from the night before. Over Peter leaving the goddamn toilet seat up, from what Amanda could hear through the pillow jammed over her head. It seemed that Grace had gotten up to pee in the early a.m. and had gone for a swim instead. They had eventually stopped shouting and gone back to sleep, but Amanda had been unable to do the same.

She reached for her pack of smokes, smiling in spite of her postnap wonkiness at the image of her mother dropping into cold toilet water by the dawn's early light. It hadn't been terribly funny at seven in the morning, when she'd finally given up trying to get back to sleep, but it was a classic. Devon would laugh his ass off. She stood and opened her window, then scooted her chair beneath it so she could smoke without polluting her room too much. She wasn't worried about getting caught; her mother knew she smoked (and had the audacity to disapprove), but Amanda didn't like the stale smoke smell in her clothes.

She lit up and leaned back in the rickety chair. Hot air wafted through from the parking lot, smelling of oil and baked asphalt. From late spring to fall, the complex would be an oven on sunny days; the wind off the bay never seemed to make it this far inland. She hawked, spit out the window, took another drag. Thought.

She'd spent most of the morning at the library, surfing for information about psychic ability. Ninety-nine percent of what she'd found had been total drivel—the sheer number of sites was staggering, almost thirteen million if you googled *psychic abilities*, and it seemed like most of them had something to sell (besides an assload of psychic reading ads, there was also a big market for books and videos promising to help people discover their own latent abilities), but she'd read some interesting things, as well. There were even a few serious, grown-up people who believed in it, who didn't sound entirely bugfuck—although some of them spelled *magic* with a *k*, which didn't exactly contribute to their authority. She'd found out that precognition was the most commonly reported form of ESP, and that something like 70 percent of the experiences occurred within dreams. Also, that it was usually calamity, a death or a natural disaster, that was foretold; the ratio of bad news to good was like four to one. There was a lot of theory online too, about whether the perceived future could be changed—although some of the suppositions had gone into quantum physics, and she'd gotten a little lost trying to decipher phrases like *the feasibility of retro-causality*. In any case, stories similar to what had happened to her and to Bob Sayers's brother weren't all that uncommon. She'd e-mailed some of the more promising site addresses to Devon, since he had a printer and wouldn't charge per page, as the library did. She'd checked out a couple of books, too. Her mother had been promising to buy a computer since she was like thirteen, but she would bet cash money that *that* wasn't gonna come to pass—

A rap on her door.

"Yeah," Amanda called. The door opened—and it was Peter. Grinning like a monkey. He'd be handsome, she'd often thought, if he never spoke; dark hair and eyes, wolfish jaw, nice teeth. Of course, he couldn't say two words without labeling himself an undereducated, narrow-minded bigot, and his casual cruelty toward just about everyone made it impossible to like him. Grace had picked herself a real winner this time around.

"Hey," he said.

"What?"

"Your mom had to go in early," he said. "Jason called in sick, so she had to cover."

"Oh," Amanda said. "OK. Thanks."

He stayed in the doorway, still smiling that wide, toothy grin. "So, what are you doing?"

She shot him a disparaging look. "Having some alone time, do you mind?"

"I don't mind," he said. He shifted his weight, leaning against the doorframe...stared at her. "You thinking about your boyfriend?"

Jesus Christ. "No, I'm not thinking about my boyfriend," she said, dripping as much sarcasm as she could. She took another drag on her cigarette, feeling the first inklings of unease. It was Sunday. The bar closed early, but her mother still wouldn't be home until after midnight.

"I'm going to have a beer," he said, completely ignoring her obvious hostility. "You want one?"

"Don't you have to work or something?" she asked.

Peter shook his head slowly, still staring at her, still grinning. "I did some work this morning looking over a work site, and they don't need me at the dock. I've got tonight free and open, not a thing to do."

Like she cared. "Well, no thanks," she said, as sourly as possible, turning more toward the window. Here's my back, asshole. Leave. Leave.

He didn't move. She didn't look at him, concentrating on the view from her window—a scraggly tree, a patch of graying bark dust littered with dried cat crap and cigarette butts, a corner of parking lot shimmering in the late-day sun. The moment stretched, stretched, moved from uncomfortable to unnerving. This was stupid; this was her house, her room, she should tell him to get the fuck out, but she didn't, and still, he didn't move.

"I've got some pot," he said. His voice was softer than it should have been. "You ever smoke pot? I bet you do. This is some primo shit, too; it'll totally knock you on your ass. We could get high, watch a movie or something. You know, just hang out."

It was too creepy. Her sarcasm failed completely as alarm bells started to clang, as the room got smaller. She'd always though he was a total fucking dog, but she hadn't really *believed* it, not till now. *Out, get out, right now.*

Although she'd had no plans for the evening, had no desire to leave the apartment after her sweaty nap, she butted out her smoke and stood up.

"Thanks, but I've got to get going," she said. She forced a smile in his general direction, grabbed up her cigarettes. Her bag and shoes were by the door. She'd go downtown, get coffee or something, read one of the library books, and wait for Peter to clear out.

She took a few steps toward the door, expecting—hoping— that he would move, but he didn't. His muscular arms, bare and scarred and tanned, were casually folded across his chest. He had a good six inches on her, and beneath his beer gut was the hard, well-developed body of a dockworker. She didn't want to retreat, didn't want him to think she was scared, but he was suddenly close enough to smell, smoke and sweat and cheap, heavy after- shave. She backed up a little, afraid to try to push past him. God, what if he grabbed her?

"Where to?" Peter asked. He was still smiling, acting like he was really enjoying their conversation.

"Meeting friends," she said. "Downtown."

"Aren't we friends?" he asked. He actually looked her up and down, his gaze dropping to her chest, her hips, back to her chest. She wasn't wearing a bra.

"I'm going to be late," she said, struggling to seem casual, aware that her heart was beating loud and fast. "Look, Mom already knows I'm going out. Didn't she tell you?"

The lie was automatic and hopefully credible, and Peter's smile faded slightly. She seized on the line of thought and ran with it. "You can call her if you want."

"I don't want," he said. He took a half step into her room.

"Or I could call her," she said, making her voice hard. She met his eyes, but only for long enough to see the sudden spark of anger there, of sneering disappointment. He mastered it quickly, found a smile again, raised his hands slightly like someone try- ing to avoid a fight.

"We don't want to upset your mother at work," he said. He backed off, just a little. "Some other time, right?"

She quickly moved past him, mumbled a *sure, right*, and headed for the front door. It seemed a million miles away, a million miles of bad carpet and cheap linoleum when any second his heavy hand might come down on her shoulder. She grabbed her bag, opted for her clogs from the pile of shoes, caring only that they were the easiest to get on, and was outside in less than a minute. She hurried across the lot, not daring to look back, feeling sick with tension...and, strangely, guilt. No vague innuendos, no questionable looks; her mother's boyfriend had been inviting her to fuck.

Oh, man. She wanted a smoke; she wanted to sit and smoke and think about it, figure out what to do, but somewhere far from Peter. Should she tell her mother? Sure, but...Grace already knew that Amanda didn't like her boyfriend, and she had accused Amanda of trying to break them up in at least three drunken rants in the last six months. Sober, she could be reasonable... but in any condition, she wouldn't take the news well. Amanda couldn't count the number of times she'd heard her mother, totally shit-faced, declare her love for Peter.

It was still hot out. She figured it was maybe five thirty by now, but it wouldn't be dark till nine; he'd be gone by then. She'd go down to the Coffee Klatch; they were open until nine every night in the summer. She wanted to talk to someone about what had happened, but there was nobody to call. Devon and his Uncle Sid were having dinner with Carrie, Sid's girlfriend, and her family tonight, some barbecue deal. There were three or four people she knew well enough to have coffee with, friendly acquaintances, but no one she trusted like Devon.

Shit. Shit, shit, shit. As if she didn't have enough trouble in her stupid life without that dickhead making things a thousand times worse. Amanda dug for her sunglasses and hurried, in spite of the heat, in spite of the uncomfortable bounce of her unsupported breasts, to get away from her home.

><

Eric Hess was sitting on the curb and smoking and thinking about home when he saw the girl walk past a block over, headed down the hill. He glanced back at his dad's house, considered the consequences if he didn't show for dinner—Jeannie would pout and wiggle her tits, and his father would do the whole point-his-finger thing and talk about respecting *his* rules under *his* roof, and then it would be over.

Worth it? He watched the girl disappear past a hedge, thought about how she'd looked at the picnic, all pale and soft, smoke spilling from her dark lips as she talked to her friend, and decided it was. He stood and flicked his smoke into the gutter, wondering what her name was as he started after her. Something cool, like Chloe or Thora. She had to be another tourist's daughter, no way this hick shithole could produce that kind of alternative. Or maybe it could. What the fuck did he know?

Not much, he thought, finally reaching the corner that intersected his street with the one she'd been heading down. He took a right, making a point of looking at the street name. Devlin. He lived at the corner of Devlin and Blair. Well, *lived*, that was one way of looking at it. They'd been in Port Isley for a week—nine to go before he could return to the strange, treacherous grind that was his life in Boston, and he expected all of them to be as boring and shitty as the first—and he'd only ventured into "town" on his own a couple of times. He didn't particularly want to interact with anyone, fakey smiling at strangers or whatever. Mostly, he walked to the park by their house and sat and read and smoked.

He listened to music and he jerked off and he watched action movies on cable. He'd successfully avoided his father so far, which hadn't been too difficult—Dad spent his days working on the boat and every fucking night boinking his prom queen wife, who was only, like, six years older than Eric and screamed like a porn star when she came. Or faked it, more likely.

The girl was a full block ahead of him, but he didn't hurry too much. He liked watching her shuffle along in her slipper-shoes, clogs, liked the sway of her soft ass, the determined set of her shoulders. There were a couple of girls he hooked up with every now and again back in Boston, both smart girls, both kind of fucked-up. This girl was like that, he thought. He hoped. Fashion girls weren't his bag, too skinny and bitchy and they laughed too much at everything. He liked 'em morbid.

It was early evening, the sun still in the sky but dropping, and the air was getting cool. The girl had a flowered bag she wore over one shoulder, kind of a vintage-looking thing. She gave him a profile a couple of times, looking toward the bay when the trees opened here and there, and he liked the shape of her nose. When she finally turned enough to see that she was being followed, she didn't slow down for him. He wouldn't have expected her to.

She led him down the shaded hill to the small town's epicenter, if such a word could be used, a couple of streets that ran along the water, that had restaurants and businesses. For another half block they were alone, and then they started passing a few people, walking to their cars or whatever, couples, a family. There were some kids carrying ice cream cones, and most of the faces he passed looked happy, relaxed, smiling, but he couldn't imagine why. Except for a smoke shop that didn't card and a good-sized used bookstore, there was a lot of nothing in Port Isley, as far as he could tell. Jeannie had apparently read some fucking article about summering in the Northwest, and it was just like that weird old TV show, only his stepmom Jeannie wriggled her model bod instead of bobbing her head, and Dad did what she wanted. Anything for his blushing bride, even if it meant spending two months in some backwater rich-people's tourist town, so she could feel like she was properly spending her new husband's money.

The girl ignored everybody, keeping her head down. Introverted. He was more extro himself—he was a good-looking kid, he knew that, knew that people cut him slack when he smiled and made bullshit small talk—but he wasn't looking to make any friends, either, so he kept his focus on the girl, followed her across a back parking lot to a coffee shop. He had enough friends at home, where he *should* be the summer before his senior year, only Dad had insisted on his fucking visitation and his mother had bargained him away, because she was pretty much a cunt and she wanted to travel Europe and pretend she wasn't anyone's mother. Both of his parents were bright and intensely manipulative people; he even admired them, at times, for their strangely clever maliciousness, but he'd grown out of being their puppet a few years back, since right after the divorce. Before the split, when they'd been one silent, dysfunctional family unit, his parents' expectations had been few—as long as he kept his grades up and didn't embarrass them publicly, they left him alone. Now his mom wanted a sounding board for her every neurosis, and his dad required him to submit to long, personal discussions about utter bullshit that ended with awkward hugs. They were supporting him financially, however; college was paid, and as much as he resented their general negligence of him as, like, a person, he wasn't an idiot. So, summers with Dad in sunny LA, private school in Boston with Valium-popping mom. One more year and he'd have a private apartment just off campus; it was already a done deal...

The girl went into the coffee shop, a generic-looking place called Coffee Klatch. Eric followed her inside. Into a heavy coffee smell hanging over shelves with mugs and coffeepots and assorted random shit for sale, and the high-pitched squeal of the espresso machine's steamer frothing milk. There were half a dozen small tables inside, the type that seated two uncomfortably. He'd been in the exact same shop on both coasts.

She went straight to the bar in the back, where someone else was ordering…he joined her, the two of them making up the line. She was tall for a girl, like five seven or eight, even. As close as he was, he could see the roots of her dyed hair, an ashy brown against the burgundy-black of the dye. She smelled like cigarettes and baby powder.

"Double iced espresso," she said, her voice low and a little husky. She rummaged in her bag, dragged out a battered black wallet, and waited while the woman turned to the machine and scooped up a plastic cup. Eric reached for his own wallet and saw he had, like, eighty bucks on him. Dad left a twenty on the counter every other day, usually with a note explaining that he and Jeannie were sightseeing (read: out fucking on the boat) and would be back with dinner later, takeout seafood from some ritzy place by the pier; Jeannie didn't cook, of course. All he'd bought since coming to Port Dullsville were smokes and some yellowing paperbacks, so he was relatively flush.

The girl got her drink, doctored it heavily at an extension to the counter, and sat at one of the tables while Eric ordered his coffee. He'd already decided that he'd try the direct approach. It usually worked.

He walked to her table, stood next to her chair. She was digging through her bag again, but she looked up when she realized she had company, her expression careful, ready to be defiant. Her eyes were green.

"Hey," he said. "Is your name Chloe?"

"No," she said.

"Huh. You kind of look like a Chloe. I'm Eric. Would you mind if I sat with you, just for a couple of minutes? I mean, if you're not meeting anyone."

She hesitated, but then nodded. "Yeah, I'm not. Meeting anyone."

Eric sat, leaning back in the spindly chair. "So…not Chloe?"

She smiled, a little twitch of a thing. "Amanda."

Eric nodded. "That's a good name."

"I'll thank my mother for you," she said. "You here for the summer?"

He nodded. "You too?"

Her smile curved, a sardonic thing. "Nope. I call this shit-hole home, thank you for reminding me."

Nice. She was funny. This close to her, he could see how flawless her complexion was, pale and creamy. She had a baby face, but her gaze was sharp. Her mouth was a little too wide.

"So…you'll be around?" he asked. "Is this where you hang?"

She raised her eyebrows. Her tone was slightly derisive. "Where I *hang*?"

"Not the local lingo?" he asked, and hit her with his best smile. "So, now I look like a total dickhead or something? Dickhead, that's the shiz, right?"

She smiled back at him, and he decided he had to know her better. Something about her eyes, when she smiled…he could see her vulnerability, beneath her punk-rock front. He could see that she was slightly damaged.

"No, you're fine," she said. "Yeah, I come down here a lot. Can't smoke, though, so I usually end up on one of the benches by the pier. If it's nice."

"If it's not?"

"Library," she said. "Under the overhang, front steps."

"Home's no good?"

She leaned back a little, matching his posture. The glimmer of openness was gone, just like that. "You a therapist or something?"

Time to leave her wanting more. He stood up, picked up his coffee, and gave her another patented Eric Hess grin. Didn't want to look like an asshole, either...

"Just interested," he said, sincerely. "I gotta run. I'll see you."

"Chances are good," she said, her tone dismissive; she was already busy rummaging through her bag again. Good. She was interested, he could tell, so she was hiding a little bit. He understood the need, appreciated her as another fucked-up person in the universe, just making her way...and knew that she'd likely spend the next week hanging around the places she'd mentioned, hoping to run into him again.

Mission accomplished. He took his time walking back out into the dying day, pleased that he'd decided to follow the girl. Amanda. Amanda. He set his still-full coffee on the curb in front of the shop—what the fuck was a klatch, anyway?—as a good-bye gift, so she could see why he'd really come in, and started back up the hill.

CHAPTER

9

Sadie came hard, felt herself fluttering around Josh's thickness as he pulled his magic fingers away. He gave a few final pumps, gasped, and buried his head against her collarbone. Pulsing, pulsing...and they slumped together, Sadie's bare ass against the damp, icy-cold wall of the walk-in, her skirt hiked around her waist, Josh supporting himself against one of the wire shelves.

"Mmm." Sadie smiled, laughed a little as she caught her breath. His skin was so young and tight, lightly tanned and smooth over long, lean bones. A flop of thick, shining gold-brown hair hung over his eyes, his head down as he breathed deeply, radiating warmth in the humid cold. He was all she could have asked for in a summer fling. Pretty to look at, smart enough not to be embarrassing, too young to take seriously.

She pulled herself away from the moment long enough to glance at her watch. Ten to four. Shit. Randy would be in soon. He was cooking Monday through Thursday for the season. The restaurant opened at five. And Rick had said something about coming in to do inventory, probably right around then...there was still another hour of prep to do, at least, and she didn't want Rick wondering why it wasn't done. Wednesdays were tricky, since it was her night to work in the kitchen. He was always dropping in. Keeping you out of trouble, he'd chortle, pecking at her cheek. He had no idea.

"We gotta get moving," she said, carefully edging herself toward him, making him pull out. She immediately clenched her vaginal muscles; no panties today in anticipation of their rendezvous, and she didn't want essence of Josh running down her thighs while she put together the cassoulet. She'd want to get to the bathroom, pronto.

Josh reached down, pulled up his pants by the belt, the soft clink of the metal pieces half-buried in the heavy, constant thrum of the refrigeration system. She smoothed down her skirt, watching him.

"You still want me to do the salads?" he asked.

"Yeah. Randy'll do the filet when he comes in, and the bisque's already on."

Josh nodded and started to turn away.

"Hey," she said, catching him around the waist. "That was nice."

He grinned, leaned in to kiss her. "Sexy Sadie," he whispered, and though the nickname was tired, she smiled in turn. At least he knew the reference.

Together, they walked to the door of the cooler, brushing at their clothes, Sadie running her fingers through her hair. If either had turned, they might have seen Rick on the other side of one of the narrow glass doors that fronted the walk-in, where the chilled side dishes and desserts would be set out for the waitstaff to reach in and grab. Rick with his hands tightened to fists, an expression of near wonder on his face.

>‹

In spite of her day—the sheriff had been in a mood, they'd had twice the usual number of crank calls, and there were rumors of a statewide benefits cut—Annie was full of energy when she

went off duty, psyched for her date with John. She signed out
at six and hurried home to shower and change for their date
at seven o'clock at Le Poisson. She chose a sleeveless summer
dress, nice but casual, opting for the big, lacy shawl thing over
her shoulders, her last birthday gift from her brother and his
wife. She had nice shoulders, she thought, drooping the shawl
low, looking in the mirror on the back of her closet door. Of
course, John had seen them already—along with a few more
private areas—but she saw no harm in accentuating her better
attributes. Saturday night with John had been really good for
her, had lifted her spirits after that long, miserable almost-affair
with her college prof, and she wanted their first "date" to go just
as well.

I feel pretty, oh so pretty, her mind hummed as she locked up
the apartment and got into her well-used Toyota, the old blue car
starting with barely a sputter. She'd be right on time.

John Hanover. Who would have thought? Until a week or so
before, she'd never considered it, never considered *him*, mostly
because of Lauren. They hadn't been close, but fairly friendly—
two professional women in a small town, both wending their
way through academia. They'd met for lunch a few times. She'd
liked Lauren well enough, but wasn't surprised when she'd heard
about the divorce. Just the way she'd talked about herself, her
ambitions and interests…it was like she hadn't wanted to include
John in her depiction of herself, in what she presented to the
world. That was pretty much what John had told her on Saturday.
He'd been so…so *real* about it, too. Realistic and angry and sad
and OK with feeling all those things. Like a grown-up. Now that
she'd looked at him, really looked—

—*really fucked his brains out*, she thought, smiling, down-
shifting her car as she came to a stop at the bottom of the hill. No
reason to be coy. Now that they'd done *that*, she was wondering

how she'd never looked at him before. She knew *why* she'd never looked; Annie didn't pretend to be some pinnacle of morality, but she had a few principles, and screwing a married man wasn't one of them.

But how? How *did I never notice him before?* He was startlingly appealing in an intellectual way, like one of those actors who always played smart, deep guys. Kevin Spacey, maybe. His wit and charm made him handsome. Average body but well endowed where it counted. And the way he looked at her when she was talking, when they'd been together in bed…like he was concentrating on her, really working to see who she was, to *know* her.

Thinking about it gave her a happy chill. She didn't want to jump the gun; she knew there were men who had taken faking sincerity to an art form—God knew she'd dated her share—but she thought John was different. The connection between them on Saturday night had been so intense, so…so perfect.

Slow down, girlie-girl. You barely know the man.

True enough, but that didn't stop her from feeling like a future with him was somehow inevitable. It was so *strange*. She was a levelheaded kind of girl; overly direct sometimes, but not impulsive. Certainly not the type to sleep with someone before the first date. And the sex had been…well, extremely satisfying. She'd been uncharacteristically assertive, in ways she'd only ever imagined, and it had paid off.

Maybe he brings it out in me, she thought, and smiled again, turning onto Front. Le Poisson was on Front, parallel to Water. Parking would be murder on the weekend, but Wednesday was a relatively slow night; she quickly found a spot less than a block away. She took a second to check her makeup and fluff at her hair in the rearview, then got out, wrapping her shawl around her shoulders. There was almost always a breeze this close to the water, and though the lowering sun was still bright, it was already starting to get cold. The salt wind ruffled her hair, and she hurried to the restaurant, concerned for her 'do; ironically, the just-tousled look didn't stand up to actual tousling.

Just as she reached the door, a beautifully carved mahogany affair with a massive brass handle, John caught up to her.

"Allow me," he said, opening the door. He smiled at her, seeming slightly out of breath as she slid past him. He smelled nice, like some mild soap. Subtle.

They only had to wait for a moment before being seated. The last time she'd been in had been a few weeks back, a Friday night, and the place had been packed. Tonight, Poisson was barely half-full, the muted conversation from the dozen or so tables low and pleasantly background. The soft lights and candles made the dark, heavy woods of the room glow, like some romantic restaurant from a movie.

Leticia Barker seated them near the kitchen, handed them menus. Tish was a quiet young woman who lived in Port Angeles and who played weekend hostess for the restaurant and waited tables during the week. Annie noted that she seemed more subdued than usual. Her shoulders were up, too, her body language tense.

"How are you, Tish?" Annie asked, after the girl had listed the specials—a wild rice cassoulet with herbed prawns, salmon steaks with lemon-dill pesto, pork medallions in garlic, filet mignon. Yum.

"I'm well, thank you," Tish said. "How are you? Can I get you something to drink?"

Her smile seemed a bit strained, but Annie let it drop. She didn't know her all that well. John opted for a microbrew, and Annie got a glass of the house Chardonnay. Tish said she'd be back shortly and hurried away from their table—directly to another, with an apologetic smile. Annie looked around, realized that Tish was the only waitress on. And there was no one behind the mirror-backed bar at the far wall, so she was doing the drinks, too.

No wonder she's tense. Annie had waited tables just after high school, a twenty-four-hour greasy spoon that had been horribly understaffed—one waiter per twelve tables, something like that. She still had panic dreams now and again from that place, that she was standing in a vast room full of diners that had all arrived at the same time and she couldn't find the menus.

"Looks like she's by herself tonight," she commented.

John looked up from his menu. "What?"

"Nothing, never mind." If John hadn't ever worked in food service, he didn't likely notice that kind of thing. She'd often thought that everyone should be forced to serve food to the general public for at least a day at some point in their lives, to gain some measure of empathy for the waiters and waitresses of the world. It was a difficult job.

"So, how's life since Sunday?" John asked, sitting back in his chair. He was wearing a dark suit jacket over a handsome dress shirt, no tie, new jeans. He looked good, crisp but not overdressed.

"Not bad," she said. "The last of the TV crews have packed and gone, which is a relief. Other than that, same old...well, more of it, I suppose."

"It's been busy?"

She nodded. "We've got a few people who call in pretty regularly, with ongoing complaints about a neighbor's dog or the volume of a stereo or wild kids or what have you...frequent flyers. Usually, we get a couple of calls a week. Maybe a couple a day in the summer. Since Monday, we've logged complaints on, like, eighteen or nineteen separate calls, only a handful of them from our regulars."

"Wow."

"Weirder than usual, too," she said. "One lady called to tell us that her next-door neighbor's cat has been spying on her. Another guy said he thinks his daughter has taken up witchcraft and wanted to know if that was against the law so we could arrest her."

John smiled. "No kidding? Do you have to go check them all out?"

Annie sighed. "Usually, no. Like I said, we've got our regulars, mostly retirees that don't have hobbies. Half the time they just want someone to listen; five minutes on the phone calms them down. But like I said, most of this stuff has been coming in from new people. And the sheriff has been on edge since the Billings thing, so he wants all of us out and about, actively fielding practically everything that comes up. Letting ourselves be seen, you know."

"So you actually had to investigate a spying cat?"

"That one, we passed on," Annie said. "Is paranoia like that common? It is paranoia, right?"

"Feeling that you're being spied on by a cat?" John asked. "Could be a lot of things, depending on what her other beliefs are. Not to mention her medical history. Does the cat talk to her? Can it read her mind?"

Annie liked that he was taking it seriously. "I'm not sure. Ian fielded it. He did say that she called her neighbor a 'lecherous old man.' I guess it's his cat she was calling about."

John shook his head. "Sounds like a delusional disorder—paranoid—but it could be organic, could be schizoid…there's no way to be sure without knowing more."

"Delusional disorder—sounds dangerous," Annie said.

John shrugged slightly. "Again, it depends. On the cause, the severity, the extent of disruption to her life, how she reacts to things in general. There's not a lot of black-and-white when it comes to psychology."

"That would drive me nuts," Annie said, then laughed at the sort-of joke. "I'm a big fan of clear-cut and simple. The law is kind of like that—for all its strange gray areas, it's based almost entirely on precedent. And police work is definitely pretty straightforward. Not all the time, but most."

John was smiling. "Yeah, that'd be nice. Unfortunately, people are fairly complex creatures. Of course, that's what makes them interesting."

Tish appeared, set their drinks out, and promised to return.

"How about you?" Annie asked. "Anyone really crazy lately?"

John's return smile was less than amused. "Actually, I've also been getting more calls than usual. I came in this morning to a backlog. Clients I haven't seen in a while, wanting to meet. And several prescription requests."

Annie sipped her wine. "I thought psychologists couldn't write prescriptions."

"Can't, but I make referrals. There's a guy in Port Angeles who's a psychopharmacologist—specializes in psychotropics, antidepressants, antipsychotics, like that. He actually called this afternoon to ask that I start steering referrals to one of his colleagues, all the way over in Kingston. He says his phone's been ringing off the wall for more than a week now, mostly from clients in Port Isley who want their meds upped."

"Huh," Annie said. Interesting. "Seems to be an increase in mental illness around here."

John nodded. "It's not uncommon after a sensational death in a small community. A lot of people get freaked-out."

"Is that a medical term?"

He smiled and nodded again, his voice low. "Yep. Us therapists use it more than any other. Along with *dysphoric* and *totally bugshit*. Makes us sound like we know what we're talking about."

Annie laughed. They picked up their menus, chatted about what they were going to order, moved on to local gossip for a moment or two—the big Victorians that had been rented out for the summer, the roadwork being done out by the lighthouse, the community theater.

Tish showed up and took their orders. Annie went with the seafood bisque—a Le Poisson standard for her—and the salmon steak. More calories there than she needed, but she'd skimped on lunch. John opted for calamari and the pork medallions, and they went back to talking about the theater. Miranda Greene-Moreland's open poetry night would be worth seeing. Dick Calvin, one of John's neighbors, in fact, had proved to be the reading's big hit last summer. The generally peevish old man—he was probably pushing eighty by now—was a retired ferryboat captain and had scared generations of Port Isley's children with his perpetual scowl and curt manner. He had his house egged every Halloween. And he had surprised everyone with a short series of simple but lyrical odes to his late wife, Annelise, who'd apparently died when they'd both been in their twenties.

Tish showed up with their appetizers and hurried away again.

"I talked to him a month or so ago; he was out seeding his lawn," John said. "He said he was planning to do it again this year. 'If anyone's fool enough to come listen, I guess I'm fool enough to go up again,' he said."

"And the soul of a poet," Annie said. She shook her head. "I'm definitely going, then."

"We could go together," John said. He hesitated, smiling. "You know, if you want. If it's…"

"Applicable?"

"Exactly."

She grinned back at him. "I don't know, that's practically a whole month from now. Longer. Kind of jumping into things with both feet, aren't we?"

"Maybe so," he said. "Something to think about, though."

"Yeah, it is," she said, feeling almost absurdly giddy. She couldn't remember feeling so...so *excited* about a boy since about junior high. "And I will. I am."

John nodded, his gaze warm, and dug into his calamari.

"Speaking of neighbors, have you met yours yet?" Annie asked. "The rental next door?" She spooned into the creamy bisque, brought up a tiny bay shrimp and part of a scallop. Heavenly.

"No. He—or she—is a real hermit. Haven't even seen him. Or her. Although I heard the car pull out late the other night. After midnight, in fact."

"Really," Annie said. She took another taste of soup—and crunched into something.

Crab shell or something, big, though. Frowning, she pulled the offending bit out of her mouth, looked at it, turned it around—

"What is that?" John asked.

Annie shook her head. It was semitranslucent, about the size and shape of a small fingernail...in fact, it was exactly the size and shape of a fingernail. A woman's pinkie, maybe. A sliver of dark-red flesh clung to it.

Tish was walking by, an empty tray in hand. Annie caught her gaze, still frowning.

"Is everything all right?" Tish asked. She looked even more strained than before.

"Something in my soup." Annie held it out for the waitress to see before putting it on her napkin.

"Part of an oyster shell, maybe? I'm so sorry. Let me get you a new bowl."

She scooped up the offending bisque, smiling apologetically at Annie. "Our usual chef isn't working tonight."

"I thought the calamari was different," John said. "Who's on?"

Tish's smile became forced. "Mr. Truman."

Annie was surprised. "I didn't know he cooked."

"None of us did," Tish said. She seemed about to say something else but walked away instead, heading for the kitchen. John and Annie exchanged looks, Annie not at all sure that she wanted another serving of bisque. She looked at the thing that had been in her bowl, feeling a little queasy. Whatever it was, it really looked like a human fingernail. Really.

From the kitchen, they heard a raised voice, angry, masculine. Tish came back out a beat later, her face red, carrying a new bowl. She looked like she was about to cry, but she managed a weak smile as she set it down in front of Annie.

"Tish," Annie started, not sure how to intervene, only sure that she needed to try. "Did he—was that Rick yelling at you? Mr. Truman, I mean?"

Tish nodded, her eyes bright. Annie felt for her. "Is there anyone else back there?" she asked gently.

Tish shook her head. She lowered her voice, leaned in, and spoke all in a rush. "He sent Randy home—the cook? And when Katie started asking about it, he sent her home, too. He said if she didn't like how he ran things, she could just…she could go home, too."

The flush in her cheeks suggested that his language had been a bit more forceful. "He told me to stay out of the kitchen. Said if I wasn't putting in an order or picking up, he didn't want to see me. I wouldn't say anything normally, I mean he's my boss, but he's—he's kind of scaring me."

Annie had heard enough. "Go ahead and eat," she said, nodding at John as she stood up. "I'll be back in a minute."

John started to stand also, but Annie waved him off. "I don't want him to feel…overwhelmed. I just want to talk to him."

"I'm a good talker," John said.

Annie nodded. "I'm sure. But cold calamari is the worst. And I can handle this. I'm the law, remember?"

She said it lightly but meant it. Rick was kind of a blustering jerk, but he was also on the town council; he toed the line. A few choice words from a PIPD officer—even one in a summer dress—would probably keep him from beating up on his waitresses, at least. Having John along wouldn't help.

Annie touched Tish on the arm. "Just keep out of the kitchen for a minute or three, OK?"

Tish nodded uncertainly, then went off to attend to one of her neglected tables. Annie smiled at John—he looked as uncertain as Tish, but he smiled back at her—and walked to the kitchen door, already figuring how she'd handle it.

Unofficial, like I'm just coming in to say hi to the chef, but firm, direct eye contact...

She pushed the heavy swing door, and a clean and well-lit kitchen opened out in front of her—two massive stoves, an industrial grill, twin rows of counters, a walk-in refrigeration unit. The back wall opened to the right, but she couldn't see what was there; prep area, probably, sinks and counters. A single piece of fish was on the grill, spitting and hissing, and there were several big pots steaming on the stove, but no one was in attendance.

To her immediate right was a small room with a dishwasher in it, a massive steel unit with a stray hose attached, but no one operating it and no Rick. A hall ran off to the left, curving around the walk-in and out of sight. There was an office in back, she remembered; a few years ago, she'd taken a vandalism complaint from Sadie Truman there. Someone had broken one of the front windows.

Prep area or office? Annie hesitated, thinking it might be better if she just waited—he'd have to come out for the fish, sooner or later—and heard a noise from the adjunct at the back of the kitchen. It sounded like a sigh and was followed by soft talking. A man's voice, low and almost soothing in tone...Rick?

Thought she said he was alone back here. Huh. Annie started for the adjunct, eager to get back to John. She liked that he hadn't insisted on coming along; a lot of guys would have. It was a nice change, to meet someone mature enough to leave off with the whole macho thing. Or, even better—maybe he actually respected her opinion, and—

The smell hit her. She slowed, maybe twenty feet from where the wall opened up, trying to pick apart the unusual and unpleasant scent that had suddenly drowned out good kitchen smells. Raw meat, perhaps, but thick and too heavy, like a butcher shop dumpster. Wasn't one of the specials filet mignon? Or maybe it was the pork. Anyway, she was glad she hadn't ordered it, if that was what it smelled like raw.

"Mr. Truman?" she asked, walking forward again—

—and then he was stepping around the corner of the adjunct, quickly covering the short space between them, crowding her back. His face was red and sweaty, his expression thunderous.

"What are you doing here?" he barked. "This is a private business!"

Flustered, Annie stepped back. "I'm—excuse me, I'm sorry, I just wanted to come back and…and talk for a minute. I realize you're busy, but maybe we could go to your office…"

She trailed off, looking at him. At the clean black apron he wore over a dark polo shirt that was positively stiff in places with unidentifiable stains. At the minute specks of—of something that spattered his face. Food? Mud?

Blood?

Alarms clanged in her head. Her gut gave a sharp, shuddering twist, her instincts informing her deeply, wordlessly to get out, *get out*.

And there was another sound from the back, from where Rick had been. That sighing sound again, a pitiful, weak flutter of noise.

Rick and Annie had both turned toward the sound. Now Rick looked at her again and smiled. A slow, wide, entirely unpleasant smile that made his face look rigid and inhuman. The flecks of dried matter on his skin stood out now that she really looked at him, red and bright under the fluorescent light. His hands were clenched.

"I couldn't wait," he said. "I thought I could, but I couldn't."

"Couldn't wait for what?" She barely heard herself speak, her thoughts coming fast and hard, trying to organize, to make sense of all the pieces. Rick, spattered with blood, talking and acting like this, someone sighing...the thing in her bisque that looked like a fingernail.

Gun's in my purse. Vincent had been adamant that his people carry at all times; her .38 was in her lacy summer purse, which was at the table next to her chair, and she felt an intense burst of self-reproach for not even thinking of it until now.

Call it in. Get out and get some backup, and keep talking, keep him talking. She slid back another step, very carefully. The lights were too bright, seeming to call attention to her retreat.

Rick frowned, his expression darkening. "As if you didn't know," he said. "I'm sure all of you knew. He couldn't have been the first, not the way—not the way she was taking it."

Not the way she was...Sadie? Annie had heard things, here and there, about Mrs. Truman and some of the young men she hired—and she worked not to let it show on her face, the way he was watching her...

She backed up another step but also shifted to the left, trying to see around him to the hidden corner. "Who's back there, Rick?" she asked.

His eyes welled up, his shoulders sagging. "Anyway, it's over," he said. He seemed exhausted. He stared down at the floor, at his shoes, still but for the single tear that spilled over one blood-misted cheek.

Annie stepped to the side again, keeping her gaze fixed on Rick. He didn't have a weapon, but neither did she, and he was built like a truck. On the other hand, he seemed calmer now. Subdued. Maybe she should—

"Help," a sighing, plaintive voice called from the back, barely audible, miserable and shaking—and male. Not Sadie.

Still watching Rick, Annie took two, three sidling steps left, shifting casually toward the back—and saw what was there, the picture startlingly clear and terrible, the overpowering smell of meat becoming an awareness of what had transpired.

Like a scene in a movie, she thought, trying to fit a reality over what she was seeing. Her glance away from Rick turned into a long, wavering stare as she struggled to process, struggled not to vomit.

A long counter ran the length of the kitchen's back wall, the adjunct ending in a pair of heavy stainless steel sinks. There was a wide cutting block slanted toward one of the sinks, a fire exit in the corner—and blood everywhere. Splashed on the counters, trails of it drying on the sink fronts, on the floor. He'd made some attempt to clean up—there were diluted pink streams snaking around the floor drain, pink smears on the counters— but all that was scenery, a backdrop to the real horror. Great hunks of meat, some of it skinned and dressed, some of it still recognizable as human—a woman's bare leg, sticking out of the sink; the flayed rib cage atop the butcher's block, one shoulder and upper arm still attached, one small, flat breast hanging off like a limp sack—seemed to cover every available surface. On the small countertop to her right she saw a cutting board with a heap of hammered flesh circles laid out, a pile of minced garlic next to a long, dirty knife. A meat hammer was nearby. She saw a huge colander of peeled shrimp by what looked like a cross-section of a human thigh, the rounded, bloody bone and raw muscle tissue contrasting sharply with the pale skin still attached. And in the corner, tucked against the fire door, a person drawn up in a fetal position. A young man, his hands pressed to his groin. Fresh blood seeped from the red pool of his hands, from what seemed to be a thousand cuts along his bare arms and shoulders.

"Help," he whispered again, rolling his head toward her, longish stands of hair sticking to his battered and bloody face, and Annie took a step toward him, unable to deny him, *kid's dying*, and with a terrible, guttural scream, Rick was striding at her, his hand flashing out to the cutting board, his face red and grinning once more.

"Leave him alone!" he screamed, and Annie had ample time to realize she'd made a mistake before the knife he'd snatched up punctured her skin, her chest, her right lung. He drove it in with both hands, and the pain was bad, way beyond bad. Her whole body trembled with it, shock waves of it shuddering through her as her legs went away, and she fell to the floor. The knife ripped and tore as it left her, as her body weight and his grip on the knife's handle fought for dominance; the knife won. She looked up, saw Rick, saw that he was weeping, saw her own blood dripping from his hands.

"He fucked her," Rick sobbed, but his tone was that of a petulant child. "He doesn't get help."

Stabbed me. She gasped, tried to think—to cope with the pain long enough to understand the situation, to remember what to do, to breathe—and in a matter of seconds the black and bright darts of light that floated in front of her were joining together, making everything else irrelevant.

10

Bob was pouring his fourth drink of the night when the phone rang. It was his employee, Nancy Biggs, and she was almost frantic with the news; there had been a multiple murder at Le Poisson. She'd gotten a call from her brother's wife, Mary, who went to church with Leticia Barker's aunt in Port Angeles—it was a drive for her sister-in-law, but she liked the minister there, Nancy explained breathlessly—and Leticia worked at Le Poisson, and was still there with the police because someone had gone crazy and stabbed the owners. Mary had gotten a call from the aunt, who'd heard it from her sister, Leticia's mother, and Mary had called Nancy because of Nancy's connection to the press—and Bob was going to go down there, right? Because he had to, it was big news, a murder spree in little Port Isley!

He managed to get off the phone by promising to call her as soon as he learned more. After a second's hesitation, he downed the shot of Old Crow—no hurt in getting himself fortified, at least a little—and was out the door in under three minutes, shoes to coat to keys.

The last dregs of sunset illuminated the sky, making everything orange and strange as he drove down the hill. A cluster of local police cars, marked and plain, were badly parked in front of the restaurant, effectively blocking traffic. Maybe twenty or thirty people were gathered by the doors, talking, clustering, trying to see inside. Most appeared to be summer people. Local cop Ian Henderson blocked their way, his expression unusually grim.

Bob parked two blocks away and hightailed it back, popping a mint as he walked, wondering how close the grapevine had gotten to the truth. Rick and Sadie Truman, stabbed? Good Christ, *why*? Granted, they were as well liked as any snobby rich couple in a small town. Rick was a blowhard and Sadie was uptight, but surely neither had inspired active *hate*.

Or maybe they did, he thought, moving into the gathered watchers, searching for a familiar face. As many a noted author had liked to point out, small towns were full of secrets, of grudges harbored and loves unrequited. Of course, what Nancy had relayed to him could be entirely wrong, or backward. The way gossip got garbled after three or four or ten tellings, maybe Sadie and Rick had stabbed a customer. Bob couldn't help a smirk at the thought; that seemed more likely, somehow. *Maybe someone complained about the food. Or tried to skip out on their tab.*

He spotted a good source in the front line of the small crowd—Jamie, talking on a cell phone—and edged toward him. Jamie owned the gas station by the high school, was a solid family man with a working brain, and he was also one hell of a gossip. Bits of conversation swirled around Bob as he started for Jamie; what he heard dried up the last of his smirk.

"—in an ambulance, one of the guys said he probably wouldn't survive, but—"

"—you see him when they brought him out? There was so much blood on him, and that *smile*, it was just—"

"—like that thing in Seattle last year, with that one couple? They were swingers or something, and they picked up this man who—"

"—heard he killed one of the customers. And a policeman, I didn't quite—"

"Hey," Jamie said, putting away his cell phone as Bob approached, his face pale above the collar of his dark dress shirt. "Crazy, huh?"

"What have you heard?" Bob asked.

"Not a lot," Jamie said. "I just got here a few minutes ago. Deanne and I had reservations for eight. Mom's with the kids. Anniversary. I just told her not to come. I'll have to pick up something on the way home…"

"Someone was killed?" Bob prompted him gently.

Jamie nodded. "Oh, yeah. Sadie Truman's dead. And Annie Thomas."

Bob felt his stomach go hollow. "Annie?"

Jamie nodded again, added something equally insane. "Rick did it."

Bob was still trying to absorb the news when the door to the restaurant opened. John Hanover stepped out, his expression bleak, his shoulders hunched. He wore a shirt that was too big on him, someone else's—he held a plastic bag in one hand, with what looked like his suit jacket stuffed inside—and he blinked and squinted, as though surprised at the time of day, or the people, or both. He looked terrible.

Bob excused himself from Jamie and went to him. John seemed lost and was entirely willing to let himself be led away from the group. Bob steered him toward the street with a hand on his arm—realizing, as they walked, that John smelled of blood.

More gossip, more whispering as they passed through the watchers, the hushed voices pointing John out as one of the customers, as a witness, as a doctor. John seemed oblivious, his expression blank and dazed.

The shadows were getting long, the evening starting to chill. Bob was about to ask John what he needed—a ride home, a drink, a willing ear—when John spoke, his voice soft and strained.

"Annie's dead," he said. "I ran into the kitchen when he started yelling, but it was already too late."

"Who did it, John?" Bob asked. "Was it Rick?" He was more concerned for his friend than for getting the scoop—but he still wanted the story, he couldn't deny it in spite of the small measure of guilt that went with the admission. No matter that he was the only reporter on the scene, or that the fluff-filled *Press* was every two weeks; he'd worked as a journalist for most of his adult life. Wanting to know the five *W*s became habit after a while.

John nodded, gazing out at the street. "She was trying to help the kid, I think. I'm not sure, but that's what I think. Rick said *leave him alone*, that was what I heard, and we ran in and she was already down. Annie."

John turned his haunted gaze to Bob but didn't seem to see him. "I should have gone with her," he said. "I wanted to."

Bob was fitting the pieces together. "Annie went to talk to Rick, and he—stabbed her?"

John kept talking. "We—it was our first real date. And the waitress said he was acting—she said she was scared of him, and Annie told me that she could handle it. Talking to Rick, I mean. And I let her go."

"You couldn't have known," Bob said.

John nodded, but his expression made it clear that he begged to differ. Bob thought about pushing the point, then let it slide. John would come to his own conclusions.

"You said she was trying to help the kid," Bob said. "What kid?"

"Josh," John said. "The waitress said his name was Josh, he worked at the deli. He was sleeping with Sadie, apparently. So,

Rick chopped her up. Sadie…and he castrated Josh, but he was still alive, and I think Annie was just trying to, to—"

John's face crumpled. He turned away from Bob, his jaw working, a low, strangled sound issuing from his throat. Bob waited it out, debating whether to lay a hand on his shoulder, to offer what limited comfort he could; he wanted to help but reflexively resisted the idea of intruding on another man's grief. Before he could decide, John managed to pull himself back together. He took a deep, shuddery breath and turned to face Bob again, wiping at his eyes with the heels of his hands. Bob could see dark-red rinds of blood beneath John's fingernails.

Probably Annie's, Bob thought, and felt cold.

"What a fucking nightmare," John said. He looked and sounded miserable, but the expression of blankness, of shock was finally gone. "Rick Truman had a psychotic break. Or maybe he was always borderline, and finding out about his wife was a stressor, I don't know. Maybe he invented the whole thing. He killed Sadie, though, in the kitchen. And he was torturing her supposed lover to death when Annie walked in."

"Christ."

John nodded, his expression turning. He looked physically ill for a moment, and when he spoke again, his voice was throaty and quavering.

"There were—he was putting them in the food," he said. "Annie found a fingernail in the bisque."

Bob felt ill himself—but as before, he also felt guiltily energized by the news. Horrible, horrible of course…but Jesus, what a story! And on the tail of Ed Billings's killing spree. The modern media machine was about to descend on little Port Isley, God help them all.

"What happened to Rick?" Bob asked.

"After he killed Annie, he went into some kind of catatonic state, just dropped the knife and laid down," John said.

"Somebody called the police. I tried to help Annie, me and this woman, but I—there was nothing we could do."

He shook his head as if to clear it. "One of the other diners used to be a PA or something; he helped the kid. Might have saved him, I don't know, he was in pretty bad shape. The EMTs showed up, they took the kid—Josh—and Rick away. Vincent and a couple of his people went with Rick. I don't know if they Mirandized him or not, I didn't really catch that part—I was talking to someone when they took him out…"

He stopped talking, as though he'd run out of words, and Bob could see that the reality of it all was still hitting him. He could see it in the dark anguish of John's gaze, wet and confused. He decided that he would get anything else he needed from some other source.

And this week's edition is already run, anyway, that selfish part reminded him. He told it to go fuck itself.

"Do you need to stay here?" Bob asked. "To talk to the police?"

John shook his head. "I already talked to Vincent. I told him I needed a shower. He said I could come down to the station after…or he'd send someone to get my statement, I don't…I don't remember…"

"Come on, I'll drive you home," Bob said.

John took a shaking breath, then nodded. Bob patted his arm and motioned in the direction of his truck; they started walking, the evening's first stars springing up far above.

Bob wondered when the reality of the situation would hit *him*—he'd known Rick and Sadie since his first day in Port Isley and had been half in love with Officer Annie, in a pleasantly hopeless way—and decided that he'd really rather not be sober for the awareness, when it came. He'd have to hope that reality would be kind in its generally dreadful timing.

Either that, or I can go on a bender until the autumn rains hit, until it's too late to care as much. He knew better, knew that grief didn't work that way…but strangely, the thought gave him some small comfort.

>‹

Tommy had finally found the bat handler and was trying decide whether to round up some people to run an instance to find another Hanzo sword when he got a whisper from Jeff. Private, not in the line of chat.

nother guy went craZ & kild wife, it said. *dwntwn. rick trueman, ownd la poison.*

When? Tommy typed, as quickly as he could.

2nite, 2-3 hrs ago.

Tommy started to ask how he'd found out about it but hadn't finished when the next message came.

kild her, put her N soup, no shit. she was screwing ths guy & he chopt off guys dick 2 & did kill a cop.

No way, Tommy sent.

4real. Can U get out? Im going dwn.

Tommy automatically glanced toward his bedroom door, cracked open. He could hear clattering in the kitchen downstairs as his mom and Aunt Karen cleaned up from dinner and had their drinks of whatever. There were two older couples in the house, too, probably already in bed. They went to bed crazy early. It was almost ten thirty, which was usually when his mom expected him to brush his teeth and get settled, at least in the summer. He could stay up later if he had a good enough reason, a show he really wanted to watch or a quest he needed a few extra minutes on, but no way she'd let him leave the house at this hour, for any reason.

I could go anyway, he thought, and was guiltily thrilled by the idea, one he never would have had even, like, a year ago. Leave a note on the desk, saying he ran over to Jeff's for a book or something, then out the front door. They'd never know. Port Isley was so small, and Aunt Karen only lived halfway up the hill; ten minutes to get downtown, tops. It was enticing…but only a little. He might get back before his mom realized how long he'd been gone, but she'd definitely find the note before he made it home. And she'd be super PO'd if he left without telling her.

And it'd be wrong, he thought, but the thought didn't carry the same weight it once had, when he'd been younger. That realization was somehow more alarming than anything else.

Another moment's pause, and he tapped out, *can't, doors blockd*, his heart thumping. There was no way Jeff could find out he was lying. No way he could think of, anyway.

pussy, Jeff said, as if he'd intuited the lie, and then *L8R*, and he was gone, presumably off to see what he could of the new killings. They'd been up to the place in Kehoe Park a couple of times, seen the flowers and stuff, but Tommy had felt uncomfortable about it. Not like Jeff, or Jeff's friends. They'd made a lot of jokes about ghosts, and about fucking. They said *fuck* a lot, way more than his friends at home. And they'd made a big deal of riding their bikes over the spot where the body was supposed to have been. Tommy hadn't told his mom about any of that—and he decided he didn't want to be the one to tell her about Le Poisson, either. If Jeff was right, it was just too creepy.

Pussy, he told himself, but then put it out of his mind, returning to his game. It was too late to start a new quest, even a short one, but he could do some mining, get some money that way. Or maybe work up his fishing skill. He concentrated on the busywork, telling himself that it didn't matter that he'd seriously considered leaving his room, leaving the safety of his family for the wide, dark summer outside, where things were happening.

CHAPTER

11

Amanda waited around the pier for three days, morning to night, telling herself she was just avoiding Peter, but mostly wanting to see Eric again…and for three days, she'd sat and smoked and picked apart their too-brief conversation from the Klatch, remembering that smile of his. Having no close girlfriends to talk with—she'd been kind of tight with this one girl all through junior high, but she had moved two years ago and they'd lost touch—Amanda had spent those long, idling hours reading and posing on one of the park benches, her sunglasses perched on the bridge of her nose, a cigarette always burning so she could do the French inhale thing that looked really cool. She'd told Devon about meeting Eric, of course, but had quickly grown bored with his graphically sexual innuendos and relentless teasing. It was weird, but ever since the picnic, things had been a little strained between them. Like he was disappointed or something but was trying not to show it. Trying too hard, maybe.

She hadn't told Devon—hadn't told anyone—about what had happened with Peter, with him hitting on her. She knew Devon, knew he'd push her to go to the cops or Willie T at the high school to get Peter busted. Which he deserved, totally, but she couldn't bring herself to admit that she couldn't handle things herself. Plus, she *thought* her mom would kick Peter out on his ass if she told…but maybe not. Lately, Grace had been really into Peter, God only knew why. Amanda didn't want to think about it.

She'd just keep away from him, make sure they were never alone together. In a few more months, she and Devon would have their own apartment and real lives in the city, and her mother never needed to know that anything had almost happened. Which it hadn't.

Amanda found out about the murders at Le Poisson on Wednesday night, when her mom came home from work with the news. She'd called Devon immediately, and they'd agreed to meet early on Thursday, which sort of messed up her plans of hanging around the pier all day, but she was starting to think that the mysterious Eric hadn't been as cool as he'd seemed, initially. She was interested, but she wasn't going to wait by the phone, so to speak, even if she didn't have anything better to do. The murders, at least, were a distraction.

She and Devon exchanged details on the walk down the hill Thursday morning, what little they'd heard and overheard. Annie Thomas and Sadie Truman, dead. And Josh Waites, alive but mutilated. He'd worked at Truman's deli and had been totally hot; she and Devon had both thought he was slamming. If the rumors were true, Rick Truman had cut off Josh's dick and served it to his dinner customers, along with most of his wife's guts.

Even before they got to the bottom of the hill, they could see the news vans lining up on Bayside and overdressed reporter types wandering around, setting up shots, tapping on laptops while camera guys moved equipment around. Devon pointed out a man who just had to be Tim Bishop off Channel Five, talking on a cell phone with a scowl on his icky-tan face. They had to wait in line at the Klatch forever for some guy to buy like ten lattes, and the woman after him ordered six more, both of them all wired up with phone gear and carrying iPads. A well-dressed, overly made-up woman with a notepad approached them outside after they got their coffee, a determined smile on her face, and

Devon said, "…because she was a paparazzi *whore*," kind of loud before she even opened her mouth, which made Amanda almost snort coffee out her nose. The woman kept right on walking. It was funny, but also surreal and unpleasant, seeing all the reporters and cameras around, knowing why they were there.

They walked toward the old middle school, back up the hill and west. During the summer, town kids used to gather on the school's playground, passing time under the giant wooden play structure in the heat of the day. A lot of kids still did, over at the new school—but the old site, right by Kehoe, was where the stoners hung out now, pretty much year-round. The vast basement was mostly open to the air, half-filled with broken chunks of concrete, but it was partially covered and mostly empty at one corner, creating a shady cave that could hold a dozen kids comfortably…if you didn't mind perching on a pile of rocks, inhaling the mold smell along with your drugs. Amanda got high there every now and again—seemed like there was always someone with a soda can pipe and time to kill hanging out in the basement—but she didn't like to linger. Too dirty and spidery.

It was still early—well, almost eleven, but early for going to the middle school—but there were already six or seven people sitting in the basement's cool shade, most gathered around Cam Trent and her boyfriend, Greg. Cam's mother was on the PD, and Cam was therefore a total pothead and slutbag, but she also knew everything about everything that went on in town.

"Hey," Devon said, as they climbed down the carefully placed slabs of broken concrete that made up the stairs. They shuffled past the piles of rubble at the basement's entry, joining the group. There were a couple of candles burning in the corner, as usual, fighting with the thickest of the darkness, although you could mostly see by sunlight filtering in.

"Oh, look, the hag and her fag," Cam said.

"Yeah, sorry we're late, we were both fucking your dad," Devon said, and got a few laughs. Missy and Keith were there, and they made room. There were a few grease monkeys hanging out, and two of them took off, one of them muttering darkly, glaring at Devon as they exited. Most of the car guys hated Devon because he was gay, and because he was always making jokes about crankshafts and pumping pistons, shit like that. No great loss.

Greg was loading a fat bowl, which made the rounds while Cam recounted what she'd heard—nothing they didn't already know, except that Rick Truman was locked in a psych ward for observation. Amanda wasn't planning to smoke—she hadn't had any more weird dreams or anything, and she wasn't hip on inviting any—but when the pipe came to her, she gave a big internal shrug and lit up, unable to resist. It had been, like, two *weeks*. And that whole conversation with Bob Sayers had put things in perspective; something had happened to her, for real, but it was like that story about his brother. Onetime deal.

They settled in, listening as theories about the town's sudden bloodlust were introduced. Keith put out the idea that Mr. Billings and Rick Truman were buddies who'd made some kind of psycho suicide pact, only Rick had chickened at the last minute. Cam said she'd read this stuff on the Net about how this one murder in Scotland set off like five more in a month, a few years back. Devon told the story about all those kids in Japan or somewhere who'd committed suicide by jumping into a volcano back in the thirties. Like, a couple/three hundred of them, over a period of months. Liz Shannon, who was a total hippie flake, went on about the moon being in Scorpio or some such shit for a few minutes, but she was an idiot, just a voice droning in the dim, nasty basement. It was cool and quiet, and Amanda's coffee was just the right temperature, tepid and creamy and not too sweet, and she lit a cigarette and felt herself relaxing as Liz prattled on.

Amanda made a big deal out of not having any close friends, but she felt accepted, mostly. Everyone here knew her mom was an alkie, they knew she listened to weird music and kept a journal and liked to wear safety pins on everything, and no one really gave a shit. Most of them, anyway. That was cool, it was like, like *community,* they were all connected because they all lived and worked in the same space…

She took a deep breath, realizing how high she was. It had been a while, and Greg always had awesome shit. His brother dealt.

"Astrology's a load," someone said. Greg Taner; he had his arm around Cam and his tone was mostly good-natured. Greg was on the football team, but he wasn't one of the Dicks. Just kind of a dork. With good pot.

"Didn't you ever see any of those shows where, like, everyone in a class gets their own private astrology printout, and they go on and on about how true it is, and then the professor tells 'em they have their neighbor's printout?" Greg asked. "You know what I'm talking about?"

A couple of people laughed, and Liz shook her head. Even in the dim light, Amanda could see that she was blushing. "I got my chart done, and there's all kinds of stuff in there that's, like, totally specific."

Devon chimed in. "Let me guess—you're loyal and honest, you hate to be uncomfortable, you avoid conflict…"

Greg snorted, a big, dumb grin on his face. "You like rainy days and walking on the beach."

"You believe in it, right?" Liz asked, looking at Amanda.

"What?" Amanda stared at her, her brain taking a second to catch up. "Do I believe in *astrology*?"

"Yeah. You had a premonition, right? So you *know* there's more to this universe than the things we can see and touch. The stars have things to tell us, if we—"

"No, I don't fucking believe in fucking *astrology*," Amanda said, too loud, and just about everyone laughed, and she glanced over at Greg because he laughed really funny, kind of loony—and she read things in his face, in the blurry dark that shadowed his face. She didn't see—she just *knew*, watching him laugh, knew things about him that she hadn't known before. She knew he ate frozen waffles almost every morning, drenched and sopping with imitation maple syrup. She knew he and Cam were fucking, and he liked to do it doggie-style the most, because he loved the way she flipped her hair over her shoulder when he pounded into her, and she knew that Cam was the third girl he'd ever been with, and the only one he thought had a good body. She knew he was going to enlist in the marines in the next month or so, shortly after a knock-down fight with his old man about... about...

"You saw something, didn't you? You said you did, at Pam's, everyone said you did," Liz said, a whining, pleading sound in her voice, and Amanda looked at her and saw that beneath that tousled blonde face, Liz thought about killing herself often, regularly, and she had a cat named Duchess, and she wanted to cry now because everyone was laughing, but she would push it down, push it down, she wouldn't cry in front of them, she *wouldn't*.

Amanda didn't panic, because she was high, and because the awareness seemed natural and wasn't accompanied by visuals, and because knowing that Liz wanted to kill herself made her feel fucking *awful*, and it seemed important that she not say the wrong thing. Everyone was watching; she knew she should be funny and mean, but she didn't want Liz to have to...to *hurt* like she did.

"What everyone says doesn't matter," she said, and smiled, made it as sincere as she could manage, aware that she was tripping but it was all good, she could deal, she would deal. "We all believe in something. Whatever floats your boat, right?"

Liz smiled uncertainly, and Amanda also knew that the wannabe hippie girl was going to lose her virginity and get pregnant on the same night, sometime in the summer because there was the smell of cut grass, *outside, she's outside and she doesn't love him but she hopes he'll like her now and it hurts, stings, kind of, but she doesn't say so, she doesn't want to ruin anything—*

"I gotta get out of here," Amanda said, and dropped her coffee and stood up. She couldn't deal, after all, and she didn't want to make a scene like at Pam's, but she couldn't stay, didn't want to sit and know all these things, and why the *fuck* did she get high, what was she *thinking*? A half dozen faces turned to her, all looking up and some of them smiling, some of them not, and Cam and Greg laughed but she didn't look at them. She forced a grin and said, "Need some fresh air, bitches," not looking at any of them, making their faces just ovals in the dark. She didn't want to know any more. She grabbed her bag and turned and stumbled back toward the sunlight, up the mud-caked steps and into the ruined field where she'd once gone to school. It had gotten hot out, and the sun had washed the colors from the world. She walked quickly back to the nearest street, the little dead-end Eleanor. There were only a handful of houses across from the wrecked demolition site, and she found herself staring at the one near the corner, the small blue Cape Cod, the one with the perfect lawn and the roses. Dick Calvin lived there, but he'd probably be dead soon. Within a week or two, because lately he couldn't stop thinking about…about…

Almost got it like with Greg; if I concentrate, I could I bet I could—

"Shit shit shit," she whispered, and there were footsteps behind her. Devon, of course. She turned, not sure how to explain what had happened, not sure what to do—should she go to the hospital or something, should she lie down, drink water, go back to bed? She was freaking, big-time—and she saw Devon's anxious face and knew that he felt a little put out with her theatrics, and he was worried…and she also knew that some men were going to beat him up and throw him into the bay and he was going to drown. She could see his pale, bloated face in the morning light as he floated out from under the old ferry pier, his pretty eyes fixed and staring and terrible, his hair shifting gently in the lap of the cold water.

He grabbed her, which was good because she'd started not to be able to breathe, and even as she felt his fingers wrap around her arms, she was falling, her legs going weak. Devon dropped with her, supporting her weight to the ground, and she took a few deep, whooping breaths and started to cry.

"The *fuck*, Devon," she wailed, and held on tight, seriously afraid for her sanity.

><

Karen got six separate calls the night of the killings at Le Poisson, five of them from friends and neighbors looking to pass along details. Sarah drank wine and listened to her sister exclaim over the unfolding story, relieved that Tommy was home and safe. She briefly considered going upstairs to tell him—she thought it might be a good idea if he heard about it from her first—but decided morning would be soon enough. Particularly after the sixth call, which was a cancellation for the following week. A semicelebrity couple, some radio DJ and his new bride, had been planning to take their honeymoon in Port Isley and had booked a week at Karen's house. The man called to say that the killings would be big news for a while, and he and his wife were looking for something a little quieter. Karen had bitched for two hours straight, and Sarah had gotten more than a little tipsy, providing encouragement and support, agreeing that the world was going to hell. Despite the grim circumstances, it had been nice to connect with her sister. And nice not to be the one in need, for a change.

The next morning after breakfast there was another cancellation—and calls from two different news channels asking if Karen would comment about the killings. Sarah sat in the kitchen nursing her hangover—too much red wine gave her a bitch of a headache the day after—and listened to Karen start up again, a rehash of her rant the night before as she put away pastries and stored quiche from the morning brunch. She needed the income, was counting on it, she wasn't in the red, by any means, but most of what Byron had left her had been put back into Big Blue, and she didn't want to dip into the savings account...

"I mean, what kind of people, you know?"

Sarah blinked and played back the last bit of conversation. Something about the gall of the media, to drive away her business and then call to get her opinion on the matter.

"I totally agree," she said. "I'm sorry, I'm all out of focus."

Karen gave her a half smile. "You *do* look like shit," she said, keeping her voice low. Both of the couples currently staying at Big Blue had gone out after brunch, but Karen had apparently gotten used to keeping her voice down since opening the house.

"Thanks so much," Sarah said, and took another sip of coffee. There was a clatter on the back stairs; Tommy bounded into the kitchen a minute later. She just had time to register that he was fully dressed—his hair still askew from sleep, but his shoes tied and he was wearing a clean shirt—before he scooped up a cheese Danish and plopped down next to her. Usually, he slopped around in his pajamas until noon.

"Did you hear about the murders?" he asked. Casually.

Sarah raised her eyebrows. "You heard about them?"

Tommy poured a half glass of orange juice. "Yeah, last night. Some people were talking about it on the trade channel. This morning, too. There are already a bunch of news vans in town."

He took a sip of juice and looked at Sarah. "Jeff and some other kids are going to go down to where the reporters are, to see if they can get interviewed. Can I go?"

Some people were talking about it. Jeff Halliway, thank you again. Sarah glanced at Karen and saw that her sister was staying out of it; Karen picked up a bottle of wood polish and a roll of paper towels and headed back into the dining room.

"You want to get interviewed?" she asked, stalling.

"Nah. I just thought it'd be something to do," he said, and hooked his finger into the center of the Danish, pulling out the cheese part. "It sounds like half the town is already down there."

Sarah hesitated. He was old enough to ride his bike to and from the park at home, and regularly hung out with his friends after school. He was only twelve, but tall for his age, and smart about being safe. On the other hand, Port Isley wasn't really familiar territory, and twelve was so very young...

And people were murdered, don't forget. It wasn't a field trip to the library. Port Isley was having a run of bad luck, no question, and while the events of the past two weeks didn't seem connected, she wasn't feeling encouraged about the sanity of the vacation town's residents.

"I'll be back before lunch," he added.

He's not a baby anymore, she thought, and sighed. She supposed she should be happy he was getting some outside time.

"Take the cell," she said. "Call me when you get where you're going. And sunblock before you leave. Especially your nose and the back of your neck."

"OK." Tommy drank off his juice and stood up, smiling at her. The smile was sweet and full of good humor, and she wondered at how unpredictable kids could be. A week ago, he was all wide-eyed wonder at the prospect of a murder scene. Now it was business as usual…and his sudden nonchalance struck her with a clear glimpse of the young man he was becoming. As always, the recognition was a mixed bag—pride, mostly, but there was some nostalgic sadness in it, too, and vague anxiety for the upcoming teens.

He was gone a moment later, back up the stairs, and Sarah strongly considered going back to bed for a little while. She could see if Karen needed anything and then crawl back under the covers, flip through one of the courtroom thrillers she'd picked up at the bookstore the other day and just drift…

The kitchen phone rang, the noise startlingly loud. Sarah waited for the second ring, hoping Karen would bustle back in, but no luck. She actually groaned as she pushed herself out of her chair, vaguely remembering how she could drink like a fish when she was in college and still go jogging the next day. Getting older wasn't much fun.

She cleared her throat, picked up on the third ring. "Good morning, Big Blue," she said, trying to sound cheerful.

"Karen?" The voice was doubtful. The voice was that of her ex-husband, Tommy's father. Sarah closed her eyes.

"No, it's me," she said. "What's up?"

Jack breathed into the phone, a sound she recognized instantly and found intensely annoying. It was his hesitant, I'm-not-sure-how-to-say-this breathing.

"Your sister's little town is all over the news this morning," he said, and did his little breath thing again, a pause, a measured exhale through the nose. "I wanted to see how you were. How Tommy is."

Sarah waited for the ache to settle in, or the anger. It was always one or the other when they spoke.

"We're fine," Sarah said, sitting back in her chair. "Karen's had a couple of cancellations, and there's a lot of morbid gossip going around, but I suppose that's to be expected. Small town and all. Tommy's curious, but he doesn't seem anxious. To me, anyway. He's actually out with some friends, but he'll be back for lunch. If you want to call back."

"Ah…OK," he said, and did he sound a bit disappointed, perhaps, that she wasn't reacting the way he'd come to expect? She expected to feel happy, realizing that she'd thwarted him somehow, denying him his ego stroke…and again, nothing. She felt like he was Tommy's father and deserved her civility for that, but she owed him nothing else. Not her friendship, certainly, after how he'd behaved. And not her…her *engagement*.

I don't have to care about him anymore, she thought, and realized that it was already a done deal. Karen walked back into the kitchen, raised her eyebrows at her. Sarah shook her head, smiling a little.

"Are you sure you're all right?" Jack asked. "You sound…different. Distant."

"I'm great," she said. "Should I tell Tommy you're going to call? I know he wants to talk about his visit next week. He's excited about watching fireworks from the boat."

"Sure, fine. You're still bringing him on the thirtieth, right?"

"Right."

"We're really looking forward to having him," Jack said.

She felt a slight sourness at his casual use of *we*, but only because she thought he was probably lying. From Tommy's reports and her own brief observations, Sarah suspected that Vanessa had no idea how to interact with her new husband's son—and, in fact, resented having to share Jack with anyone else.

"I'll tell him you'll call," Sarah said. "Listen, I should run. Karen needs help with the dishes."

"Oh, sure," Jack said. "OK. I just wanted to tell you, if you need anything, or you think the environment up there is getting too…well, stressful, and you want to bring Tommy sooner…"

"I'll keep it in mind. Really, we're good."

"OK." His disappointment was obvious now, and she wondered how she hadn't ever noticed before, that he *liked* knowing she was still a mess because of him, or at least expected as much. "I guess I'll let you go…"

"Thanks, Jack. Bye."

She hit the hang-up and looked over at Karen, feeling shockingly OK with her relationship to her ex…and more than a little confused by how suddenly this OK-ness had come. It was where she wanted to be, where she'd hoped that time would eventually take her, but she hadn't even come *close* to this kind of acceptance in the months following the dissolution of her marriage. She'd faked it pretty well, even convincing herself, at times, but this was different. This was…this was *permanent*.

"You feel all right?" Karen asked.

"I think I should drink more often," Sarah said, shaking her head, which still throbbed ever so slightly. All things considered, she felt amazing.

✂

Devon and Amanda walked to Devon's house, where, at Devon's insistence, Amanda took one of his uncle's muscle relaxants, drank a glass of water, and curled up on the couch in the den. On the way to his home, she continued to "see" things—get feelings about houses and the people inside—but she was so upset it all blurred together. Which she welcomed. It was the closest she could come to blocking the knowledge that kept coming at her.

After Devon had buzzed around her for a few minutes, getting her a blanket, offering food, she started to calm down. By the time he perched himself on the arm of the couch by her feet, she felt like it—the episode, the whatever-it-was—was over. She felt exhausted, like she hadn't slept for a week. Devon folded his arms tightly and studied her, and all she felt looking back at him was what she could see on his face—confusion and worry.

Thank fucking God. She didn't see him beaten and dead and floating by the pier...but she *had* seen it, and she had to decide what to tell him. All she'd been able to get out on their dizzying journey to his house was that she was losing her mind.

"Can you talk about it yet?" Devon asked.

Amanda sat up a little, crossing her own arms. "I started having all these psychic flashes," she said. "I started...knowing things, in the basement. I knew about Greg's life, and Liz's, all this stuff I didn't know."

"Like what?"

"Like...I knew all these details."

Devon nodded slowly. "Like..."

"Greg eats waffles for breakfast. And he likes fucking Cam doggie style. And Liz has a cat named, uh, Duchess. And she thinks about killing herself, like, a lot."

Devon smiled. "Doggie style, huh? I would've pegged them for missionary."

"The Lawn King on Eleanor, the old guy? He's going to kill himself."

Devon nodded again, his smile fading. "You got high, right?"

"Yeah," she said. "I think that set it off, or something." She drew in a shuddering breath. "I thought I was losing my mind. Everywhere I looked, I saw—I knew all these things about people. And I—"

She faltered, thinking about the one thing she actually had *seen*. She took another deep breath; she'd just tell him, say the words…and then she saw the look on his face. The very wary look.

"You don't believe me?"

"No, I do," he said. "You definitely…you were flipped out, no question. I just—I thought after we talked with that reporter, you were saying how he was totally right, how you must have just had a bad dream about Brian Glover and the Dicks and your subconscious made it *seem* like the same kind of thing…"

"I know," Amanda said. "But today, just now, I'm telling you, I *knew* stuff."

"But you *were* high…right?"

Amanda sat up straighter, hugging herself tighter. "I was high at Pam's party, too."

"Right, you were…" He trailed off, still looking at her with that expression, a careful arrangement of his features. "I'm just trying to figure this out, is all."

The pain was a dull knife, turning in her gut. "You think I'm *imagining* all this?"

"Seriously, you had a psychic flash at the party," he said. "But the stuff since then, you were asleep or you were stoned. I'm not saying it didn't happen, I'm saying that maybe…maybe, like, your neurotransmitters got fucked up a little, after what happened, and now when you're stressed or whatever…"

He left the obvious unstated, and maybe what he was saying had some validity, but she had to defend herself.

"Maybe I was wrong about the rape, but the feelings I was having—" she started.

"Feelings," he interrupted. "You *feel* that Greg and Cam do it doggie-style, you *feel* that the Lawn King wants to off himself. You didn't *see* anything."

"Devon, when you came out after me, I saw that you were getting frustrated with me—with my *theatrics*." She used the word that she'd seen in his face and watched him react now, his eyebrows going up. "You were excited because something had fucking *happened*, and you were worried, and you were thinking that I needed to get over myself.

"And I saw you..." She shook her head, not even sure what tense to use. "I knew that there are these men, and they're going to beat you up and throw you in the bay. I saw you, in the water. I *saw* it."

"What men? I was in the bay?"

Amanda nodded, and the anger that had inspired her to blurt it all out like that fell apart. Her quavering voice, when she spoke, reflected her dismay. "I think you're going to—I think they're going to kill you."

Devon looked incredulous. "Why?"

"I don't know," she said. She suspected it was because of him being gay, but she didn't *know*. She wanted to be as clear as possible.

"You saw it—saw *me*—like you did Lisa Meyer?"

He leaned closer and spoke in his serious voice. "Amanda, this isn't a joke, or a, a fucked-up goth fantasy or something, is it?"

She felt her eyes well up anew. "No, it's not."

She saw confusion and fear and anger cross his face, imagined she could feel his internal struggle—had his best friend cracked up, or was she turning psychic, or was she a selfish, crazy pothead bitch? She waited, and when he finally spoke, his voice trembled almost as badly as hers had. To her almost infinite relief, in spite of what they were talking about, because it meant they were still friends. "Smoke break?"

"Oh, *fuck* yes," she said, and meant it so fiercely that it was funny, and they both laughed a little as they stood up. But the good feeling didn't last, and by the time they lit up, standing in the narrow shade of Devon's back porch next to a butt-filled coffee can, Amanda's stomach hurt again, and she didn't know what the fuck she was going to do.

><

Thanks to a surprise "family" getaway, Eric had been stuck on a fucking sailboat for three days, listening to Dad fuck Miss Big Tits, and the whole boring, annoying time, he'd been thinking about Amanda. Soft-skinned, green-eyed Amanda. It was almost weird, how much he was thinking about her, and the second Dad docked late Thursday morning, Eric started looking. She said she hung out by the pier, but he thought she meant the old one down on the crappier part of the waterfront, not the marina. He headed that direction and spent a couple of hours sitting on a bench, smoking and watching boats far out across the bay, rereading his battered copy of *The Basketball Diaries*. He texted some of his friends back home and heard from one of his crew that a chick they knew had OD'd, so that was something, but no news otherwise. Eventually he got hungry and decided to head home, swinging by the coffee shop on the way for a hopeful look inside, but no luck. There were news vans parked all over the place, which was mildly interesting, but not enough to actually pursue. He got himself an iced coffee and a poppy-seed muffin and started up the hill...and fate put her in his path. He was just over halfway home when he glanced down one of the side streets and saw Amanda walking into a house, leaning on some guy's arm. He wasn't sure, but it looked like the same guy who'd been with her at the picnic, who Eric assumed was gay—he dressed totally gay and did that kind of pose thing that gay guys did when they were standing around, a hip thrust out, an angled wrist. Not that Eric had anything against fags. The way he saw it, just because he wasn't into dick didn't mean no one else should be. Live and let live.

They disappeared inside the house, and Eric parked himself on the curb at the corner, where he could see her when she came out. He had smokes and sustenance and a book to read, and partial shade from a stone fence; he would wait. What he wanted, what he always looked for in a girl, was an adventure, a crazy adventure he could fall in love with for a while. Amanda was his type, and she was built like Marilyn Monroe to boot, which kicked ass over some of the skin-and-bone Emos he'd fucked back home.

About two hours later, she walked back outside by herself. She was wearing a knee-length black skirt and a plain gray shirt and had black jungle boots on. She put on sunglasses and started in his direction, and he felt his heart thud happily in his chest. He liked looking at her, watching her move. He liked knowing that she was totally unaware that he was watching her or that they were about to meet again.

"Hey," he called out when she neared the corner opposite where he was sitting. The shade had totally enveloped him, and she lowered her head and took off her sunglasses as she walked across to meet him.

"Amanda, right?" he said, and stood up, pocketing the book.

She'd pushed the sunglasses back in place, and he couldn't see her eyes, but he could see that her nose was red and she wasn't wearing makeup. She wasn't smiling, either.

"Where you going?"

"Home," she said.

"Can I walk with you?"

She hesitated, tilting her head slightly as though studying him. "Ah, yeah, I guess."

He smiled, but she still didn't smile back. As they started walking, he registered her body language, tense and closed off, the way she held her shoulders. He'd gotten the impression that she'd dug his line at the coffee place, but maybe he'd read it wrong.

"Are you OK?" he asked.

"Actually, I'm not," she said.

"What's wrong?"

"What isn't," she snorted, but added a minute later, "I'm probably losing my mind, is all."

"I like that in a girl," he said, sincerely.

She sighed but seemed in slightly better humor when she answered, "You've got crazy bad timing, you know that? Where've you been, anyway?"

Eric scoffed. "My dad's boat. A surprise sail to the San Juans, so he could take his new bride to her first wine tasting. We just got back this morning."

"Sounds swell," she said.

"Sucked."

"You missed the big news. A guy went nuts and chopped up his wife and fed her to a bunch of people at his restaurant," she said.

"No shit?" That explained the news vans.

"Nadas shittus," she said.

"Is that Latin?"

She finally looked at him, a slight smile on her face. "You hassling me? Because I've already had a fucker of a day, and I don't need to be hassled."

He couldn't quite tell if she was kidding, which he liked. They walked for a minute in silence, and he tried again.

"So, you're losing your mind? How's that going?"

"Sucks cock," she said.

"Voices telling you what to do? Obsessive hand washing? Paranoia?"

Her smile was gone. "Psychic flashes, of all things. I always thought they were total bullshit, and then I had a real one—seriously, with witnesses and everything—and now I may be having more of them, or I may just be so freaked-out from the first one that I only *think* I'm having more."

He didn't think she was kidding, now, but played it cool in case she was yanking him. "That's really interesting," he said. "So, like, mind-reading, or seeing into the future…?"

She stopped walking for a beat, stared at him, her expression defensive. Whatever she saw in his face, she apparently realized that he wasn't trying to be an asshole. "Both, I guess. The first one, I saw a girl get killed. And like two days later, she was dead. Now, though…"

He waited, watching the way she bit at her lower lip, like she was deciding what to say. She was sexy cute.

"Now I don't know," she finished, and they started walking again. "I saw a bunch of stuff today, and I don't know if it's true or just, like, my brain fucking with itself."

"What did you see?"

She frowned behind her dark glasses. "Bad shit," she said. "My friend, Devon? He thinks maybe I blew a fuse when I saw Lisa getting killed, and now I'm getting all these signals that seem like the same thing but aren't."

"What do you think?" he asked.

She hesitated before answering. "I think it was real," she said, her voice soft. "But if I'm losing it, I *would* think that, wouldn't I?"

The conversation was weird but engaging. She wasn't all simpery or dumb about it, and if she was staging some psycho fantasy play, she should go into acting, because he totally bought it. "Is there any way to, like, test it? I mean, the things you saw or whatever, is it stuff you could check into, to see if it's true?"

"I don't know," she said, and sighed. "Maybe some of it. Nothing was really specific, and the stuff that was—I mean, I thought that this one girl has a cat, and I thought of the cat's name—I could check on that, but even if it turns out to be true, maybe I knew it before, you know, and just forgot. The other stuff . . a guy I know might enlist in the marines. An old man who lives on Eleanor might kill himself. If that happens, I guess...I guess it could all be true."

She seemed unhappy, and confused, and he suddenly felt really good, really happy that he'd found her, that she was sharing this with him. That she was turning to him for support. It was like they already knew each other.

"Or, you're crazy," he said, and smiled at her. "Look at the bright side, right?"

The smile she gave back made his heart thump again, and Eric suddenly felt quite sure that they really had been fated to meet, that there were forces in play, or whatever. If she was a nutjob, that was cool. If she was psychic, even better. Either way, he won. There was no question they'd be fucking within the week, and the summer wouldn't be boring anymore, and she *was* beautiful, a beautiful, strange adventure just waiting to happen.

12

Phillip's office was small but comfortable, blond bookshelves and soothingly neutral artwork. John slouched in the leather arm-chair next to the window, exhausted by their session, exhausted by the retelling of Annie's murder.

"Do I need to remind you that it's a process, what you're going through?" Phillip asked.

John stared out at the windswept car lot. Sun flashed off metal. "Yeah. Remind me."

"Shock. Traumatic stress. Stages of grief, guilt, regret...I've known you for a while, John. You liked this woman. There had to be something there, for you to be so taken."

John nodded, his throat hitching. "Yeah."

"That's a lot of work ahead," Phillip said. "You tired yet?"

"I was tired before," John said. "I was planning to call you, anyway. I've been thinking about Lauren, a lot. And women in general. Then this thing with Annie..."

He'd told Phillip about seeing Annie at the picnic, about spending the night with her, about her death...but he didn't know how to convey the *experience* of her, or how hopeful he'd felt, being with her. He thought about her half smile and her bright, golden-brown eyes, and how she'd looked, standing barefoot in his kitchen, drinking coffee with him. How dynamic and friendly and interesting in the bedroom, when they'd been together, when he'd been inside her and they'd locked gazes and

he'd felt something pass between them, something real and possible. It had felt so good, to connect with a woman again.

Then he thought about the blood, and that brought it on, the
loop that had played again and again in his mind's eye, that had
not turned off since he'd walked into the kitchen of Le Poisson.

When Rick had screamed, they'd all heard. A dozen diners
had turned toward the kitchen, the room going still for a beat,
the shouted words hanging in the sudden lull like some mad
riddle. "Leave him alone!"

John hadn't paused to see the expressions of his fellow diners, although his imagination had since provided his little mental movie with worried frowns, with shared glances of concern
and mumbled surprise. He had been on his feet and through the
swinging kitchen door as soon as he'd registered Rick's voice—
not the words but the tone, the shrill, petulant fury—and had
been just in time to see Rick in the room off the back of the
kitchen, mumbling something as he dropped a bloody knife, the
clatter somehow muted. Rick dropped to the floor, disappearing
behind the steel legs of a long counter that ran the length of the
room.

John stepped closer, saw that the room was splashed with
blood; it was everywhere, and someone else was near Rick. For
some reason he saw the pattern of her skirt, first, before he understood that it was Annie there on the floor, holding her stomach
with folded arms, more blood spilling out from beneath their
trembling hold. He saw the flowers on the dress, sodden and red,
and then he was moving, fast, grasping for the compression-to-
breath ratio, finding it as he fell to her side, ripping his jacket off,
bundling it, looking for the wound. She shifted, her poor bloody
arms falling away from her belly, and he realized how bad it was.

He pressed his jacket against the worst of it. "Call nine one
one!" he shouted. "Get over here, somebody get over here!"

He heard someone, a woman, scream, heard more people coming in, a shocked babble of rising voices. He rolled Annie to her back and saw her eyelids flutter, and there was more blood, rolling out of her mouth in a dark stream. Less than ten feet away, Rick lay on his side, holding his knees and grinning and shaking, making small, animal sounds in the back of his throat. The expanding pool of blood unfurled long fingers toward him.

An older woman in a light linen pantsuit knelt next to John, reached out to hold the compress against Annie's abdomen. Her knees were immediately soaked red. "I've got it," she said, her voice brisk but calm. He found out later that this woman had worked for better than twenty years as a trauma nurse in a Los Angeles hospital. "Is she breathing?"

John bent over Annie's face, over her half-open eyes, touching his fingers to her neck—but there was nothing, nothing at all, and the gurgling, spluttering cough that erupted from her relaxing throat, that misted warmth across his face, was the part of the memory loop that became slow-motion. That was when it had finally occurred to him that there might be no hope.

He'd started CPR and known within a minute that she was gone. Besides the terrible mess beneath his locked hands, the salty-slick taste of blood when he'd breathed for her, he just knew. The nurse had probably known too, but they'd done what they could, they'd kept it going. A few people ventured to their end of the kitchen, and someone had started shouting that there was another victim, and someone else had screamed, and a man had stumbled past them, vomiting, his dress shoe sliding in Annie's blood, leaving a red, broken skid mark. John didn't look up, only kept up the compressions, *thirteen-fourteen-fifteen, tip, pinch, breathe, lock, one-two-three*, kept counting, his shoulders aching, telling himself that there were miracles, that people survived terrible traumas every day, surely worse than this. He was still telling himself that when a pair of EMTs pushed him out of the way. He stumbled to his feet, watching them work, watching Annie's slack face bob and tremble as they pumped and prodded. He wiped wet hands on his brow, looked and saw that his hands were bloody. He realized how he must look, and turned, wondering where the woman in the pantsuit had gone, where Rick had gone, his numb gaze taking in what was in the kitchen's back corner, although he wouldn't really see it until later, in the dark and silence of his lonely bedroom. A cop he didn't know had led him from the kitchen to an office in the back, away from the two men bent over Annie's still body. Before they'd turned the corner, John had seen one of the techs shake his head.

There'd been questions and more questions, and a quick exam by another EMT, a brisk, masculine woman with leathery skin and cold eyes, and finally they let him wash his hands and face, let him go...but the mind's-eye movie really ended when that EMT shook his head, confirming beyond doubt that she was gone—and then promptly looped back to Rick's angry, terrible shout. There was no one image that stood out, that seemed more or less important than any other, but his mind couldn't let it rest. Like if he just went over it again, and again, some detail would stand out. Something would explain what had happened, how it had happened...

Phillip was watching, waiting for him. He was a good therapist, a colleague John had known for better than a decade, and John respected his opinion. Trusted it. John dragged himself back.

"I can't stop thinking about what happened," John said.

"It's only been what, four, five days."

"I know, but..." John closed his eyes for just a second and saw Annie in his kitchen, smiling over the rim of her cup. Saw Rick, dropping the knife. When he spoke, he barely recognized the anguish in his voice. "How do I get through this?"

"You got anything in the house?" Phillip asked. "Ativan, Xanax? Klonopin?"

John blinked. "You telling me to get high?"

Phillip leaned forward in his own chair. "I'm telling you to cut yourself a break," he said. "This is a terrible thing, what's happened. Stop me if this doesn't ring true, but it sounds like you were finally taking some steps away from what you were with Lauren. Opening yourself up, letting your guard down."

John felt his eyes well up again. "Yeah."

"And lightning struck," Phillip continued. "Of course you're going to think about it. You're going to remember it and replay it and analyze it, probably for the rest of your life, so give yourself a chance to, to *acclimate*. You and I both know that you're strong enough to get through this, but you don't have to do it all today, or this week, or this month. You can't, anyway. It's a process. I said it before, I'll say it again if you want, but you know that. You bury it and suffer later, or you let it happen."

John nodded, still struggling against tears. He wasn't ashamed of crying, he was just goddamn tired of it; his eyes hurt. His heart hurt.

"So, you do what you can," Phillip said. "Take a vacation, if you need it. Get sleep. Eat decent food. Go for walks. And if you want to turn your brain off for a little while, don't beat yourself up about it."

John nodded again, feeling like a child, grateful to be told what to do. "Lauren might have left something in the medicine cabinet..." Right before they'd split, she'd gotten herself a scrip for Xanax.

"I'll call over to Arnie, get him to phone something in to your pharmacy," Phillip said.

"I got a call from him just the other day," John said, remembering with a pang that he'd been telling Annie about it, over their dinner. "Last week. He asked me to start sending referrals over to the new guy in Kingston."

"Actually, I've been overbooked myself," Phillip said. "Mostly people from Isley."

"Me too," John said, and sighed. "Though a few of my regulars are taking breaks, so it's not too bad." He was thinking of his last appointment on Wednesday, his incest survivor. Marianne. Marianne was divorced, middle-aged, and overweight and had struggled mightily with unipolar depression and a variety of dysfunctional behaviors throughout her adult life, mostly thanks to an uncle who'd repeatedly molested her when she'd been in her early teens. John had been seeing her five times a month for better than three years, since she'd moved to Port Isley, and had only caught glimpses of the sturdy, confident woman she was, beneath her little-girl voice and constant stream of self-deprecating jokes… except in their last few sessions, she'd been…better. Stronger. And Wednesday, she'd told him that she was tired of letting her past dictate her future, in a clear, grown-up tone that told him just how much better she really was. They'd agreed to move their sessions to once every two weeks, but he wouldn't be surprised if she went to a call-as-needed by the end of the summer. Maybe sooner. He wished he could take credit for the change, but as far as he could tell, she'd just decided to get better.

People do recover, he thought. *They move on. I will, too.*

"Leave him alone!" Rick screamed, as he was pushing the knife into her belly, gutting her…

"Give yourself the same advice you'd give to a client in your situation," Phillip said. "Take care of yourself. Let yourself heal a little. We can start some cognitive work when you're ready. It *is* going to get better."

"Just like that, huh?"

Phillip smiled his gentle smile. "Don't forget that you've got resources, you've got friends. Use your support system. And I'll make time, whenever you need it. Just call."

John looked at the clock on the wall, saw that his fifty was almost up. He knew he could push it; Phillip staggered his appointments to allow for certain situations, but he wanted to get home, wanted to spend his last day off getting himself together. He was eager to go back to work. When he was with a client, he was the observer, the advocate; he'd learned how to leave his own baggage at the door of his office, a carefully practiced skill that had allowed him brief periods of relief when things had been at their worst with Lauren, and he believed—hoped desperately— that work would save him again.

Phillip stood up with him and walked him to the door. Usually, they chatted for few minutes about work-related stuff, articles of interest they'd read, colleagues they had in common, but John couldn't think of anything to say. That made him feel like crying again, which made him think of the EMT who had shaken his head over Annie's bloody corpse. *Not gonna happen*, that head shake had said. *Don't bother.*

"Take care, OK?" Phillip asked.

John nodded and let himself be embraced. Phillip thumped him on the back and let him go. John hunched his shoulders and headed for the lot, squinting as he stepped out into the day, the sunlight an assault. He was as tired as he could ever remember being.

CHAPTER

13

Independence Day was a holiday that Miranda Greene-Moreland had mixed feelings about. There were a few—Thanksgiving (because of the oppression of the Native Americans), Christmas (because she didn't believe in the Western interpretation of God), and Easter (same reason)—that were probably her most troublesome, ideologically. She preferred to celebrate the solstices and made a point of telling everyone so when she handed out gifts every year. The Fourth didn't have any unpleasant political or religious connotations for her...but it was *their* day, and every year they made a point of reminding her. That made Independence Day the worst, hands down.

Another explosion boomed through the woods, and Miranda and Terrence, one of the retreat's yearlong participants, both jumped. They were in the kitchen, making sandwiches for the firework excursion; the entire retreat was heading for the lighthouse at dusk, to see what they could of Port Angeles's show—and to get away from their crazy neighbors for a little while, who spent every Fourth of July getting ridiculously drunk and blowing things up from morning until well after midnight. Every year, she ended up calling the police. They always promised to send someone over there, but she had no idea if they ever did. One year, she'd gotten so mad that a few of her artists and she had driven over there at two in the morning (on the fifth!), ready to give Cole Jessup what for...only they'd pulled up to the compound's security gate and honked and no one had come, even though they'd heard drunken laughter in the woods. Someone had fired a bottle rocket in their direction, they'd had to leave for fear of bodily harm, and Chief Vincent had as much as shrugged when she'd complained, saying that it could have been an accident.

Terrence fluttered a hand to his chest. "I wish they'd stop *doing* that," he said.

Miranda shook her head, her mouth a grim line as she spread aioli on the sandwich bread. "If wishes were horses," she said, which had been a favorite saying of her mother's, and automatically hated that she'd said it. The vague feeling of irritation that came with the reminder that she was, in fact, turning into her mother added to her already high stress level. Shots and whistling bombs and chains of firecrackers had been going off in the woods since early morning, disrupting the community's spirit, making work impossible.

Except for Darrin, of course. She had no doubt he was in the studio today. Her intense young artist from the East Coast could work through anything, it seemed, and had proved to be her most prolific summer guest, as well as the most popular. He liked to talk about art and the creative process sometimes while he was working, and several of the community members had taken to gathering around while he spoke, listening to his thoughts about the flow of the universe as he sketched or colored one of his brilliant pieces. Miranda had taken her needlepoint and sat in on a few of his sessions and found him to be absolutely *inspiring*, if a bit...dark, she supposed.

"Which salads are we doing?" Terrence asked, heading back to the fridge with an armful of condiments. "Potato, pasta, and...?"

"Berry melon," Miranda said promptly. She'd just bought fresh, organic blueberries and raspberries from the farmers' market in Port Angeles, and the cantaloupe left from breakfast would fill them out nicely. "If you'll rinse the berries, I'll—"

Boom! Miranda instinctively ducked as the roar of an explosion echoed around the camp, much too loud to be all the way over on Jessup's land unless they'd bought a cannon. *Probably did, bomb shelter crazies—*

Terrence screeched and dropped his armful, mustard, onion, and a packet of sliced provolone hitting the floor. The mustard jar broke, spicy brown goop splattering across the kitchen floor, decorating Miranda's bare ankles beneath her long, embroidered skirt.

"Oh, my God, I'm so sorry!" Terrence hurried to the sink and grabbed the dishcloth, hurried back to kneel and wipe at the floor. Miranda sighed and went to help him.

"I'm such a klutz, I'm so jumpy, and that was so *loud*, it didn't even sound like a firecracker…" He dabbed at the splayed strings of mustard, while Miranda carefully picked up the larger pieces of broken glass, the vinegar-mustard smell making her want to sneeze. "That was, like, an MX missile or something. They're never this bad. Do you think they're on our side of the line?"

"Oh, I have no doubt," Miranda said, dropping the glass into a paper bag.

"Do you want me to call the police?"

"Why bother?" Miranda said, grabbing a handful of paper towels. "By the time they get here, those crazies will be back on their side, saying they'd *never* trespass, the trees are clearly *marked*, Officer." She ran the towels under the sink and started wiping her ankles, *tsk*ing with annoyance when she saw an oily speckle of mustard on the hem of her skirt.

Terrence went to the sink to rinse out the dishcloth. He turned back to her, a slight smile on his face. "You know, last night I was telling some of the new people about the whole history with

Jessup, about the cats and everything? And Darrin was throwing out these ideas about things we could do. You know, to mess with the A-team over there."

Miranda stood up from cleaning her skirt, frowning, imagining slashed tires or broken windows. "I don't think that's appropriate, Terrence. We're..." She searched for an analogy and found an appropriate one. "We're not rival summer camps, are we?"

"Some of the ideas were funny, though," Terrence said. He finished wiping up the mustard, putting the rest of the things back in the refrigerator as he spoke. "Like, tie-dyeing their laundry. Or putting all these bumper stickers on their trucks, like, 'I Heart My Pomeranian,' or 'The Goddess Is Alive, and Magic Is Afoot.'"

Miranda couldn't help a smile at the thought...and a string of loud pops from somewhere close in the woods wiped it from her face. The clock read just after two. So, only five more hours of listening to the survivalists celebrate, before the trek out to the lighthouse.

"It *is* tempting," she said. "But if he brings it up again, tell him it's not a good idea. That sort of thing is beneath us. Besides, I don't think..."

James was standing in the doorway to the back porch, and the expression he wore made her forget about firecrackers and bumper stickers. "James? What is it?"

He swallowed, and she could see his Adam's apple go up and down, could see the light sheen of sweat on his face. He looked as though he might vomit. He leaned against the doorframe, his body sagging against it, and took a deep breath.

"I think I found them," he said. "I mean—I think, they're out past the kiln. They look like—just—I mean, the tails. I heard the explosion and started walking toward the line, and I heard at least two people, running away. And I almost stepped on them, they're just laid out, side by side—"

"Speak clearly, darling," Miranda said, not unkindly.

He swallowed again. "The cats' tails, Miranda. Eight of them."

Terrence let out a muffled cry, his hand pressed to his lips, and ran out of the kitchen. Miranda only stared at James, and for the first time since forming the retreat, she thought very seriously about killing Cole Jessup.

><

Amanda took an extra-long, cool shower in the late afternoon, carefully shaving her armpits and legs, washing her hair twice and using her mother's good lotion once she got out, rubbing it everywhere she could reach. Eric was going to come by the apartment around six, and they would walk up to the lighthouse together to see the fireworks. After having a little private time.

Boyfriend, got a boyfriend, her mind sang happily, as she wrapped herself in a towel and crossed the narrow hall to her bedroom, to the drowsing fan of hot, tired air blowing around her room. Her mother was at the bar, and Peter hadn't been around for a couple of days, so she and Eric would have the place to themselves. She still felt a little weird about Eric seeing the apartment—they'd hung out almost every night for the last week, all their "dates" at his house, which was practically a mansion—but he'd seen the apartment's outside, and she'd already explained how it was with her mom and Peter. Eric came from money, but he wasn't a snob. He was...he was so cool, about everything. He liked a lot of the same music she did (Nirvana, duh, but also Jack White and Franz Ferdinand), and some of the same movies. He was really into uberviolent video games, which

There was a long pause. "Uh, *yeah*, we have plans," Devon said. "Don't you remember? After the picnic? You said we should stake out the fairgrounds, just in case anything happened."

"Yeah, but after last week, you said you thought it was my fucked-up brain, *remember*?" she shot back, her defenses snapping into place. "And Eric's coming over. We're going up to the lighthouse, to watch the fireworks."

"Sounds romantic," Devon sneered. A couple of days after Eric had walked her home that first time, the three of them had gone out for coffee together...and while both boys had been civil, there'd been no real friendliness between them. Eric had been focused on her, and Devon had been overall unimpressed with him—commenting later that he seemed nice and was good looking, in an urban white-boy way. She'd gotten the impression that Devon didn't think Eric was all that smart but was being tactful in not saying so—although his disdain was evident by what he *hadn't* said, and she was a little irritated that he hadn't at least pretended to be happy for her.

That day at the middle school, when she'd seen him drowned and dead, she'd been so scared, so afraid for him. And he'd been scared too, and he'd believed her. But with Eric to distract her and a growing certainty that the old reporter dude had been spot-on, after all, about her brain trying to convince her that she was seeing real things, Devon's sudden jealous-queen bit was a little tired. He'd already told her, straight up, that he thought her mind was playing tricks on her, and every conversation they'd had in the last week, he'd been a little more certain each time, a little quicker to remind her that she'd smoked some superstrong pot right before seeing what she had, about him being dead. She hadn't even bothered to tell him about the strangely vivid and realistic dreams she'd been having, although she and Eric had talked about them a couple of times. There'd been no more nightmares, not exactly, but deep, emotional dreams, like visions from a reality her mind hadn't created. Like...like the visions, but not as whole. She mostly couldn't remember them when she woke up, anyway, although a few of the weirder images had remained—a little boy in a hall of mirrors, a grinning woman with blood in her hair. Others. The interesting part was that she kind of *felt* like those shadowy people, in her dreams. Felt the high-strung anxiety of the little boy, trying to find his way through the mirror maze, which was dark and empty for some reason. Felt a kind of self-righteousness, a grinning wildness within the bloody woman. In the dreams, she saw them and *was* them, all at once. She doubted the dreams were psychic or anything, but they definitely seemed like part of whatever her brain was up to, lately.

Something I might have shared with my best friend, she thought, and sighed. "Don't be a dick, Devon," she said, letting her defenses down a little. "Are we fighting or something? Because I feel like you're mad that I've been busy lately. And after all the weirdness about what I saw and everything, I don't want you to be mad at me."

He didn't say anything for a few seconds. "I'm not *mad*," he said finally. "I just—I mean, this is a big thing in your life, what you've been seeing, and we've been friends for a while, and I guess I'm kind of...I feel like I'm getting shut out of this totally important thing for you so you can play hide-the-bone with the new guy, you know? I mean, you've been seeing him like every *day*."

Amanda leaned back against the wall, letting the shirt fall open. The apartment seemed stuffier than usual. Even with the fan blowing directly on her, she was already sweating from the heat. "I know, I know. But he's...he's only here for, like, another month, and I'm really liking him, OK? And you're right, about me being an ass. Let's hang out tomorrow, OK? I won't make any plans."

"We *had* plans for tonight," Devon sniffed.

"For a stakeout that we've pretty much vetoed the need for, right? And which you haven't mentioned for, like, ten days or something?"

"Whatever," Devon huffed, but he was only pretend offended, she could hear it in his voice. "And tell me you're using protection, by the way."

"Well, *duh*."

She could hear a grin in his voice. "Are we a Magnum Plus? Or does Mr. Eric suffer from the teeny-peeny? You never said."

"Fuck off." She hesitated, then added, "We'll be up at the lighthouse later, if you want to sit on our blanket."

"Fireworks are for fags. I've got a hot date later, anyway."

On the computer, she silently finished. "You still with, uh, gguy7?"

"I'm so over him," Devon said. "Actually, my new Romeo is local. Like, meet-me-in-Kehoe-so-you-can-suck-my-cock local."

Amanda remembered Devon's blind, staring eyes, filled with water, and felt a touch of apprehension…and hurt, that he'd kept such big news to himself. "You gonna tell me his name?"

"Can't. It's strictly on the DL." Devon sounded pleased. "You wouldn't believe me, anyway."

That was her cue to start pumping him for details, but Eric would be over in twenty minutes. Less. "You're so gay. I'll call you tomorrow."

"Whore," he said breezily, and she hung up on him, smiling—

—and there was a knock at the front door. Eric was early.

She tossed the phone on her bed and ran her fingers through her hair, fluffing it up. "Just a sec!" she called, throwing her makeup back in the bag. She dropped the bag on the floor, next to a stack of books, and did a last look around as she hurriedly buttoned the bottom half of the men's work shirt. It wasn't what she planned on wearing to the lighthouse, but fuck it, they were going to have sex before they left, anyway—and she thought she looked kind of sexy, wearing just a big men's shirt. The room was appropriately cluttered, but not dirty. She'd done the dishes and picked up the living room, too.

"Hold on, I'm coming," she said, hurrying down the hall— and as she turned to face the front door, it opened, and there was Peter, stepping quickly inside, closing the door behind him. He still held the key in one hand—and he slipped it into his pocket as he grinned at her, his eyes dark and roving. She reflexively crossed her arms, blocking his view.

"Hey," he said, his voice low and insinuating. "I left something here. Thought I'd drop by and get it, if that's OK with you."

"Whatever," she said, backing away, back toward her room. Eric was coming; he'd be there any minute.

"Where you going?" he asked, and stepped closer—and dropped his hand to the front of his jeans. He rubbed his thumb over the bulge there, still smiling. "Don't you want to help me look?"

"Jesus, Peter," she said, unable to believe he was touching himself, feeling sick and shocked…but not entirely surprised. "Get your shit and get out, right now."

She wanted to sound tough and mean, but her voice was shaking, her thoughts tumbling—why hadn't she done something, said something to her mother? Grace had been in a crappy mood lately, distant and irritable, but she should have talked to her, anyway. There was no lock on her bedroom door, but the bathroom had a lock, a wimpy little door lock, but she just had to keep away until Eric came, and—

—and what's he going to do? Knock? Go home when no one answers?

"Come here," he said, and took another step, and she turned and ran, and made it about three steps before he grabbed her arm, almost jerking her off her feet. He pulled her to him, grabbed her in a rough embrace, and she shrieked, a startled, angry sound. Peter clapped a hand over her mouth, talking soft and fast.

"Don't be like that, baby, you're going to love it; I bet you love to suck dick, don't you?" His breath was sour with beer and cigarettes. "With your pouty little baby mouth. I'll make you come, too, I'll eat you out till you scream, you'll fuckin' love it."

He lowered his hand while he was talking, cupped his hand around her left breast, still holding her waist tight with his other arm. Tight enough that she could barely breathe.

"I'll tell my mother," she gasped, realizing how stupid that sounded as she said it, how ineffectual, as if the threat would be enough to make this stop.

Peter smiled, squeezing her breast. "I already told her about how you've been when she's not around," he said. "Dressing up, flirting, asking me to sit by you. A little crush on Mommy's boyfriend. She was mad, but I told her it was normal, I told her to let it alone, that it would pass once you realize I'm *her* man. And she said if you tried anything else, she'd pack your fuckin' bags, so you might want to think about what you want to say to her. About whether you want to say anything at all."

She could actually see her mother's face, tight with anger, could see how he'd set it up, *no wonder she's been such a bitch—*

"Now we can do this fun or you can make me hurt you, but we *are* going to fuck, Amanda-pie." He used her mother's nickname for her, from when she'd been a baby. Hearing him say it made her feel ashamed and dirty, like he'd already raped her.

"Let me go," she said, looking into his eyes, searching for mercy. She'd never liked him, but they'd been nodding acquaintances for months; he was her mother's boyfriend, for fuck's sake—he *couldn't*, could he? It sounded like a plea, it *was* a plea, and there was nothing in his eyes but determination and raw lust, and she could feel his erection against her stomach, a hot urgency, pressing. He leaned in to kiss her, still holding her breast—and she'd been in shock, maybe, but at the thought of his tongue in her mouth, she jerked her head away, bringing her arm up, pushing at his face as hard as she could.

"Let go, I'll call the fucking cops, you let me go *now!*" she shouted, and he grabbed her wrist and squeezed tight. She gasped with pain, looking into his flushed face, and saw clearly that he wanted to hurt her, that he was OK with that—that he had expected it.

"You do that," he said, and his grin was a terrible thing. "You can tell them that I fucked your brains out, and you said no—and I'll tell them what really happened, I'll tell them that you begged for it, and I'm only human, right? And when I felt bad, after, said I was going to tell Grace, you changed your tune. They going to believe *you*, you think? The slut daughter of the town lush?"

Amanda stared at him, determined to fight but frozen suddenly by the reality of the situation, the possibility that no one would believe her—

—and someone knocked on the door.

"Eric!" she screamed, and Peter squeezed her wrist tighter, and she screamed again, as loud as she could. Immediately, there was pounding at the door, Eric calling her name, and Peter let her go, an expression of rage contorting his features, his gaze darting to the door and back to her as he pulled away.

"Amanda!" Eric shouted, and started kicking the door, and Peter stuffed his hand into his jeans, readjusting himself, plastering a smile on his thwarted face.

"You just made a mistake," he said, almost too quietly to be heard over the pounding. He reached for the door, still glaring at her, flipped the lock, and jerked it open. Eric half fell inside, and Peter pushed past him, was outside and gone before Eric righted himself.

He looked at her, confused, looked back outside. She heard a door slam, heard Peter's truck peel out of the lot a beat later.

"You OK?" Eric asked, and suddenly he was there, putting his arm around her, puffing his chest out as he looked back toward the parking lot, his expression grim. "Did he—was that Peter?"

Amanda nodded and leaned into him, expecting tears to come, but there weren't any. She felt strangely resigned that she'd just been forced into some nightmare confrontation with her mother, that her date with Eric was fucking ruined, that she wanted to shower for ten hours, but even if, she'd still be able to feel the warmth of his hand, the insistence of his hard dick at her belly. Overshadowing these things, she saw her life as the tiny, insignificant thing that it was, really. She'd been lucky, but she just as easily could have been violated and her life ruined and the world would have kept turning, turning.

Eric held her, and she felt how much he wanted to protect her, the sense of it suddenly so strong that she felt like she was inside him, loving her...

No. Not love. Infatuation...and something else, a kind of need that she didn't know, that was beyond her experience. The feeling was as mysterious and fathomless as some oceanic trench. It wasn't love...but it was something, a connection, more than she'd ever had with a boy, and she was thrilled that she'd inspired such a depth of emotion, even if she didn't understand it...or understand how she knew, exactly.

It doesn't matter, she told herself, and let him comfort her, thinking that knowing such a thing wasn't so bad.

><

Karen and Sarah had packed a picnic dinner for the guests staying at Big Blue, and they had all gone to the fairgrounds together,
two aging couples and the two sisters. Tommy was off with his
father in Seattle, and Karen was surprised to find that she missed
her nephew. She'd never particularly cared for children, but
Tommy was bright and good-natured, and she'd gotten used to
having him around. Sarah, too.

Sarah donned a hooded sweatshirt and stood with the others. "Are you coming?"

Karen looked over the table, at the piles of picnic plates and
empty containers. The guests would walk directly back to Big
Blue after the fireworks, and she didn't want to return to clean
up by herself. It was silly, she knew, in a town Port Isley's size,
but she disliked being by herself outside at night. Too many years
in the city, she supposed. Besides, the way her stomach was bur-
bling, she thought she might need to visit the bathroom soon.
She'd overindulged on the brie.

"I'll pick up here," she said, "be along in a few minutes."

"I can help."

Karen glanced around. Someone had started a bonfire in the
pit near the bathrooms, and another group had turned up their
music, classic rock spilling through the gathering dark. There
were still a few dozen people milling about; there'd be no short-
age of groups to walk with in the next hour.

"No, you go ahead," Karen said, and lowered her voice
slightly. "I think they could use a guide," she added, nodding
toward her two couples, already starting for the road. The young-
est of the four was in her sixties, and all of them had drunk wine.
The Kasdens were from California and were celebrating their
forty-fifth anniversary, and the Jacksons were summer regulars.
Thurman and Maz Jackson were a sweet couple and had always
been as sharp as knives, but this summer, both of them had

seemed…confused, perhaps, was the best word for it. Thurman in particular. He'd taken a walk the day before and come home nearly three hours later, drawn, his hands shaking, saying only that he'd taken "a wrong turn or two." It didn't seem to have occurred to him that he could have asked directions, or used someone's phone. Karen had been saddened to realize that this would perhaps be their last summer at Big Blue.

"You should be the guide," Sarah said. "You know the way better than I do, and you're friends with the Jacksons…"

Karen smiled. "Enjoy the show, sissy. You're on vacation too, remember? And I need to use the restroom, anyway."

Sarah grinned. "Too much fruit in your pie? Need to sit for a while, make some brown water?"

"Don't be crass," Karen said automatically. Sarah reveled in being gross around her, knew that it bothered Karen no end, although she'd been depressed and anxious for so long after she and Jack had separated that it was nice to see her regaining her sense of humor, however crude. Sarah had mentioned a number of times how strange it was that she suddenly seemed to be over Jack, but Karen wasn't surprised. Sarah was much stronger than she gave herself credit for; she always had been.

"Oh, OK, *Mom*," Sarah said. "She used to say that all the time, you know."

"Not to me," Karen said.

Sarah was already walking toward the guests but shot a smile back at her, her light hair tied in a loose ponytail. She looked like a teenager sometimes. Karen watched her walk for a moment, fading into the gloom—and felt her gut rumble again. She hoped it was just her and not the food, or she'd have some unhappy houseguests.

Bathroom first, she decided. She picked up her purse and headed for the squat block building at the park's far edge. A little boy with a sparkler ran in front of her, his face lit by happiness, and somewhere in the deepening night, a mother called for him in a worried tone.

She was almost to the bathroom when someone called out.

"Hey! Hey, excuse me, can you help me?"

There was a teenager standing at the back of the building, where the trees began. Light from the bonfire cast flickering shadows over his face. He couldn't have been more than seventeen, just a few years older than Tommy.

"I dropped my mom's cell phone back here," he said, and smiled, a quick, embarrassed smile. "I've got a flashlight"—he held up a dark cylinder—"but I can't find it. Do you have a cell? Maybe you can call her number, we can find it that way."

Karen considered her disgruntled bowels—considered, too, that she didn't know the boy—but another look at his anxious, youthful face and she was reaching into her bag, stepping off the worn path to the bathrooms, moving toward the trees. She pulled out her phone, smiling at the young man. It would only take a minute.

"What's the number?" she asked, raising her voice slightly to be heard over the music, something by AC/DC—and the teenager stepped back, disappearing into the shadows behind the building, and then a hard, sweating hand grabbed her wrist, and she dropped the phone as she was jerked away from the light.

CHAPTER

14

John was pleased when Bob Sayers showed up on his doorstep just after sunset on the Fourth of July. He'd made no plans for the holiday, except to relax; it had been a long, surprisingly difficult week. His workload had gone from easily manageable to barely so in a matter of days, and while he welcomed the break from his mind-movies of Annie's murder, he felt more than a little overwhelmed by the sudden step-up in intensity of some of his clients' issues. One of his regular clients had been arrested for beating up his ex-wife, a turn John had truly never expected. Dale had grown up in an abusive household, but had worked hard to deal with his temper; he hadn't had a physically violent outburst in years, since a college bar fight. After his divorce, Dale had been struggling with his anger...and had been doing pretty well, John thought. Except that the ex-wife now had a broken collarbone, wrist, and two ribs, plus about eighty stitches; Dale had beat her with a belt after learning that she meant to remarry. John had visited his client in county lockup, a strained conversation in a cold, stale room. Dale had seemed honestly baffled by his own behavior, like he couldn't understand what had happened, or how. Which made at least two of them.

John had also had to refer one of his retired files, a woman he hadn't seen in years, to a psychiatrist he knew, to put her through a full medical workup—the pleasant, outgoing woman he remembered had begun to exhibit symptoms of an acute psychosexual disorder. In barely a month's time, she'd progressed from sudden, inexplicable fantasies to picking up strangers and taking them home with her. Such a sudden change without any apparent trigger suggested something physiological, an organic problem. He was worried about her; Nina McAndrews had sold John and Lauren their house and had come to see him a few years later for about six months, when she'd separated from her husband; overall, she'd struck him as fairly well adjusted, if a little repressed. They'd never talked about her sex life—like a lot of Catholic ladies of her generation, Nina had felt uncomfortable talking about "those" things—but he'd never had any indication that she was headed toward such extreme behavior, either.

Dale and Nina were perhaps the most dramatic examples, but many of his clients were in trouble just lately, it seemed, and he'd been busy—not just seeing people, but digging through file notes and articles and the latest DSM for help; he was dealing with things he'd only read about, or seen as a resident: signs of late-onset schizophrenia, borderline personality disorders, megalomania. For the first time since moving to Port Isley, he'd had to stop taking new patients. Candice was in a dither over the mountain of paperwork, insurance companies wanting estimates, forms to fax, addresses to bill...

"Think you can handle it all?" Bob asked. They sat on John's back porch, drinks in hand, and listened to firecrackers off in the distance, only the die-hard and drunk still setting them off. It was probably after midnight. The woods of the park were cool; both men wore long sleeves.

John sipped his beer and leaned back in his sagging lawn chair. "Yeah, I can handle it. It's my job, right?"

Bob hesitated, then said, "I mean, after what happened with Annie."

It was the first time his friend had brought up the murders since arriving. John sighed, sinking farther into his chair. "Work is solace," he said. "You're a man's man, you're supposed to know that."

Bob chuckled. "I suppose I do. I've written six months of editorials in the last two weeks."

"How are you holding up?" John asked. Bob had been friendly with Annie.

Bob studied him for a moment, his gaze unreadable in the heavy shadow—the only light came through the living room window, pale and diffuse.

"I don't know," Bob said finally. "I've been drinking too much, but I guess that's nothing new. Been kind of…introspective, I guess. I've certainly been keeping busy, with the paper…" He trailed off for a second, then added, "And some research I've been doing. For the last week or so, I've been pursuing some crazy thoughts, I guess you'd say."

"Really," John said. A deliberate opening for Bob to elaborate, if he wanted.

"You going to analyze me, Doc?"

John grinned. No getting anything past Bob Sayers. "Heaven forbid. Talk if you want. I promise not to give advice unless you pay me."

Bob sipped from his drink. He'd brought a bottle of whiskey over—he said beer was for doctors and sailors—and had been drinking it neat all evening, although John had yet to see any sign that the aging reporter was drunk. "You ever heard of anything called mass psychogenic illness, or MPI?"

"Group hysteria?" John asked. "You think…you think that teacher and Rick Truman, killing those people…"

"And other assorted weirdnesses," Bob interjected. "People aren't acting themselves lately, have you noticed?"

John thought about Dale and Nina…and a dozen others he'd seen in the last week. It was tempting to wish there was some common cause.

"Well, yes, but it's not unusual for a tragedy in a small town to have an effect on the community," John said. He felt like he'd been saying that a lot lately. "Sometimes a profound one."

"I wonder," Bob said. "You said yourself that your caseload has doubled, right? I finally got around to checking the police blotter, something I'd been neglecting since Annie…since that night. You realize our crime rate has gone up about a hundred percent in the last month? Compared to June last year? Domestic abuse, vandalism, harassment complaints…granted, it's summer, but as far as I can tell, things've *never* been this bad."

"Right, but two sets of murders in just a couple of weeks…" It was his turn to trail off. A great number of his current appointments had been made before the first murder. If there *were* some commonality…

He promptly shook the idea. "Insanity isn't contagious, Bob."

"Not necessarily insanity," Bob said. "I got online—amazing, what's out there now—and found some interesting things."

"About mass hysteria," John said. He remembered reading a fairly recent article on sociogenic or psychogenic illnesses—groups of people, usually in small, isolated communities, who suddenly started to exhibit the same psychosomatic symptoms. There'd been a group of kids at a summer lunch program in Florida, back in the early nineties, who had all been convinced that they were suffering food poisoning—of the 150 children there, almost half were vomiting and fainting, any number hospitalized, and all because one of the kids said they felt sick, and someone had said *poison* a little too loud. Turned out the pre-packaged food, the servers and tables, the kids themselves had tested clean…but the rumor had spread, the perceived sickness spreading with it. The article had cited a couple of other examples.

"That's where I started," Bob said. "I *surfed*, I believe the young folks still say—I looked at anything having to do with groups of people, all being affected in some negative way. Chemical spills, mercury poisoning, copycat killers…you know, there are clusters of suicides that pop up every now and then, bunches of teenagers all cutting their wrists or turning on their cars in closed garages? Just because they heard about some other teens doing it?"

"The Werther effect," John said, nodding. His college roommate had done a paper on it, concerning the impact of media coverage on teen suicides. The name came from a book written by Goethe in the late 1700s about a young man named Werther who shot himself after a failed romance—and upon its publication, a number of young male readers followed suit, even dressing in the clothes that young Werther had preferred. "There's a whole set of ethical choices that the media has to make when anyone commits suicide. They have to be especially careful with teenagers killing themselves. Developmentally, they're particularly susceptible."

"Don't teach your grandpa how to suck eggs," Bob said, his expression amiable. "I was on a paper for something like half a century, wasn't I? I was asking if *you* knew anything about it."

John grinned. He didn't sit around analyzing his friendship with Bob or why he liked the man so much—he tried not to, anyway—but he thought that the fact Bob said things like *don't teach your grandpa how to suck eggs* had something to do with it. "So, you think people are catching crazy? Is that what this is about?"

He said it lightly, but Bob seemed to really consider the question, his lined face set in thought. "Maybe, maybe not," he said finally. "I mean, there *are* cases on record. Isolated communities swept up in bizarre epidemics—the Salem witch trials, obviously, but there are others. Near some village in Africa—next to Kenya, I think—thousands of people were caught up in laughing fits sometime in the early sixties. This lasted for months, people suddenly breaking into episodes of uncontrollable laughter." Bob drank, then added, "Not that it was funny. There was also a lot of crying reported, rashes, pain, breathing problems…"

MPI again. "Let me guess," John said. "Political instability?"

Bob nodded. "Change of borders, change of power. The popular theory is that everyone was just stressed as hell."

"Port Isley isn't exactly isolated," John said. In the park, a string of loud pops and a teenage shout of glee.

"Why, 'cause you can drive out of it? Because you can be in Seattle within an hour, assuming you can catch the Angeline ferry on schedule?" Bob scoffed. "We don't feel isolated because we've got computers and cell phones and cable news, but we *are* pretty much alone out here. Port Angeles's our closest neighbor, and she's a twenty-minute drive on a good day."

"I didn't mean geographically," John said. "Psychologically. Having phones and the Net and the news does make a difference when it comes to that kind of hysteria. We have input from the rest of the world, especially with the summer people here. Not to mention better science. And no common religion. Besides which, no one is actually *sick*, per se."

"Yeah, I noticed that," Bob said, and sighed. "It's probably nothing."

"It *is* interesting," John said. Assuming you accepted the premise that an entire town was going off the deep end, trying to unravel the *whys* and *wherefores* was a challenge, at least. "You really think there's…something going around?"

"You're the shrink; you tell me," Bob said. "Are people crazier than usual?"

John was reflexively ready with a *no, of course not,* but the beer, the relaxed attitude, feeling not-bad for the first night since Le Poisson, he gave it some real thought. He was getting more business, that was true—a lot more. And not the standard feed of depression, divorce, midlife crisis, what he'd mostly dealt with since putting out his shingle. People were generally too complex to fit neatly into categories, and he felt he did his clients a disservice by pigeonholing them...but it seemed, lately, he'd spent an awful lot of time just trying to find the *right* labels, to figure out what was going on, to try to provide some help. For lack of a better term, people *were* acting crazier.

Not all of them. Marianne, his incest survivor, had canceled her last appointment with a smile in her voice. Four, five of his regular patients had cut their times, come to think of it, all for reasons of improved mental state. If there was a psychological bug going around, it wasn't making everyone sick.

"Are *you* feeling...different?" John asked.

"Drinking too much, like I said," Bob said. "I've been thinking about my life, remembering things...nothing else, unless you count my dust-covered reporter's instincts stirring." He smiled and sipped his whiskey. "A last gasp, perhaps."

Lauren, John thought, asking himself the same question. Before his too-brief relationship with Annie Thomas, he'd been thinking a lot about Lauren, about women in general...he'd been feeling something, no question; he'd even been planning to talk to Phillip about it. But since Le Poisson, thinking *differently* had been par for the course. He'd been traumatized, for fuck's sake.

*Annie's dress, her bleeding red dress...*John promptly took a healthy swallow of his own beer. He wasn't drunk, but his pleasant buzz was starting to fade, and he wanted it back. "Actually, I've been feeling pretty crazy myself, lately," he said. "But I think that's to be expected."

Bob was about to say something else when the phone in John's shirt pocket chirped and vibrated, a startling burr of motion. He held up a hand and fished the cell out to see who was calling so late. His voice mail listed his cell in case of emergencies, though he couldn't remember the last time a patient had called the number on a weekend.

The listing was Good Samaritan, Port Isley's tiny hospital.

"I should take this," he said, and stood up on Bob's nod of acquiescence, opening the cell as he walked to the back door, nearly tripping over one of Lauren's flowerpots that he had yet to toss.

"This is John Hanover," he said, stepping into the bright kitchen, and the woman on the other end started talking, her words high and too fast.

"Dr. Hanover, it's Sarah Reed, Karen's sister? Karen Haley? She was your patient for a while, after Byron died. Her husband, Byron. We met at the picnic, I was there with Karen and my son, Tommy. I'm sorry to be calling so late. Karen really needs you, can you come? Can you come right now? To the hospital?"

"I remember you, Sarah," John said. He kept his voice soothing and low. "Take a breath and tell me what happened."

"Karen was aa..." A shuddering breath, and when she spoke again, he could hear the tears in her voice. "Attacked. She was attacked and, and sexually assaulted a few hours ago at the fairgrounds. By a group of boys."

John felt suddenly sober. "Oh my God. Is she hurt, is she badly hurt?"

"She's hurt," Sarah said. "And the police keep trying to talk to her, this Chief Vincent, he keeps asking all these questions and she's, she's really not doing very well. And she needs to see someone, now, and you were her doctor, she's always spoken so highly of you...will you come? I'm sorry, I know it's late, but I don't know who else to call. Do you think you could come?"

John checked his watch, assessed his ability to drive. "I'll be there in twenty minutes."

Sarah let out a soft sob. "Thank you, thank you so much," she said, and hung up.

John stepped back out on the porch. "I'm sorry, Bob," he said. "I've got to cut out for a while. You're welcome to stay—the guest room sheets haven't been changed in a while, but it's not like they go bad or anything, right?"

"What's up?" Bob asked, rising from his chair.

"Ah, an old client of mine, she got hurt," John said. "And it sounds like the cops are being insensitive. I have to go down to Good Sam. There's leftover pizza in the oven; have some pizza, watch a movie or something…" His thoughts were racing, jumping ahead to finding his keys…*chew some gum in the car, bottle of water on the drive*…he didn't see the look on Bob's face.

"Was she raped?" Bob asked.

John stopped thinking about his keys and stopped and looked at his friend, replaying what Bob might have heard from his end of the conversation. He was pretty sure he hadn't mentioned anything specific, although he supposed there might have been some inference—

"Gang-raped, by a bunch of teenage boys?" Bob asked, stepping closer. His lean, weathered face was too pale. "At the fairgrounds?"

"How did—could you *hear* that?"

Bob's expression tightened at John's inadvertent confirmation. "I'll tell you on the way to the hospital," he said. "If you wouldn't mind giving me a lift. I'm not in much condition to drive."

"I don't think the, ah, family would appreciate having the press show up," John began, but Bob was shaking his head.

"It's not like that," he said. "This isn't a story. Or it is, but not one that'll ever see print. It's—I may have information for the police, that's all. I won't be bothering her family."

John stared at him a moment. If Bob was drunk, he still saw no sign…and the reporter's expression was set. "Yeah, OK. You'll tell me what this is about?"

Bob nodded slowly. "People aren't acting themselves," he said, seemingly as much to himself as to John. "Let me hit the head; I'll meet you at the front door."

"Sure," John said, telling himself that Sarah's voice must have been audible to Bob somehow. It didn't seem possible—

—*isn't possible*, his brain affirmed.

—but what other explanation made any sense? Maybe there had been some gang rapes in Port Angeles or over in Jackson, something he hadn't heard about. Of course, that must be it. He settled on the thought with relief; Bob had heard something about some other related crime or crimes, maybe from the police, for the paper. For a moment, John had thought…

He shook it off; it wasn't the time for flights of fancy. Karen needed a friendly face. He'd done a rotation through a rape counseling center as a resident, liked to think he'd at least been competent…he hoped he could be useful.

Karen Haley. Goddamnit. He knew that rapists were troubled, broken people, that many had been victims of abuse themselves, as children…he'd never had any sympathy for their actions, but he'd tried to understand, through his filters of training, how they had come to be, what he might do if he had a client with those tendencies.

Dead men don't rape, he thought now, remembering the scrawled graffiti from some random wall in the city, and found that he agreed too fiercely to wonder at his sudden change of heart.

><

Bob told John about the girl, Amanda, and her friend, whom he'd met and talked with at the picnic, as John drove them to Good Sam. About how Amanda had foreseen the rape, just as she'd predicted Lisa Meyers's death...and his impressions of the two young people as honest and sincere. The doctor was skeptical, to say the least. Bob had always suspected that John was a little too bright in that way that precluded real open-mindedness—the intellectual liberal curse, perhaps, to believe that they knew everything because they'd read an article about the law of large numbers and a book or two on the invention of God.

Still, John had the decency not to point and laugh, and Bob didn't take offense at his less-than-enthusiastic response; John was preoccupied, worrying about his patient, and Bob had more than enough to chew over without trying to convince anyone of anything. That little punk-rock girl, all of seventeen...Bob kept trying to make the scenario plausible, imagining that Amanda and Devon had planned everything, perhaps even paid their cohorts to attack a woman, to substantiate their story—maybe they meant to sell it; maybe Amanda was plotting to become the next John Edwards, or whatever psychic marvel was popular these days, and they'd set Bob up as their credible witness. The idea was far-fetched, but certainly not as out-there as precognition. There was the even simpler explanation, that it was a coincidence. Rape wasn't common in Port Isley, but it wasn't unheard of, either.

The thing was, he believed Amanda Young's story. Not because he was open-minded, although he fancied that he was, or because he believed that there was more to life than what the sciences had figured out, although that was true, too. He just thought she was telling the truth.

And she's seen two separate events before they happened, now; at least two. And what did that mean? Only that he wanted to talk to her again, as soon as possible. And he needed to find Stan Vincent, to see if that kid, Brian Glover, was a suspect yet.

They pulled into Good Sam's main parking lot, adjacent to the ER. There were a handful of hybrids and SUVs parked close to the entrance, summer folk, probably escorting their firecracker-injured kids through the urgent care. There were also two PIPD units parked at the reserved spots in the front, next to one of the hospital's ambulances. One of them was the chief's.

What am I going to tell him? Bob considered his options as John pulled into a space at the end of the line. Stan Vincent had always struck him as a pragmatist; walking up to him and announcing that a psychic had fingered the rapist wasn't going to fly. On the other hand, if there was a chance that Amanda might have seen something else, or was going to, maybe it'd be better to tell the truth, to establish that she shouldn't be dismissed as a crank...

Bob felt a tightening of his gut. If he'd believed their story, he could have prevented what had happened...but to be fair, how *could* he have believed it? What sane person would have?

"I may be a while," John said. He and Bob both climbed out, John pocketing his car keys. "Do you want to meet up later, get a ride home?"

"No, I'm good," Bob said. "I'm barely a walk from here. You do what you need to do, don't worry about me."

They started for the front entrance, hurrying. "Call me tomorrow, let me know..." John tried a smile. "Let me know if your teenager needs a therapist, I suppose."

Bob smiled back at him, sure that his own looked just as distracted. "I have to find her, first. I'll keep you updated."

They walked in together and immediately saw Chief Vincent and one of his officers, Ian Henderson, standing by the pay phone at the far side of the room, talking. Bob could see their tension, their expressions, their stances betraying them, and hoped he wasn't about to make a mistake. Bob and John exchanged farewells, and John hurried to the front desk. Bob popped an Altoid and walked toward the policemen, still not sure what he was going to say.

"Chief," Bob said, nodding in greeting. "Officer Henderson."

Vincent's eyes narrowed. "What do you want?"

Bob raised his eyebrows, startled by the obvious antagonism. "Just to talk a minute."

"I don't have a minute," Vincent snapped. "You want a story, call the office tomorrow."

"I...ah, I may have some information for you," Bob said. "About the attack."

Vincent glanced at Henderson, back at Bob. "What attack is that?"

"The rape," Bob said. "A woman was raped, is that right?"

"How did you hear about it?"

Bob looked to Henderson, saw Vincent's grim suspicion mirrored on the other man's face. Both men were looking at him as if *he'd* raped someone.

"I was at a friend's house, and he got a call—"

"Who's your friend?"

"It doesn't matter," Bob said. "Look, was the victim able to identify her attackers?"

Vincent's gaze narrowed further. "You didn't answer my question, Mr. Sayers."

He didn't anger easily, but the chief's rudeness was starting to get to him...and it was also deciding his course of action, as far as how truthful to be.

"Brian Glover and a couple of his buddies were talking about attacking someone, at the town picnic," Bob said. "I heard some other teenagers discussing it."

Stan Vincent was suddenly close enough that Bob could feel his breath across his face, hot and sour. "Who? What teenagers?"

Bob took a step back, kept his expression impassive. "Some kids, I don't know."

"And you didn't report it?" Henderson asked.

Bob couldn't help a stab of guilt. "No. I mean, it was just kids, talking."

Vincent's eyes were cold and hard. "Talking about beating and raping a woman."

"If I'd really believed it, I would have called you, obviously," Bob said. "And I'm not saying this Glover kid *did* do it. I'm just telling you what I heard."

"From 'some other teenagers' you don't know, is that right?" Vincent asked. He made no effort to keep the sarcasm out of his voice.

"That's what I said."

Vincent stared at him another moment, then nodded, once. "I'll want you at the station, first thing in the morning. Don't make me come get you."

Bob stared back. He had no idea how to respond. Vincent finally looked away, to the other cop.

"Let's go," he said, and Henderson nodded, and both men started for the doors.

Bob watched them walk away, troubled by the brief encounter, by Vincent's behavior. He wasn't sure what he'd expected, but the anger, the abrupt dismissal...Stan Vincent wasn't acting like himself either; not at all.

"What the hell is going on around here?" Bob murmured aloud, unable to imagine what the answer might be.

>-<

Amanda woke up as soon as she heard the car pull into the lot, headlights splashing across the wall in lengthening slats. She blinked at the digital clock on top of the TV, saw that it was just after four in the morning. Eric had left around midnight. He'd wanted to stay, but Amanda couldn't think of a more embarrassing, personal, awful scene to witness: Grace would be shit-faced, as usual, they would fight, she was sure, and it would suck.

She sat up on the couch and turned the TV off, surprised that she'd fallen asleep; the fireworks had still been going strong when she'd dozed off. Postadrenaline crash, maybe. She'd been keyed up for a couple of hours after Peter had gone. Eric had wanted to call the cops, but Amanda knew she had to tell Grace first. Her mother would never forgive her if she called the police on her boyfriend without at least warning her. It was Saturday, which Grace always considered a license to drink excessively—but Amanda hoped it wouldn't be too bad, that she'd be clear-headed enough to at least hear her side of the story. She had no doubt that Peter had shown up at the end of Grace's shift to spin his own version of things. He might even come home with her, which would make the fight all the more ugly. She was glad she'd sent Eric home.

Amanda and Eric had stayed in. They'd smoked and talked and eaten and had finally had sex in her small bed as late twilight passed into dark, as the fan buzzed in the corner and the fireworks started in earnest. The assorted trash families that lived in the complex loved nothing more than to make shit explode, and the parking lot had been overrun with them, shouting and laughing in between the pops and whistles. Eric had been tender and gentle with her, touching her hair and face as they'd done it, and she hadn't gotten off but it had been mind-blowingly intimate and therefore amazing, anyway. She'd been able to feel the way he wanted to protect her and how good he felt inside her...she hadn't shied away from the emotional connection, from knowing what she couldn't know, and she'd felt…engulfed by him, as he smiled into her eyes. It had been thrilling and frightening and beautiful.

Amanda folded her arms across her stomach, a hard, heavy knot, as a car door slammed. A key scraped in the lock, and the headlights pulled away, the car's engine rumbling loudly in the predawn quiet; it wasn't Peter, then. One of the waitresses usually gave Grace a lift when she'd had a few too many.

Her mother opened the door and saw her on the couch, waiting—and gave her a look of such deep unhappiness, of anger and bitter regard, that Amanda felt suddenly very, very lonely.

It's over, Amanda thought. The loneliness bloomed into sorrow. Grace had never been very good at the mothering thing, but she had tried; there'd been a few good years in there, before the drinking had gotten too bad, when it had just been the two of them. "Us against them, Manda-pie," she'd say, and hug her tight-tight-tight.

It wasn't fair…but then, it had never been fair.

"So," Grace slurred, closing the door, tossing her keys on the coffee table. She threw them too hard, and they skidded over the edge. She unshouldered her purse, let it fall on the floor. "So, you wanna fuck Peter, issat it?"

"He attacked me," Amanda said, aware that it was useless.

"Right, right," Grace said, her smile sad and sneering at once. "You come on to him and try to fuck 'im behind my back, and now he *attacked* you."

"I never came on to him. He's lying."

"I gave *birth* to you," Grace said, her eyes welling up. "You were my *baby*."

"He's a liar," Amanda said, her voice clear and cold. "He came in here and fucking grabbed me. He was going to *rape* me."

"I see how you are with him," her mother said, like she hadn't said anything. The tears spilled over, her mouth curved in sudden rage. "The way you look at him, the way you're always *touching* him."

Amanda stared. "What?"

"He tol' me about you, calling him when I'm at work, pushing up against him—showing him your tits—"

"*What?*" Amanda couldn't believe what she was hearing. "I would *never!*'"

Grace nodded, grinning now, her eyes shining. "Oh, yes. I've seen it. I tol' myself it was a crush, that you'd never do that to me. I'm your mother; I'm the only family you have, after your father left me all alone…"

The mood shifts were fast, even for Grace. She bit at her lower lip, tears spilling again.

"I know I haven't always been perfect, but I thought we were friends! I never thought that you would—that you could—" She broke down, sobbing.

Amanda watched, wondering. For most of her short childhood, she'd cried when her mother's tears had started to fall. But they fell so often and almost always meant nothing the next morning. Her childhood had been pretty much over by the time she was twelve. Devon had printed out some stuff for her once from Al Anon, about how alcoholics were emotionally stunted by their drinking, unable to grow past the age they started, often as teens. Amanda had seen it play out every day of her life. Grace, drunk, creating dramas from nothing, from the air. Anger and blame, remorse and self-recrimination, tears and more tears; there were promises made, to do better, and sloppy, showy hugs, and always another drink, to celebrate. It was all about Grace, and Grace's problems, and what she needed, and what she wanted. What Amanda wondered at now was how clearly she

could really see it, the jagged, broken selfishness that her mother
wore like a cloak, so wounded that she couldn't allow anything
else to grow, either.

"Mom," she said, and felt her throat lock up anyway, understanding the reality of what was happening. "Mom, this is no
good. We can't talk when you're drunk."

"You're not putting this off, sweetie," her mother said,
abruptly spiteful through her tears, vicious. "He told me what
you were wearing when he came by. He told me what you said,
how if he didn't dump me you'd say he, he molested you."

"And you believe him?" Amanda asked, feeling calmer than
she'd expected—but more hurt, too, the ache like a rotten tooth
in her stomach. How could her mother even *think* that of her? "I
can't stand him; don't you know me at *all*?"

Grace stared at her, swaying slightly, her mouth turned down
in an ugly grimace of crocodile sorrow. "I thought I did. Maybe
when you were little. But you're a grown-up now, all grown up,
aren'tcha? You want to be a grown-up, you can pack your shit and
get the fuck out."

"You believe him," Amanda said, answering her own question.

"He told me weeks ago that you started flirtin', and I
thought he was—I thought he'd made a mistake. I didn't know,
then. But I been watching you, the way you look at him. The
way you're pushing yourself at him." She was drunk enough to
repeat herself, to forget what she was saying, but the words hurt
all over again. "Showing him your tits, like some whore. And
he came in tonight and said what you did, how you tried to kiss
him, and then screamed when one of your friends knocked on
the door."

The suspicion was on Grace's face in every line, every wrin-
kle. She looked old, witchlike, and her terrible smile quivered
with the effort she was putting into holding it. "It was a setup,

wasn't it? I think you set him up, so you'd have a witness, so you could, could…" She grasped for the word. "*Support* your lies. That's what he thinks, too. But he loves me, he loves *me*. Not you. He wants us to move in together, and you—I don't want you here when that happens. I mean it. I can't trust you."

"Mom, listen to me," Amanda said, standing so that she could meet her mother's jittery gaze, so that she could make her mother *see* her. "He hit on me a couple of weeks ago. When I told him I'd tell you, he backed off. Tonight, he was going to do it, he was going to *rape* me. He would have if Eric hadn't shown up. He told me that he was going to tell you I was the one who asked for it. He even told me how my story would play to the cops, if I reported it—how he'd make it look like I was trying to stay out of trouble by accusing him." Even thinking about it now, she felt a chill of the dread she'd felt earlier, when he'd been touching her—understanding that he'd thought it all out, that he'd *planned* to force sex with her and get away with it. It was shocking, even for a mean bigot like Peter, that he could be so deliberately evil.

"Don't you see what he's doing? He's a bad guy, Mom, he's no good. Don't let him do this to us."

For just a beat, Grace stared at her, her face slack—and Amanda wanted to feel hope, wanted to think that she'd gotten through, but her mother's feelings radiated from her like a dark aura of heat, of betrayal and mistrust. Her expression meant only that she was too drunk to process her daughter's words.

"*You're* the liar," her mother said finally. "And a whore, prob'ly. Who's your friend, anyway? Somebody else you're fucking? It's no wonder your father left. I'da left, too, if I'd known what you were gonna turn into."

Amanda felt empty inside. "That's great, that's really great. That's awesome parenting."

"You're so mean to me," Grace said. Fresh tears had sprung up. "I don't need you around always telling me what a fuckup I am. Why don't you get your shit and get *out*?"

The last was nearly screamed. Grace had made the threat in the past, when she'd first caught Amanda smoking and again when she'd found weed in her bag last year, but those had been weepy, showy scenes; this time was different. Grace was different. Amanda's emptiness filled with fear, with not knowing what would happen, where she would go. Devon? Eric? One of the cheap motels down on the highway? It was four in the morning. "Can I pack a bag, at least?"

"Pack a bag, take some money out of the tip jar," Grace said. "Take all of it, because it's all you're getting from me. Just be gone when I get up."

Her mother stared at her another moment, a caricature of bitterness, of self-absorbed addiction. "You were looking for an excuse to leave, anyway. Always were."

The last word; Grace staggered toward her bedroom. The cheap interior door didn't slam, but Amanda heard the lock click, heard her mother talking to herself in a loud, unsteady voice.

She sat back down on the couch, distraught and disoriented. It had all happened so fast. She took a deep breath, then another. Tomorrow morning Grace might regret kicking her out; she could wait. But even if Grace took it back, there was no reason to stay.

She'd pack some things, take the money—her mother stuffed most of her tips in a jar on top of the fridge, for groceries and bills; at any given time, there was a couple hundred dollars in the jar—and try to sleep another few hours, although she couldn't imagine how, knowing that she was officially homeless. She'd go get some coffee, then find Devon. Devon would put her up, she knew, and his Uncle Sid was a decent man; she'd have a roof over her head for a while, until she could figure out what to do next. She had her savings, too; she could…could…

Her own tears came up, and she let herself topple, falling into the battered old couch with a soft wail. Even a month ago, she couldn't have imagined this. Grace had been a pretty awful parent, as far as parents went, but there'd never been any question about Amanda being welcome in her home—in *their* home.

Everything is changing, she thought, which made her think of what she'd been seeing, what she'd been feeling, ever since that horrible vision of Lisa Meyers's death…and she felt quite strongly now that *everything* was connected somehow, the death and strangeness in her life and in Port Isley.

Amanda cried for a while, then got up to start gathering her things.

CHAPTER

15

To add insult to injury, after their tasteless, despicable prank, leaving the cat tails on the grounds of the retreat, Cole Jessup's compound of drunken crazies had detonated fireworks until three in the morning. By the time they stopped, Miranda was too angry to sleep. She finally dozed off around four and woke up just after seven, unrested and too angry to lie still. James was snoring gently as she slipped on a tracksuit in the faint, early light from their bedroom window and went downstairs to make coffee... but when she reached the kitchen, she paused only long enough to put her shoes on, then went outside.

Tom Corwin, the community's unofficial handyman, had removed the cats' tails after the police had come; he'd buried them near the herb garden. Miranda's mouth twisted in a small, bitter smile; the *police*, weren't they just the most helpful organization? They'd sent some part-time officer she'd never met before who'd arrived a full three hours after she'd called. The officer had seen the tails and had listened to everything and taken some notes and promised to get back to them, and Miranda could see in the young man's bland sincerity that nothing would be done. The crazies would deny everything, and the police would drop the matter, perhaps advise her to consider a civil case, and her sweet kitties would still have been murdered and hacked up by one of those crazies.

Her stomach knotted. Most of the tails had been nothing but bone and desiccated skin, a few sad tufts of fur. For *years*, someone had been keeping them, God only knew why, or why this psycho had suddenly decided to...to *taunt* her with them. How could anyone be so malicious, and for no reason at all? Had she ever done *anything* to deserve such cruelty?

The woods were peaceful, alive with small creatures and morning birds rustling through the brush. Miranda walked slowly, holding herself against the chill. She walked without paying particular attention to direction, thinking about Darrin Everret's proposals for settling the score. They'd all talked about it the night before, at the retreat's picnic, over several shared bottles of wine. The most popular idea was to sneak over to the compound late one night and paint everything bubblegum pink—the front gate, the trees, any of the buildings they could get to without waking everyone up. It was a funny idea, but even drunk and in shock over her kitties, Miranda couldn't bring herself to advocate the plan. Besides the fact that playing such a prank was beneath their dignity, there was also the issue of retribution—Jessup and his people would know who did it, and if they weren't above killing cats, God only knew what they might do to take their revenge...

Besides which, it's not enough, she thought, stepping over a fallen tree. *Not nearly enough.* She'd thought about slipping poison into their food or water and writing a note to make it look like some kind of cult suicide. She'd imagined those hard, lined faces, soft with bloat in the summer heat, the woods silent and peaceful as the crime scene people shook their heads, as the reporters referenced Heaven's Gate and the People's Temple. She'd thought about blocking their doors and setting a fire; even if they managed to escape, they'd have nowhere to live and might move away. And if they didn't get out, if the flames consumed them all...well, things like that happened sometimes, didn't they? People died.

As gratifying as the dark dreams had been at one in the morning, they really *had* been harmless; there were children at

the compound. She would never harm a child, even a child destined to grow up as damaged and dull as its parents. Still, she
felt that circumstances demanded she do *something*, and if the
police wouldn't help her, what choices did she have?

She'd reached the line of stakes that divided her land from
that of Jessup's—hadn't she been headed there all along?—and
stopped at the first of the wilted orange ribbons, folding her
arms tightly, feeling how tired she was. Tired and unable to sleep,
because of this man and his repulsive brood. She imagined that
there was a palpable difference in the atmosphere between her
territory and his, the woods on her side of the line natural and
inviting and filled with light; stepping past the boundary stakes
as she did now, without really thinking about it, the morning
stillness became the watchful silence of a dark and slinking
predator, tensing for attack.

She didn't continue on, only stood in Jessup's woods and
let herself feel how strongly she'd come to hate him—and as if
the gods had been waiting for her to confirm her heart's truth
before guiding her further, she heard the crunch of underbrush
from Jessup's side, heavy steps approaching. She started to back
up, feeling a flush of panic at being caught out trespassing...but
then stopped and waited. She wanted a confrontation, she realized, had wanted one for a long time, although she hadn't known
it until right this very second. That she was a woman alone on
crazy people's land didn't occur to her, or not as more than a
passing thought. They had trespassed on her land at will, since
the very day she and James had purchased it and begun planning
their society of artists and artisans. Why should she cower, why
should she back away?

Cole Jessup himself appeared a moment later, dressed in
dark-green fatigues with a matching canvas cap and carrying
a rifle. She recognized him from his broad shoulders and the

choppy salt-and-pepper hair jutting out from beneath the cap. She saw him before he saw her, and planted her feet more firmly, her rage making her strong and solid, an oak before his blustering wind.

Jessup's blank face turned in her direction, and he stopped walking, blinking in surprise. Only for a beat, though—and then he raised his weapon and trained it on her. She wasn't surprised or frightened—only angry, angrier than she'd felt in as long as she could remember. Her body shook with it.

"Get off my land," he said, his low voice threaded with venom.

"Or what?" she asked, and somehow, she was smiling, a grin that felt carved into her face. "You going to shoot me, Mr. Jessup? Kill me, for doing something *you* do whenever you feel like it?"

"Get off my land," he repeated. The gun didn't waver.

"And how would you explain it to the police?" Miranda asked. "You going to say you were afraid for your life? Afraid of a *woman*?"

She took a step toward him as she spoke, seeing him through a veil of red that pulsed before her eyes. "You going to cut me up, like you did my kitties?"

"I don't know nothing about your cats, you crazy hippie bitch," Jessup muttered, but the way his gaze darted away from hers told her that he was lying. "You're trespassing. Get the fuck off my land, *now*."

She took another step away from her side. "Know nothing," she sneered. " 'Don't know *nothing*.' You think I'm afraid of *you*, you ignorant bastard, 'cause you're the big man with the gun? Because that doesn't mean—"

The rifle thundered, the sound deafening, and Miranda fell backward with a scream, her arms wheeling for balance. She hit the ground, a sharp stick ripping the seat of her pants, punching into the back of her thigh, and for just a second she thought the abrupt pain she felt was from a bullet, that he'd actually *shot* her. Shocked, her ears ringing, she looked up into Jessup's cold, grinning face.

"You should be afraid," he said, his words barely audible through the clamor in her ears. "You come on my property again, I'll kill you. That goes for all your faggot friends, too, and any more fucking cats you send over here to shit on my land."

His lips curled, his expression one of disgust. "Fucking faggot tree-huggers." He spat. "Coming out here, acting like your shit don't stink. Thinking you're better 'an us. My family's owned this land for three generations. You don't tell me *anything*, I tell *you*."

He was furious and insane; she could see that in his eyes. She didn't move, barely breathed, and hated him more than ever, for what he'd done, for who he was.

Jessup held her gaze a beat longer, then turned and walked quickly away, his stride stiff and angry. She couldn't hear the twigs breaking beneath his boots, but as the deafness subsided, she could hear her own ragged breathing and the pounding of her heart.

>‹

Eric and Amanda and Devon were smoking on the front porch when the old truck pulled up in front of Devon's house, parking at the curb. An oldster got out, saw them, and started walking toward them, his hand raised in a gesture of greeting.

"Who's that?" Eric asked.

"The reporter," Amanda said. She stubbed out her smoke and stood up. Devon immediately followed suit, and Eric did the same, trying to recall what she'd said about the reporter. The guy hadn't believed her story, he remembered that much.

Eric stepped in front of Devon, taking his place at Amanda's side—noting Devon's thwarted expression with some satisfaction.

The oldster approached with a smile, but he didn't look happy. His face was watchful behind that slight curve of his lips, and when he stopped in front of them, Eric could see that he was impatient, tense.

"Devon, Amanda," he said, nodding, turning his gaze toward Eric. "I'm Bob Sayers," he said, and stuck out his hand. Eric shook with him.

"This is Eric Hess," Amanda said. "He's a friend of mine."

"Did something happen?" Devon asked.

Sayers nodded. "Yeah," he said simply.

"Was it Brian? At the fairgrounds?" Devon asked.

The reporter let out a deep breath, like he'd been holding it. He nodded. "I talked to the police when I heard about the attack. Local woman named Karen Haley. She owns Big Blue, the Victorian over on Exeter. Three boys raped her behind the fairground bathrooms last night, just after dark."

He looked at Amanda, his gaze unsettled. "Like you said."

"Oh my God," Devon said. "No fucking *way*."

"What did you tell the cops?" Amanda asked. Her voice shook a little, and Eric slipped his arm around her, pulling her close. She leaned against him.

"That I'd heard some kids talking, saying that Brian Glover and a couple of his friends were planning something," Sayers said. "I don't think Stan Vincent would have believed anything else. He was...he didn't seem himself."

Devon turned to look at Amanda, his eyes wide. "This—what you saw, this means—what you saw about *me*, that's going to come true, too, isn't it?"

"Oh, fuck," Amanda said, and stepped away from Eric, closer to Devon. Eric had to fight an urge to pull her back, his body almost aching from the sudden absence of her. She slid her arm across Devon's back, and Eric felt a burn of jealousy, the intensity of it totally unexpected.

"I think we should talk," Sayers said, looking at Devon and Amanda. "Can I take you out to breakfast? Or lunch, I guess. My treat. All of you," he added, glancing at Eric.

"Yeah, OK," Amanda said, still holding Devon's hand. "You're coming?" She looked at Eric.

"Sure," he said, and shrugged for effect.

Amanda took his hand again, walking them to the reporter's beat-up truck.

><

The waitress at the Hilltop Inn seated them in a corner booth and poured them all coffee. The restaurant was nonsmoking, which sucked, but at least they had privacy; breakfast was pretty much over, and the lunch rush hadn't started yet. Only townies ate at Hilltop; the summer people went to Café Fresco, where they could get free-range egg-white omelets and organic espresso. Hilltop's décor was generic pancake-house bland and the air conditioner was set too high, but the food was cheap and plentiful.

"So," Bob said, as soon as their server disappeared. "Tell me what's been going on since the picnic."

He was looking at Devon, who'd done all the talking when they'd first met, but he only stared back at the reporter, his eyes kind of unfocused. He looked like he'd been punched in the stomach.

Amanda had already decided on the ride over not to hold anything back, even the shit she wasn't sure about. She'd probably come off like a psycho, but if she could keep anyone else from being hurt or killed, it'd be worth it.

"A bunch of stuff," she said, and Bob turned his attention to her. "So far, it's been like three different, uh, categories, I guess. I mean, there are things I see when I'm dreaming, and stuff I see when I'm awake…and then I've been feeling some other things. About people. That part seems to kind of tie everything together."

"How do you mean?"

She frowned, not sure how to explain. "I didn't feel anything at first—I mean, with the Lisa Meyer thing, I saw what happened, but I didn't *feel* like Lisa or Mr. Billings. And I didn't feel like I was getting raped, thank God. But that's all changing. When I see people in my dreams, now, it's like I *am* them, for just a couple of seconds. It's like, superempathy, I guess. Seeing their future is…" She searched for the word. "…*incidental*, if that makes any sense. Same when I'm awake."

Bob had pulled a pen and a small notebook out of his coat. "Give me some specifics."

"Well, *I'm* going to bite it," Devon said. His tone was light, casual, but he wasn't smiling. From the twitch in his jaw, Amanda realized that he was extremely angry. "Beat up and dropped in the bay. How's that for specific?"

"Why are you so pissed?" Amanda asked.

Devon's expression was one of disbelief. "Are you fucking kidding me? How about, I don't want to *die*, is that a reason?"

The reporter looked back and forth between them, then settled on Amanda. "You saw this?"

"Yeah. Like a week ago. That was also when I started feeling things about people. Or when I first noticed it, I guess."

"Did you feel me being dead?" Devon snapped.

Eric was trying to hold her hand, and she shook him off, aggravated and deeply stressed. "Jesus, Devon, it's not my fucking fault!"

"I know, I know," he said, staring down into his coffee cup. "I'm just really freaked, OK?" He added a mumbled, "Sorry."

Amanda nodded, wishing she could smoke. She was exhausted and wired and fucking homeless. "We'll figure something out," she said, although the phrase didn't really have any meaning; she just had to say something.

"You saw this while you were awake?" Bob asked.

"Yeah. I was…I was high, actually. And we were with some people, hanging out, and I started knowing things about them, which was not good. So I took off. When Devon followed me, I saw him…I saw him like that."

He jotted something in his notebook, which was weird, like she was suddenly important…which she was, she supposed, if her new "gift" was permanent. *How fuckin' surreal.*

"So, what did you, ah, sense about these other people?"

She recounted the details as she remembered them, what she'd felt about Greg and Carrie, then all the random shit she'd dreamed. Except for the stuff about Greg Taner doing Cam doggie-style; that was just too embarrassing to say out loud to a senior citizen. Same with how she'd felt having sex with Eric, how she'd kind of gotten into his head. She couldn't imagine how that kind of information would be useful, anyway. He wrote down Greg's name, most interested in the part about him enlisting in the military. Presumably because it was something he could actually check on.

"Oh! And the Lawn King, he's going to try to kill himself," Amanda said. "He wants to, anyway."

"Lawn King?"

"That mean old guy, lives in the house on Eleanor. The one with the manicured lawn? Dick, ah…"

"Dick Calvin," Bob said, frowning. "You're sure about that?"

Amanda shook her head. "I'm not sure of anything. I'm seeing all this fucked-up shit. And my mother kicked me out last night because her numbfuck boyfriend tried to get into my pants, and he spun this fat lie about it, and she sided with him."

"I can talk to your mother," Eric said, practically the first thing he'd said all day. "Tell her what I saw, if you think that'll help."

Jesus, what a terrible idea. "If she doesn't believe me, no way she's going to care what you think," Amanda said.

"I can be pretty convincing," Eric said. "I mean, I heard you scream."

"No," she said. "Seriously."

"Do you think I should leave town?" Devon asked. "That'll keep it from happening, right?"

"I don't know," she said. "Maybe."

Devon nodded eagerly. "If I'm not here, I can't exactly drown in the bay, can I?"

"Do you think these futures are set, or do you sense that they can be changed?" Bob asked.

"I don't *know,*" Amanda said, too loud, feeling like her head was going to cave in. Everyone wanted an answer, or needed to be reassured, or wanted to know the nature of this thing that had totally come out of nowhere. "What the fuck do *I* know?"

Bob set his pen down and took a sip of coffee. Devon looked miserably introspective. Eric tried to hold her hand again, and she let him, feeling somehow both grateful and annoyed by the gesture. The waitress came back, and they all fumbled through the menus, ordering little. Amanda wasn't hungry at all, but her stomach ached from too much caffeine and not enough food.

When the server had gone again, Bob looked at her with a speculative expression. "Have you tried to make it happen? One of these flashes?"

"Like, on purpose?" Amanda scoffed. "I've pretty much been hoping it'll never happen again."

"Understandably," Bob said. "But considering it seems to be getting more...*severe*, maybe having some sort of control would help."

"I don't think it works like that," Amanda said. "I think it just happens."

"You should try it," Devon said. "I mean, maybe you can figure out *how* to stop it, if you know how it works. And you could try to see—you could see if anything has changed."

"How should I—I mean, what should I do? I'm not going to smoke any more pot, no way. Last time was…" She thought about the dim, musty dark of the middle school basement, the feelings gathering around her like nightmares. "It was too much."

"If marijuana does it, maybe if you just try to relax, that'll be enough," Bob said. "Take some deep breaths, close your eyes… don't focus on anything in particular. See what comes to you."

"Right now?" Amanda asked, looking around the mostly empty restaurant. There was a middle-aged couple in a booth on the far wall, and a single, haunted-looking young man at the counter near the front, staring at a cup of coffee, but they were otherwise alone.

"Sure, why not?" Devon said. His voice held an edge of desperation.

Amanda let go of Eric's hand and nodded. "OK," she said. "Just—don't all stare at me, OK?"

She closed her eyes and started to breathe slowly and evenly. She could smell coffee and a greasy sausage smell. She could smell smoke in her clothes. A sound like a knife or fork, scraping a plate, somewhere behind her.

This is stupid, she thought, and then, *They're totally staring at me.* She took a deeper breath, shifted in her seat, trying not to think about being a freak with no home. A moment passed, and her self-consciousness grew into embarrassment, like she was trying to do a magic trick and wasn't pulling it off…Devon was getting impatient; he wanted to hear that he wasn't going to die, that she saw him alive and well and—

waiting in the park, seeing him duck out from the shadows, a hot fumbling in the dark and telling him that he had to leave town and hoping that Mitch would at least act like he cared

—he won't, he doesn't want to admit that he likes it best blow jobs he ever had—

She opened her eyes, staring at Devon. "Mitch?"

Devon's eyes widened. "What?" he asked, his voice small, breathless.

"What did you see?" Bob asked.

"Mitchell *Jessup*?" she said, and Devon sat back in his chair, shaking his head slightly. If she'd needed further confirmation—and she didn't, she understood exactly what was happening—she would have seen it in Devon's shifting gaze, the nervous lick of lips. Mitchell Jessup was one of Cole Jessup's fucked-up sons. He lived out in the woods with the other gun nuts. Amanda was not a little shocked; all the Jessups and their survivalist pals were notoriously homophobic. And sexist, and racist, and usually not very clean.

Gah. She'd *felt* how it was, from her very brief contact with Devon's thoughts—sweating and salty and coupled with a kind of brutal, sexual degradation, for both of them.

"Is that who's going to…to hurt Devon?" Bob asked.

"Not unless his dick is bigger than most," Amanda said, and Devon had the good grace to look embarrassed, at least. Bob finally caught on and dropped his gaze. He took another sip of coffee, then cleared his throat.

Eric chuckled.

"So, you can feel things when you try," Bob said. "That's good; that could really help."

"Help what?" Amanda asked. She was finding it hard to even look in Devon's direction. "How is knowing people's personal shit going to help anything?"

"Honestly, I'm not sure," Bob said. "But maybe you'll get feelings from places, too, or we could go somewhere there are a lot of people gathered. You might see something else we could use..."

He trailed off, fixing her with a steady gaze. She saw the red lines in his eyes and knew he was a drinker, and that he was about to tell her the truth. The awareness made her feel almost giddy, like she was flying in a dream.

"What it comes down to is, I feel guilty as hell that you came to me when you saw someone getting raped, and I talked you out of taking action," Bob said. "I thought I was doing a good thing, and I was wrong."

"You didn't know it was going to happen," Amanda said.

"That's true, but I still wish I'd done different." He sighed. "There's a lot of insanity going around Port Isley these days, and I have a feeling that things are going to get worse before they get any better. Maybe I'm wrong—I hope I am—but if I'm not, and if you see something else, something we can prevent..." He held up his hands, a why-not gesture.

Amanda nodded. It wasn't really a plan, but it was something she could *do*, besides resigning herself to the random trauma of her life. "So we should just, like, wander around, trying to see things?"

"Don't include me," Devon said. "I'm out of here *today*."

Amanda turned to him, feeling unpleasantly startled by his statement, like she'd just heard a loud, ugly noise. "Where are you going?"

"I have a cousin in Portland. She's been inviting me to come stay with her for a while now. You know, Claire? She can help me get set up."

"What about Seattle?" Amanda asked. "I mean, we were going to go in October, anyway. You could go early, find us a place..."

"It's too close," Devon said. "Look, we can worry about that later. We're talking about my *life* here."

Mine, too. Amanda thought of all the times they'd talked about their apartment together, about how they'd always have wine in the cupboard and cheese in the fridge, parties on Friday nights and a window box of flowers and a kitten they were going to call Snookie, whatever the sex. She thought of all the times when her mother was screaming-puking drunk, when imagining her new life in a real city was all that kept her from falling apart. He was right, of course; it made sense for him to leave, but it still hurt to have her small dream so utterly abandoned.

"Maybe I could go with you," she said.

"Maybe," Devon said, his expression saying otherwise. "I mean, I should go right away, since you didn't see when I'm— when it happens." He flashed a nervous, insincere smile. "It could happen tonight, right? But you could come down later, once everything's cool with my cousin. Like in a few weeks. A month or so."

Amanda couldn't think of anything to say to that.

Bob's expression was quite serious. "I think you should stay," he said, looking at her. "It might mean someone's life. I have a friend, he's a psychologist, lives on the same street as Dick Calvin. I'll talk to him, get him to go see Calvin; if he's really suicidal, you may have just saved his life."

Amanda nodded, thinking of what she'd just done, seeing how it was with Devon and his hot, empty sex with Mitchell Jessup...and felt a real stir of power for the first time. She was seeing things, she had *made* herself see things, and as totally fucking out there and upsetting as her visions had mostly been, she was who was seeing them. Her, Amanda Lynn Young, with her stupid grind in stupid Port Isley, who'd never expected better than to get the fuck out and get a job and have a life. Something was finally happening, to her and to the town, something she had a part in. Like, an important part. It was as if she'd fallen into some kids' adventure story, only without the dragons or talking animals.

Just murder and rape and very bad dreams, she thought, and wondered what was going to happen next.

><

Ethan Adcox was initially kind of excited when the cops showed up at the Safeway and asked him to come down to the station. After all, it wasn't like he was in trouble or anything. He did some super minor shit, stacked cases of beer behind the loading dock every now and then, occasionally swiped a few bucks from Pop's wallet, but nothing worth getting the cops interested. Nothing they knew about, anyway. They'd walked right into the storeroom while he was talking to the new girl from the deli section, Trina—she was kinda fat but had a nice smile, and he hadn't gotten laid in, like, *months* (fourteen of them, to be exact), and his complexion wasn't so great lately that he could afford to be picky—and been all serious and grim and shit, saying they had some questions. He started to make some noise about losing his job, but they said they'd already talked to Mr. Addison and that it wouldn't take too long, depending on what he had to say. Trina's eyes had gone wide—she was local but homeschooled; her mom and dad were Jesus freaks—and his nervousness about marching back through the store with a police escort was counteracted somewhat by the understanding that she would totally put out for a bad boy such as himself, if for no other reason than to piss off her parents. All the other employees and shoppers had looked at him like maybe he was a serial killer, which was also cool. Half an hour of sitting alone in the tiny, windowless room at the police station, however, wondering what they wanted to talk to him about, that wasn't so cool. He kept thinking about what Todd had been telling him a couple of days before, about what Brian wanted to do...that was just talk, though. Brian was always saying crazy shit. But if it wasn't that, why *did* the cops want to talk to him?

Because someone saw me, he kept thinking, and as the minutes slipped past, the thought was getting harder and harder to dismiss. Five times in the last month, Ethan had taken late-night walks, walks that took him past open windows in his neighborhood...bedroom windows, at houses where some nice-looking women lived. He'd watched them sleep, thinking about how easy it would be to slip inside and touch them, or make them touch *him*, and he'd whacked off, thinking about it, and though he'd only picked houses that had bushes or something near the windows, and none of the women had woken up, maybe someone else had seen him. Someone out walking a dog or jogging or something. By the time the door opened and Chief Vincent walked in, Ethan's initial excitement had completely fizzled, and he'd sworn to never, ever go for another late-night walk.

Everyone knew Stan Vincent, the town's police chief; he gave talks at the high school every year about drunk driving and seemed like a decent guy—Ethan wasn't pro-pig or anything, but Vincent's message was pretty much go ahead and get shitfaced, everyone does it, but getting behind the wheel when you're plowed is just plain dangerous. He wasn't all moralistic about it, he didn't talk down to them, he was just, like, matter-of-fact. Which was kind of cool. Ethan's friends all talked shit about Vincent, fucking stick-in-the-ass supercop, but Ethan had never had any run-ins with the man personally and figured they were talking out their asses. Seemed to him, nobody got hassled by the man who didn't deserve it.

Vincent moved to the other side of the crappy metal table and sat down, smiling slightly. It wasn't an inspiring smile; there was a look in his eyes very much like the one Pop got when he'd been drinking and brooding, a combination that usually meant a couple of punches in the gut for Ethan. Ethan's fear ratcheted up a notch.

"Thanks for coming in," Vincent said, sitting back in his chair. He set a little notebook on the table. "You know why you're here?" He was acting all relaxed and friendly, but his eyes said otherwise.

"No. Ah, sir," he added.

Vincent grinned, a terrible grin because Ethan could see the disgust in it, like the chief was looking at a slug or a worm. "Mind if I ask what you were doing last night?" Vincent asked. "About, eight, nine o'clock?"

Ethan felt a giant wave of relief. His last visit to a window had been three days before, and way after midnight. "Me and my dad were at a barbecue, watching the fireworks," Ethan said.

"Where?"

"Some guy he works with, John…" Ethan scrambled for the name. "Liston? Lipton? Something like that."

Vincent nodded slowly. He picked up his notebook, fished a pen out of his pocket, and jotted a few words down. "If I check that out, I'd find people willing to say you were there?"

"Yes, sir, absolutely." Ethan couldn't have been more sincere. "From, like, six till after eleven. I remember, 'cause when we got home, it was almost midnight. I looked at the clock and everything."

Vincent didn't say anything for a minute, long enough for Ethan to wonder if the chief believed him. He remembered seeing in a movie somewhere that people being interviewed by the cops often kept talking, desperate to fill up the silence, and he told himself he wouldn't do that, but as the seconds stretched, he found he couldn't stop himself. "We could see the fireworks from their back porch. Port Angeles's fireworks? And we watched the whole show. There were, like, fifteen, twenty people there."

"And do you know where your buddy Brian Glover was last night?"

Ethan blinked. "Brian? What'd—why?"

Vincent didn't answer. "You hang out with Brian fairly often, don't you? Brian, Todd Clay, and Ryan…" He flipped a page in the notebook. "…Thompson, is that right?"

Oh, shit. "Not that much," Ethan said, trying to sound casual, not sure if he was pulling it off. This *was* about Brian, and likely Todd and Ry, too. *Holy shit. They did it.*

Ethan and Todd had drunk some beers Thursday night, when Ethan had gotten off work. Brian was still grounded for getting shit-faced at the picnic, and Ryan had been off at some cousin's wedding in Bellingham, so it had just been him and Todd, sitting in Ethan's car outside Kehoe Park. Drinking and talking.

"So, you're not friends?" Vincent asked.

"We hang out sometimes," Ethan said. Supercop obviously knew that much. "But I been pretty busy with work and everything, lately."

"You know where they were last night?" Vincent asked.

Brian says we should find ourselves some pussy, Todd had told him Thursday night after they'd each had a few, and Ethan had laughed and said something about how pussy was hard to come by, lately, and Todd had said that Brian had a plan. *He says if we do it somewhere public, like on the Fourth or at the carnival, maybe, no one will hear anything.*

"You're talking about…about raping someone?" Ethan had asked, not laughing anymore.

Todd polished off his fourth beer and let out a tremendous belch. "Jesus, Ethan, it's not like that. We're just looking for a little fun, all right? Give some lucky lady the ride of her life."

Ethan had forced a laugh, played it off cool, but he hadn't thought it was cool, not at all. Ethan's first and only girlfriend, Bonnie, had been molested by her stepfather when she'd been, like, twelve. Not the same thing as rape, but in the same ballpark, and it had surely fucked *her* up, big-time. Ethan had come away from their brief, tumultuous relationship with a clear understanding that molesters and rapists were the jagbags of the universe. When Todd had called him yesterday, to see if he wanted to go to the fairgrounds with them, Ethan had begged off, vaguely grateful that his dad had insisted he go to the stupid backyard barbecue. Not that he thought they were *really* going to do anything, but Ethan didn't want to be around if they did. Todd was an OK guy most of the time, but Brian was kind of psycho and always looking for a chance to prove it. And Ryan was up for anything, anytime.

"No, sir," Ethan said now, although he couldn't meet Vincent's eyes. "Like I said, I don't see them so much anymore. 'Cause of my job, and everything."

Vincent's stare, when he finally looked up, was cold and scrutinizing. *Shit*, Ethan thought again. They'd done it, they'd grabbed some woman and attacked her. He wondered why they'd dragged his ass in, instead of Brian's...then realized that he was the only one in the bunch who was eighteen. Brian and Todd and Ry would all have to have their parents involved.

"You know something," Vincent said. He tapped the end of his pen on the notebook, still leaning back in his chair like he was chatting with an old friend, but his voice had gone dark, matching his gaze now. "You know something, and you're going to tell me, or I will cut your fucking balls off and feed them to you."

Ethan stared, shocked. "What?"

"You heard me," Vincent said. "I'd give you a chance to think it over, but to be honest, I'm not in the mood to wait. I've had a long fucking day already, Ethan. I'm tired. So, out with it. Unless you think I'm kidding."

Ethan swallowed, his mouth too dry, his brain numb like it had just jumped into the bay in December. He didn't want to test Vincent's threat, no way, but not ratting on his friends was so deeply ingrained it was practically a character trait. "I'm—I don't know what you're talking about."

"Sure you do," Vincent said. "It's all over your face. I understand you don't want to tattle on your shithead buddies, but let me tell you—you break the law in my jurisdiction, and you *will* pay the price."

Ethan tried again. "I wasn't there, man, I don't know what happened, swear to God—"

Vincent stood up abruptly and took a single, swift step around the table, his expression murderous, his hands clenched into fists. Ethan ducked away, almost falling out of his chair, but Vincent was faster. He punched Ethan in the side of the head, hard, smashing his ear. Ethan let out a scream as the chair tipped over. He threw his hands out to catch himself and watched as one of Vincent's black boots came down on the fingers of his left hand, and then his fingers were screeching as loud as his ear.

This can't be happening, he thought, and then that heavy boot drove into his stomach, and he curled himself into a ball, not thinking anything, just trying to breathe.

"You think I don't know what you say about me?" Vincent asked, and kicked him again, a brand-new explosion of pain to contend with. Ethan drew in a shuddering breath and puked, bile and energy drink and bright-orange bits of cheese puff pooling on the floor in front of him. The pain and the smell of his partially digested breakfast made him retch again, a terrible, painful lurch that brought up the rest of what was in his stomach. Vincent stood over him, his face hard, his shoulders high and tight.

"Your balls are next, Ethan," Vincent said, and pulled a big folding knife out of his front pocket. He flipped out the blade, four inches of shining steel, and knelt next to Ethan, carefully avoiding the puddle of vomit. "Not my choice, you understand, but when you attacked me, I had to defend myself. You might bleed to death before we can get you to the hospital, but them's the breaks, right?"

Ethan shook his head, tried to speak, and retched again. Long strings of viscous spittle hung from his lips and chin, sticking to the floor.

"Tired of you goddamn people," Vincent muttered, grabbing the waistband of Ethan's jeans. He pulled him closer, dragging Ethan's head through the pool of puke. "You sit there with your mouth shut when all I'm asking is for you to do the right thing. You don't care about the law, you don't give a shit about this town, making me look bad, and all I do is run around cleaning up your selfish goddamn messes...and does anyone say thank you? No, you all think I'm some incompetent asshole, that I can't get the job done. But things are changing, you better goddamn believe it—"

"Todd told me," Ethan gasped. "He told me that Brian said they were gonna get some pussy, them and Ryan. I didn't have nothing to do with it, swear to Christ!"

Vincent hesitated, the knife still in hand, his other hand jammed into the front of Ethan's jeans. Ethan actually felt the cop's fingertips brush against his shriveled cock, and for just a second, Ethan thought he was going to keep going anyway, but the strange light in Vincent's eyes seemed to fade slightly, and he sat back on his heels, carefully folding the knife back up before sticking it in his pocket.

"That wasn't so hard, was it?" Vincent said, and smiled at him. "Let's get you cleaned up, son. You all right?"

Ethan didn't answer, too busy thanking God for letting him keep his balls, *crazy, Supercop's gone totally fucking nuts!*

"You're all right," Vincent answered himself, pulling Ethan into a sitting position. "I'll kill you if you tell anyone about this. You know that, right?"

Ethan nodded, wiping at the tears on his face. He had no doubt whatsoever. "Yeah," he said, and Vincent clapped him on the back.

"I'm just trying to protect my town, you understand. There's a greater good here to consider; it's nothing personal. And no one would believe you, anyway."

Ethan nodded again, holding his throbbing ear with one hand, his stomach with the other. "Yes, sir," he said.

"Good boy," Vincent said, beaming at him like a proud father off some TV show. "Good boy."

>‹

John had stayed at the hospital for several hours. He'd talked to Karen, who'd still been in shock, whose battered face had made him want to weep, and he'd talked to the doctor—besides the black eyes and swollen jaw, she had a cracked rib, a sprained wrist, and multiple contusions and abrasions on and inside her vagina and rectum—and he'd talked to Sarah, Karen's sister, and held her as she'd cried. Then he'd gone home, slept poorly for a few hours...and found himself heading back to the hospital after a shower and a cup of coffee, feeling like he hadn't done nearly enough. Feeling more involved, perhaps, than was safe...but what did that even mean, if he truly wanted to help? The open look of relief, of gratitude on Sarah's face, when he stepped into Karen's room, told him that he'd made the right decision.

Sarah said she had managed to catch a few hours' sleep of her own, curled in a hospital chair; John urged her home, to change clothes and pack a bag for Karen, promising to keep vigil while she was gone. Stan Vincent had been back, Sarah said, at the crack of dawn, with a handful of photos he wanted Karen to look at, but Karen had been sleeping; the doctor had finally sedated her in the early morning hours. Sarah said that Vincent had actually suggested they wake Karen up to look at the pictures; she'd only been able to get rid of him by swearing that she'd call the very second Karen opened her eyes.

John assured her he'd fend off any overzealous policemen, and they'd talked for a few minutes about what she needed to do; she'd already decided to send Karen's guests away and cancel those scheduled to arrive for the next few weeks, and she wanted to get it done as soon as possible. John supported the decision, which seemed to make her feel better about it. She discussed the matter frankly with him, treating him as if they were old friends...which again affirmed for him that he wasn't intruding on a private tragedy, that he was actually being helpful. Not that his motives were entirely altruistic; it was the first day of his weekend, and he didn't want to sit home alone, drifting on Ativan, waiting for work to start up again and save him from himself and his thoughts of Annie.

Karen didn't wake while her sister was away, her bruised face at rest against the stiff, white hospital pillow, and John spent that time thinking about last night's conversation with Bob. About the town going crazy. About the girl who'd foretold the attack, Amanda Young. According to Bob, she'd also known about Ed Billings's murder and suicide spree. It surprised him a little that Bob was so quick to credit that kind of thing, mass madness, psychic ability...although he had to admit, he'd been a bit unnerved last night when Bob had related details he shouldn't have known about the rape—that it had happened at the fairgrounds, that the attackers had been teenagers. John suspected that the girl was plying for attention and had worked out some elaborate prank to get it. As for the rest of Port Isley...coincidence. Tragedy inviting tragedy. He watched Karen sleep and assured himself that the rest of the summer would be uneventful. Surely the town had exceeded its seasonal lunacy quota.

When Sarah returned, she brought coffee and sandwiches. They talked in low voices as Sarah set out the makeshift picnic on the counter beneath the window, plus napkins and paper plates she pulled from a grocery bag. She'd already talked to Karen's current guests and left messages for the people she couldn't reach directly.

"What about Tommy?" John asked. "When's he coming back?"

"Day after tomorrow, Tuesday," Sarah said, handing him a sandwich on a paper plate. "It's roast beef, is that OK?"

"Yes, thank you." He was absurdly touched that she'd bothered to stop and pack food for him. He set the plate down, not particularly hungry. Outside, the sun was shining brightly, glinting off metal in the parking lot, but the hospital's air conditioners fed cold, antiseptic air into the room from next to his seat, making the view seem unreal. "Are you...will you tell him what happened?"

Sarah sat across from him, her chair close enough to the industrially padded loveseat he'd taken that their knees almost touched. "Actually, I was hoping you might have some advice," she said. "About what to say, I mean. I don't want to traumatize him, but I don't feel comfortable lying to him, either..." She put her own plate aside and put her hands in her lap, her fingers restless. "We have a pretty good relationship, but he's been through so much in the last couple of years…Jack and I splitting, moving out of Seattle…" She smiled a little. "He's doing so well, though. And he's so smart."

"It sounds like you already know what to do," John said. "I don't think you need to go into details or anything. Tell him that Karen got hurt, and she's very sad about it, but that she'll get better."

"She will, won't she?" Sarah asked. Her eyes were worried.

"Absolutely," John said, sincerely. She'd never be the same, though. And while she might succeed in getting past the event, the brutality of the rape, the violation of self…

She will be haunted, John thought. Doomed to remember. Would she experience a loop of images, repeating? How long would it be before she could close her eyes and not see their faces, looming over her in the dark, not imagine their stupid, pawing hands on her body? Her experience of herself as a sexual being had been redefined by force, perhaps irreparably damaged.

Someone should kill those fucking kids, he thought, the hate burning in his gut, suddenly, startlingly clear and savage and all-encompassing. *Hurt them, beat them, rip them apart and bury them in pieces—*

"John? Are you OK?"

He focused on Sarah, saw her concern, and slowly shook his head, still burning inside. He didn't trust himself to speak. The depth of the feeling frightened him, badly, because he wasn't like that, he didn't think like that.

Annie's murder, Karen getting raped, he told himself. Projection, guilt, stress. Perfectly normal…and it *felt* normal, as if the intense desire to kill was a natural part of him, one he had somehow never noticed before, and that was wrong, too, all wrong. He suddenly felt like he couldn't breathe.

Panic attack! His mind screamed helpfully. *Panic attack!*

Sarah leaned forward and touched his arm. Her fingers were warm. Her eyes were beautiful, direct, and deep blue. "Hey," she said.

He closed his eyes, concentrating on inhaling, exhaling, on the touch of her hand. He made a conscious effort to relax. To not think of Karen or the boys who'd raped her, or to think of when, exactly, Rick had driven a meat knife into Annie's soft, flat stomach, or to berate himself for having those thoughts; he was letting those thoughts go, he was letting go; he inhaled, exhaled, more deeply now…and felt a steadying gratitude to the woman sitting with him. She seemed to understand what he needed and kept her peace, sliding her hand down to hold his. Their fingers interlocked. After the briefest of hesitations she moved from her chair to sit next to him, put her other arm across his shoulder, rested her head against him.

Long seconds ticked past. Her breathing was slow and even, and she smelled sweet and mild, like vanilla, her shampoo, perhaps, and he imagined that she had closed her eyes too, was… was *resting* with him, sharing what limited physical comfort was appropriate between two relative strangers. He knew he should let go of her hand, should smile and say something appreciative; that the time had come to acknowledge their moment together as shared grief, to set it aside and perhaps talk about what steps were next. They weren't friends, after all; they barely knew each other. She had called for help because her sister had been a client of his, because he'd been a resource she could utilize to help Karen. But there was no awkwardness in their half embrace, no indecision or tension in the gentle pressure of her body; they were here, they were together, and he wanted to keep touching her, keep accepting her, her *gift* to him. She pressed closer, and her breathing seemed to thicken. His senses were filled with her, the bad thoughts far away, and he wished they could be closer still, that she would climb into his lap and look into his eyes while he—

John let go of her hand, making himself smile at her as he pulled himself back.

"I'm sorry," she said, and sat back slightly. She was flushed, her eyes slightly dilated. She looked almost frightened. "I'm... sorry, I didn't mean..."

"That's OK," he said. "Really. I feel like I should apologize. I'm not usually so..." He stared at her, not sure how to finish his sentence, either. What were they apologizing for?

For not being ourselves. For acting like teenagers on a hormone high.

Sarah laughed, a small sound, and said what he'd been thinking. "I have *not* been myself, lately."

"Right there with you," John said, which felt like the understatement of his life. In about three minutes, his emotional pendulum had swung from wholeheartedly wanting to kill, to actually take life, to wanting to...

He didn't dodge the thought, determined to face whatever was happening to him. He'd wanted to go to bed with her. As much as he'd ever wanted anything. And it seemed so natural, so *reasonable* that they should sleep together, comfort each other with their bodies, as if getting to know one another first was an unnecessary prerequisite.

Just like with Annie.

"Maybe I *should* start seeing you, professionally," Sarah said, drawing him away from the thought. "Seriously. I've been feeling so...so different since I came here. It hasn't been bad, but it's just not *me*."

"I could refer you to someone," John said, his voice distant to his ears. He was already too involved personally to consider treating her. *Why? What's happening?* "It might be helpful to have someone to talk to, while you're taking care of Karen's affairs, supporting her emotionally," he added, the encouragement reflexive. "That's a lot to deal with."

Sarah hadn't really met his eyes since they'd moved apart, but she did now. Hers were summer-sky blue, the rich afternoon clarity of a late day in July. "I couldn't talk to you?"

"I don't think that's a good idea."

She turned her head and looked at Karen, sleeping. "That's too bad," she said, her voice soft. "I feel comfortable talking to you. And I can't tell you what it means to me, that you're here. To me and Karen."

"We can still talk," John said. "I'd like that. I only meant I'm not taking on any new clients right now."

"I understand," she said. Her disappointment was obvious, and it actually pained him to see it. Before he could think, he was talking. Telling her the truth.

"I don't know what's happening to me," he said. "A friend of mine was killed, recently, a woman, and I keep thinking about it…everything is so muddled, and I've been able to keep a professional distance from my clients, I've been working, but you…just now, I was so angry about what's happened to Karen, enraged, actually, and then I thought—when you touched me, I felt—"

He shook his head, willing himself to shut up. He wished he could explain, that he understood enough about his state of mind to be *able* to explain.

Sarah studied him a moment, her gaze direct. "You wanted more, didn't you? With me. Wanted to…wanted to be closer."

He didn't try to deny it. "I'm sorry."

She took a deep breath and looked down and away. "I felt the same way. That's what I was talking about, about feeling different. What just happened, between us—I've never felt like that—that fast, I mean—with anyone. Not since high school, anyway."

"It's the situation," John said, affirming it as much for himself as for her, really working to believe it. "The trauma—people react in ways they wouldn't, normally."

"It's not just *this*, though," she said. "This is just the latest thing, you know?"

John nodded slowly, thinking about Annie. He was about to ask what else she'd experienced, but she was looking at Karen again. Her eyes welled with tears. "Sometimes I'm so goddamn selfish."

"It's not selfish to keep having a life, even when something terrible happens," John said, jumping at the chance to be back in the role of therapist. He groped for it like a drowning man, grasping for salvation. "Don't beat yourself up."

She wiped at her eyes and nodded. "Right, OK."

What's wrong with me? Why was he spouting therapy? Why wasn't he able to be in the moment without stopping to analyze it? Why was he *like* this? He was confused, a little scared, even… but he wasn't here to make things worse. He was sure of that much.

"I'm sorry," he said again. It would undoubtedly be best if he left, made his excuses and got out before he suffered another flash of insanity. "Maybe later, I can come back…"

"You're not leaving, are you?" Sarah asked, her expression stricken. "Don't leave. I mean, if you really have to, if you have somewhere to be, I understand…but I'd really—"

She interrupted herself with a sharp, unhappy laugh. "Listen to me. I do want you to stay, but I'm—it's fine, whatever you want to do. Really."

Her obvious distress moved him. He wanted to touch her again, to hold her and tell her he would stay as long as she needed him…which he knew was crazy, he *knew* it, and yet the intensity of the feeling was only slightly diminished by the realization.

And he had to actively fight the urge to reach out and touch her again.

People aren't acting themselves lately, have you noticed? Bob's words. How had he dismissed them so easily?

He forced another smile and picked up his plate. *Karen, I'm here for Karen.* He'd repress the hell out of everything else until he could get home, get a chance to work through whatever was happening to him.

Maybe to everyone, he thought, and didn't care for that thought, not at all.

"I'm afraid you're stuck with me for a while," he said, and she smiled warmly, and he wanted her, still. And he thought that he'd better be very, very careful.

CHAPTER

16

Dick Calvin climbed onto the stepstool beneath the opening for the attic, reaching for the poorly knotted rope to fit around his neck. He'd learned how to tie a hangman's noose in his late teens, back when knowing how to tie different knots had been an integral part of working the piers, but he wasn't as dexterous as he once had been. Between the arthritis and the eyesight, he couldn't tie shit anymore.

He'd just touched the loop of rope—and there was a knock on the door. He hesitated, twisting the thick nylon braid between his fingers. He wasn't expecting anyone, and he didn't have any friends...unless he counted Cecil, which he didn't. He couldn't.

Dick felt a familiar wave of deep unhappiness. Cecil had lost most of his marbles a few years back due to a series of strokes and didn't know his own name anymore, let alone Dick's; the few times Dick had made it out to the nursing home in Port Angeles, ol' Cecil had only stared at him, his poor, sagging, frozen face shaking a little, his eyes haunted by a confused and silent stranger. Cecil wasn't going to be knocking on any doors, ever again...and lately, Dick couldn't stop thinking about him, about the Cecil he'd known at twenty, or at forty; hell, the man he'd known only a few years before.

A man's man, Cecil Weston. Cecil had been the sort other men privately held up as an example for themselves—because he was responsible and straight-thinking and he didn't hold truck with idiots or fools. He also told a good joke, a rare commodity, and wasn't quick to judge anyone. Cecil had served honorably in Korea, come home and married his high school sweetheart, and raised three good boys on a ship worker's salary. He'd even aged gracefully, putting a life-is-for-the-living face on his widower status—his pretty, funny wife had died from the big C shortly after his retirement—dating a nice lady from his church four or five years after Hazel had been laid to rest. He'd mourned his wife, of course, but he'd done it in private, the way it was supposed to be. A good man, with a lifetime of good memories to help him grow old…and *blam*, the first clot hit, worming into his fine brain and settling in, a massive CVA that blew out half his lights. He'd just gone to bed that fateful night, and by the time his oldest son used his key the following afternoon, it'd been far too long…doctor said it was a wonder he was still breathing, considering, and just like that, Cecil Weston was doomed to diapers and delirium for the rest of his days. His kids had pooled their money, got him into a nice place; as much as they loved him, they couldn't take care of him at home. But the nursing facility still smelled like piss, and even if the staff got slightly better than minimum wage, they didn't *know* him, didn't care about him. They looked at Cecil Weston and saw the living, breathing parody of the man he'd been, a series of systems to be fed and wiped and pitied until his body wore out or broke. And all those memories, lost…

Knock-knock-knock.

Dick scowled. The neighborhood kids knew better than to come to his house scrounging for jobs or selling their stupid crap. He knew a few people on the street by sight—the doctor, the young couple a half block down—but they'd have no reason to knock on his door. People generally annoyed him, and he didn't mind saying so. Last time he'd had a drop-in visitor, it'd been Annie Thomas, asking about the girl in the park; before that, he couldn't recall. Crazy world, now, sin to every side and no end in sight...and maybe a man like Cecil could have handled it, he *would* have handled it, would have found a way to navigate the chaos of the young century and his old body and done it smiling, remembering his life with Hazel and the boys, taking his lady to quiet dinners and regaling her with tales of the sea. Dick had tried to tough it out, tried to keep himself busy with his yard and his occasional scribblings, but he could see now that he'd been kidding himself, that the world had little use for the likes of him. His own sweet Annelise had died better than a half century ago; his strongest memories of the only woman he'd ever loved were as thin and translucent as smudged glass. But to lose even those, to wind up like Cecil...

The reality was, he was doomed either way. If his brain didn't give out, something else would; some tired, damaged piece of him would stutter to its inevitable halt, and if he was lucky, that would kill him. Chances were far better that he'd rot to death alone in some low-rent hospital bed, robbed regularly by the migrant orderlies and condescended to by some creaky, dried-up nurse. Or worse, a perverted Nancy boy, who maybe got a little tickle from sponging off old-man cock. But even if he beat the odds, if he stayed hale and healthy until his final day, passing peacefully in his bed after a good night's sleep, he wasn't half the man Cecil Weston had been, not half. He'd lived a sour, solitary life and left no mark on the world. Sick or well, what memories did he have to fill the long nights when he couldn't sleep? And really, who would give two shits when he was gone?

Knock-knock.

Persistent bastard. He had a brief urge to go down and tell the intruder where he could stick his sample case or whatever the hell he was selling. Interrupting a man at his home, where maybe his peace was all he had; shameful, it was downright shameful.

He slipped the noose around his chicken-skin neck, pulled the rope tight. Not much slack; he had it solidly tied to the rafters—maybe his hangman's knot was off, but he could still tie a competent anchor bend, arthritis or no—and needed the drop to be short, what with the stool being so low to the ground. His toes would almost touch as it was. The ladder he'd used to put up the rope was locked away in the shed, the bills were paid up, the garden weeded and watered. He'd written a will and left it propped on the kitchen table, donating anything of value or interest to the township of Port Isley. Not that anyone would care, but he'd tidied up as best he could. It's what Cecil would have done, if he'd known what was coming.

Knock-knock-knock.

"Oh, for Christ's *sake,*" Dick snapped, and pushed away from the stool, giving it a kick for good measure.

➤◄

John knocked again, though he felt fairly certain that Dick Calvin wasn't home. The old man's car, a battered beige Ford sedan, was in the tiny detached garage, but Calvin was active; he spent an hour or three in his yard every day that it wasn't raining; there was no reason to suspect that he hadn't simply walked down into town.

Either that, or he's already dead.

John sighed, looking out at the bay. The view from their street was fantastic in the evenings, the water lit up in ripples of golden light, but the sight provided little distraction. The thought that Calvin had killed himself…he wasn't certain he was ready to go there, not yet.

There *was* something going on. Considering his overwhelmed practice, considering the murders, he thought Bob's theory—that the citizens of Port Isley were being influenced, somehow—needed to be revisited. Emotions *were* heightened, people seemed to be having impulse control problems, issues with morality and id…his current halfhearted explanation, dreamed up on his way home from the hospital, was that they had fallen victim to some mildly psychedelic spore or pollen, some new variation that had come with the season, and even *that* felt crazy. Psychic ability was a step further than he wanted to go.

So why am I here? he thought, turning back to the door. A hand-lettered card—No SOLICITORS, it read, in neat block letters—had been taped inside the curtained pane.

He answered himself, gazing at the unwelcoming card. Because he didn't want to reject anything out of hand. Not after his day at the hospital, the intensity of the feelings he'd had. He had been mostly saved from his bizarre emotional turbulence with Sarah when her sister had woken, and a very tense, very forceful Stan Vincent had shown up a third time, carrying his photos; Karen had agreed to look at them and picked out two of the boys who'd attacked her—she wasn't certain about the third—and John had again been struck by a rage he didn't expect and couldn't rationalize, watching her sweet face tighten and then crumple when she looked at the pictures.

John shook his head and rapped on the door once more. When Bob had finally caught up with him—John's cell had rung about a minute after he'd turned it back on—the reporter had recounted his morning meeting with the teenagers…and had asked John to go check on his elderly neighbor, see if he could assess Calvin's state of mind. John had only stopped at home long enough to use the bathroom and find out that Bob had called his voice mail three times before heading back out. Perhaps Dick Calvin *was* suicidal—the spore explanation would account for all kinds of abnormal thoughts and behaviors—but the idea that someone had *sensed* that about him...

Is probably no crazier than the rest of it. When he'd finally left Sarah and her sister, he'd meant to go straight home and spend the evening at his computer, writing his way through the disorder, making lists of things to consider, to research...but the urgency in Bob's voice, when they'd spoken—the reporter believed this girl, who believed that Dick Calvin was planning to kill himself— suddenly it seemed like too much was happening too fast for John to take his time.

Way too fast, he thought, recalling his lingering good-bye embrace with Sarah, his tryst with Annie, and the brutal end to which she'd come. John knew a guy from med school who'd gone into etiology, studying disease causation. Dwier, Kurt Dwier. John had his e-mail somewhere, or could find it easily enough, get a phone number. Kurt had done some work at the CDC; he'd have some ideas about how to proceed.

And you'll say what, exactly? "Hey, Kurt, long time no see. Listen, people are acting out of character around here. That is, some of them. There have been murders. I've been having strange thoughts, too...I feel really unfocused...or, rather, too focused, too caught up in myself. With my processing, as it were. Do you think it might be some kind of pollen?" The Kurt Dwier he'd known at school—a short, grinning redhead with a penchant for burping replies to questions—would calmly, rationally hang up on him.

He needed evidence, something real and tangible to back up his claims. Stats from his files, crime data, hospital records...he could make a case. He had to do *something*. His training and vocation gave him a clear picture of how bad things could get for Port Isley, assuming there was some mind-altering agent at play. How many people in any community were slightly less than balanced, leaning toward trouble? How many would only need a slight nudge to send them over?

What's actually happening out there?

John turned on the small porch and looked out at the immaculate yard. Tall or fragile plants didn't grow well in Port Isley, blasted as they were by the winds, but Calvin had nurtured a number of low, hearty flowers in perfectly symmetrical beds that ran along the sides of his home. John recognized marigolds and what he thought was peony; his mother had been a weekend gardener, although her efforts had never been so picture-perfect. The lawn was as flawless as ever, the last of the day's light against Kehoe's trees casting long shadows across the manicured green. If Dick was suffering from suicidal depression, it hadn't stopped him from keeping up appearances.

He's fine. He walked down the hill, that's all. John would go home, get some notes down. He would get *organized*—even the word was soothing, images of neat lists and bullet points calming him, allowing him to momentarily disregard his concerns—and come back in an hour or so.

He turned back toward his house—and saw a handful of teenagers emerging from the old school basement across the street, the girls giggling, the young men swaggering and playing cool. On impulse he changed direction, walking toward Dick's backyard. He didn't feel like being sized up by a gaggle of stoned kids, and the path that ran behind their homes was actually quite pleasant by twilight in the summer, cool and thick with shadow. There was a man walking toward him through the dusk, a stranger. John slowed his step. The man was on the tall side but hunched slightly, his head down; he didn't see John, didn't seem to see anything as he walked, his gaze on the ground. The guy was too thin, and pale. He didn't look familiar, either, although the dark of the woods masked him somewhat, turning his eyes into black pools.

The stranger finally looked up when they were less than a dozen feet apart, and John saw that he was fairly young, probably no older than thirty. Surprise registered on the younger man's face, his body straightening, his hands coming out of his pockets. He was close enough for John to see a flurry of emotions cross his gaze—the stranger was startled, angry, fearful, guilty...then carefully blank, although John believed that the man had been crying, from the raw, red look around his eyes.

Imagination, John told himself. Maybe he had allergies. And why would he be angry or afraid?

Or guilty?

Both men stopped walking and regarded one another. John put on a polite smile and stuck out his hand, stepping forward. The main trail through the park was a good fifty meters west of the small track that connected his house to Dick's; the man was trespassing, and while John saw no reason to call him out for it, common sense dictated that whenever possible, you tried to meet the people who were lurking behind your home.

"Hi," he said. "Going for a hike?"

The stranger didn't back away, exactly, but seemed to hunch away from John's outstretched hand, jamming his own back into his coat pockets.

Don't touch, John thought, lowering his hand. Overhead, high in the trees, the wind was picking up. The crash of the branches was like the ocean, the airy surf loud enough to almost drown the stranger's low, soft voice.

"You're the doctor."

"I don't know if I'm *the* doctor," he said. His voice sounded bright and amiable, which made him feel like some cocktail party dork, but he couldn't seem to help it. "I'm *a* doctor. John Hanover, I live in the last house on the block."

He nodded toward his house, although the back porch was hidden by a turn of the track. The stranger didn't turn to look—but seemed to understand that more was required of him, that an introduction was now mandatory.

"David Mallon," he said. He didn't smile. "I took the rental. The gray bungalow."

Ah. The mysterious neighbor. That explained what he was doing back here. John refreshed his own smile. Not that he particularly wanted to chat, but he'd always felt it paid to be friendly with neighbors, to at least be able to call them by name; you never knew when you might need help. "You're right next door, then. Are you here for the summer?"

Mallon nodded. "That's the plan." Still no smile, and his posture continued to be defensive, his shoulders up, his whole body leaning away from John's. Like he thought John had a cold and was afraid of catching it.

"You here for the water or the architecture?" John asked, and at Mallon's blank look, added, "Our summer people fish, sail, or like Victorians, for the most part."

"Summer people," Mallon said, and finally smiled, a faint thing. "Is that what I am?"

"Not necessarily," John said. He couldn't tell if Mallon was offended or amused. And suddenly, standing here and chatting with him, trying to *analyze* him, seemed like a monumental waste of time. "I'm sorry, I'm a little distracted today; I have some things to take care of…it's nice to meet you. Maybe we can try it again sometime?"

Mallon nodded, but as John started to walk past him, he didn't move, didn't take the natural opportunity to end the conversation by continuing his own way. John considered stopping for about a quarter of a second, to ask if Mallon was all right, but the lure of getting home (getting *organized*) was too great. He simply nodded at the young man—an introvert, obviously, and possibly a mysophobe—and kept walking, his thoughts turning back to his jumble of thinking. He would write it down, quantify and simplify. Events, his clients, something about emotional evolution...

By the time he reached his back porch, he'd entirely forgotten Mallon.

><

Devon was gone. He'd packed a bunch of his stuff into the ancient Volvo wagon in his uncle's garage—Sid was still out of town on business, and the Volvo was technically Devon's, a gift from Sid for his sixteenth birthday; Isley was too small to ever drive anywhere, though Devon drove it to Port Angeles sometimes—and he'd left a long note for Sid, explaining that he had to go to Portland (he'd intimated a boyfriend emergency for Claire, who was also Sid's niece), and that Amanda would stay for a while (homeless)...and then he'd said good-bye and hugged her and driven away. Amanda had watched his car turn down the hill, heading for the winding route that would lead him to the interstate, his taillights barely flickering at the stop sign. Somehow, the day had passed; it was full dark and starting to cool on this side of town. Back at the apartment, the heat would just be starting to pick up, turning her bedroom into a stifling cave.

Ex-bedroom, she thought, but her homelessness didn't bother her half as much as watching Devon drive away. Eric, who'd been conspicuously silent all day, was probably still sitting on the porch. He had hung back while she and Devon were embracing and saying their final farewells, offering a disinterested wave to her best friend in the world as he'd deserted her.

Not deserted, she told herself, still watching the empty street. *Not abandoned*. What choice did he have? It wasn't like she could ask him to stay in Port Isley, to hold her hand and comfort her through this—this fucked-up *weirdness*—after she'd seen him floating in the bay. And he was only going to Portland. It was six, seven hours away, tops. Sid was pretty easygoing; he treated Devon like an adult and likely wouldn't be too freaked that his nephew had taken off. And he'd let Amanda stay for as long as she needed; Sid Shupe was one of those rare adults who actually helped people instead of just talking about it. He'd even offered to let Amanda move in once, after Grace had pulled her last DUI.

She sighed, noting that her daylong abuse of caffeine had left her with a sour stomach and a jittery, grainy feeling. She didn't feel like crying for a change, but she was bone tired. How long before the threat was gone, before it was safe for Devon to come back? How long would she participate with Bob's Let's-Save-Isley idea before she decided to blow town, to make the certified jump from homeless teen to self-sufficient young person?

Eric was suddenly standing behind her, his long-fingered hand slipping around her waist. He'd ducked home while Devon had been packing, and she'd felt kind of...relieved, really. Devon had been chattering away, nervous as hell about leaving—and about being near her, she'd sensed, not in a supernatural way but because every time she moved closer to him, he found a way to be on the other side of the room. By silent consent, they hadn't spoken about his hookup with Mitchell Jessup, which was just as well. She was pretty much creeped out by the concept, and he was obviously embarrassed. In spite of the awkwardness, though, she'd been glad for some alone time with him, because she didn't know when she'd see him again, and their friendship was, like, the only truly solid thing in her life. But then Eric had been back in less than an hour, just showed up and walked in, like he'd been invited. He'd been too quiet, mostly listening to Devon's anxious monologue, occasionally trying to touch her. He'd been weird all day, staring at her every time she looked at him, and he was kind of...*stilted*, the way he talked. Like he was carefully thinking about everything he said before he said it.

She tensed for just a second when he moved even closer but then made herself relax. With Devon gone, she didn't exactly have a support network anymore. And Eric was still totally hot, even if he was acting stupid today, and he obviously wanted to help her. For the most part, she liked the touching and his intensity. She'd definitely liked it last night.

She had to think of Peter then, and her mother, and how the night had ended. It seemed like a million years had passed already. She didn't want to think about it, not at all, and she grasped for a diversion. Bob had said he was going to do some research, talk to his shrink friend, and then call her at Devon's sometime in the evening. Sid wasn't supposed to be back until Monday or Tuesday. She and Eric were alone.

The urge to fuck his brains out was sudden and all-encompassing. Without another thought, she turned into his embrace, sliding her hand to the front of his jeans.

They broke apart long enough to get inside. Barely. And for a few moments, at least, their bodies locked perfectly together, and she was free from thought, from everything but his touch.

CHAPTER

17

It was dark, a half moon hanging low in the sky over the black, glittering bay, the trees in the park softening their afternoon symphony. The wind had become a breeze, a warm one. John figured it was the first night in a while that hadn't turned cool after the sun disappeared, which meant the dog days had finally come to Isley. From this high up on the hill, one couldn't hear the tourist sounds from the waterfront, the summer night parties that spilled from the bars and restaurants and piers, engines of cars and boats revving, laughter…but John knew they were down there, retired baby boomers and dot-com merge consultants and the idle well-off, interacting with the user-friendly locals. The glow from so many lights made it hard to see the stars.

John stood on Dick Calvin's porch again, this time waiting for Bob and the police to join him. Bob had insisted, after hearing that the crotchety old man still wasn't answering his door. John's certainty, that Calvin wasn't home, had faded for no reason that he could name, and he found himself pacing up and down the low steps, occasionally glancing up at the too-faint stars, wondering if Amanda Young had actually foreseen Calvin's suicide.

When the phone buzzed in his pocket, he started. He was wound up, agitated, tired; the combination made him jumpy.

"Hello?"

"John? It's Sarah."

John felt his heartbeat pick up, just hearing her voice. "Hi, how are you?"

There was a brief silence, long enough for him to worry, and then she sighed. "I'm all right, I guess. I'm home—at Big Blue, I mean. Karen kicked me out; she said I needed some real sleep." She laughed, a soft, wry laugh. "Except I'm not sleeping. I'm not even tired."

"Oh," he said, already guessing why she'd called. *Say no. Say you're busy.* If earlier at the hospital was any indicator, they'd be in the sack before the door closed behind him.

"Do you think you could come over? Just for a little while?"

"I'm, ah, doing something right now..."

"If you don't want to, that's OK," she said quickly.

"No, it's not that. I really am busy."

"Later, then?"

It didn't seem to be in him to lie to her. "I could. I'd like to see you. I'm...I'm not sure that's such a good idea, though, considering...considering what might happen."

Another silence. He thought she would ask what he meant, but she surprised him. "Would that be so terrible?" she asked.

"No," he said. "No, it's not that I don't want...ah, it's just..."

Just what? Just, we may regret it? Just, we're two single, lonely people and there's no reason not to touch each other? Not to fuck?

The images that flashed through his mind were explicit. Not the gentle lovemaking he'd envisioned earlier, not at all.

sweating sucking fingers sliding screaming

He cleared his throat, forcing the images away, willing his stirring erection to stand down...and abruptly thought of Nina McAndrews, his client and one-time real estate agent, who he'd sent out of town for a full medical workup.

"It's like I start thinking about it, you know, it, *and even the words in my head make me—I get, um, aroused." Nina, huddled*

in the corner of his couch, as far from him as she could get. She wouldn't look at him. "I can't—once I start thinking about it, I can't stop, I have to—I have to do something about it." Nina, crying. "Oh my God, what's wrong with me?"

"I'm starting to think that there may be some...some chemical influence here, in Port Isley," he said, taking a breath. "Something that's making people act rashly, or out of character."

"Really?"

"Yeah," he said, feeling himself steady. Saying it aloud sounded strange, but not crazy, not impossible. "Don't you? I mean, I don't know you that well, I don't want to presume anything, but earlier, when you said you haven't been yourself..."

"Wow," she said. "You think—that would explain...Jesus, that would explain a lot of things." She sounded almost relieved. "What do you think it is?"

"I don't know. I don't know anything for certain...some biological agent, maybe..." He thought of the open Word file on his desktop, the random, unclear jumble of theory and supposition that he'd tapped out after visiting Dick Calvin's a few hours earlier.

Even as he spoke, Bob's battered truck pulled up in front of Dick's house.

"Ah, I have to go," he said. "I'm sorry. I'll call you back later, or—"

"But what is it?" she asked. "Should I be worried? Should I leave Tommy with his dad? He's supposed to come back on Tuesday, but if you think—"

"Sarah—"

"I need to *know*," she said. "Don't tell me that there might be something—something *toxic* here, then hang up." She sounded close to tears. "Tell me what's happening. I feel like I'm all alone, suddenly, I feel—" Her breath shook. "Please, John."

Bob got out of his truck, closing the door gently—and a PIPD patrol car pulled up behind the truck, its bar lights dark.

"I'll come over," he said. "As soon as I'm done here. We can talk, I'll tell you what I know. What I think. But I have to go now, OK?"

"OK," she said, on another shaking breath. "OK, good. I'll be here."

A lone cop got out of the patrol car—one of the summer officers, a tall, spindly young man John didn't recognize—and joined Bob at the foot of the walk, talking into the radio clipped to his shoulder. John turned his attention to the two men as they started toward him—and realized that he could hardly wait to see her. Her face, her voice, her touch; whatever the consequences, he didn't care.

Bob was talking to the young cop as they reached the steps, spinning a plausible tale. "...and when he didn't show up, I called John, asked him to come check."

Bob smiled tightly, nodding at John. "John Hanover, he lives in the last house on the block. *Doctor* Hanover."

The officer blinked at John. He was early-to midtwenties but had perfected a world-weary, jaded air, the kind that veteran cops always seemed to wear. His voice was bland, pleasant, bored. "Uh-huh. You friends with Mr. Calvin, Doctor?"

"Well, we're neighbors," he said, realizing how stupid that sounded as he said it. Obviously they were neighbors. Bob had just said so. "I came by two, three hours ago; there was no answer. Same when I tried again, just now."

"Uh-huh," the cop said again. He turned his attention back to Bob. "Has Mr. Calvin been sick, or...do you have any reason to be worried about him?"

Bob shrugged. "Honestly, I don't know him that well. He writes a column for the paper, we talk sometimes. Last time I saw him, he seemed a little down. Ah, depressed. I don't know about what. We agreed to meet up tonight for a drink; he was supposed to come by my place. Like I said, when he didn't show, I called his neighbor."

The cop looked to John again, who nodded, hoping he looked as cool, as innocent as the reporter. The story sounded reasonable to John, but the officer's gaze had gone calculating, skeptical.

Paranoid?

"Uh-huh," he said, and stepped past John, muttering an *excuse me*. He rapped on the door, waited. Rapped again.

Bob cast a look at John, his eyes worried.

"Mr. Calvin!" the cop called, and John jumped. The cop put his hand on the doorknob. Turned it. The door opened, a sliver of stuffy dark beyond the frame. Thick, warm air swelled out.

"Step back, please," the officer said.

"Maybe I should come along, make sure—" Bob began.

"You will wait *here*, sir," the young man cut in, his voice too loud, his suspicious gaze hopping between the two of them, and John realized that he was nervous. His right hand had dropped to the black nylon holster on his hip. He wasn't touching his weapon but looked like he was thinking about it.

Bob held up his hands, an OK-by-me gesture. The cop pulled a flashlight off his belt, clicking it on as he touched the radio at his shoulder once more.

"Sam-Two entering the premises at seven two two seven Eleanor, ten-twenty-three…"

He disappeared inside, leaving the door open behind him. John and Bob moved back from the front steps, pitching their voices low. John told the reporter some of what he'd experienced earlier in the day, and his reasonable belief that he wasn't the only one.

Bob nodded. "It's weird, all right. When I take a step back, look at what I've been thinking…well, more the *way* I've been thinking, I guess. I haven't noticed anything really bad, in myself—well, past the drinking. I'm kind of obsessed with this theory, though—this story. I can't stop thinking about it, about how and why and what I can do to fix it. I spent most of today reading, downloading articles, trying to find patterns…"

He turned and looked at Dick Calvin's front door. The wedge of darkness inside hadn't changed.

"You really think he's dead?" John asked.

"I don't know, Doc," Bob said. "I hope not. Amanda seemed pretty sure that he wanted to kill himself, though."

John hesitated, then asked, "If we're all affected, do you think it's possible that you believe this girl because…" *How to put it gently?* "Because you've been, ah, influenced?"

"Delusional, you mean?" Bob smiled and clapped a hand on John's shoulder. John could smell a shadow of whiskey on his breath. "More things in heaven and earth, boyo. In this case, I hope she was wrong. I hope we're all wrong."

John nodded. "That'd be—"

Nice was blotted out by the shout from deep inside the house. The young officer sounded panicked. "Doctor! Get in here, right now!"

John broke and ran, faintly aware that Bob was right behind him. Up the steps, the cop was shouting again, *Upstairs, hurry!* It was dark, only ambient street light from the windows to guide them to the stairs. John took them two at a time, using the banister to haul himself faster.

There was a bright line of light at the floor, the flashlight—the kid had dropped it—and by its sharp wedge of light, they could see the policeman supporting a long, inevitable shadow that hung from the roof, a body, Dick Calvin.

"Ah, *shit*," Bob moaned, and they ran to help the panicked officer. Before they even cut him down, John knew they were much too late.

>+<

It was almost one in the morning before the soft tap came at the door. Sarah woke from her light doze at once and hurried to the door.

She smiled when she saw him and stepped aside to let him in. He only stood there. His hair was rumpled, his color pale; he looked very tired, and worried.

"I'm sorry it's so late," John said. Behind him, the street was silent and still.

"That's OK," she said. "Please come in."

He didn't budge. "One of my neighbors committed suicide."

"Oh! Oh, John, I'm so sorry," she said. She took a step toward him but saw that he didn't want her to some any closer, the way he leaned away from her.

"I don't know what to do," John said. "I can't seem to think straight. There are people killing each other, getting hurt, but others— the effects are so varied, I can't imagine *anything* that would do what it's doing." He shook his head. "If I hadn't felt—ah, different myself, I wouldn't have believed there was any unusual influence. Even now, I keep half convincing myself that I'm just really stressed out."

He smiled bleakly. "Bad things happen, all the time, every- where. Just because a bunch of them seem to be happening here, that doesn't mean anything. Not necessarily. And violence, mur- der—those things don't happen in a vacuum. People are affected, vulnerable, anxious…prone to inventing the answers they need, when there are no sane answers available…"

He trailed off, and she could almost see him warring with himself, trying to decide if his theory was based on anything past wild speculation.

"So…what's the next step?" she asked, leaning against the doorframe.

"I don't know. I can call the state, get them to send out some people to test the soil, the water…I've got a college friend who worked for the CDC for a while; I'll try to get in touch with him. And I'm meeting a girl tomorrow morning, a friend of a friend, she might know something…"

He grinned, a self-conscious, slightly hysterical smile. "She's psychic. How's that for a logical approach to contagion? Maybe after I ask her to divine the source of our trouble, she can put me in touch with my grandmother."

Sarah hugged herself against the early morning air. She didn't know him well enough to know what would best soothe him, so she said what she felt. "I think keeping an open mind takes work," she said. "But if you're looking for an answer to an inexplicable problem, it's kind of the best policy."

"But what if the problem is only *in* my mind?" he asked, his expression stricken. "What if we're just making up excuses, looking for ways to, to accept how we're feeling? How can any of this be *real*?"

The way he looked at her then, she felt a hot, pulling need deep inside and found that she didn't care if what she wanted was wrong, if what they both wanted was wrong. They both wanted it; that was what mattered. Suddenly, that was *all* that mattered.

"Come inside," she said, and he gave in and stepped through the door. They didn't speak again until he said her name, whispered against her neck sometime later.

CHAPTER

18

Bob called Amanda early, and they agreed to meet at John's office. When he called John at home to confirm, there was no answer, but he got through on the cell. Ten o'clock. John didn't work Mondays; they would have privacy—and Bob wanted Amanda to be able to concentrate, somewhere quiet where she felt safe.

At a quarter to ten, Bob pulled up in front of Devon's house. Amanda and her boyfriend were on the front step, smoking. Amanda had said that Devon had gone, that he'd taken off for Portland, but it was still strange to see her without him. Her boyfriend, Eric, was quiet, with that vague insolent sullenness that seemed to attach to too many teenage males. Obviously, Amanda wanted him to be present, although Bob wished she'd left him behind; the kid seemed jealous every time she turned her gaze to anyone besides himself, and he was constantly touching her, distracting her. They drove to John's office mostly without speaking.

John met them in the small waiting room, wearing the same clothes he'd worn the night before. He looked like he hadn't slept, but his smile was open and sincere as he shook hands with both Amanda and Eric. He led them back to his office, pausing along the way to grab a few sodas out of a minifridge next to the empty receptionist's desk.

John's office was as Bob remembered—soft colors, soft furniture, and a window that looked out over Water Street. He could see the tall masts of sailboats at the far end, although the marina's pier was blocked from view by the third story of the hardware store, the tallest building on the downtown waterfront.

Amanda and Eric sat on the pale-green sofa adjacent to John's desk. John sat across from the couch, his office chair turned toward them. Bob stayed standing. He reflexively scanned the papers on John's desk, saw the words *traumatic bereavement* at the top of one of them, heavily underlined.

"Thank you for coming in," John said.

"Not a problem," Amanda said, her tone neutral. "Although— maybe this is a dumb question, but why did you want to meet me, anyway?"

"Our mutual friend here believes you have a gift," John said. "I didn't think—I thought he might be wrong, but after last night, I wanted to meet you myself."

"What happened last night?"

John shot a look at Bob, then took a deep breath. "I'm sorry to tell you this, but Dick Calvin committed suicide yesterday."

Amanda's soft, round face twisted. Eric put his arm around her, but she pulled away from him, turning an accusatory glare to Bob.

"Why didn't you say something?" she asked.

Bob shook his head, suddenly uncomfortable with his decision to let John break the news. "I figured we'd be talking about it soon enough," he said. "I thought with John here, we might be able to come up with some ideas, about how to handle things better from here on."

"I know it's a shock," John began, but Amanda interrupted him, still looking at Bob, her voice rising.

"No, it's not, I *told* you he was going to do it. You said we could save him, you said I might have *saved* him!"

"I was wrong," Bob said, wishing for a drink. John didn't step in, only watched patiently. *Thanks, Doc.* "And I should have told you already, I was just..." He resorted to the truth. "I thought John would be better at it, I guess."

"So what's the use of knowing anything?" Amanda snapped. For the anger in her voice, she looked miserable. "Why fucking bother?"

John was professional, his tone confident. "Because if there *is* something going on in Port Isley, and if you can actually see some of it—see things that other people can't—then we can use that information. We might be able to stop more people from getting hurt."

"Right, like we stopped the Lawn King from hanging himself," she said.

John raised his eyebrows. "How do you know he hung himself?"

"He did, didn't he?"

"Yes, but how did you know that?" John reached over to his desk and picked up a legal pad and a pen. "Did you see it? Tell me what you saw, or thought, exactly."

Amanda hesitated, shooting another unhappy look in Bob's direction...then told him the same things she'd told the reporter only the day before—about sensing things, about getting into people's heads, about Devon and the kids she'd gotten stoned with, about her dreams. She said that when she'd sensed what she had, about Dick Calvin, she'd just known. "Like, if I said, how did Elvis die, you'd say..."

John blinked. "Uh, cardiac arrest brought on by an overdose and—"

"On the crapper," Bob said, and Amanda nodded at him.

"Like that," she said. "I just knew."

John wrote quickly as she talked, only glancing at the paper occasionally. Bob was impressed that he managed to write in a mostly straight and even hand. Practice, he figured. He'd known a couple of reporters who could do that, one of them with a cigarette in his writing hand, watching people talk while they took down what was said. Bob had never gotten the hang of it, himself, though he'd fashioned his own private shorthand over the years…

Pay attention, old man. The devil was so often in the details.

"OK," John said, as her brief story dried up. "And Bob said you've had some success *trying* to see things. Have you done any more of that?"

"No," Amanda said. She shifted on the couch. Eric watched her, intently focused on her; Bob got the impression that if asked, the kid wouldn't be able to remember John's name or how they'd gotten to his office. "I mean, it's—it's like eavesdropping, or something."

John nodded. "Do you think…do you think it's possible that this empathy you're experiencing is a reaction to what's been happening in Port Isley?"

"What do you mean?"

"When I got here this morning, I looked up some things," John said lightly. "About what sudden, unexpected violence can do to the people who are affected."

Traumatic bereavement, Bob thought.

"What, some of them turn psychic?" Amanda asked.

"Not exactly," John said. "But sometimes our perspectives can be skewed, by events beyond our control. Violence, murder, suicide—sometimes these things are so hard to accept, to even face, that our minds try to find a way to make sense of them for us. It's a way to deal with pain."

Amanda looked at Bob again, and he saw that her defenses had snapped shut as quickly as that, neat and solid as a European bank's. "He thinks I'm full of shit," she said. "Is that what *you* think? Is that why you wanted me to meet with a shrink?"

John held up his hands, a placating gesture. "Hold on, that is *not* what I think," he said. "You knew about Dick Calvin. I can't just discount that, can I? I'm trying to keep an open mind, believe me, but to do that, I've got to look at all this from more than one angle."

Amanda was still staring at him, and Bob shook his head, firmly. "He doesn't think you're lying, and neither do I. We're just trying to work this out, that's all. To be fair, you didn't believe it either, when this first started."

"She's not lying," Eric snarled, and if Amanda was pissed at the unspoken hint of disbelief, Eric seemed positively homicidal. He stood up, glowering at the two men, his lanky body poised as if to fight. "This is *bullshit*."

Amanda stayed where she was. "No, it's OK," she said. When Eric didn't sit down again, she added, "You can leave, if you want."

Eric hesitated, then sat. He didn't look happy about it. He slumped away from them, his posture telling them all what he thought.

John studied Amanda a moment, then sighed. "With my background being what it is, my training, I have to look at it from a psychological point of view. Strong, unpleasant emotions like guilt or grief or fear, witnessing violence—these things can have an intense effect on the people who experience them. I'm not trying to discount what *you're* experiencing, I'm only looking for a way to explain what's happening."

"Show him," Eric said, turning back to Amanda. "Do it. Tell him something you couldn't know, about *him*."

His tone was almost vindictive, but Bob didn't disagree with the proposal. He'd hoped that she'd be willing to demonstrate her ability to John, to wipe out the doctor's uncertainty once and for all. And wasn't that why Bob had suggested John's office, a calm environment, so she could focus?

"I'm not a fucking monkey," she said. "I don't *perform*."

"It's not like that," Bob said. He moved to the couch, crouching in front of Amanda, wanting to be sure she could see his sincerity, his belief. "We don't know what's going on in Port Isley. Maybe nothing at all, maybe it's just a bad summer, a dark summer. A run of coincidence, hard luck, law of averages…I don't believe that, but I don't *know*, I don't think anyone *knows*. What I *do* know is that for whatever reason, you've been tuning in to these things. And we need your help."

Eric snorted, a mean half laugh, but Bob ignored him. "I'm sorry about Dick Calvin, I really am. You know it's not your fault, right?"

Amanda looked away.

"I know how you feel," Bob agreed. "If I'd *acted* sooner, or if John had gone by to check on him earlier…maybe things would be different. Maybe not. All we can do now, though, is move on from here."

He glanced at John, back at her. "Can you show him something? Tell him something? Think of it as practice. It's like you've got a new tool, a powerful tool, but to know how best to apply it— to even know what your skill might apply *to*—we need to push the perimeter, a little."

"*We?*"

"You," Bob amended quickly. "And only if you want to. It's your choice."

Amanda didn't look convinced, but after a moment, she nodded. "OK."

"Try doing what you did yesterday, with Devon," Bob said. "Only…John, come over here, sit by her. Try focusing on John specifically. Don't pull away from whatever comes to mind, don't let yourself be surprised out of it. Tell us everything you think, no matter how small or seemingly unimportant."

Bob moved out of the way so John could sit. The doc looked slightly embarrassed, but game. Eric seemed even more angry, and his expression further soured when Bob suggested that Amanda hold John's hands.

The teenage girl turned to face John. She took both of his hands in her own and then closed her eyes, breathing deeply. They waited, all of them watching her. After a long, silent moment, one of her hands twitched, and she started talking, her eyes still closed.

"You were with her last night; you barely slept at all, and you're afraid you might be in love with her, because you're also afraid that you're sick, that the whole town is sick, so maybe those feelings don't mean anything," she said. "Uh, you want to take a shower, you don't want to be sitting so close to anyone when you haven't showered. You're worried that you smell like—" She cleared her throat, her face reddening slightly. "Like Sarah, to be specific. You've never believed in psychic ability, but you trust Bob, and with the strange, strong feelings you've been having about Sarah, and...Lauren? Annie, for sure. Annie's dead but you aren't looping anymore, whatever that means."

She opened her eyes but stared down at their hands. "Anyway, you think you might be wrong, about everything, but you don't know and your brain just keeps trying to make the pieces fit, and they won't. Also, you think you're getting a headache because you skipped breakfast."

John's eyes had widened. Bob felt a deep satisfaction, saw it mirrored in a spiteful way on Eric's triumphant young face. John let go of Amanda's hands and sat back a little. The expression he wore was one of deep awe and not a little embarrassment. Bob wondered faintly who the hell Sarah was.

Amanda smiled, was transformed from pretty to beautiful in that instant. "Ka-*pow*," she said. Eric laughed, but the sound was high and anxious.

John was speechless for what seemed a long time, then he sighed and nodded and looked at Bob.

"OK," he said. He looked at Amanda again. "That's some talent you got there."

She was pleased with herself, Bob could tell, her eyes bright with it. "It's getting stronger," she said. "I've been pretty freaked-out, overall, but I'm starting to...to get the hang of it a little better, I guess."

"You got all that, just now," John said.

She nodded. "Yup. Other stuff, too, but that's what—that's the biggest stuff. Like, where your head's at. So to speak."

"Just out of curiosity, what other stuff?" John asked.

"Um...something about a guy named Phillip? He's, like, your...colleague? And I *think* you were wondering if there's anything in the office for the headache..." She trailed off and frowned. "The smaller stuff isn't as clear. There's—"

"What do you mean by smaller and bigger?" John interrupted. "In what way?"

Amanda looked at John like he was a moron. "What do you think? Bigger, smaller. Uh, more important in your brain, less important."

"OK," John said. "Just trying to clarify, that's all."

Amanda relaxed, nodded. "OK. So. There's also, like, this *static*, underneath that. Like, with an old radio? Some of the signals are totally clear, and some are coming in on different channels that aren't so clear, and most of them don't send out anything. Does that make sense?"

"Sure, why not?" John asked. He looked slightly dazed. "You get this kind of...of *depth* off everybody?"

"I've only done it on purpose twice," she said, and her sincere smile crept back. "I think I could, though. If I tried. It's, like..." She shook her head. "The power, or ability or whatever, is changing. Evolving."

"In what way?"

"It's stronger, I'm pretty sure," she said. "I mean, it's getting easier to pick up people's…I don't know, inner dialogue?"

John nodded. "Bob says you've had some precognitive experiences. Did you get anything like that just now?"

"No," she said. "I don't think so, anyway. But the dreams I've been having…a lot of the same imagery keeps repeating, and it feels real. Like the other stuff, anyway. And I don't think it's happened, yet."

John stood and walked back to his desk, picking up the notepad he'd written on earlier. "A smiling woman with blood in her hair. A big fire. A boy in a darkened house of mirrors. Gunfire. A woman bathing an infant."

The whole list was creepy, but that last sent a shiver down Bob's spine. Not a scary image in itself, but considering the rest of the list…he hoped that they'd find a way to track the young mother down before she did anything…irreparable. And so far as he could see, Amanda was the only chance they had. She'd *seen* these people, or been them, or however it worked; she was the key.

"How can we use this?" Bob asked, looking at John, then Amanda. He felt hungry to make it happen, to *do* something. Amanda was willing, and surely John could figure out how to make the most of her ability. "How can we track them down?"

John put the notepad down, shaking his head. "I'm not sure," he said. "And I'm not sure that our primary focus should be on rescuing these people, necessarily—"

"What the hell do you—" Bob began, and John held up one hand.

"Not these *specific* people," he said. "I mean, of course we want to help, we *should* help. I think our big goal should be tracking the source of…of whatever's going on here. If we can pin down the X factor, the influence, then we'll have everything we need to call in some *real* help. We can get the town evacuated, get the CDC involved, whatever government labs are applicable...we could save *all* of them."

He turned back to Amanda. Eric had finally let a few air molecules pass between them; for the first time since Bob had met the kid, Amanda's boyfriend wasn't glued to her side or some other part of her.

"I've been considering the possibility that everything that's been happening here is due to some chemical influence, a poison, something biological," John said.

"Yeah, I got that," Amanda said. "Like, spores or something."

"Do you think—is there a way that you can think of, to track down something like that?"

Amanda thought, her sharp gaze looking inward. After a moment she shook her head. "I don't know," she said. "I haven't had any feelings about places or things, only people. I think you're right, though, about everything being connected."

"What if we start with a timeline?" Bob asked, the thought suddenly occurring to him. "You said you've been overbooked, lately—what if we try to figure out when the first, ah, cases popped up? Maybe we can trace it that way."

John was nodding. So was Amanda. "Yeah, that's good," John said.

"Plus, like, hospital reports, and police reports, stuff like that," Amanda said. "You guys can get those things, can't you?"

"Already on it," Bob said. He didn't mention that he'd been too drunk, digging through the police reports, to notice any common denominators among the recorded incidents, or even to make note of the dates. No matter, he told himself. They'd be looking through all of it again.

John flipped through some of the loose papers on his desk. "I had a list started...there's a social services worker in town; I thought I could ask her about anything unusual. And I was thinking we could talk to some of the local clergy, see if they can give us an idea about what their parishioners are up to..." John paged through the papers for another moment, then gave up, a look of irritation on his face. "I might have left it at home."

"We'll start a new one," Bob said. He felt good, hopeful; they had a plan, of sorts. A place to start, anyway.

"What should I do?" Amanda asked. "I mean, I can't exactly go around trying to read everybody in town; that'd take forever."

Eric watched her talk, his gaze fixed on her moving mouth. He still hadn't touched her again, even sat away from her a little, as though *afraid* to touch her. Considering what she'd told John about himself, Bob thought he understood. Having a girlfriend who read minds made lying or cheating pretty much impossible, and if she was tapping into feelings...Bob didn't know anything about the kid, but he'd been seventeen himself, once. Surely the major components of male adolescence hadn't changed *that* much.

John frowned, a thinking face, and crossed his arms. "Let's get some facts down, times and events," he said. "And I'll make a few calls, see if we can get someone out here to run tests. Once we have something substantial, we can go to the police."

Bob thought about Stan Vincent, how he'd been at the hospital. "I don't know that the local cops are going to be much help," he said. "Chief Vincent seems...unreasonable."

"If we have evidence, though, he'll have to listen," John said. Bob considered pointing out that his statement was wishful thinking at best, but let it slide; if Vincent wouldn't step up, there were the state cops. Even the feds, if it came to that.

John turned back to Amanda. "You could go with us, try to get a read off whoever we talk to," he said. "Until then, you should keep a journal. Write down everything you see. The police have those sketch-artist computer programs; maybe we can find some of the people you've been dreaming about that way."

"There's the poetry night, next week," Amanda said. "Bob said it might be a good idea to go somewhere there are a lot of people, see if I can, uh, pick up anything big…"

"Hopefully, you won't have to," John said. "By then, we should have this thing figured out."

Bob didn't feel as certain as John suddenly seemed, but the doc's confidence was heartening, and contagious. If their suppositions were true, if Port Isley had been infected somehow, they'd make a case for it and get the proper authorities involved. A whole town couldn't self-destruct without anyone from outside noticing, not in this day and age…or even people *inside* the town, for that matter. He'd made the connection, and if an aging, drunk reporter could see that something strange was happening, there were bound to be others.

"We'll figure it out," Bob affirmed, and Amanda and John both nodded, and Eric only watched Amanda, still not touching her.

CHAPTER

19

Darrin Everret heard a soft tap on the door of the west studio and smiled, sure it was Kim. The sculptress usually came by well after dark to avoid being seen by Miranda or any of her minions. Ms. Greene-Moreland frowned on fucking, it seemed, by her "guests," and since Darrin wasn't paying, he had no real choice but to play along. In front of Miranda, anyway...although he had the feeling she'd look the other way in his case. He knew he was the retreat's darling—he had more talent than any three of the rest of them—and he'd only just discovered a passion, a genius for long, rambling, brilliant monologues about the artistic experience. Almost every day that he worked—which was pretty much all of them, he'd never been so productive—he had an audience now, three or four of them listening to him talk about the process while he was creating. Sometimes they worked alongside him; sometimes they just sat there in awed silence, watching him put lines on paper, listening to his theories and assertions.

He dropped his pencil in the tray, brushed off his hands, and ran them through his hair. He'd been banging the sculptress since their first week. Kim was homely but fantastically enthusiastic in the sack and wasn't as vapid as she'd first seemed; she read a lot of books, and there was an actual sense of humor behind those myopic brown eyes. A little talent, too. Her pieces weren't total shit, anyway, like what most of the others churned out.

Darrin was cool with the Kim arrangement, but he also had his eye on Jane, one of the poets. Poetesses. She was boring as hell, her poetry was depressing and uninspired, but she was also much prettier than Kim, better body, face like a cheerleader's. Jane had become a regular at his daily discourses, along with Kim and Brandon, the collage-mixed-media guy. Brandon had a big, fat hard-on for Darrin, which was funny but also pathetic. He was an ex-Mormon and still half in the closet, but so obviously attracted to Darrin that it was almost painful to watch, to see his longing gazes, his confused, blushing attempts at conversation.

"Yeah," Darrin called. Maybe it was Jane.

Maybe it was Jane *and* Kim.

Miranda Greene-Moreland stepped into the studio, gowned in some ridiculous green muumuu, wearing oversize hoop earrings with little dolphins dangling in the middle.

Say good-bye, hard-on.

"There you are, Darrin," she said. She smiled, showing her stained, unlovely teeth. "I hope I'm not breaking your concentration...?"

"Of course not, Miranda." He'd been about finished, anyway. The alien landscape in front of him was a forest, the perspective fish-eyed, shades of pencil and charcoal creating a sense of oppression. The crowded leaves in the forefront confused the eyes, creating a trap, pulling the viewer down to the base, primal immediacy of the hungry, fleshy trees.

She stepped closer, peering at his strange trees. She raised a hand to the base of her throat, an oh-my expression if ever he'd seen one.

Extraordinary, he thought.

"Darrin, this is just...the perspective, the way the leaves crowd in..."

Extraordinary. Amazing?

"*Astounding*," she said, and he chuckled. She wasn't predictable, not at all.

"No, really," she added, as though he'd been disagreeing, and went back to gazing at the drawing. "Just *extraordinary*."

Darrin bobbed his head in acknowledgment, properly humble. He was fully aware that his work had progressed from good to fucking *exceptional* since he'd come to the Greene-Moreland retreat, but Miranda and her dud husband were paying the bills. He knew better than to snap at the hand that was stroking him.

"So, what brings you out this way so late?" Darrin asked. "I thought you were an early-to-bed person."

Miranda smiled. "I am, usually. But I've been thinking about some of your ideas, and I wanted to talk about them a little more."

"My ideas?" Darrin's impromptu philosophy discussions covered everything from religion to best types of pencil. Miranda had sat in once or twice, but the days had been blurring a little lately—he hadn't been sleeping well—and he couldn't remember what he'd talked about when she'd been there.

"For revenge," she said, and her smile turned slightly wicked. "For getting the crazies back."

Darrin stared at her for a beat. Crazies?

"Oh, the survivalists," he said. "The…Jessups?"

"Cole Jessup, that's right," she said, and leaned against one of the dusty stools by the wedging table, where Kim and the other sculptors worked their clay. The sculptors had more room in the big studio, where the pottery wheel was, but Kim had pretty much moved all her tools and shit here, to be where he liked to work. There was dust all over the place, and dried bits of clay always crunching underfoot. "I think Mr. Jessup and his friends could use a little lesson, after all."

Darrin gave a tentative smile, not wanting to appear too eager. She'd been pretty clear about her thoughts on the matter…

although he'd considered carrying out some guerilla retaliation on his own, after the cat tails had been laid out behind the kiln. That shit was just *asking* for it. "Anything in particular you have in mind?"

Miranda laughed. "I don't really think along those lines. I'm not a planner like that, you know? I'm *emotional*. And honestly, I don't think I should be directly involved. You know, with the details. If you're asking me, though…something humiliating would be best, don't you think?"

Darrin grinned. Now she was talking. He'd get Brandon and Kim to help him, maybe Terrence; he had a decent sense of humor (what queen didn't?). A few drinks, a midnight recon and attack…he'd always liked that kind of thing, papering trees on Halloween, unscrewing salt shakers at restaurants, although he'd thought he had outgrown most of that shit. Thinking about it now, though, considering the possibilities, knowing he had the go-ahead from his stick-up-the-ass, self-important patroness…

Epic; this is gonna be epic, he thought. "When should we do it?"

"Oh, you should wait a bit," Miranda said. "The Event is coming up next week. I don't want anything to, to *distract* our community before then."

He could hear her capitalize the *E* in event. Some dork-ass open poetry night she'd scheduled for mid-July, which everyone at the retreat would be forced to endure. Waiting sucked; he didn't want to wait that long, but he wasn't about to argue with her. "Right, yeah. Of course."

"And you'll be careful, you'll take someone with you as a lookout, won't you?" She gave him such a stern, motherly look that he almost laughed. "It could be dangerous."

Darrin nodded soberly. "Don't worry, I'm all over it. You know, when I was in high school, some guys I knew used to go out and do stuff like this, and this one time—"

"Only don't take Terrence. He crumples under pressure."

"Oh, ah, sure."

"You don't think me a hypocrite, do you?" Her frown deepened. "After all my talk about being an adult, for me to even *condone* this kind of thing…it's inappropriate, isn't it?"

"No, not at all. I mean, what they did to your pets. I love animals, their…" He reached for the turn of phrase she'd used more than once, telling her boring stories over dinner. "Their essential innocence, you know? How they're so completely *themselves*."

"That's exactly what I always say," she said, her eyes wide.

"And for those assholes—I'm sorry, excuse me, but it's so infuriating—for them to murder them, and then…then *taunt* you with it." He shook his head, playing the offended sensitive artist that she believed him to be, though actually, he fucking hated cats. Disgusting animals. "They deserve a little payback for something like that."

"Still, you won't tell the others, will you? That it was my idea? Only I'd feel terrible if word got around that I'd encouraged conflict, of any kind." She gave him a sweet smile, and for just a moment, he could see what she'd looked like thirty years younger. "I have my reputation to think about."

"Hey, as far as I'm concerned, you don't know anything about it," Darrin said.

Miranda seemed to relax, her puckery old face softening. "You would do that for me?"

"Consider it done."

"And you'll let me know, the night you choose," she said. "So I'm not *surprised* by anything."

Talk about control freak. Darrin smiled warmly at her. "Absolutely. I'll take care of everything, you just focus on the, ah, *event*."

She brightened. "Five of our community members will be reading," she said, "not including myself. It's going to be a wonderful night for all of us, for the town. For some of the locals, it will be the cultural highlight of the season."

Miranda Greene-Moreland happily chatted her way out the door. It wasn't until after she'd left that it occurred to him to wonder what had changed her mind about retaliation against Jessup and his crew...and to decide that event or no, he would be paying the survivalists a visit in the next night or two. He wouldn't "distract" any of the artists; he'd do his first run solo. Nothing too creative, just broken windows or slashed tires. He'd want it to look like kids, but effective. And it was certainly due. Miranda was pretentious and dull, but Jessup and his people were fucking assholes; they needed a beat-down.

Kim showed up before his planning went any further, a lascivious smile on her uninviting, flat face as she locked the studio door behind her. For the sake of his newly burgeoning erection, Darrin stopped thinking about Miranda Greene-Moreland.

>←

Georgia Duray stood in her small, neat kitchen, watching a grilled cheese sandwich burn on the dented griddle on the stovetop. She wore a grin that she wasn't really aware of...nor was she aware that her hand kept drifting up to touch her hairline, where blood had dried to a sticky film after Nick had beat her with one of his battered cowboy boots. Her husband of almost six years was drunk, of course, passed out upstairs in front of their ancient TV, but the black smoke starting to rise from the burning sandwich would take care of that quickly enough...she thought she had maybe two or three minutes until the smoke alarm kicked on.

Georgia had known when she'd married him that Nick had a problem with his temper, much like her own father had, and knew from the talk shows that he'd probably watched *his* dad beat on his mother when he was a kid. He didn't talk about it, but that kind of thing was generally learned behavior—so said the sincere-faced doctors on those afternoon shows—and would continue to cycle from generation to generation until someone made a conscious effort to stop it. Georgia touched her lower belly, where she imagined her jelly-bean-size baby was curled up sleeping, and again felt the *rightness* of what she'd decided to do; since Nick obviously wasn't interested in changing—he'd gotten worse, in fact, since she'd announced her pregnancy only a month earlier, drinking and then picking fights practically every other night—it was up to *her* to break the cycle.

She'd changed, though. Quiet, sweet little Georgia, five foot two and a hundred pounds, timid to the point of transparency, had become responsible for a life besides her own, and she meant to protect it. After the last beating, three days prior—a series of shoves and slaps and pinches that had finally culminated in a silent, spiteful rape, all because she'd forgotten to unload the dishwasher—she'd had an idea, a dark, breathtaking idea, and that idea had blossomed into a plan.

The smoke from the burning bread and butter was thickening, had begun to pool at the ceiling. Georgia watched cheese ooze out of the sandwich, sizzling when it touched the scratched surface of the pan. It was time.

She pulled her silky pink flowered robe tight around her body, turned, and walked out of the kitchen to the front hall. She stood at the bottom of the stairs, the scuffed tile cold against her bare feet, looking up to the open doorway of their bedroom. Inconsistent blue light from the television played across the wall and the carpet, and she heard screams and gunfire from whatever movie he'd passed out watching. The basket of laundry and a pile of folded towels sat on the landing at the very top of the stairs, and with the lights down, the fishing line she'd stretched between the rail and the wall—some previous owner had installed a safety gate at the top step, and the screws were still sticking out of the wainscoting's base—was invisible, at least from where she stood. Nick, drunk and angry as she expected him to be, would never see it. He wouldn't take notice of the things on the lower three steps, either, a place they regularly put things to take up later—the stack of library books, the box of picture frames she was going to store in the attic, a bag of hangers. Why would he? There was nothing unexpected.

The burning smell was strong, smoke trickling out of the kitchen, rising toward the second-floor landing. The smoke wouldn't wake him up—she knew for a fact he'd consumed almost half a fifth of the cheap bourbon he liked, the one with the medal on the label—but she was pretty sure the alarm would. She placed her hands on her soft belly, an inch or so beneath her navel, not nearly so nervous as she'd expected. She noticed her grin and grinned wider. She was a smart, nice person, and she was going to be a good mother. Nick was a bad man, everyone knew it; they knew he was a drinker and an abuser. He'd go to hell for what he'd done to her. Maybe there had been love, once upon a time, but that didn't change the obvious fact that the world would be a better place without him. He didn't deserve life...and the baby didn't deserve him for a father.

The sensor finally caught the first whiff of smoke and started to sound, urgent, demanding attention. Georgia waited, going over her list of things to do. The list was very short, which seemed best; she'd kept the plan simple, sure that she would mess up anything too complicated.

After what seemed an eternity of the piercing alarm, she heard Nick in the bedroom, a muffled curse. She heard him get off the bed, heard his stumbling footfalls, and there he was, leaning against the bedroom door's frame, his hair sticking up, an ugly expression on his bleary face as he stared up at the smoke detector. He couldn't reach it, she knew, without a chair or a footstool.

He took a single step forward—and then stopped, finally noticing the smoke. He looked down, saw Georgia.

"What the fuck you doin'? Did you burn something?"

Georgia didn't answer.

"Jesus, Georgia, get the fucking stepstool up here!" He staggered to the top of the stairs, the ugly expression just for her, now. "Stupid bitch. What the fuck are you cookin' this late?"

"Grilled cheese." She knew her grin was back and didn't care if he saw it. She had to raise her voice to be heard over the alarm, but that was all right. "I was dizzy, see, after you hit me. After you hit me with your boot. And I started the sandwich, because you told me to make you one, and then I guess I passed out. I didn't even hear the alarm."

He stared at her, blinking, his hands clenching into fists. "You can hear it now, can't you?"

Georgia shook her head, which still ached, badly. "I'm unconscious, Nick. I can't hear anything."

"You are so fucking *stupid*," he said, and started for her—

—and his foot caught the line, and down he came. It happened fast, his arms flying out, his expression turning from ugly anger to ugly surprise. His head hit the wall, his foot slid on the pile of towels, and then he was crashing down, limbs slapping against the rail, and she heard a snapping sound and one of his legs seemed to turn sideways. He somehow managed to miss the books, but the heavy box of frames was in just the right place. Glass broke, and the bag of hangers seemed to explode like a jangling bomb, and then he was at her feet, his right leg twisted under him. There was a bleeding gash in his throat, and the way he held his chest, the gasping, spluttering breath he took and the way his eyes rolled suggested that maybe he'd punctured a lung, or at least had some internal injuries. Serious ones, probably.

He panted, let out a groan, panted more. The alarm continued its bright serenade, although there seemed to be less smoke now; it was hard to say.

"Help," he gasped, and sounded weak, like he was badly hurt. It was going better than she'd even hoped.

The box of frames had been overturned and crushed, shattered glass and broken wood sticking out everywhere. Georgia bent down and used the edge of her robe to pick up a long, jagged shard of thick glass from the floor, careful not to cut herself, careful not to touch the glass with her bare fingers. She leaned over her husband. The cut on his throat was bleeding heavily, but not quite heavily enough.

"Help," he whispered; she could barely hear him over the bleating alarm, and she nodded, and inserted the glass into his wound, and pushed.

Nick screamed, but the sound was too raspy, too broken to be very loud, and he flailed his arms. He belted her hands away, hard enough to hurt, but the pain didn't bother her. That seemed fair. The glass stuck out of his neck, bobbing and weaving, and as he dropped his arms, gasping ever louder, she leaned in and kind of *slapped* at it, with the heel of her hand, still wrapped in the robe. She was surprised how easily it cut. There was a brief resistance but then a kind of *tearing* feeling, and then he was gurgling blood, grabbing at the piece of glass, jerking it out. It fell on the tile by his head and broke.

He tried to scream again, and then he tried to speak, and then he grabbed his bleeding neck and tried to roll over, but there was nothing for him to do. The blood from his throat continued to pulse out, and she saw a spreading stain on the front of his ratty T-shirt a bit lower down, another piece of glass poking through his shirt near his stomach. She watched as a pool of red formed on the tile around his shaking upper body, watched as the panic, the awareness of what was happening brightened his muddy eyes. Not much longer, she thought.

She stood and stepped over him, watching her feet. It wouldn't do to get blood on them, or glass, and she didn't want to disturb the mess on the stairs. She cautiously moved up each step, remembering the night after her best friend's bachelorette party when he'd called her a stupid slut and pushed her into the heavy kitchen table and she'd dislocated her shoulder…then she was grinning again. Not as stupid as he thought. She unknotted the fishing line and carried it to the bathroom, dropped it in the toilet, flushed. Back down the stairs, she warily stepped over her husband—he was unconscious or dead now, and the pulse of blood had become a drool, and the puddle had become a lake— and headed back to the kitchen. The smoke had definitely started to thin out, but that was all right; the alarm would keep going for a while. By now, the neighbors were probably starting to wonder.

The grilled cheese, solidly burned to the pan, was still smoking. Georgia picked up the spatula, took a deep breath—and then let herself fall, dropping the utensil, staggering a bit as she crashed to the floor so that it would look right, should someone find her before she "woke up." The story would tell itself, she was pretty sure. If the house caught on fire, she would come around just enough to crawl to safety, but she thought rescue would occur before then. Their closest neighbors, the Desmonds, were retired and nosy; they were probably already calling the police to complain about the noise or headed over to see what was happening. They knew that Nick drank, and likely knew that he smacked her around sometimes…but she had no doubt that she'd be able to produce a few tears if any questions were asked. The baby had lost his or her father, after all, and that *was* sad.

Georgia closed her eyes to wait, thinking of baby names.

CHAPTER

20

Dream Imagery

The woman with the blood in her hair. Smiling. Thinking about...something burning? Note: Haven't seen this one for three days at least (since 7/7?)

The boy in the hall of mirrors. Maybe 12, 13? It's dark, he thinks he's being followed, he's scared. Feels sick.

The mother bathing her child. Her hair is tied back, she and the baby—2-3 mos?—are both crying. She (mother) weeps from exhaustion.

Big building fire at night. Person watching is a man. Young?

Woman hiding in bushes, sounds of screams and gunfire (can't see anything but leaves). Early. She has to pee. Someone yelling "Get down!"

Precog/One Time Only

Lisa Meyer (nothing about Billings murder/suicide, tho—also nothing about Le Poisson).

B. Glover/Dicks assault.

Devon, drowned.

Lawn King suicide.

Greg Taner, enlist?

Liz Shannon loses virginity/gets pregnant(?)

Amanda stared down at the notebook, trying to think. Should she add another category for thoughts and emotions? She kind of didn't want to, considering how much of it there was...

plus, Devon fucking Mitch Jessup, that time she'd kind of gotten "in" to Eric, John having sex with Sarah, whoever *she* was. Thinking about having to discuss that stuff with grown men made her uncomfortable.

There were several things she didn't want to put down...or didn't know how to put down. Bob and his drinking, for one. She could write that on the way home from John's office, right before Eric had gotten all freaky, she'd felt Bob's deep, persistent desire to be pouring alcohol down his throat...but who would that help? Bob knew he drank, he knew he'd been drinking too much, and he was either helpless to stop it or he just didn't care. And John's confusion, his super brainiac chaos...he was entirely aware of what was going on; he didn't need her to spell it out. He was way smart. Obviously, they were both experiencing mood shifts, changes of thought, difficulties with control...had she changed, too? If anything, she felt stronger lately. Like, cooler, emotionally. She thought that even six months ago, Grace kicking her out would have wrecked her—same with Peter's attempted rape, or even Devon leaving. Now, though, she felt like she was coping really well, not letting it get through to her...changed, though?

Well, not counting the whole totally psychic aspect...

She almost smiled. Sudden access to ESP probably qualified as a change. Now that she thought of it, maybe there were other people in Port Isley who'd gotten, like, powers in the last month or so. Why not? There was all kinds of stuff she couldn't explain—the last few days, wherever she'd been, she'd felt...it was like there were these free-floating pockets of anxiety that she kept blundering into, that didn't seem to be connected to anyone in particular, random feelings of tension, strain, fear...and of *secretiveness*, of things hiding, of things held back. Like there was this incredible energy of restraint, of strong feelings that were being clamped down on, hard, and she didn't think she could explain that to anyone, it was such a weird, unformed feeling. If Devon were here, he'd understand what she meant...

Devon. She looked around his room, where she'd been sleeping since Sid had come home; Devon's uncle had pointed out that if she was going to be around for a while, she might as well have a door she could close. Thank God for Uncle Sid. It was a comfortable room, dark colors, good smells—faded cigarette smoke, hair product. Devon's spendy unisex cologne, the one she always teased him about, telling him it smelled like lemon soap and anal lubricant. She'd talked to him exactly once since he'd been gone, for about two minutes. He'd been on his way out somewhere. He'd sounded...busy. Out of breath almost, to get off the phone, to get moving; his questions were rote, and he cut off her answers. She'd hung up feeling depressed and lonely. And he hadn't even been gone a full week.

Not that she was alone. She had Eric.

She sighed, leaning back on Devon's too-soft bed. Eric. The sex continued to be devastatingly satisfying, which made it hard to work through some of the other parts. They still hooked up at his house, at random hours...his dad and stepmom were perpetually out, cocktails or dinner or boating, though she *had* finally met them. Yikes. His father was a stereotype, a business-guy dad from an eighties comedy flick. He winked all the time. And his fake-boob wife was practically a teenager, which was just creepy. It was hard to believe that they were Eric's family, that he had any connection to them at all.

After their visit to John Hanover's office, after Bob had taken them back to Devon's, Eric had kind of flipped out over what had happened. He'd gone off on her about privacy, about how it wasn't cool that she hadn't told him that she could read minds, how it wouldn't be cool if she tried to read *his* mind, how he'd be offended, blah blah blah. It had been more like a tantrum than a real fight…and she'd felt it coming off him in waves, then—his very deep feelings for her, and his fear that she would leave him if she knew. She didn't call him on it, obviously—considering what he was yelling about, the timing would have been fuck awful— but she'd been a little freaked-out herself. Mostly because his deep feelings were so *dark* to her, so hard to understand. She got a sense of that profound need she'd felt before, lust and longing and something like terror at the thought of losing her, and she didn't know what to do with that. She felt those things too, sometimes. Sort of. Other times, the realization that he was about a hundred times more invested in "them" than she was made her feel like running, as fast and as far away as she could get.

Not today, though. The novelty clock on Devon's wall said she had about half an hour before they were going to meet up. Whatever her brain was up to, her body wanted as much Eric as it could stand…they were both seventeen and willing to try anything; it couldn't possibly get better. And he was her boyfriend, and she wanted to be with him. It was cool, walking with him to get coffee, smoking together, listening to music in his basement…touching him, letting him touch her. The feeling of calm closeness that almost always came after the sex, too, the feeling that everything—fucking *everything*—was going to work out, that was like a drug, that was bliss. Why would she run away from that?

She picked up the notebook again, reread, considered adding more detail—the man at the fire, for instance. She got the impression he was young, but that was more a guess than anything else. He was so close to the flames that his shirt was actually hot, and the front of his hair was frizzled away from the heat; she could feel these things, although she couldn't see him, physically, only the fire. The man wasn't really thinking anything, just feeling how beautiful and consuming the fire was, watching it devour, watching it birth smoke and sparks, watching the night light up...

Her power, her gift, as John had called it, was big and getting bigger. She could even trace the evolution, kind of: her first experiences had been more like movies, only as they'd progressed, she'd started to *be* there, first as part of the scenery—when Brian Glover raped that poor woman, at the fairgrounds—then as, like, a participant. Or, rather, *the* participant, inside the person experiencing the situation. Maybe she would have more waking visions like the one she'd had about Lisa Meyer, or Devon, maybe the circumstances had to be just right, she had to get high first or something, she didn't know. When she wasn't with Eric, she spent most of her time online—Devon hadn't taken his computer, thank God; he'd said his cousin had a laptop he could use—continuing to look up aspects of psychic ability (new favorite word: clairsentience; new favorite concept: mirror neurons) and case histories. She'd even taken the Zener card test, the one where she had to guess the symbol, and scored totally average. Which had actually been a little disappointing. What she'd been seeing, in her dreams—when she tried to describe it, it sounded like mind-reading, but that was an oversimplification; it was mind-*inhabiting*. She'd have thought she'd ace a *card* test, for Christ's sake. And maybe having *that* particular talent would let her see something technically *useful* for a change, names or addresses, dates, possible reasons for why this was happening, all these people feeling and acting so differently...why *hadn't* she known about the cannibal fest at Le Poisson, or that Mr. Billings was going to go home and kill his wife before he killed himself? What other disasters wasn't she seeing?

She looked at her list of dream imagery. The gunfight, the big fire...the mom and baby. Plenty of potential for death and disaster, if any of it was real. But for as specifically as she experienced each image—the woman crouching in the bushes, worrying that she was about to pee herself as weapons cracked impossibly loudly, people screamed, and she held her purse like they would take it from her when they pried it from her cold, dead fingers—their meanings were as vague and untraceable as...well, dreams. What lady? Where? When? The scared kid in the hall of mirrors, that had to be at the carnival that came each August; they had a fun house...but easily thousands of kids went through there. It was in Isley for a full week, a magnet attraction for a half dozen port towns. The lights were out; there seemed to be no one else around—maybe it was closed and the kid had sneaked in. Or maybe there was a power outage. He thought someone was following him, but maybe it was his kid brother or a buddy, sneaking up to scare him.

You don't think so, though. No. The things she felt were strong and mostly unpleasant, and John had told her that she needed to start trusting her instincts, and she thought that the boy in the fun house was in trouble.

She'd talked to Bob last night; he'd said that John had gotten someone from the state to come in and take soil and water samples. Amanda felt fairly certain that they'd find nothing. She didn't know why she thought that, she just did...and she was starting to think that what was happening was, like, a destiny thing, that there was nothing any of them could do about any of it, and she didn't know why she thought *that*, either.

And it's not true, she told herself. Devon was safe. Wasn't he?

Feelings without reasons, random affirmations out of nowhere based on nothing, on air. Bob and John had been compiling stats, making lists, trying to work out a time line; John wanted to go to the police before the end of the week. Amanda already knew that the cops wouldn't even entertain the notion. "Officer, sometime in June things started to change...*and they're still changing!*" Uncanny, not so much. Even with a stack of bizarre incidents to back up their theory, there was no commonality, there was no *reason* they could point to, to explain the changes in Port Isley.

"He's here," Amanda said aloud, surprising herself a little. That night at Pam's party, a million years ago…she'd thought, *he's here*, and she'd started crying because she was already totally freaking on the Lisa Meyer thing, and she'd been confused… but what had her stoned brain been trying to tell her? Was there some significance? She hadn't even thought about it since telling Devon, a day or so after…

She turned a page in the notebook, wrote the two words down at the top of the page, underlined them. *He's here…*tapped her pen on the innocuous words…jotted beneath them, *influence = man?*

She tried to follow the thought but got nothing; she had no sense that she was having some brilliant insight; maybe, maybe not. She looked at the clock again, a ticking black cat with eyes and a tail that moved from side to side, and decided that she wanted to clean up a little before meeting Eric. A wipe-down, some deodorant, mouthwash. She closed the notebook and dropped the pen on top of it. She didn't know if anything would come of the effort she was making to keep track of what she saw—but it felt good to be involved, to be actively participating in her life. Since that first time, that first terrible vision, she'd wished for nothing more than for things to go back to the way they were, before…and now…

Now I want to keep it, she thought, looking into the mirror over Devon's toothpaste-spattered sink, looking into herself as she worked her fingers through her hair. How many people had the opportunity to really do something, to make a difference? She didn't know what to expect anymore, everything was different because *she* was different, and that was as liberating as it was frightening as it was exciting.

She smiled at herself, liking the light in her eyes. She'd always hoped she might be special, that she *would* be, and now it was true.

>‹

A few days after Tommy got back, Jeff came over early, like nine in the morning, and asked if he wanted to go inner tubing down at the old piers with some of the other kids. Tommy immediately agreed. Mom was being weird, which he had pretty much expected—Aunt Karen getting hurt and all; Tommy felt a little weird himself. Dad had told him before he left that his aunt had been attacked and assaulted; his mother had said the same thing, used the same words. It sounded better than beat up and raped, he figured, but he understood what had happened. He felt bad for her.

What he *hadn't* expected was to come home from his entirely boring visit with Dad and Vanessa to find his mother all excited and happy about John Hanover, the geeky doctor they'd met at the picnic who was over *every night*. They tried to hide it. The doctor showed up at midnight and was gone by like, seven, but Tommy wasn't as clueless as they obviously thought.

He swallowed a sudden foul taste, thinking of the muffled sounds he'd heard just last night. Disgusting. The guests were all gone; Aunt Karen practically never came out of her room, and Mom was flitting around like a schoolgirl, all smiles and blushes...which was even extra weird, because since he'd come back, she'd been all over him asking him about *his* feelings, asking if he felt different about anything, when *she* was the one who was obviously different. She was too...*happy* wasn't the right word; he liked to think that happy wouldn't bother him...

Stupid, maybe, he thought, walking next to Jeff, listening to the slap of their sneakers going down the hill, cool rubber on warming asphalt. By trying to hide the affair, she was lying to him, and that made him feel...it made him feel like punishing her by not thinking nice things about her. Even the guilt that accompanied the thought was fleeting. She was acting *stupid*. She barely knew the guy.

The sun was still mild, but he could already feel it revving up to be another scorcher. In addition to not asking anyone's permission to leave—his mother hadn't been up; she'd been sleeping in a lot just lately, so he'd left a note on the kitchen table—he hadn't put on any sunblock. He hadn't forgotten, he just hadn't done it, and feeling the warming sun on the back of his neck, he felt a kind of nervous satisfaction that he couldn't explain.

I'll tell her I forgot because I was so tired, he thought. *I'll tell her that I couldn't sleep, because of all the fucking noise.*

It only took about ten minutes to walk down the hill, and unhappy thoughts about his mother kept him mostly distracted from Jeff's random comments about the town, about the kids, school, and this and that. There were a lot of people out and about, more as they neared the bottom of the hill—summer people, Jeff informed him with a sneer—brightly dressed, carrying to-go coffee cups, wearing sandals and expensive shades. Tommy liked not being grouped in with the tourists, although technically, he supposed he was a summer person, since they'd leave at the end of the season. Back to that little apartment without a yard and seventh grade at a school where he would be the new kid, where his mom would be the new teacher. All of which would suck, but he guessed that would be the end of ol' Doctor John; at least there was that. The idea of some *stranger* kissing and touching and, and *fucking* his mother...gross. It made him want to throw up.

As the two boys got closer to the old pier, the crowd thinned dramatically. They headed east along Water and were quickly past the nicer eateries and shops, past the historical buildings and the town's trio of small parking lots, all crammed with expensive cars. As picturesque as Port Isley's main thoroughfare was, twenty minutes straight along the water down the exhaust-stinking road and the view became a gas station, a warehouse, and the run-down Seaside Motel with a gravel parking lot. There was a kid at the motel, standing in the shade of the front office, smoking a cigarette.

"Hey, that's Trevor," Jeff said, perking up as they got closer. "His uncle works there. Trevor!"

Trevor shot them a cool, disinterested look, exhaling smoke. He was tall and skinny and looked a little older, maybe fifteen. Tommy had seen him before, hanging around at Kehoe Park right after that girl had been killed, but they hadn't spoken. Trevor had a mean smile, curved and smirking. He'd been the kid who'd come up with the idea to ride bikes over the place where they'd found the body. Tommy had met guys like him—not many, thank God, and he'd never had to hang out with any of them—and was pretty sure that Trevor probably laughed whenever someone got hurt and talked shit about people that weren't around. It was written all over him.

"Is he coming?" Tommy asked quickly, his voice low. They were still approaching Trevor, who didn't move to meet them. Jeff shrugged, his attention fixed on the older kid.

"Hey," Jeff said again, and Trevor finally gave him a nod.

"We're going tubing," Jeff said. "You wanna come?"

Trevor deliberately looked them up and down, then took a drag. "Tubing on what?"

"Ah, Mike T. and Jeremy are meeting us down there; they're bringing their stuff," Jeff said. "You got a smoke?"

Trevor ignored him. "You the new kid?" he asked, looking at Tommy hard. Like he thought he was Clint Eastwood and Tommy was a street punk.

Tommy held his ground and his silence, only nodding. He instinctively knew that whatever he said, Trevor would find a way to use it to make him look dumb.

"Your aunt runs Big Blue, doesn't she?" Trevor asked. From the way his eyes sparkled, he already knew the answer.

"Yeah," Tommy said, waiting for the inevitable. Wondering if it was going to bother him.

"She got raped, right?" He shook his head in mock disparagement, stealing looks at Tommy's face. "Got fucked by practically the whole football team…cops arrested 'em and everything… that's rough, man, that totally *sucks*."

Tommy wasn't as big as Trevor, but he was tall for his age, and sturdy. And his dad had taught him how to throw a punch last summer. In spite of his suddenly hammering heart, the fearful knowledge that he'd never been in an actual fight, not once, he decided immediately that he wasn't going to put up with any shit.

That's how bullies work, his father had said, after Scott Morgan had threatened to beat him up at his old school last year, when his parents were still together. *They'll try to intimidate you. But if you stand up to them right away, let 'em know you won't put up with their bullshit, they'll back off, look for an easier target.* His father had been on his second beer after dinner or he wouldn't have cursed like that in front of him, which made the advice all the more valued, all the more credible. Tommy had never had cause to apply the principle—Scott Morgan had been expelled for fighting some other kid, not a week later—but had always wondered if he would, when the appropriate occasion arose. If he'd have the *balls*.

"Yeah," he said, through an actual flash of red brought on by speaking, and the abrupt rage spoke for him, the words spilling out of his mouth without his thinking them first. "She got hurt;

that's right. Did you feel a need to discuss it? Because I really don't want to."

His heart was still thumping overtime, but he welcomed the rush of adrenaline, the feeling that maybe it would be good to fight, to curl his fingers in and wrap his thumb around them and drive it into this mean kid's narrow face...and maybe Trevor saw it, because he dropped his gaze first, dropping the subject of Aunt Karen along with it. He looked back at Jeff, like Tommy was now beneath his interest.

"Any girls coming?" he asked Jeff.

"Mike's sister, probably," Jeff said. "If she does, she'll bring some of her friends."

Trevor scowled and dropped his butt on the ground. He let it burn. "Isn't his sister, like, ten?"

"Kylie's eleven," Jeff said. "And I think some of her friends are older. Hey, maybe Jenny Todd will show up with the Luther kids. Kylie's friends with Valerie Luther, right?"

Why are you trying to impress this guy? Tommy thought, looking between the two older boys. Trevor was an asshole. He didn't want to spend the day hanging out with an asshole.

"Huh," Trevor said. "Nothing better to do in this loser-fuck town, I guess."

They started walking again, Trevor promptly falling behind, trailing after as he lit another cigarette. Jeff seemed pleased that the older boy was coming with them. Tommy didn't like it, but with the weird, powerful anger leaking out of him, the first hesitant feelings of pride welling up—*it worked! I did it, and it worked!*—he felt like he could handle himself.

Another five minutes walking, past an abandoned cannery, down a short, steep hill next to an ancient parking lot to a strip of dirty, gravelly sand. Jeff talked the whole way, trying to sound cool, cursing more than he had before Trevor had joined them.

The beach was small and smelled kind of rotten. There was a much nicer beach down below the lighthouse, where the summer people went to tan and picnic; the sand there was fine and clean, meticulously maintained. Aunt Karen had taken them down there a few weeks ago; over lunch, she'd said that the beach was fortified by community tax dollars, the sand actually towed up from farther south down the coast each year to replace what winter always took. Tommy found the idea fascinating, that they'd been sitting on a beach that would mostly be gone come November. That night he'd had a bad dream that he was standing on a tiny shelf of rock at the base of a high cliff with the deep ocean lapping at his ankles and nowhere to go, and waves were starting to rise out in front of him, vast, towering waves…he remembered the dream because he'd woken in a burst of terror as the first freezing wave had been about to crash over him, and then he had lain there in the dark for a minute, feeling nightmare echoes. The waves had been scary, but the other fear was deeper, harder to name—it was just the *water*; the dark, cold, powerful blue had stretched out in front of him like eternity, so big that it could hide anything, anything at all…

Here, where the ferries had once docked—before the service had been moved to Port Angeles twenty years back, Jeff had told him on the way down the hill—the dark, glass-strewn rocks were littered with cans and bottles and assorted bits of trash. And there was the pier, massive and old, chipped concrete and gray wood extending out over the water, supported by rows of greased piles. The smell worsened and defined, became an oily, fishy kind of rotten, but Tommy didn't really notice it after a minute or two. There were a bunch of other kids down by the piles on the rough sand, standing amid a collection of inner tubes and bright plastic beach toys, buckets, rafts, and a couple of beach balls. There were two guys around his age. As they got closer, Tommy could see that there were three girls there too, and one little kid, a boy, maybe five or so. There was also a much older girl, built like a woman from a sports magazine. She wore shades and a striped swimsuit top and a piece of gauzy light fabric wrapped around her hips.

Jenny Todd, I presume, Tommy thought, still happy with himself for standing up to Trevor. Still a little surprised, too, by how much he'd wanted to pound Trevor's face in. Presumably someone would do it, eventually. His dad was fond of saying how people always got what was coming to them, and Tommy wanted very much to believe that; it just seemed fair.

The waves out in the bay were tipped with white, but the water at the base of the pier was mostly still, the lap rhythmic and slow. It was shallow, too. There wasn't a cloud in the sky. Tommy could feel his exposed skin sucking up the heat. Another hour and he'd be a lobster. He'd make a point of sticking close to the pier. Under it, maybe.

They approached the group, Trevor still hanging back, acting indifferent. Toward the end of the pier, a man with fishing gear leaned against the rail, looking down at them. Looking at the teenage girl, Tommy figured as he got a closer look at her himself. She was tall and had long legs and round hips and big breasts; she had a heart-shaped face and a pretty smile; she had shining reddish-brown hair piled on top of her head, with long wisps of it curling down the back of her neck. She was the prettiest girl he'd ever seen in real life.

Jeff introduced him around, kind of, but Tommy missed some of the names, working to appear cool and clever and witty by the way he stood, trying to stare at Jenny without staring. He had half an erection from the very slight glance he'd dared at her breasts, and willed it to go away, told himself that she was at least seventeen, that the smile she gave him was friendly, nothing more. Much as he might wish otherwise. He'd known about masturbation for quite a while, and he wasn't a fanatic or anything, but he'd been more into it just lately...like, a lot more. And he didn't think it on purpose, but he *did* think it, that Jenny was going to have a starring role at some point in the very near future, like tonight.

"Hey, Jenny," Trevor said, nodding at the beautiful girl, and she smiled pleasantly enough at him, too, but there was zero interest in the look. She might have been smiling at a mailman or a waiter or something. Tommy felt a weird kind of satisfaction that she wasn't interested in the older boy, either. She pulled out a lime-green cell phone about a second later and started tapping keys.

"Sissy, will you keep an eye on Jay?" she said, and one of the girls nodded eagerly. Jay's sissy, Valerie, was maybe nine, had frizzy hair and a rounded, unformed body and a missing tooth. Another girl volunteered to assist, and they promptly surrounded the little boy, who was rubbing handfuls of dirty sand on his stomach for no apparent reason. Her babysitting duties delegated, Jenny walked away from the group, still punching keys. There was a blanket and a couple of bags of stuff in a relatively clean patch of sun, next to the rocky wall separating the beach from the parking lot above. Jenny knelt on the blanket, nearly knocking over a tall can of energy drink, arranging her long legs just so...

Tommy wasn't the only one looking. He glanced away long enough to see that Jeff, his friend Mike, and Trevor were all watching her, various dazed expressions on their faces. Jeremy, a glasses-wearing, quiet kid who seemed younger, was more interested in claiming the best raft. He and one of the little girls were already exclaiming over the chill of the water.

Tommy caught a small movement from the pier. The fisherman was still looking down, but he was watching the kids—them, not Jenny. He had thinning, sandy hair. His bland, middle-aged face was red, sunburnt maybe, and the look he wore…

"Who's that guy?" Tommy asked. The look he wore was creepy. He looked *hungry*. But as soon as he realized that they were all turning to look at him, he backed away from the rail, suddenly deeply interested in his fishing rod. He jammed a shapeless sun hat on his head and looked out over the bay.

"Some perv, probably," Jeff said. "Come on."

They set out the rafts and inflatable tubes, the girls giggling and shrieking as they positioned themselves on the plastic toys. Tommy got a clear, purple-tinted ring with a patch on the side and rubber handles. The water was uncomfortably cold, but the handles allowed him to pull his butt mostly out, and his feet quickly went numb. After a few moments in the reflected sun, the cold felt good.

They floated around the end of the pier, the waves keeping them from drifting too far out. They paddled out to the drop off, Tommy getting chills even looking out to where the water turned black. Thinking about that dream he'd had, about the depthless ocean. Thankfully, the water was too cold and choppy there for them to linger.

The sun had grown hot, and everything seemed hazed out in shades of brightness, and Tommy realized he was having a good time, that he liked being out on the water. Jay, the little kid, got splashed and started screaming that he wanted to make sand castles instead, so he and his sister and the other girls paddled their rafts back to the beach. Trevor tried to smoke, sitting on a big blue foam board, and immediately dropped his lighter in the water. Jeff and Tommy and Mike all cracked up. After several choice curses, Trevor wondered aloud if Jenny had a light, and kicked himself back under the pier, muttering about "fucking little kids" as he went.

"Trevor's kind of a dick," Tommy ventured, when he was sure Trevor was out of earshot. Jeff didn't say anything, but Mike nodded vigorously.

"I heard he got busted for stealing a couple of weeks ago," Jeremy said, floating on a flat foam mat shaped liked a frog. He pushed his glasses up on the bridge of his pudgy, peeling nose. "He took some stuff from the hardware store. His mom had to go down to the police station and get him."

"Aw, Trevor's all right," Jeff said.

"No, he's totally a dick," Mike said. "He pushes people around all the time, and that's the second time he's gotten caught. My dad says he's a bad egg."

"A bad egg?" Jeff smirked. "That's stupid. Who says *bad egg*?"

Tommy was about to volunteer that he'd used the term himself, a perfectly acceptable descriptive when you didn't want to say *asshole* in front of your parents, when from the beach came a high, squealing scream. Tommy looked over and saw that Jay had stripped out of his SpongeBob shorts and food-stained tee and was running bare-ass naked across the sand, laughing while his sister shouted after him to stop. Jenny's blanket was empty, she was nowhere to be seen, but it didn't look like an emergency or anything; he was just being a little kid, and now the other girls were chasing after him, calling his name. Jay shrieked and ran faster, his pudgy little legs kicking up sand, his babyish arms pumping, his round butt shiny white, practically glowing in the sun. He should be falling down; he was wearing sandals that appeared to be on the wrong feet, but he was losing them, fast. It was kind of funny.

Tommy shaded his eyes, looking up at the pier, where the fisherman had been hanging out all morning—and saw that the fisherman was watching Jay, and that he had his hand in his pants and was moving it rhythmically, his glassy-eyed stare fixed on the little boy. They were close enough to the pier, it was maybe fifteen feet up and not far from where they were floating, that Tommy could clearly see what he was doing—but he couldn't believe it; he couldn't believe that someone would do that, right in the open like that.

A little kid, Tommy thought, and felt sick.

"Hey," Tommy said, then suddenly he was screaming it. "*Hey!*"

The fisherman turned and looked at him, still jerking it, and he was staring right at Tommy as he shuddered, his mouth falling open, his tongue sticking out just a little…and then he had his hand out of his pants and was scooping up his gear, turning, running away.

"Was he jacking *off*?" Jeff asked. "He was, wasn't he?"

Everyone was staring at Tommy. Even Jay had stopped running. Jenny and Trevor appeared from under the pier a beat later, blinking in the sudden brightness, both of them holding cigarettes.

"I didn't see," Jeremy said. "Was he?"

"That's fucked-up," Mike said, and it was Tommy's turn to nod, and then they were all paddling toward shore, Tommy dropping into the icy water as they got closer, his good feelings about the day turning confused and falling away as they dragged their floats onto the sand, and everyone was talking at once. Then Jenny was telling everyone to shut up, she was trying to call the cops, and Sissy was holding her little brother wrapped in a sandy towel, her eyes filled with tears. Jay started crying that he wanted to go home. Tommy could relate; he just wasn't sure where home was, exactly; not today.

>‹

Friday morning, John and Bob went to meet Amanda at the closed deli half a block from the police station. John was tired; Bob had picked him up at his house a few hours after he'd gotten home from Sarah's, which meant he'd slept, including last night's nap, five hours? Not so bad, except he couldn't remember the last time he'd had a full eight. Research, caseload, his long, lovely nights with Sarah...six, seven days? As they walked toward the deli, Bob was telling him about what he'd heard only that morning, rumors of orgies out at the artists' retreat, but John was trying to focus on the meeting ahead, on presentation, on objectives. What had seemed so clear only a week before had become clouded—and at the same time, the deep connection he'd made with Sarah had actually clarified some things for him, had made him reconsider the nature of the influence. They'd talked a lot about the possibility—the *probability*—that the intimacy they were experiencing had been boosted chemically by whatever was happening to Port Isley and its inhabitants...but Sarah had pointed out, and rightfully so, that if that were true, the things occurring could not easily be categorized as wholly bad or destructive. Considering how fulfilled he felt spending time with her, how mutual the attraction was, it was hard to argue. He found it hard to argue with her about much of anything, he was so consumed by their sudden, incredible affair.

I'm fine, he told himself, gripping the thin file he carried more tightly. At least well enough to take action. Hadn't they found evidence? They had enough, he was sure they had enough.

There had been four suicides in Port Isley since about the first week of June, including Ed Billings and Dick Calvin. Last year, there had been one. All year. There had been four murders in the same six-week period—Lisa Meyer; Ed Billings's wife, Darva; Sadie Truman; and Annie Thomas. Last year, and for two years before, none. Zero. Even accidental deaths were up within the city limits, two in the last week—a local had fallen down his stairs during a small house fire, and another had perished in a single-car crash; both men had had blood alcohol levels over .15. Bob had learned that the car crash victim had been in AA, had claimed to be sober for better than six years, and had attended his meetings religiously...up until sometime in June. There had been Karen's rape and a handful of other probable sexual assaults—things that hadn't made it to police report stage, that likely never would. Like what had happened—almost happened—to Amanda with her mother's boyfriend. They'd kept the research focused on what they could prove, but Bob had dug up a lot more, through conversations with the families of hospital workers, chats with friends and neighbors. Sexual abuse and domestic violence were up, and there were undoubtedly a half dozen ugly scenes playing out unwitnessed and unreported for every one that Bob had heard about.

But how many stories are there out there like ours? Sarah had asked, her voice soft in the darkness, the feel of her naked skin like cream, like velvet, clichés that didn't even touch the epiphany of her body against his. *How many others like us? Letting go of sadness, anger, old defense mechanisms? Embracing the good people we find?*

John let out an involuntary sigh, remembering what had followed. On a purely intellectual level, he knew that what was happening between them couldn't be love. This was neurochemistry in action, hardwired instinct plus a projection of hope, beliefs about intimacy...but he also felt an excited flutter in the pit of his stomach every time he thought of her, and he couldn't make himself not feel that.

She *did* have a point. If there were others like them, connecting, then the changes weren't all bad. But people discovering themselves wasn't something they could quantify, nor was it the kind of stuff even Bob could get, asking around.

The reporter had proved to be extremely adept at hearing things; he had a wide network of people who liked to gossip and was friendly with any number of summer residents besides. John supposed he shouldn't have been surprised—Robert Sayers had been a regular byline in a major city newspaper when John himself had been in diapers—but the casual finesse with which Bob drew people out and got them talking was remarkable. John had thought that he'd have the edge, considering his career choice—

and how much Bob drinks

—but his own questions had turned up little. The Catholic priest he'd spoken to had wanted to tell him more, he was sure of it, but in the end, the good father had clammed up, saying that the only thing happening in Port Isley was God's will. And the social worker had been a brick wall, start to finish. He'd learned that church attendance was up all over—so much so that the local Baptist minister was thinking about applying for a permit to hold Sunday services at the fairgrounds—but that wasn't particularly helpful. John had turned the interviewing over to Bob and spent his very few spare hours compiling the notes Bob gave him and figuring out how to run a probability-statistics program on his aging computer. If he'd run it right—and he was pretty sure he had—they had more than enough to convince Stan Vincent, and then the chief would…he would do something. Maybe it was the lack of sleep, but John couldn't seem to imagine much further than their meeting with Vincent. They would lay out the facts, the *facts*, and Vincent would nod slowly, understanding filling his eyes, and then…

He'll know what to do. John was sure.

They turned the corner on Main, and there was Amanda, alone. She sat cross-legged on the curb in front of the deserted deli, smoking, reading a book, wearing all black except for her half-laced, screaming-orange high-tops. She looked up and saw the two of them approaching, dog-eared her paperback, and slipped it into a flowered bag.

She stood up, dropping her cigarette to the pavement. "This is a bad idea," she said. She ground the butt into the cement with her toe. "He's not going to listen."

John held up the file. "Two-hundred-percent increase in violent attacks in a three-month period, better than eighty percent of those in the last six weeks. Five weeks, really. Massive increases in medications prescribed and purchased, hospital ER reports, complaints filed...ah, church attendance, counseling sessions scheduled...vandalism..."

He looked to Bob for help, his brain too tired to remember any more, but Bob was looking at Amanda.

"You get a feeling for this?" he asked. "About Chief Vincent?"

She did a head shrug, tipping to one side and back. "Maybe. I don't know. I think it's just what I think."

Bob nodded. "When I saw him at the hospital, he seemed... hostile, I guess. Not like himself."

John had to smile at that. "We can welcome him to the club, then."

Bob snorted, and Amanda grinned.

"I suppose you have a point," Bob said. "Still. We could go to the county sheriff's, bypass the problem entirely."

"The evidence is important; it's how we'll get people from the state or the feds to listen," John said. "But I'm counting on the fact that the chief lives here, that he's well aware of the increase in violent crime...and that he may be experiencing symptoms himself. When he sees the numbers, realizes how bad things are, and that there's a possible *reason* for how he's probably been feeling..."

They looked mollified, if not convinced. Sarah had agreed with his logic when he'd discussed it with her. She'd stopped worrying about the effects of the agent on herself or her son— her belief was that whatever was happening, the people who were inherently stable would remain so—but she *was* concerned about having Tommy in an unsafe environment. John wasn't sure how she'd come to her conclusions, but she seemed committed to them.

Maybe she just doesn't want to leave, he thought. Karen had made it clear that she wanted Sarah to stay for as long as she could.

And maybe she doesn't want to leave me. The thought was intoxicating. If they could convince Stan Vincent to take them seriously and then to take over, to deal with what was happening, he could shift his focus back to work, where it belonged…and to Sarah and what was building between them. She was going to talk to Tommy, soon—they'd both agreed that until they were sure they wanted to continue their relationship, it was better that he not know the depth of their involvement—but John had never felt more certain of anything.

"Let's do this," he said firmly, and Bob nodded once, and Amanda sighed, and they started for the station.

21

Ian Henderson watched the trio of locals walk out of the chief's office, their faces red, their expressions resentful and angry. He'd recognized Bob Sayers and the shrink, John Hanover, when they'd come in, asking to speak to Vincent. Henderson had spent the next ten minutes trying to place the teenage girl, stealing looks through the wide window to the chief's office from his desk. He wouldn't have admitted it, but he was also keeping an eye on the meeting. On the chief.

Vincent was standing at his door, watching them leave—and when he saw Henderson watching, he waved him over.

"Got a real winner this time." The chief gritted his teeth as though he were trying to smile as he ushered Henderson in.

"What did they want to talk about? That was Grace Young's daughter, wasn't it?"

Vincent ignored the questions, went to his desk, and picked up a handful of papers. He walked to the garbage can and deliberately dropped them in. He was trying to appear casual, but his every move radiated anger and strain. "Town's falling to pieces, swear to *Christ*. I expect bullshit from the summer people, you know?"

Henderson raised his eyebrows, waited.

"It would seem that we're not doing our jobs," Vincent said. He paced back to his desk, turned, seemed not to know what to do with himself.

"They said that?"

"They said exactly that," Vincent snapped. "They apparently didn't think I'd *noticed* that crime is up, that we're having an over-the-top summer this year." He grinned his tense facsimile of a smile. "And get this—it's all because of the spores."

"*Spores?*"

"Spores or pollen or fairy dust. Something in the air or the water, making people *feel* things. Last week it was an alien invasion; that kid with his tinfoil hat." Vincent shook his head. "What do you think's coming next? I'm betting government conspiracy."

Henderson nodded but felt an inkling of concern. It had definitely been a whackjob summer, people calling or coming in to talk about some extremely strange shit. Besides the death count, the number of public and private disturbances being reported, the vandalism at the docks and out at the cemetery...it sure as hell seemed like *something* was up with the citizenry, local and summer. Just in the last couple of days, even. A middle-aged tourist woman had freaked out at the grocery store, crawled into the meat case, and started tearing open packages of hamburger, rolling in it, moaning. She kept saying that the blood would make her young again. Trent and LaVeau had fielded that one. When they'd tried to pull her out, she'd snapped at them with her teeth, like a dog. They'd actually had to call the paramedics in to shoot her up with something. A gay couple had come in a few weeks back, reported harassment, notes on their door, late-night calls— yesterday, someone had smeared feces all over their front porch. And some skeeze had masturbated in front of a bunch of local kids down at the old dock. That was only the weird stuff, too.

Spores...he vaguely remembered watching a show some years back about the Salem witch trials—how maybe all those people were accused and convicted because there had been this one kind of mold on the crops that made everyone crazy for a little while. Wasn't he just thinking that Vincent was acting different, that he'd changed?

"They wanted to know how I'm *feeling*," Vincent sneered. "How the fuck do I know? I feel fucking *stressed*, and is it any wonder, with all the shit going down? Like I don't have enough to do without taking our town's *emotional* well-being into account."

"People have been...ah, more tense lately," Henderson ventured.

"Of course they have! I'm right there with 'em!" Vincent had started to pace again. "Spores, aliens, Saturn rising. All the nutcases are out and about, and maybe there *is* a reason."

He stopped to look at Henderson. "Bottom line, though, who gives a shit? I mean, really. What matters isn't how people *feel*, I feel all kinds of crappy. I'm understaffed for this shitstorm of a summer, I can't seem to get to the goddamn budget for next year—hell, my *wife* left me—but that doesn't give me the right to just, just fuck *off*, does it? Do whatever the hell I feel like?"

He spread his arms, his expression echoing his words: *Does it? Huh?*

"Ashley left?" It slipped out before he could think twice. Vincent was a solid family man. He didn't go on and on about his wife and kid like some, but when he did talk about Ashley—a petite, shy brunette who sometimes brought double batches of homemade cookies to the station—it was always with warmth and respect. And he obviously doted on his little girl.

"She took the baby and went to her mother's for a while," Vincent said, looking away. His hands fell to his sides. "Said I was letting it all get to me, and she didn't want Lily to..."

He trailed off, shook his head, and then he was walking again. "Ah, we'll work it out," he said. "Maybe I *am* going crazy, maybe they're all right, there's a conspiracy or something. Thing is, it's what we *do* that matters, isn't it? Isn't that the fucking *point*?"

"Fucking A," Henderson said, thinking of Annie, who'd died trying to do the right thing.

"We've got to keep the citizens in line, keep it tight," Vincent said. "And if they fuck up, we've got to make sure they're held responsible for their actions." Henderson nodded along with him. "It's our yard, am I right? Our yard, our house, our *business*."

That sure as hell hit home. The two of them had led the team (if you could call Frank LaVeau and Dave Miller a team, anyway) that had collared the trio of teen rapists. The very hour that county got wind of the arrests, Wes Dean had been in motion, moving the kids and their squawking families to the county seat to await processing. To the sheriff's house. Rick Truman was in Seattle being held on aggravated murder—the lawyers were trying to hammer something out to save him from a needle in the arm—and Sheriff Dean had managed to turn the wrap-up on Poisson over to the SPD, gotten a friendly city judge and an assistant DA to make it happen by piecemealing out the forensics to Seattle's lab and assigning some suck-ass lieutenant to run the interviews. For whatever reason, the sheriff had a hard-on for Vincent. Jurisdictional strife could get nasty, and was so common that it had become a cliché; Henderson had seen grown men bicker over whether a warrant would stand like snot-nosed preschoolers screaming about who got to play with a toy—but the animosity that the sheriff directed at the police chief seemed both sincere and personal. With the way Dean had been fucking them lately, Henderson could get behind the idea of cutting him out of the loop.

"*Our* business," Vincent repeated. Henderson nodded again and felt a renewal of fierce loyalty to the man. So what, the chief didn't want to kiss ass anymore? He was a strong, brave cop trying to do what was right, and why the fuck had Henderson wanted to be an officer in the first place, if not to take care of business? To protect and fucking serve?

"You're with me on this, aren't you, Ian?"

"You know I am," Henderson said, and clapped his hand on Vincent's shoulder, which seemed much thinner than it should be. "All of us are, Chief."

Vincent's smile was finally sincere. "We'll do whatever needs to be done," he said. "And we'll just see what happens, next time the sheriff decides to drop by to play catch."

Henderson laughed, thinking of how good it would be to stick it to ol' Western Dean, not thinking at all of spores or mold or some TV show he'd seen a million years back about seasons of insanity. Not that it mattered, anyway.

><

Sarah hung up the phone, one hand pressed to her heart. She immediately started for Tommy's room, feeling dazed. Feeling hurt. Guilt would come next, she suspected.

Upstairs, Karen was asleep, so she stepped quietly down the hall. Tommy's door was closed, and she stopped in front of it. When had he started to close his door? Why hadn't she noticed?

Because of John, she thought, and yep, there was the guilt, right there. It had taken less than a week for her to fall madly, passionately in love with John. She'd thought she'd been doing a good job since Tommy had come home from his father's, making sure he was OK, focusing on being the mom of an almost-teen, but she'd only been going through the motions; she'd taken her son at his word that he was fine and gone back to counting the hours until John was with her. That too-brief moon-shadow time in the dark of her bedroom, touching him, being touched.

Selfish, she told herself. *Selfish and blind*. She believed John's theory, that emotions were being heightened somehow, that the citizens and natives of Port Isley were being affected; people might have died, her own sister had been raped...and all she'd been able to focus on were her feelings for John, so sudden and surprising that she'd let her common sense take a vacation. She'd chosen to decide that everything was fine because *she* was fine.

Are you, though? She couldn't look at his closed door any longer, by herself out in the hall. She tapped. "Tommy? Got a minute?"

A long pause, then a reluctant, "Yeah."

She opened the door and stepped inside. Tommy was at his computer, his back to her. On his monitor, a ghost was running over dark fields. She winced, looking at the dark, angry red of his neck. He'd come home two days ago with a bad sunburn and a distant countenance after going out with his friends without permission. She'd rationalized the minor act of rebelliousness: he'd just come back from time with his father; he was pushing boundaries. And he *had* left a note. He hadn't had much of an appetite for lunch or dinner, which she'd chalked up to the sunburn. She'd given him aspirin and run a soda bath and hadn't suspected that anything...that anything terrible might have happened.

"Pause your game?" she asked.

"Just a second." He typed something out, taking his time, and she felt a surge of intense frustration, there and gone in a second—and it finally occurred to her to wonder what she meant to say to him.

He turned and looked at her with a carefully bland expression and worried eyes. He couldn't hide his anxiety from her... *at least there's still that*...and a small, rational thought floated through her head, that everything was crazy and going too fast, that no one was OK, that she should pack up her son and her sister and get out, get away. People weren't supposed to feel so much or change so quickly—

"*What?*" Tommy said, and that single word was so sullen, so petulant, that she snapped back to the moment. To her relationship with her son.

"The police just called," she said, and was gratified to see him drop his gaze. She was ashamed of the petty satisfaction but couldn't seem to help it. "They wanted to know when I was going to bring you in to make a statement. About what happened at the pier."

He didn't speak, didn't look up.

"Why didn't you tell me?" she asked, and she sounded whiny to her ears. "Why didn't you say something?"

No answer, and she took a step closer to him. "Were you— were you scared to say anything, or maybe a little embarrassed?"

"No," he said. "It just wasn't a big deal."

A grown man masturbating in front of children? She couldn't imagine that he hadn't been distressed. He obviously didn't want to talk about it; he was still staring at the floor. She didn't want to handle this wrong, but she wasn't sure what to say. "Honey, I know that you're—you're growing up, and I couldn't be more proud of you, you know that, right?"

"Yeah." He didn't look up.

"I just—if something bad happens, I really want you to tell me. It's my job to protect you and make sure that...that if you want to talk about something, you feel like you can. To me."

He mumbled something, still staring at the floor.

"What?"

He finally looked up, and his expression was as unpleasant as his tone. "I said you've been so busy lately, with that guy. That doctor. I didn't want to *bother* you."

Sarah crossed her arms, and it was her turn to look away. She took a deep breath. "Did you—did you see us, or..."

"I heard you, OK?" The red in his face deepened, and the words spilled out, angry and miserable. "I keep hearing you, and it's, it's *gross* and you don't even *know* him."

He had completely changed the subject, and she got it, then, understood what he was telling her. She hadn't told him about John, so he'd decided to keep something from her. Her guilt intensified, but there was some relief, too. He'd had a reason, he wasn't growing up and away from her, *he won't keep anything like this from me again*. Even telling herself, she knew better.

"I should have told you," she said. "I'm sorry. When Karen got hurt, John—Dr. Hanover—came to help her, and he and I—"

"I don't want to *hear* about it, Mom. God!" His embarrassed shock was melodramatic, so essentially teenage that it might have been funny to someone watching. She wasn't laughing; what must he think of her? What did twelve-year-old boys think about sex?

"I'm trying to tell you that we're—that it may be serious between us," she said. "I know it's happened fast, but we're not—it's not casual, I wouldn't want you to think that I do that kind of thing without—"

"I don't want to talk about this right now," he said.

"Honey, I really think—"

"Seriously," he said, and now his look was pleading. "Later, OK?"

No, it's not OK, she said, but only inside. She didn't want to push him, and she'd always respected his boundaries as best she could, and she didn't know what to *say*; that was the problem: she didn't want to make things worse. She needed to think, to decide what to do. She needed to talk to John.

"OK," she said. "Later, though."

He went back to his game. She was dismissed. She stared at him for a few more seconds, frustrated and worried and terribly wistful, then turned and walked out. She left his door open behind her, but halfway down the stairs, she heard it close.

><

After Stan Vincent had pretty much tossed them out of his office—Amanda had been right, the police chief had as much as told them they were full of shit—they'd gone to Bob's house, where he'd put in a call to the county sheriff. The lady deputy he'd spoken with had sounded harried and indifferent to the idea that crime was up in Port Isley; she'd offered to mail him a report to fill out, or welcomed him to download one from their website. John had needed to get back to work—he was surprised and discouraged by the lack of authoritative interest—and Amanda, not even slightly fazed, had gone back to Devon's, to do whatever it was that teenage girls did when they weren't giggling in public. Not that Amanda was the giggling type; Bob couldn't remember ever meeting such a sarcastic young person. She hadn't been able to get much from the police chief, saying that in spite of his surface bluster, he was closed off beneath, tightly controlled. She'd called Vincent a clenched fist, and Bob thought that an apt metaphor for a lot of people around Isley lately, those that weren't actively high-diving off their sanity boards.

"Sanity boards," Bob said to himself, and shook his head and poured another drink. If that was the best he could come up with, he *should* be drinking. It was late afternoon, anyway; no reason to hold back. Wasn't like he had any place to be, anyone else to impress. He wanted to stay home and relax—

—*drink*—

—and figure out what else he could do, what any of them could do. He understood that someone like Vincent wouldn't *want* to accept such a vague, circumstantial theory about an increase in general craziness, but the way Bob saw it, *wanting* didn't have much to do with anything. There was evidence, there was a giant bump in the crime rate—and it was a new millennium, for Chrissakes. There were gases and drugs and fanatics willing to use those things on people. Hell, corporations, *governments* used those things on people; seemed to him, the cops should be open to those kinds of ideas. And it seemed to him that Stan Vincent had to be affected, too, to be so quick to dismiss what they'd laid out.

After they'd left the police station, after Bob had put in their call to the sheriff, they'd talked over some other options. Bob had suggested that they wait on the water and soil tests, see if they could come up with hard data, then go see the sheriff...but they wouldn't get the results for another week, probably, and Amanda seemed to think that they wouldn't prove anything, anyway. She couldn't say why, but considering her mysterious and powerful talent for knowing things, Bob and John had both lost enthusiasm for the idea. John had pitched calling the press back in, but Bob had been lukewarm on the proposal. The evidence was undeniable, but crime was up everywhere lately, times were tough, and the impression that people were changing, in all different ways...unless you were one of them, it wasn't really much of a story. Bob had reminded them that if they could get hold of Poppy Peters, he might have some ideas, but their mayor had been conspicuously absent the last couple of weeks. He wasn't in his office and hadn't returned any of Bob's calls. Frustrated by a lack of direction, they'd all agreed to meet again for Miranda Greene-Moreland's poetry night in the hope that Amanda might be able to find some of the people from her dreams.

"Dreams," Bob muttered, and downed his shot. He started to lean back into his tattered old couch—the TV remote was tucked between the cushion and the arm, and he thought there might be a ball game on—then remembered the notebook, Amanda's notebook. She'd given it to them after their dismal meeting with Vincent; Bob was supposed to turn it over to John after he'd taken a look.

He rose unsteadily and walked to the kitchen. The spiral-bound notebook was on the table, where Amanda had left it. He took it back to the couch, nearly tripping over his shoes at the end of the scarred steamer trunk he used as a coffee table. Cursing, he lowered himself to one of the tired cushions and opened to the first page of the cheap notebook. *Dream Imagery...*

He studied the list, frowning over Amanda's descriptions, considering each one as fully as he could. He'd had a bit too much booze too fast, maybe, hadn't eaten since breakfast...he'd live it up, order a pizza, one of those meatball-garlic specials from Rad's. It might kill his stomach, but fuck it, he had an economy-size bottle of antacid in the kitchen, and no one lived forever. He'd call it in as soon as he was done with the notebook, which suddenly seemed like tedious work.

He frowned at the page, annoyed by his attitude. He'd brought Amanda and John together; he'd been pushing his hypothesis since the day he'd thought of it—this was happening, really happening, and getting drunk was a distraction. He knew better, but getting drunk was also a relief. Drinking helped him shoulder the responsibility of *knowing*, because it made him care less; it made him want to eat pizza and watch the game and worry about everything tomorrow.

"Goddamnit," he said, and dropped the notebook on the trunk, disgusted with himself. Why wasn't he *doing* something?

What can *you do?* Obviously, if people were feeling sick or afraid, they'd try to do something about it—go to the doctor, leave town, go to the cops, *something*. He wasn't a detective or a social worker, he was a reporter, an editor; there was nothing *he* could do—

—people changing, not much of a story...unless you're one of them.

Bob sat up straighter, wishing he hadn't had so much booze as the remembered thought held, began to grow. An editorial, maybe...hell, he could run a full page, *front* page. He had no doubt that John's statistics readout was news. The numbers were compelling. Follow it with a few questions, *get John to work 'em up: notice any strange behaviors in loved ones, unusual feelings of anger, sorrow, like that...*then a call to action, a demand for a town meeting. A demand for a proper investigation, carried out by someone besides himself and a psychic teenager and a lovesick psychologist.

Bob spotted a pen on the trunk, fumbled it up, and opened Amanda's notebook to a blank page somewhere in the middle. He didn't want to lose any of this, and he was drunk enough to be afraid that he would. *Been drunk enough not to have thought of it until now, Holy Christ.*

He started writing, pausing after a moment to pour another drink. The paper was supposed to get a run past the council before it came out, but maybe he'd do a last-minute kind of thing, bypass any possible censorship. If they were wrong about what was happening, he'd lose his job, no question...and he'd look nine kinds of fool. But the risk of embarrassment, next to actually halting the unprecedented disaster that seemed to be engulfing Port Isley...perhaps stopping that crying mother from doing whatever she meant to do with her crying child...

Bob downed the drink quickly, writing furiously, his hope growing.

CHAPTER

22

Tuesday night, John left the house at around seven, deciding to walk to the community theater rather than drive. Summer parking was always bad, and though it was still hot, there was a steady breeze. A lot of other people had the same idea; he passed any number of families and groups of people walking down the hill, mostly summer folk dressed in light, casual clothes, all headed for Miranda Greene-Moreland's poetry reading. He found himself studying their faces as he walked, wondering what secrets lay behind their closed expressions, behind their expensive sunglasses.

Maybe none at all, he told himself. Perhaps the assumption that everyone was being emotionally influenced was erroneous; John certainly felt the effects himself and had noticed behavioral and philosophical changes in most, if not all, of his clients... but if the influence was a kind of pollen or some other natural occurrence—as he still believed, regardless of the lab results he'd received only yesterday—it stood to reason that there might be a nucleus from which the effects radiated, a zero point. Not necessarily, but worth looking into. *We could print out a map, try to chart the more intense changes by residence, maybe...*

He put the idea on his mental list, which was slightly more coherent since Sarah had slowed the course of their affair—Tommy had apparently overheard their lovemaking and was understandably upset. Not that they'd stopped seeing one another, that wouldn't have been possible for either of them, but they'd limited their private time together to barely an hour in the very early morning and had worked to keep their pleasures silent. He was getting more sleep, at least, and told himself that his clients deserved as much…although waiting to see her each night left him teetering between anticipation and agony.

He reached Water Street and turned toward the theater, joining a growing throng of walkers. There was a slow, steady crawl of cars going in both directions and apparently no place to park. The theater only seated a few hundred, but there seemed to be a thousand people out on the street, all headed the same way. How many of them were in love, and how many harbored darker thoughts? How many, like him, were struggling to find their way amid feelings of confusion and uncertainty? He supposed they'd find out soon enough; the paper would come out tomorrow, and Bob's story would run on the front page. Bob had called on Friday night to tell him the idea, drunk and excited, sure that going "straight to the people" was the best course. John had liked the proposal a lot; it was so much more immediate than waiting for someone in a uniform to pay attention. He'd gone over the article with Bob on Saturday, made a couple of suggestions about how to format the questions the reporter had come up with, and had felt quite optimistic, which he hadn't thought was possible so soon after their ugly meeting with Stan Vincent; being called delusional by the police chief had hit a little close to home. John had called Amanda, who'd seemed as relieved and hopeful as John had felt, after reading the article. They were still going to meet him at the reading, see if anything important came up through Amanda's abilities, but John was certain that tomorrow would bring the real resolution; when the *Press* went out, the mayor, the council, the police—all would surely be inundated by calls, forcing them to take action.

Although the reading wasn't scheduled to start for nearly an hour, there were easily a hundred people already at the theater, milling about on the expansive front lawn, holding plastic cups from one of the concession booths out front. There were three stands, two that served food and one that only did drinks—beer and wine—and John noticed that the line for alcohol was thrice as long as at the other booths. He saw a woman in the line with Sarah's light hair and felt his stomach knot, his heart beat faster—but she turned, and it was only some woman.

"Doc!"

John turned and saw Bob waving, a few people away. The lawn was getting crowded. John ducked around the talkers and saw that Amanda and her boyfriend were behind the reporter. Amanda looked stressed. Her eyes were hidden by her shades, but the way her shoulders were hunched, her arms folded in front of her stomach—maybe putting her in this kind of situation wasn't such a good idea. Eric's expression was totally bland.

"Hey, glad we all came early," Bob said, stopping in front of John. His breath smelled like mints and alcohol, and he had to raise his voice slightly to be heard. "I ran into the kids on the way down."

"You doing OK?" John asked Amanda.

"Need a smoke," she said. "Come with me."

She walked toward the door of the theater, Eric in tow. Bob shrugged at John and they both followed, Bob nearly running into a middle-aged couple holding pints. Amanda veered left just before the entrance, cutting to a narrow path that ran behind a leafy hedge fronting the building. They had to lean their bodies to edge through, all the way down the front wall of the theater—and just around the corner a small space opened up, tucked between the continuing hedge and an angle of the building. The ground was littered with cigarette butts and empty cups and bottles, but it was quieter and there was enough room for them to stand facing each other. Amanda and Eric lit up, Amanda leaning against the dusty wall, exhaling with a sigh.

"That's better," she said.

"What's it like?" John asked.

"Smoking?" Amanda smiled her wry twist of a smile.

"Being around all these people," John asked.

"Weird," she said. "Tense. I don't know."

"Are you picking up specific thoughts?"

"I don't know," she said again. "I haven't tried. I mean, I think I have to try to, like, do it one person at a time. Like focus on someone."

She took another drag, shook her head. "Right now, it's like, this feeling of...of tension. Like anxiety, coming from everywhere. It got worse the closer we got, coming down the hill. It's—" She laughed, an unsteady sound. "It's pretty bad."

"You still want to try this?"

"Yeah, totally, I just wanted to smoke first, is all."

Bob had fished an old leather-bound notebook out of his back pocket, the kind where you could replace the pad of paper inside. "I thought we could sit in the back," he said. "I'll write down anything you see. Ah, sense. Unless you think it might be better to stay out here..."

"No, inside's good," she said. "I think it'll be better when everyone sits down, calms down, you know?"

"It doesn't matter anyway, right?" Eric asked suddenly, looking at Amanda. "After the story comes out tomorrow, you won't have to do any of this shit anymore."

"I don't *have* to do it now," Amanda snapped back. "I want to, remember?"

"Yeah, right," Eric mumbled, and went back to smoking. Both teens looked irritated. From the dark looks Eric kept tossing toward the two older men, John suspected jealousy over Amanda's time and attention. Eric's intense, controlling focus was always on her, and Amanda didn't seem to care for it much. Considering what he knew of her background and personality—not to mention her gift for reading people—John couldn't imagine that she'd put up with his antics for much longer.

Behind them was the sound of the front doors being chocked open, and at the window over their heads, they heard a rumble of footsteps and chatter, people going in.

"We're not even going to get a seat in the back if we don't hurry," John said.

"OK," Amanda said, and took a final drag before stomping what was left of her cigarette into the dry dirt. Eric reluctantly did the same, and they started back the way they'd come, bunching together briefly where the hedge ended and the stream of bodies poured past.

>‹

It had been a super shitty day already. She'd woken up with her period, which had bled through the top sheet of Devon's bed into his mattress pad, and she didn't think the stain was going to come out. Also, cramps, and that meant no sex—not the kind she liked, anyway. Then Devon's uncle had driven her to Grace's apartment to pack up her shit, which had filled three garbage bags and a half dozen boxes, and Peter's truck had been out front. Which sucked, for obvious reasons. Amanda had gone early, figuring her mother's sleep habits hadn't changed, and they hadn't—she'd heard snores and occasional grunts from her mother's bedroom while she'd been stuffing her clothes and books and the cat doll her grandmother had given her into cardboard boxes and plastic bags, but no one had come out. That was good, that part didn't blow, but then on the way back to Devon's, she'd picked up some of what Sid was thinking, about what kind of commitment he was looking at, taking in his gay nephew's gal pal. He was thinking that he was going to have to have a serious talk with Devon about other options for her when Devon came home...and Amanda had totally started crying, and Sid had been way nice about it. He'd assumed she was upset about her mother, and that had also sucked because she didn't know what was more real, the nice Sid, telling her that people did the best they could and sometimes it wasn't enough, or the Sid hoping she'd be out of his home soon.

So after *that*, she'd tried to call Devon when they'd gotten back to the house and he hadn't been in. So she'd called Eric, and met him at his house, and he'd been cool for exactly three minutes before he'd started groping her. Which wasn't going to go anywhere anyway because of her period, and he'd been a moody bitch ever since, and he *knew* she was stressed out, so why was he being so difficult? She'd even given him a blow job to make up for not being as wet, willing, and ready as usual, which made her feel stupid; since when had she become such a whore? She'd actually tried to read him a couple of times, to look into his mind even though she knew it'd piss him off, once when they ate lunch and once in his basement, listening to music. Both times she'd felt his irritation with her, and with himself, and beyond that she'd felt that he was also far away in his mind, thinking of something else, something she couldn't get. She wished she hadn't invited him to the reading, but now they were here, and he still had a bug up his butt over whatever it was, exactly, that he'd had a bug up his butt about since before noon, for fuck's sake.

Since about the time they'd run into Bob, she'd been having an amazing attack of nerves, of feeling like the world was going to disappear under her feet while she was walking. She had been doing what she could to keep herself focused on her body, on the dropping sun, on the feel of Eric's sweaty hand in hers, but by the time they'd hit Water Street, she'd felt inside the way the air felt, high and tight and almost breaking. She couldn't believe that nobody else was even noticing, and she sincerely wished she was old enough to buy a beer at the concession stand; she needed to calm the fuck *down*.

A press of bodies and warm air hit them as they joined the flow of people, most of them chatting excitedly as they crowded through the front doors. Amanda looked back the way they'd come, her attention caught for just a second by a lone figure across the street, watching the theater—a thin, pale-looking man, strangely familiar. She didn't have time to place him before he was out of sight, blocked by the moving mob.

John had stepped into the lead and was heading for one of the two sets of doors opening from the lobby into the theater space, finding a row in the back. Which was good, because being able to leave a poetry reading easily was always good, but also because she didn't know how long she'd be able to sit still, feeling so fucking anxious. She concentrated on her breathing, on putting one foot in front of another, on who was sitting where. She ended up in between Bob and Eric. John sat on Bob's other side, on the aisle, and for the moment, the seat next to Eric's was empty.

It was too loud to talk; people kept pouring in, filling the descending rows in front of the raised stage. Amanda took deep, even breaths. Bob asked her if she wanted to use his notebook, but she had brought her own, a small one because she was carrying her "evening" purse, a black sequined clutch with a safety pin holding the top closed. She'd worn her nice clothes, too, a dark-green linen skirt and her best cut black tank, not that anyone had noticed. She took out her own notebook and wrote *Impressions, Poetry Reading* at the top of the page and underlined it. She hesitated a moment, then closed her eyes, still breathing deeply. Sure, great, impressions. If she could get past how stuffy the room was, how loud, how insanely, obnoxiously hyped up. She'd seen enough movies and television to know that psychics had to put up, like, a mental shield, and she thought that all her concentrating on physical stuff—walking, the heat, smoking—was her version of that shield. She had to let it down, to open up to strong feelings in the crowd. She had to look for the people she'd dreamed about.

Another deep breath, and another. She felt touches of thoughts, and let them come.

know she doesn't want to but if she drinks any more of that wine, maybe she'll

missing the fucking game jesus I hope she's happy, dragging me

chicken marsala, that was a thousand calories at least and the bread was empty calories should've gotten the salad

She opened her eyes and looked around. The voices, for lack of a better term, were all from different people—and she couldn't tell by looking. She knew that the first two snippets of thought had been from men, the third from a woman, but there were dozens of each still moving all around, edging past each other, finding seats. Someone had to pee, someone was feeling sick, someone else was cheating on her husband with a man named Ray—

There, the woman in a black dress, sitting three rows up next to a guy in a polo shirt. Amanda could only see a sliver of her profile as she turned to talk to her husband. *If he finds out he'll kill him, kill us both—*

"So what are you going to *do*, exactly?" Eric asked, interrupting her, the woman's thoughts disappearing like smoke.

"Are you fucking kidding me?" Amanda snapped, turning in her seat to glare at him. "I'm trying to figure out if anyone else is going to *die*, is that OK with you?"

"You told me this afternoon, once the paper comes out tomorrow, everything's fixed," he said, and worse than his moody standoffish tone, a whine had crept into his voice. "I understand this is like, a big deal for you, I know that, I just missed you today, you know?"

He leaned closer into her. "I kind of feel like we missed each other."

So, he wasn't a total idiot. She sighed. "Just…I'm going to try to concentrate, OK? So if you could just sit there and look pretty and be quiet for a couple of minutes, I'd really—that would be, like, *supportive*."

He smiled at her, his very nicest smile. "You think I'm pretty?"

She smiled back at him. "Shut up, please."

He pulled out an ancient iPod, tucking a bud into his ear, and she felt better about him than she had all day. She jotted down *random thoughts, can't place* and *blonde in black dress having affair on husband w/Ray*, and she wondered what possible good they could do here. The small, motley group trying to save their town from some terrible fill-in-the-blank; it was a standard premise in thrillers she'd read growing up—but in books the psychic one or the computer geek (the one with special skills, anyway) was always pulling out the exact right answer at the right time, and there weren't long, boring days when nothing really happened, and there was a *villain*, there was someone or something to actually fight. Everything about what was occurring in Port Isley was so vague and intangible—feelings, impulses, control—except she *knew* that there was violence to come; there was blood in her dreams, and fear, and that meant she had, like, a personal responsibility. It had to mean something that her own "special skill" had arrived just when everything started to go to hell…

For me, the night of the party.

"Hey, did you get a chance to look at that journal thing?" she asked Bob.

"Oh, right," he said. When he leaned in to speak, she could smell the sour heaviness of his breath, even his sweat—she'd grown up knowing that smell. He'd been drinking today. "Yeah, but it was all stuff we went over before, wasn't it?"

"Except for the thing about the influence maybe coming from a person," she said.

"A person?" Bob's gaze seemed to sharpen. "What do you mean?"

She explained about *he's here* and how she'd kind of forgotten about it because she never had figured out what it meant. Bob asked some of the same questions Devon had—who was here, where—and she repeated her answers: she didn't know. Bob turned to fill John in on the probably useless piece of information, and Amanda realized that all the seats were full, and there were a lot of people still standing, or leaning against the walls, and she started searching the faces she could see for anyone familiar, searching the electric air for anything frightening, and then people started applauding, their attention all turning to the stage.

Miranda Greene-Moreland walked out on the platform wearing a terrible green dress made out of layers of gauze. She smiled her beaming smile, stopping in front of a pair of mike stands. She tapped at one of them, the loud *thump-thump-thump* cutting through the applause—

—and Amanda saw them, suddenly, three men between the front row and the stage, armed with what looked like automatic rifles. The men were rough looking, denim and work boots, their clothes dirty, and she could only see their backs, but she immediately thought of Cole Jessup and his fucked-up sons, one of whom liked getting blow jobs from Devon. They were aiming their big machine-gun weapons at Miranda and people in the front row; people all around her were screaming, falling over their seats to get out, and Amanda felt a concentrated glee coming from the three men, one of them laughing aloud at Miranda's obvious terror, and two of the men had erections—

"Good evening, and welcome," Miranda said, and the clapping was dying down and the three men were gone, vanished, like they'd never been there. It was going to happen, though. It was going to happen tonight; *now*.

"Oh, shit," Amanda said weakly, and turned to Bob, to John, the words spilling out in fright, her voice gaining strength. "Guns, they have guns, they're going to shoot her!"

"Who? When?"

Amanda had half risen from her seat. The people in front of them had turned, were staring. Miranda said, "As always, we'll have our scheduled readings first—we have some wonderful talents this year—and then the stage opens, inviting any and all to participate—"

The first of the trio of gun-wielders strode into the theater, less than two feet from John, his weapon carried in both hands, his comrades right behind.

"Now, here! Gun! *Gun!*" Amanda shouted, and there was a second of silence, and then there were people screaming, shouting, those closest to the aisle shrinking away from the hurrying men, some people standing, craning for a better look, more ducking low. Bob grabbed Amanda around the waist, trying to pull her down, but she fought him. She had to know.

The men staggered themselves in front of Miranda Greene-Moreland, the harmless, aging poetess frozen in front of the mike stand, her gaze fixed on the dark, evil-looking weapons. Amanda was watching the exact same movie she'd just seen, down to the expression on Miranda's face.

"Here's for the tires, cunt!" one of the men shouted, the cry just audible over the screams of the crowd, and all three opened fire—

—but there was no thunder of weapons-fire, or maybe the howls of fear covered it up, because darkness was spreading across the front of Miranda's stupid dress, wet stains dripping from her chest and stomach, water running down her face.

Water?

Bob was still trying to pull her down, but she was figuring it out, she almost had it even before the smell swept through the room a second or two later. It was awful, she could smell it from the back row as people continued to shout and shove and stumble by, a nasty, musky stench. On the stage, Miranda was coughing, dry heaving, wiping at her face, and Amanda remembered Devon telling her once that there was a huge market for deer and fox urine, of all things, that hunters used it to attract targets or to cover their own scent. They'd laughed about it, and she'd made a joke about whether it smelled like Santa's workshop, but the smell filling the theater wasn't funny, it was an assault, and it had to be some kind of animal piss; there was no other smell it could be. Along with the screams and chaos of falling bodies, Amanda could hear people closer to the stage throwing up, saw some guy in front spewing chunks all down his shirt.

The terror was as sharp as knives, coming at her from all direction as the trio of men started back up the aisle. There were still people who thought the guns were real, who believed they were going to die here. The feelings were intense, coming from everywhere. Space cleared in front of the gunmen as men and women scurried out of their way, though John and Bob were both standing now, watching, figuring it out as she had.

She looked at Eric and saw that he was still in his seat and laughing—he was actually *laughing*—and then she saw him outside Devon's at night, leaning against the maple tree in Uncle Sid's backyard beneath an umbrella of soft, moving shadow, watching her window. And he was thinking about being with her, and he was thinking about eternity. He was thinking about *death*.

She shrank back from him, practically pushing herself against Bob as Eric looked up at her, his grin disappearing when he saw her face. She turned to Bob, keeping her voice low and fast. There was still enough noise to cover what she wanted to say.

"I need to go home *alone*, do you understand?" She rolled her eyes toward Eric. She didn't want him to know what she knew, what she'd seen. She needed to think. "Back to Devon's *alone*, OK? Can you walk me?"

Even half in the bag, Bob was no fool. He nodded, glancing at Eric, then back at her. On the stage, Miranda Greene-Moreland was weeping, the amplified sound filling the air as fully as the cloying reek of piss. Others were crying, those that weren't following the bulk of the crowd through the doors, and there were moans of pain coming from people who'd been injured in the mad dash for safety. The terror was fading, there was that, at least, but a new dreadful feeling was taking its place, a sense of isolation, of loneliness so vast that it would kill the world.

There's nobody else, she thought, and Eric was standing, worried, slipping his arm around her, and it was all she could do not to flinch away from him.

The poetry reading was canceled.

CHAPTER
23

Once the theater had cleared and the police had come, Bob and John walked Amanda home through the fading light. Eric was with them, but she'd made up an excuse about having a headache, playing it up all the way to Devon's. The adults stayed too close for anything intimate to crop up between the teenagers, volunteering small talk about the reading. Bob said that he was sorry the paper had gone to press; a bizarre terrorist attack on the poetry reading, that would certainly support the headline story. John was distracted. Amanda could tell he was thinking about his girlfriend, but he tried to keep up his end, interjecting points he planned to make at the proposed town meeting. He pointed out that word would get around about the assault on Miranda Greene-Moreland, that they should expect big numbers.

The four of them trudged up the hill, passing small clusters of men with pinched faces, women with their arms folded, witnesses to the drenching of Miranda Greene-Moreland and the cancellation of a summer favorite. Amanda tried to focus on what the two men were discussing, but she couldn't stop thinking about Eric, walking right next to her, who she could barely stand to look at. He was going to go bugfuck crazy over *her*, and what was she going to do? She couldn't stand the idea of being with him, having seen what was coming, or what *could* be coming—knowing that he was the type of person who would hurt her to fill some terrible emptiness inside. How could she ever trust him? Worse for her, for any sense that she was gaining control of her newfound power, how had she ever trusted him in the first place? Why hadn't she seen something before now?

Because it's building, she thought. *Whatever made me psychic, whatever is making people crazy, it's growing, it's getting bigger.* He'd been better, before, and while she was sad on some level that he maybe wasn't totally responsible for his behavior, she was mostly just scared. If the strange dream that had settled over Isley affected him the way it had affected Mr. Billings or Rick Truman or Brian Glover, she wanted to be away from him ASAP, before he went *pow*. The thing was, if she dumped him, she *created* the stalker scenario that was freaking her out. It was like one of those time-travel paradoxes—she'd seen something that probably wouldn't happen unless she rejected him, but seeing it made the rejection inevitable.

He has to go back to Boston in less than a month. I'll fake it, I can fake it, she told herself, but that meant they'd have to keep having sex, and she didn't know if she could do that. Her premonition at the theater wasn't fuzzy or ambiguous—she'd seen him watching Devon's house and thinking seriously about killing her and then himself. Telling himself all the while that he loved her. The idea of fucking someone who might, at some point, decide to murder her was in no way a turn-on.

Was there a way to make him different? To say or do something that would change his mind about how to feel? She couldn't imagine, nor could she imagine taking the time to talk it out with him, help him find his way. She couldn't even *look* at him.

When they got to Devon's, she said she felt sick, told all of them and none of them that she'd call later and was on the porch before Eric could protest. Sid was out; she had to use the key, and as she fumbled with the lock in the near dark she could feel Eric watching her, confused and unhappy.

I'm imagining things, she told herself, but still felt his gaze. She got the key turned, finally, didn't look back, closed the front door behind her, and leaned against it.

"Fuck fuck *fuck*," she whispered. Was he already crazy enough to come after her because she hadn't invited him in?

Devon. Call Devon.

The thought was a beacon in the murk. She made sure the door was locked and hurried into the kitchen, past the living room where pictures of Devon's relatives collected dust on the mantel. Next to the phone on the counter was Devon's cousin's number. She dialed it, sure that he wouldn't be there, that she'd get the recording, a bright girly voice saying that you'd reached Claire Pierson, she wasn't in, leave a number, et cetera, and Amanda was steeling herself not to sound sniffly on the message, and on the fourth ring, Devon picked up. She'd recognize his carefully cultivated voice anywhere.

"Hello?"

"Devon, oh my God," Amanda said, closing her eyes in relief. "Dude, where the hell have you *been*?"

In the brief silence that followed, she could hear people talking in the background, low music. Someone in a safe, sane apartment in Portland laughed, and Devon's tone, when he answered, was measured.

"Getting a job, actually," he said. "Excuse me for having a life."

"Oh," she said. She felt lost for a second, stupid with confusion. He'd been in Portland for less than two weeks; why was he getting a job? And it wasn't like he was poor. "OK, great. Good for you. Listen, I'm—"

"It *is* good for me," Devon interrupted. "There's a whole scene here. I've met some really cool people. I know you're in crisis and all, but you're not the only person in the universe."

Was he kidding? "Devon. I just found out that Eric's going to turn stalker because I'm like, superpsychic now, I saw him coming after me, and the whole town is falling to shit, and I don't know what I'm going to do."

She heard the muffled rumple of his hand going over the mouthpiece, heard him telling someone something, and there was another laugh, and she felt a stab of paranoid fear. Was someone laughing at her? Had Devon told his cool new people about *her*? When he came back on, he sounded slightly more serious. He'd moved into another room, too; it was quieter, his voice clearer.

"OK," he said. "What do you mean, falling to shit?"

"So, the poetry reading was tonight? Three of your survivalist buddies crashed it and hosed Miranda Greene-Moreland down with piss."

"Oh my God!" Devon broke up, laughing long and hard. He finally snorted out, "That's so funny, I don't even know where to start! Did anybody record it?"

"Yeah, I know, I know," she said, although she wasn't even smiling, thinking of the terror that had infused the small theater, that had made Eric laugh out loud, even while his deep, dark self was already dreaming of keeping her all to himself. "Hilarious. Except they used squirt guns that looked like Uzis and scared the shit out of a lot of people, myself included. I saw it, too, before it happened."

"Like another dream?" He finally sounded interested.

"No, like a few seconds before it happened; it was so weird," she said. "I went to the reading with Bob and John—"

"The reporter? Who's John?"

"Yeah, Bob Sayers, John is this friend of his," she said, feeling impatient. "And Eric, too, right? So I'm picking up all these feelings, like something bad was going to happen...except it was more like this tension that was coming from everybody. And then—"

"Tension coming from Bob and John and Eric?"

"No, everybody there, in the theater."

"So, you think *they* knew something bad was going to happen?"

"No, not like that," she said. The frustration made her heart beat faster. Her hand tightened on the phone. "More like everyone was really jacked up, but in a, a *restless* way. It's been like that a lot around here, all these people, like, trying to control themselves; they're ate up with it, but they're barely holding on."

"Uh-huh," Devon said. "So, what else? You said Eric's *stalking* you?"

"No, not yet," she said. "When those guys shut down the reading, everyone was running around and yelling, and I looked at Eric and saw him—" She wasn't sure how to say it. "I saw him watching me, and thinking some really dark shit. If I dump him, he's going to, to try to hurt me, I'm pretty sure."

"You should tell Sid," Devon said. "Seriously, tell Bob, too. *And* Stan Vincent. Tell anyone who'll listen. That's bullshit."

She didn't want to explain their field trip to the police station or how likely it was that Chief Vincent would want to help her with anything. She cut to the core of her panic.

"Yeah, but what do I tell *Eric*?" Just thinking about it made her feel panicky. "I mean, we haven't been together for that long, and…"

She trailed off as a young, gay voice drawled out behind Devon. "Hang up, sweetie, you're missing the movie."

Another hand clasp over the mouthpiece; another brief, incoherent exchange.

"Hey," Devon said. "Look, can I call you back later? This isn't such a great time."

Amanda clutched the phone tighter. She wanted to scream. "You're watching a *movie*, so you're too busy to talk to me about this?"

"Why do you always do this?" Devon snapped. "Swear to God, Amanda, that is so unfair. I know you've had a bad time lately, I know it's been fucked-up crazy for you, but I've been going through shit too, you know?"

He laughed, a brief, indignant sound. "I mean, you told me I was going to *die*. And I didn't believe you, but then when that woman got raped...it was like I was standing in the shadow of death; you don't know what that's like. I had to get out from under it. I mean, I don't blame you or anything, I wouldn't want you to think that, but I had to leave, right?"

"Why would I think that you *blame* me?" she asked, honestly perplexed amid her growing anger and despair. "You know none of this is my fault. I'm just seeing shit, I'm not making it happen."

"Didn't I just say that I don't blame you?" Devon said. He sighed. "I'm not mad at you, OK? Talk to Sid, tell him about Eric. He's in a position to actually do something about it. I'm in Oregon, remember?"

"I know, but what should I say to Eric? I just practically ran in here to get away from him; he's going to call later or come over. What should I do?"

"Fuck him, don't tell him anything," Devon said. "He's a psycho, right?"

"Yeah, but—"

"I told you what I think," he said, and she could tell by his voice that he was about to get off the phone, and her throat tightened, she felt so sad all of a sudden.

"I'll give you a call later," he said. "Or you call me. Tomorrow morning."

"I've been calling, I keep getting the machine—"

"Right, about that—I finally got a real cell, like, a week ago, so you should probably call me on that. I gave Sid the number. I'm sure I did."

"I don't think so," she said. "He would have told me."

"Uncle Sid? He wrote it down somewhere and forgot about it. He always does that. Just ask him. And tell him I'll call him this week, OK?"

She didn't answer. *Why do you always do this*, she asked herself. Do what? What was he saying?

"*OK?*" he asked again, and his impatience was like a small death, it hurt so badly. She wanted to tell him not to leave her alone; she wanted his love and understanding, but the word came out of her mouth tasting bitter.

"Whatever."

The silence was deafening. "Great," he said finally. "Thanks a lot."

"Wait," she said, but the click drowned her out.

She hung up and put her head down. The sadness was vast and encompassing because she knew that in a day or two he would apologize or she would, and they would be friends again— but she also felt that he was gone from her, that there wouldn't be an apartment in Seattle or window-box flowers or a pet cat with a funny name. She couldn't tell if she was being psychic or just finally understanding reality, so much more quickly than she would have thought possible. Nothing was certain. They would be friends again, but Devon was gone.

✷

Bob woke up at six on Wednesday morning and started what had become his morning ritual, of late—a hot-then-cold shower, a giant glass of orange juice with a splash of vodka in it, dry wheat toast, and a couple of antidiarrheal pills. Not pretty, but it worked. He'd also pick up a sweet white coffee on the way to the printer's. Caffeine was supposed to make hangovers worse, but he'd never found that to be the case; a day without coffee, that was just asking for a headache.

He hit the phone machine's message button as he poured his juice, vaguely remembering that there had been calls the night before. After seeing Amanda home—he still didn't know what *that* was about, boyfriend trouble maybe—Eric had promptly wandered off, and he and John had gone their own separate ways; John was surely headed to his new lady friend's house, and Bob was hot to get home, to write about the "unfortunate event" at the poetry reading while it was still fresh in his mind...and to get his buzz back up; the flask he'd taken to the reading had been empty by the time the cops showed up at the theater. He'd stayed up late. The phone had rung several times, but he'd been working and not a little tight by then. He figured it was people wanting to find out what he knew, which wasn't a whole hell of a lot. With Annie gone—and with Chief Vincent thinking he was bonkers—he didn't have a friendly face at the PD anymore, but it didn't take a rocket scientist to guess that the cops had taken statements and then sent someone out to Jessup's to pick up the offenders. Considering the nature of the crime, the shooters were probably already back at their heavily fortified compound. The trio of gun-wielding men had scared a lot of people, and knowing how bad the council wanted to keep the summer people happy, there'd surely be a push to have them incarcerated for their attack...but in the end, they'd squirted someone with piss. Against the law, no question, but not exactly a hanging offense.

The first three messages were what he'd expected—had he heard, did he see, what-would-happen-now. He sipped from his juice, considered, then added another splash of alcohol. Better.

The fourth call stopped him short, the bottle of vodka still in hand.

"It's Amanda. Call me as soon as you get this, OK?"

She sounded upset. The time stamp was just before ten last night...had she told him she was going to call? He thought perhaps so and felt a pang of guilt for having ignored the phone the night before, but there was no help for it. He only hoped that whatever she wanted, it would hold. The next call was another local, wanting to hear about the reading. Bob put the bottle back in the freezer and then finished his juice, figuring there was no way Amanda was awake this early; it wasn't even seven. He'd call her as soon as he'd turned the paper over to his couriers; they'd be at his office at nine, ready to fold, and she'd probably be up by then.

By noon, half the people in Port Isley would be talking about whether ol' Bob Sayers had gone off his nut. His sincere belief—and John's, and Amanda's—was that the other half would be stirred to action, ready to come together and talk about what was happening. They couldn't be the only people in town who'd noticed the sudden rise in overall...strangeness, in themselves as well as in others. Silence was the enemy, people quietly losing their minds, sure that no one else was suffering—his front page was about to change that.

Bob was walking out the back door when the phone rang. He hesitated, not wanting to miss anything important...but chances were good it was another gossipmonger, eager to hash over Miranda's public humiliation. Sometimes it seemed like half the locals had his home number. Besides, the most important thing he was going to do today, this year, maybe in his whole *life* was going to be getting this issue out. Never had he felt such a sense of urgency about the *Port Isley Press*; the story (headline: *Emotional Excesses Rock Port Isley*) might actually turn out to be the biggest he'd ever broken, a real honest-to-God lifesaver.

A third ring. Fuck it, maybe Amanda was up early. He left the door hanging open to the early morning light, the town as cool as it would be all day, and walked back to pick up the phone.

"Hello?"

"Bob? It's Dan Turner."

Damnit, he needed to get that caller ID. He'd heard from several people in the last month that Dan had finally caught the Jesus bug, in a big way. Bob hadn't had the opportunity to cross paths with Dan Turner of late; with Rick Truman awaiting trial down in Seattle, Turner had been busy with the council. Two of the members had resigned since June, and Poppy Peters had dropped out of sight. The other handful of councilmen had always been content to let Rick run the show, and it seemed they were happy enough to let Dan take over now. Word had it that he could (and *did*) quote chapter and verse at the drop of a hat.

Swell. "Hey there, Dan, how are you?"

The councilman's voice was rigid, high, and overly loud. "*So whoever is in Christ is a new creation; the old things have passed away; behold, new things have come.*"

"Oh, uh-huh," Bob said agreeably. "That's great. Listen, I'd love to catch up, but I've got to get over to Angeline to pick up the paper…"

"You don't, actually," Turner said. "There won't be any paper going out today."

"What do you mean?" Bob said, struggling to keep his voice even. "Third Wednesday of the month, isn't it? I sent a copy to your office Monday night."

"But not the copy that ended up going to the printers," Turner said. "*Their throat is an open grave; with their tongue, they speak deceit.*"

"What are you talking about?" Bob said, although he had a pretty good idea.

"You sent a *lie*," Turner said. "After what you've been putting out lately, the council decided that it might be wise to keep a better eye on you. I went to the printer's last night. I saw what you wrote. Your front page *news*."

"It *is* news, if people are in trouble," Bob said. "They have a right to know that they're not the only ones having problems."

"It's God's work being done here," Turner said.

"Well, that may be so," Bob said. "But this conversation we're having, right here and now—that's reason enough to run it," Bob said. "People are different, Dan, you're *different*, and I don't think—"

"*The Spirit of the lord will come upon you in power, and you will prophesy with them; and you will be* changed *into a* different *person!*" Turner's anger was tinged with awe. "God is with us, now. He is offering His mercy—*With your own eyes, you saw those great trials, those miraculous signs and great wonders*, that's Deuteronomy—*these* are the trials, *that's* what's happening right here and now! Every one of us is being given a choice, to walk with God or to turn away from Him. We are witness to a *miracle*, and I'm—*we're* not going to let some old lush interfere!"

"So fire me, that's about what I expected," Bob said. "But that paper is going out if I have to pay for it myself."

"No, it's not," Turner said, and if he was really trying to be a good Christian, to be pious or humble, he was missing the mark; the councilman sounded incredibly smug. "It's already been pulped. I watched them do it myself. And I explained to them that unless they want to lose Isley's business permanently, they're not to print another issue without speaking to me first. Personally."

"You think I can't find another *printer*?" Bob asked, as incredulous as he was furious.

"Not for the *Press*. It belongs to the township, not you."

"Jesus, Dan, I can take it to a copy center! For that matter, I can run 'em off myself!"

"Port Isley is burning with sin! The blasphemy of the Spirit will *not* be forgiven!"

"Can I quote you on that, Dan, or should I attribute that one to Mary?"

A strangled cry of outrage and a click. Turner had hung up.

Bob set his own phone back on the hook, gently, because he wanted to throw it and he was exercising some goddamn self-control, *not like the booze, drink, I need a drink.* He went to the refrigerator, opened the top door, took out the vodka, and walked back to the sink. He knew it was a bad idea, he knew he was fucking up but felt helpless to stop it—even felt a kind of sick self-righteousness, splashing a generous amount into his freshly washed orange juice glass. His town was falling to pieces, and he'd just been *fired.* What was booze for if not to ease those things? He drank it down in two long swallows, then leaned against the counter, feeling the fire hit his belly. He poured another one and then held it up, looking into the clear liquid.

Did he have free will? Did any of them, this summer? In less than two months, he'd gone from the occasional drink with dinner, the weekend nightcap, to daily drunks, the slide as easy and natural as falling down when you were tripped. John talked about not being able to think clearly anymore...the doc *didn't* talk about his new lady love, but Bob thought that Sarah—Karen Haley's sister, up for the summer with her kid—was John's real problem. Or maybe problem wasn't the right word...obsession, maybe.

All of us, he thought, still staring at the glass. Affected, influenced...but controlled? Did John *have* to go to Sarah, had Rick Truman been *forced* to chop up his wife? Did *he* have to drink, the way Amanda had to see what she saw, like it or not?

"I don't," he said, and poured the liquor into the sink, the smell making him wish he'd swallowed it, but he'd already had enough. For now.

No paper. No story. He'd told Dan Turner that he would find a way to get the word out himself, but suddenly that seemed foolish, like something a recently fired drunk would declare out of spite. He saw himself at a copy center, running off drafts of his big news on plain white typing paper, he saw himself standing on a corner of Water, handing them out to passersby, looking like an aging, jobless crackpot. Not that it had to be like that, but the imagery was so clear, he could see himself standing there with his stack of flyers, his eyes bloodshot with booze, pathetically demanding that someone, anyone pay attention; he could see the politely averted eyes of the men and women who walked past, the slight sneers. The pity.

It wasn't even seven in the morning yet, but for Bob, the day felt over. He wanted a drink; he wanted to get shit-faced and go back to bed and sleep until it was all over, whatever "it" was. He left the bottle of Absolut on the counter next to the empty glass and sat down at the kitchen table, feeling old and useless, not sure what to do next.

>‹

Amanda was dreaming.

She saw a great fire, felt its heat. She saw a boy in a dark maze, his breath coming fast, his heart thundering in his ears. She heard shots and screams, saw a young mother who wept while her baby screamed.

As frightening, as awful as these things were, they were familiar, and she turned and fretted in her sleep but didn't wake. There were other images and feelings, disconnected, fragmentary. Lust.

Fury. A man laughing. A woman's purse, spilled on the ground. Dark, malevolent spite. A fist, a hand, hands washing away blood.

The dream changed, and she saw a little girl in a pink dress, a faded photograph, a sense of longing as pale fingers traced the tiny, smiling face, shell, sea…and then Amanda was waking up, being touched, a hand sliding across her hip—

"Hey."

At the sound of Eric's soft voice she jerked awake, reflexively kicking herself up to the headboard. She clutched handfuls of the bedspread, pulling it to her chest. Eric was sitting on the edge of the bed, smiling at her. He had dark circles under his eyes, as if he hadn't slept.

"Hey, you."

She stared at him, blinking at the bright slivers of morning light coming around the curtain. Why the *fuck* hadn't she told Sid last night? Devon had said to tell him, but she'd decided to talk to John or Bob first, only neither of them were answering their fucking *phones*, and Sid had been out until late, anyway. He'd come home just after midnight with his girlfriend, and they'd opened wine and put in a movie. No *way* was she going to interrupt their date to tell them oh, by the way, she was a psychic, and she wasn't sure what to do about her soon-to-be stalker boy-friend, but they should probably start keeping the doors locked all the time; fuck *that* shit. Sid would kick her ass out pronto, and unless she wanted to impose on the reporter or the shrink, she had nowhere else to stay. Besides, she'd ended up crying a lot after her conversation with Devon, and her face had been all swollen and gross, and she hadn't felt like it.

She'd stayed up late writing out lists of options and read-ing about stalkers online, turning off the lights to smoke out of Devon's window, trying not to jump every time a shadow moved in the yard. Her instincts were all pushing fairly strongly toward getting the fuck out of Dodge. She wanted to be a crime fighter and all—who didn't?—but it wasn't worth getting *murdered* over, and Sid's hospitality shouldn't have to extend to personal security. She'd fallen asleep planning her escape.

"I didn't mean to scare you," Eric said. "You're cute when you're scared, though."

"What are you doing here? Did Sid let you in?"

Eric's grin was leering. "He's gone for the *day*; he left a note on the counter—said he and Carrie were going to Seattle and they won't be back till late."

She blinked and stared, trying to wake up. "So you just walked *in*? To somebody's *house*?"

His grin faded. "To see you," he said, his voice thick with feeling, his gaze eating hungrily at hers.

Anxiety replaced shock as she woke up more, as she grasped for the right approach. What should she say, how should she say it? She'd found a lot of websites about stalking behavior, they'd said to break it off immediately and totally with the person, to be absolutely clear—but the sites also said that before trying anything, an experienced threat management team should assess the risks, because sometimes the stalker would "escalate" if you handled it wrong. She doubted she'd find threat management in the yellow pages. She needed help, though; she was afraid to try to handle him by herself.

Run.

"Look, about yesterday," he said, apparently mistaking her silence for irritation. "I was being a dick, I don't know why. You still mad at me? Because I'm sorry. If it makes you feel any better, I couldn't sleep, thinking about it."

"That doesn't make me feel better," she said slowly. They were alone in the house, and no one but Devon knew what she'd seen, and he might as well have been a million miles away. "I've got to pee; excuse me."

Eric stood up so she could slide out of bed. She was wearing only panties and a tank, and she wanted to cover herself but didn't want to do anything suspicious. She kept thinking of all those movies where someone had to lie to a bad guy, and they always twitched and stammered and as much as jumped up and down pointing at themselves, sending off signals that they were full of shit. Was she walking normally? She scooped up her skirt, crumpled by the door; did she look casual? What was she going to do in the bathroom, anyway, what magical answer was going to occur there?

Need to think, she told herself, and stepped into and across the hall from Devon's room, flipped on the lights, and closed the door gently behind her. She resisted the strong urge to lock it, sure that he'd notice.

She actually did have to pee. She sat on the toilet and told herself that he wasn't stalking her yet, that as long as he thought everything was OK, there was no danger…but what the hell did she know, anyway? She wondered if she could fake it long enough to get a read on him, to figure out what he was thinking, but she was afraid. What if he caught on, what if *that* was what triggered him?

Get out, you dipshit. The voice in her mind that scolded, that pointed out the cold, hard facts wasn't interested in her indecision. With emotions and impulses jacked up all over town, who was to say he wasn't ready to kill her now, today? Better paranoid than screwed because she'd hesitated.

She stood up, pulled her skirt on, and flushed, her thoughts running slapdash as she washed her hands in cold water. Distract him, get away. Distract him, get away. She needed her bag—her wallet was in it—but that and her shoes were in Devon's room…

The window. Get him downstairs, go out the window.

There was an ivy trellis outside Devon's window; he used it to get out when he didn't want to go past Sid. She'd climbed it a time or ten, crashing on his floor after a night drinking or smoking pot—and on three memorable occasions, hanging out there while coming off acid. The ivy was mostly dead, so it was always full of spiders, but it was strong. Devon had reinforced the structure, double bolting it to the wall beneath the crawl of dried-up brown leaves; if she wanted to sneak out, that was the way to go, and she had a plan but it depended on acting *now*, right away, before she pussied out.

She opened the door, played a small smile on her face, and leaned into Devon's room. Eric was sitting on the bed again. His expression, when he looked at her, was haunted, and she almost faltered. *What if I'm wrong?*

Then you're wrong. Do it.

"Hey, I kind of need to take a shower," she said. "You know how to make coffee?"

"Yeah," he said, and he smiled. She could feel a kind of tension leave him because she didn't seem mad, and she felt guilty for doing what she was about to do. Sneaking away, there was no way he was going to understand.

"Everything's in the kitchen. There's a grinder on the counter, beans in the freezer," she said, and was sure that her smile looked forced now but she held onto it. She'd go to John's office; he'd know what to do. Bob was probably busy with the paper...

Eric smiled, and she smiled back, then turned and headed back to the bathroom.

She closed the door and quickly turned on the shower.

A few seconds passed, and she strained to hear over the running water—and there, the telltale thumping of a jog down stairs; he'd be turning right at the little carpeted landing and heading away from her. The kitchen was beneath Sid's room, other side of the house, practically. She counted slowly to ten. Her heart was pounding; what if he couldn't find something or decided he'd wait for her? What if she opened the door and he came jogging back up the stairs?

Tell him you forgot something. Shampoo. Toothbrush. Tampons. Go.

She opened the door slowly and stepped into the hall. Hesitated, closed the bathroom door; he'd wait longer before checking. She stepped across the hall. No time to change, and she'd climb barefoot down the trellis. She saw her bag at the foot of the bed and hurried over to it, grabbed her smokes off the dresser and threw them inside. She picked up her shoes, the high-tops, and stuffed them on top. Anything else she could come back for. Maybe with an armed guard.

She had a fleeting thought that she should leave him a note, a lie to smooth things over as much as was possible—Eric, crazy psychic mission at hand, will call you ASAP, sorry, love, et cetera—but besides the time investment, she didn't trust the instinct. It didn't seem wise to say anything encouraging.

I'll be out of town before the sun sets, she promised herself, and went to the window, which overlooked the backyard. She quietly pulled the curtain to the side and unlatched the window. The sun was bright and sane as she lifted the bottom pane, wincing at the scrape of painted wood. She slung her bag over her shoulder and sat on the sill, hunched over to duck beneath the raised window. A last look at Devon's room as she backed out, then she hooked one bare foot into the wide wooden latticework and shifted her weight down.

The slats hurt her feet. She went down quickly, pausing once when her bag shifted. A fat garden spider, its orange-and-green body an inch across, skittered over her hand, and she almost lost her grip in her sudden panic to fling it off. Her skin crawled, a spasm of revulsion, and then she hurried again, ignoring the strands of web under her fingers, on her bare arms, beneath her bare toes.

There was no drop; the trellis went all the way to the ground. She reached the bottom and stepped away, sparing a few seconds to brush at her hair and body in a brief, dancing frenzy, *yah*, she fucking *hated* spiders, and then she was moving across the backyard, mostly dirt and an evergreen hedge separating it from the neighbors'. She went around the hedge and across the next yard before stopping to put her shoes on, leaning against a garden shed. She'd forgotten socks, which meant they would stink by this afternoon.

John's office. She cut through a couple of more yards, skirting open spaces until she reached the corner, out of sight of the house. She told herself she wouldn't imagine the look on Eric's face when he realized she'd skipped out and then thought of nothing else on her way down the hill, occasionally throwing nervous looks back the way she'd come.

CHAPTER

24

John's ten o'clock had canceled last minute—there'd been an urgent early-morning call logged with the answering service, one of his clients breathlessly reporting that she was leaving town, no reason given—and though he knew he should be catching up on paperwork and correspondence, he spent better than half an hour just sitting at his desk, staring at his date book. Every page was heavily marked, different inks colliding, updating daily changes. He had a wait list ten deep. He had two new clients he thought would need to be hospitalized, a lawyer on the very edge of suicidal behavior and a young woman who'd begun to hear voices—and a half dozen other clients that he should be seeing more than once a week, based on their most recent sessions. Candice had been trying to keep up, but she'd called in sick three times in the last two weeks, finally tearfully admitting that she felt overwhelmed, that she needed a vacation. He'd given it to her, even knowing that he'd drown without office help. Which was what seemed to be happening.

There had been other cancellations, six since the weekend, and a couple of people had been no-shows. He knew he needed to be going through the wait list, reworking his schedule, but what he really felt like doing was nothing, leaving the open hours free. No client meant nothing to distract him from thoughts of Sarah. He tried to consider the ramifications of Bob's call, recorded while he'd been with his nine o'clock—he

knew he should call the reporter back; they needed to get reor-
ganized, decide their next step, and Bob had sounded depressed
as hell, besides—but he found himself putting the call off. He
would think of Sarah, and lose a minute or three to intimacies
remembered…

"John? Dr. Hanover?"

He'd left his door partway open, habit when he wasn't on the
phone so he could hear the next client arrive; the hesitant voice
called from the small waiting area.

"Amanda?"

He stood as she walked in. She looked bad, rumpled and
frantic. There appeared to be spiderweb in her hair. "Your cell's,
like, off," she said, and he realized that he'd left it at home before
going to Sarah, that he'd been unreachable all last night. He
couldn't remember the last time he'd forgotten his phone, the
last time he'd been so irresponsible.

Oh, can't you?

"I'm so sorry. What happened?"

"Oh, so, like, Eric's going to stalk me. I saw it last night at the
thing, and then he shows up this morning and walks into Devon's
house, without even knocking, and I totally took off, just climbed
out the window when he went to make coffee," she said, taking
short gulps of air between words. He held up his hands, slowing her down, relieved beyond measure that there was something
outside himself to focus on.

She sat on the couch and repeated the story over a bottled
water, filling in the particulars. She was scared, and afraid she'd
done the wrong thing, making matters worse. He reassured her;
considering what she'd seen, worrying about Eric's feelings didn't
need to be at the top of her list.

"Maybe when he reads the paper, or if his dad reads it," she
began, and he shook his head.

"Bob called," he said. "The council pulled the paper. We have to come up with something else."

"What do you mean?" Amanda's voice rose. "What do you mean, something else, like what? What about the big meeting?"

He shook his head again, and she stood up, her arms folded tightly.

"He's going to come after me; he's going to be—maybe I should just talk to him."

"Amanda, if he's capable of hurting you, that's nothing you can change. We'll go to the police—"

"The cops think we're crazy," she said. "And he hasn't actually *done* anything."

"He walked into Sid's house; that's unlawful entry."

She stared at him. "Whoopee fuckin' doo. You think they'll hold him based on that? You think he won't be out of there in the time it takes his father to write a check?"

"Good point," he said, and she seemed to deflate slightly, as if she'd hoped for an argument. She sat down again.

"So what do I do?"

"What *we* do, is, we get you out of Devon's house, for now," he said.

"I'm not—I can't go back to the apartment, no way."

John couldn't help thinking of Amanda's mother, Grace, without feeling both sad and angry. Amanda had been loaded down with more baggage than any kid deserved. She was a remarkable girl, not only for her psychic ability—which he believed in, he had not a doubt in the world that she had somehow been gifted or afflicted with extrasensory perception, quite probably an effect of Isley's agent X—but also because of her maturity, her willingness to extend herself for the benefit of others, in spite of the abuses she'd no doubt suffered as an only child of an alcoholic parent. He wondered what would happen if she left town. Would her perceptions fade? Conversely, if she went closer to the origin of the influence, would her abilities strengthen?

"God, you don't think he'd try to hurt Grace, do you?" Her eyes were wide. "Or Peter?"

He made himself focus. "Honestly, I don't know. I don't think so." He knew that the majority of obsessive followers suffered from Cluster B personality disorders, particularly pathological narcissism. Stalking was most often a way to express rage, to demean and dehumanize the object of one's obsession rather than suffer rejection.

"If you're afraid of him, you did the right thing, leaving," he said. "You can stay at my house. I have a spare bedroom you can use."

"But what about Eric? Won't him being all confused make things worse? I mean, I just disappeared, he doesn't know what happened."

"I'll talk to him, if you like," John said. "You don't need to say anything, or even see him again. I'm definitely going to talk to his parents. They can get him some help."

Amanda looked unhappy when he mentioned Eric's parents, but nodded. John looked at his clock—his next appointment wasn't until one—and decided he'd have enough time to pay a visit to Eric's house. He could stop at Sid Shupe's on the way there, in case Eric was still hanging around.

"You can stay here, or I can drop you where you want to go," he said. "But you shouldn't wander around alone until this is resolved. Do you have friends you can go to, other family?"

Amanda looked down at the floor. "You said I could stay at your house...?"

He hesitated. She'd be alone there...but Eric didn't know where he lived, or that she'd come to him for help. He'd call Bob, ask him to keep her company until he was done with work at six. The two of them could brainstorm, maybe work up some more ideas about what to do next. Bob could probably stand to feel useful. Getting fired was a rejection no matter what the circumstances.

"I'll take you there first," he decided. "We can go get your things from Sid's later, when he gets home. You should call his cell, by the way, explain what's happening."

At her pained look, he added, "And you can tell him to call me, if he wants."

She looked relieved. "Yeah, that'd be good."

He locked up the office, and she tried to act casual as they walked to his car, but she was also trying to look everywhere at once, obviously spooked. He felt good about helping her, and it made sense that she and Bob could work together on their small crusade to save Port Isley from itself. What didn't feel so good was the realization that he wanted to resolve all this now, today, so that nothing cluttered his time with Sarah, so that he needn't waste a single precious second of their time with explanations, with words. He wanted someone else to deal with it.

><

Harold "Poppy" Peters, the mayor of Port Isley, went for a walk almost every day, a habit he'd picked up a few months after he'd sold the store. He'd taken early retirement at the age of fifty-four, both of the college tuitions were paid, and they owned the house and both cars, free and clear; he and Shirl hadn't been rich, but certainly comfortable. Shirl had had her art classes and volunteer work; she'd had two grandchildren to chase on the weekends and some gals she'd gone and had margaritas with once a month. Poppy didn't like to garden or golf, he didn't own or want to own a boat, and his only real hobby had been drinking beer while watching football. Within two weeks of being home, it had become his default setting and might have stayed that way except that his lovingly honest wife had come home a little tipsy after her girls' night out a few weeks after *that* and commented that his can wouldn't fit in the La-Z-Boy for much longer if he didn't get off it once in a while. He'd gone out the next day to buy a pair of walking shoes, and except for sick days and that time he'd strained his back—picking up a damned pumpkin, of all things—he had gone out walking. Shirl had started going with him, and he had been happy to relearn her way about things, after all the years at the business, going in early, coming home late; the Shirley Anne Edison he'd married had still been there, a lively, eternally optimistic woman. She'd liked to play word games while they walked, or talk about changing her hairstyle, or tell him the plot of whatever courtroom thriller she was in the middle of reading. He had fallen in love with her again and actually had some idea of how lucky he was. They'd both liked to meet people—they were extroverts, their daughter said—and they'd wandered the parks and streets of Port Isley and talked to everyone they met who didn't mind stopping to chat for a minute or two. They'd always had a wide circle of friends and had quickly started accumulating more—more friendly waves at the store, more horns honked when they were out walking, more neighbors dropping by for coffee or a piece of pie. Not just the local folks, either. Shirl had said it was him, that people knew an honest man when they met him, but he'd known better. Shirl had been the draw; she'd just radiated sincerity and goodwill. People liked to be around her. When he had been approached to consider taking a seat on the city council, he'd been surprised, but Shirl had only laughed and nodded, just as she had when he'd told her that almost everyone on the council was pushing him to run for mayor. She'd believed in him, which had made him believe.

In one of their very last conversations, before the cancer had taken her—it had happened so fast, not four months after the diagnosis—she'd made him promise to take care of himself, to get enough sleep and eat vegetables every now and again and go for his walks. Consequently, even as miserably drunk as he'd been since she died, he headed out for Kehoe or Chautauqua Park every single morning, determined to keep his promise. He could see, now, that he'd been angry with her for leaving, furious, in fact, and because he couldn't punish her, he'd become a drunk. He drank because he couldn't bear to be angry with his Shirl, and because he missed her horribly, and because the best part of his life was over.

He might already have been dead—his health had been steadily failing for some time—but in June, less than six weeks ago, he'd been rambling through Kehoe Park at around four in the afternoon (morning walks went the wayside along with mornings), and he'd been soused on bourbon, nothing new there, and he'd tripped over a root and fallen down. He'd hit his head on a thicker root from the same cursed tree and been knocked cold, probably helped along by his drinking. He'd been on a small trail, an offshoot from the main path that ran behind a couple of houses bordering the park; if anyone had seen him, they hadn't gone for help. He'd slept until after dark, four, five hours later. When he'd woken up, he'd rolled onto his back and looked up at the stars, more or less sober—and everything had changed. *He* had changed. It was as though while he'd slept the dark, heavy poison in his body, the blackness that had come to him the day Shirl had left the world, had leeched into the ground, leaving him light and free as air. Shirl might have suggested that the blow to the head had finally knocked some sense into it, but whatever the reason, he couldn't remember ever feeling so calm. So *aware* of the universe and his place in it.

He'd stayed there for another hour or so, watching the sky, breathing and thinking and counting the shooting stars. He'd walked home and fallen asleep on the couch while icing his bruised temple. In the morning, he'd called Abe Bengston, his family's doc since Shirl's first pregnancy, and gotten some advice on how to quit the booze without killing himself. Abe had wanted to check him into a detox center, but Poppy had convinced the doctor to let him handle it himself, by telling the truth—his heart had been broken when his wife died and he'd dealt with it poorly, but he was ready to get better. The truth didn't hurt at all, he discovered, and neither did letting go of the anger, letting go of the insane guilt he'd been living with for the choices he'd made, the mistakes he could suddenly see so very clearly. Somehow he'd convinced the doc, who had told him how to cut the drinking and what to watch for.

He'd mostly stayed around home since, doing repairs on the house and to his life, taking his walks in the morning again. He'd had hard but important conversations with both of his children, making amends as best he could, making plans to see his grandchildren before the summer was out. He'd fixed the kitchen sink and scrubbed out the bathrooms and washed everything. A number of old friends had left messages for him in the last few weeks, but Poppy hadn't returned any of their calls; he didn't want to try to explain what had happened to him, as he wasn't exactly sure himself. For once in his life, he didn't really feel like talking.

That was what he was thinking as he walked down Devlin toward Kehoe Park. It was hot, the sun bright. The neighborhood streets were dozing and quiet. He was off to a late start today; it was actually getting close to lunchtime, but he'd gotten caught up going through a box of photos, piecing together a couple of albums to give to the kids. Shirl had been meaning to do it for about a decade, ever since the first grandson, but had never gotten around to it. Poppy had been entranced by the aging snapshots of his family, the Christmas morning pictures, the vacation shots from Yellowstone. He had wept freely, sitting amid the clutter of memories. Without the muddiness that constant drinking provided he was able to miss her, clearly and poignantly, to miss the life they'd had together, to grieve for the years ahead that they'd lost. The feelings were hard, but he cherished them, proof of his time with her, proof that she'd introduced him to the ideas of forgiveness and charity. She had been, and still was, a vital part of his life.

He was still a few blocks from the park when an aging truck pulled up to the sidewalk next to him. The tires ground against the curb as the driver pulled to a stop. Bob Sayers got out of the truck, slamming the door behind him. Come to think of it, Bob had called a few times recently.

Bob walked to the sidewalk. Poppy smiled at him. The old reporter didn't look well.

"Hey there, Bob," Poppy said. "Beautiful day, isn't it?" It was, too. The sun was outshining itself. The shade of the park would be cool and green.

"Where've you been, Poppy?" Bob asked. "I've been trying to get hold of you for weeks. I've called, gone by your office..."

"I've been home," Poppy said. As Bob came closer, Poppy could smell the acrid sweat of a practicing alcoholic. He would certainly know. "I've been a little preoccupied, I guess you'd say."

"Do you know what's going on?" Bob asked. "What's been happening to people?"

Poppy thought about some of the messages he'd listened to in the last few weeks, the unpleasantries...he'd received several calls from Henry Dawes, Port Isley's PR guy, even though Henry hadn't called him at home in better than two years, and there was also what he'd experienced for himself. Something had happened, was happening to their little town, all right.

Poppy sighed. "It's a struggle for some of us, isn't it?"

Bob came closer. His eyes were bloodshot. "What do you mean? What is it? Do you know what it is?"

"You mean do I know what's causing it?" Poppy shook his head. "No. But it doesn't really matter."

"What do you mean, it doesn't really matter?" Bob's voice rose. "People are changing, acting crazy! People have *died*, and if no one does anything, more may die! Doesn't that mean anything to you?"

Poppy could see his grief, his frustration, and felt a great empathy for him. "Of course it does. Seeing people suffer...no one wants that. I'm only saying that we all struggle. Whatever the source of our despair, the struggle is just as difficult."

Bob's jaw worked. "So what are you going to do about it? You're still the mayor, aren't you?"

Poppy shook his head. "I'm not even in the loop anymore, Bob; you must know that."

Bob's face was flushed. "Rick Truman *killed* people, Ed Billings *killed* people, a woman was *raped*. Your friends and neighbors are fighting, stealing, beating each other up, doing God only knows what else—and you know it's happening, and you don't think you should do something to stop it?"

"I understand where you're coming from," Poppy said. "But I can't make other people's choices for them, and neither can you. Things are how they are."

"So that's your rationalization for not caring?" Bob snapped. "You seeing the big picture now, is that it?"

"It's not about caring or not caring," Poppy said sincerely. "It's about accepting the truth. Life is chaos, and everyone dies. Everyone. My Shirl died, and so will I. Coming to peace with that, letting go of our attachments, loving the people we chance to know…it's the best we can do."

Bob wasn't on the same page. "You think Rick Truman was letting go of an attachment when he killed his wife? When he killed *Annie*?"

"Some people are afraid; they lash out," Poppy said. "But they're the exception, I'm sure."

"We can at least warn them," Bob said. "That's reasonable, isn't it? I wrote a story about this, this *epidemic* of violence, of madness. Dan Turner pulped the entire paper and fired me."

"I'm sorry to hear that," Poppy said. Bob was a fine writer. He'd done a heck of a job with the *Port Isley Press*. "I'm sure if you take it before the council, you'll get your job back. If you'd like, I could talk to Dan, or—"

"It's not about the job, fuck the job!" Bob gritted his teeth and lowered his voice. "People are getting hurt, Poppy. Not everyone is making good choices. I got a call from Nancy a little while ago; she said the phone's been ringing all morning, people waiting for the paper, asking for news…and passing things along. She heard from three separate sources that a man got beat up and thrown off the pier last night. No one seems to know if he died, or where he is—although everyone seems to agree he was of a 'foreign' persuasion. There was a big fire just outside town, one of those old barns by the turnoff. It's smoke and ashes now. Someone lit a match. Kids are running away or disappearing. Nancy called the police for verification on any of this—and the cops are saying that nothing has happened, no comment, matters will be 'handled.' "

He was in Poppy's face, his voice sharp and accusing. "So the police aren't going to help, and Dan Turner's gone ass up for Jesus, and better than half the council can't be reached for comment because they've left town or holed up some- where, God only knows. I'm on my way to babysit a girl whose boyfriend is stalking her, by the way. And maybe I'm not handling things so well myself. Your patronage is *not* appreciated. If I wanted to be converted, I'd go talk to Dan. Maybe some of us are evolving, Poppy, but what about the rest of us? You could talk to people. They need to know that something is happening here, now, this summer, something inexplicable and real and dangerous."

Poppy wasn't sure what to say. He believed that Bob's heart was in the right place, wanting to help…but what was happening was only change. And change, by its nature, was traumatic; it was birth, it was rebirth, it was being hurt so that one could also be healed. A forest fire. A comet. An ice age. Or something as mundane as a summer season in a small town.

"You underestimate what's inside us," Poppy said. "What's inside *you*. We agree, something is happening. But where you see apocalypse, I see…" He took a breath of his own. "Freedom. A chance for real freedom."

"That's great," Bob said, backing away from him. "What a pleasure it's been, discussing this with you."

"Don't be like that," Poppy said, taking a step after him. It hurt to see Bob so upset. He'd always liked Bob, respected him. "I don't mean to be patronizing. Let's talk about it. Why don't you walk with me?"

"I think I'd rather *do* something," Bob said. "I've already done my time talking. But call me if you wake up. Maybe when one of your own gets hurt."

The reporter huffed back around to the driver's side, started his truck, and rattled off. Poppy watched him go, frowning. After a moment, he started walking again.

➤←

The big house was quiet, Karen and Tommy both sleeping, and John asleep in her bed. She'd slipped from his embrace, thirsty from the wine, and she had to pee...and she was worried, and she couldn't fall asleep worried.

She stood in the kitchen, wrapped in an oversize flannel shirt she used as a robe, glass of water in hand, and thought about what John had told her when he'd finally come to her, after their first hungry embrace in the dark hall. He'd whispered the day's events after they'd made love the first time. It seemed his teenage psychic was being stalked, and was now staying in John's guest room...not a development that seemed so great to her. He'd apparently spent a good part of his day trying to track down the estranged boyfriend, with no luck—until said boyfriend had shown up on the girl's doorstep—well, her uncle's or her friend's uncle, she was unclear on that part—and shouted for her, and the uncle had called the police. The boyfriend had run off, but it all sounded dangerous to her; she didn't like the idea of a human target living in John's house.

A young, pretty target, maybe. The thought was beneath her, and she immediately dismissed it. John was as entranced by her as she felt by him. They both agreed it was madness, what they were feeling, what they were doing, but why couldn't there be good kinds of madness?

Tommy was her first priority, of course, his safety. If there were crazy people running around, she should leave. But Karen...Karen had been prescribed pills, and she took a lot of them. She wanted to sleep all the time, and when she came out of her room—either to shower until her skin was a blotchy pink or to get something from the kitchen—she seemed not quite there. John had seen her twice, then sent her to a counseling center in Port Angeles. A dark-haired woman from the center came over every other day now, sat with Karen for an hour or two, then lectured Sarah about vitamin combinations. Karen seemed to like her, so Sarah tolerated it; she didn't know what else to do for her sister. The times she'd tried to edge in to talking about leaving in the fall, Karen had withdrawn completely. She wouldn't feel right about leaving her or moving her…or leaving John. She loved him, simple as that.

"Simple," she whispered, then took another sip of water. Was Tommy pulling away because she'd met a man? John seemed to think it was his age, perhaps exacerbated by the effect…the effect that might or might not be influencing people in a harmful way, even he couldn't say. Not with what was between them. The stalker, though. The murders. And that terrible man at the pier. She'd taken a sullen Tommy to talk to Stan Vincent, who'd tried to insist that she not be in the interview room when Tommy gave his statement. She'd ignored him, of course, but watching her son apathetically tell the story in a few short sentences—there was a guy, he had his hand in his pants, I yelled, he ran—made her feel almost unbearably sad. He continued to answer her in half sentences, and to look away from her when she spoke, as he had throughout their one-sided conversation about moms having the same rights as dads when it came to moving on. He wouldn't talk to her, and she couldn't make him.

She should leave. They *would* leave. She'd tell the woman from the center, day after tomorrow, ask for advice on how to handle it. And she'd tell John…not tonight, at least, not tonight. She'd talk to Tommy first. Or maybe she should talk to John, maybe he would come with them.

Is that what I want? Yes. Yes, and yes, but she didn't think she could without Tommy's blessing. It was too big a step. Besides, he had a practice here, a house, a life. Would he come? Was it fair of her to even ask?

Her feet were cold. She put the water glass by the sink and pulled the shirt close, hurried on bare feet back to her warm bed, to John. Tomorrow, she told herself; she'd think about it tomorrow.

CHAPTER

25

Stan Vincent sat in his office, waiting for the call. Henderson was out cruising Route 12 where it connected to the highway, watching for Dean. The deputies would be here anytime, ready to take over the barely five-hour-old search for Max Reeder, a missing ten-year-old boy. Wes Dean would be sticking his big fucking face into Vincent's yet again, grilling him on what he'd done so far, pushing his way in, mucking things up. This time, Vincent wasn't going to step aside just because Dean thought he should.

Got my own boys now, he thought, and smiled, a grim little smile. Four of them, as dedicated to him as he was to seeing justice served. Ian Henderson, of course. Frank LaVeau. Kyle Leary. And the kid just on this summer, Trey Ellis; Trey had already proved his usefulness, making conversation over coffee, drawing out the uniforms who weren't ready to make the leap. Margot Trent, Dave Miller, a couple of others, they were mostly on board but with reservations, so Vincent left them out of the serious planning. He needed to know who he could trust if things went hard, who he could count on, and he was satisfied that his people could go the distance. They'd already handled the thing at the marina, and some other things as they'd come up...

He'd assigned Trent and Miller to head up the search for the missing child, and they were doing a damned fine job. At least fifty volunteers had shown up for the door-to-door, and there'd be a hundred more searching the woods and beaches if the kid didn't turn up by tomorrow. Max Reeder appeared not to be the only missing child, unfortunately, and wouldn't Dean just love to jump all over that, tying in the runaway from last week…or the three last month. But it was Port Isley's business, not county, and Vincent would handle the matter.

The radio on his desk blipped, and Henderson's voice spilled out. "I see 'em, chief. Three, four cars coming in. Dean's in front."

"Follow them in," Vincent said. "We'll meet you here."

Vincent stood up and paced around in front of his desk. Everything had fallen so neatly into place, it was as though his fondest wish—to get Western Dean the fuck out of his hair—were destined to become a reality. LaVeau had gone through their files of plates recorded leaving town in the last six hours and had already matched two to registered sex offenders. One of them was certainly harmless, guy named Armstrong; he'd had sex with a seventeen-year-old girl eleven years before, when he'd still been a teenager himself. No play there, but the other one, that was their ticket—Neil Elwes had twice exposed himself to grade-school kids at an elementary school in Texas back in the late eighties, flapping his penis at them through chain link while the children screeched and laughed. He'd spent some time in a hospital, done some community service, and had not reoffended. Elwes had moved to Port Isley six years ago to see an uncle through end-stage cancer and had stayed on after his uncle's death—and stayed on the straight and narrow, so far as anyone knew. The man worked from home and kept to himself, he didn't have any friends, and best of all, according to the recorded message on his phone, he would be in Bend, Oregon, until next week, visiting his cousin. They couldn't have planned it better.

Vincent stepped out of his office, nodding at Kyle Leary, who was on the phone. Leary nodded back at him. The station was quiet, every free hand out looking for the Reeder kid. Except for one of their part-timers at the front desk and Debra on dispatch, they were alone. The station was an antique in its own right; built in the forties, the two-story building was a monument to sturdy, handsome architecture. The air-conditioning sucked, though, and the showy, period ceiling fans actually served a purpose, pushing the stuffy air around a bit. Vincent liked the heat; it felt like movement, like action, like things getting done.

Leary hung up, stood, and moved to meet him.

"They here?"

Vincent nodded. "Five minutes, give or take. Was that Trey?"

Leary grinned. "Kid's got a pair, don't he? All taken care of."

Vincent nodded, not ready to smile yet. Poor Mr. Elwes was going to be the focus of a statewide manhunt pretty soon, considering what Wes Dean was going to find in Neil's closet. Nothing like trying to explain a box full of boy porn, latex gloves, condoms, and duct tape. Young officer Ellis was also going to make a point of breaking the glass pane set next to the front door so that there'd be sufficient reason to walk in. None of it would hold up if Elwes got himself a half-decent lawyer, but it'd take some time to sort everything out; enough time for Vincent to figure out who'd really snatched up Max Reeder. He was sure he could find him if Dean would fuck off. All they had to do was drop the name; Dean would do the rest.

Once that fucker's gone, we can get some actual work done; we can get down to brass tacks. He had some ideas about staking out the parks, getting more cameras set up to track down the bad guys—including, maybe, the sicko who'd taken Max Reeder, the real offender…assuming that was what had happened, which he did; things were too batshit crazy for him to dismiss his gut instincts. Vincent was already in the early stages of organizing a neighborhood watch, one that included blunt instruments, as needed; he thought he might get the Jessups involved, maybe a few of the dockworkers. The streets would be safe if they had to walk down each and every one of 'em…and once everything was firmly in hand, Vincent's family could come home.

He felt his heart break a little, thinking of Lily. He'd apologized enough to Ashley; she understood that he was under tremendous stress, and she would come back when she realized that he would never hurt Lily, never *would* have except that he'd been on the phone to one of his boys after what had happened in the marina and it had been very, very important to get things done in a certain period of time, to make sure that no one went to jail for taking out the trash. The trash in that case had been a seedy Mexican dope peddler who'd been working the docks, and some local boys had taken offense. Someone had called the station, and LaVeau had caught it, and there had been decisions to be made, serious, life-changing decisions. And Lily kept talking, repeating the same nonsense phrase over and over again, trying to crawl up his leg, and he'd been trying to hear what LaVeau was telling him, and she wouldn't shut up, she wouldn't stop pulling at him, grinding her grubby heels into the tops of his feet, tearing the skin there, hanging from his pockets. When he'd snapped he'd only pushed her, he hadn't *hit* her, and she needed to learn that there were times she had to listen to Daddy, that Daddy's voice was the law. That was just a safety issue, really. Ashley should have been on top of her anyway, *would* have been except she'd run to the store for "half a second" about half an hour before, leaving him to watch the baby, who was still screaming and rubbing at the spreading bruise on her back when Ashley finally came home. Kid had landed on one of her own goddamn baby dolls, that was bad luck, just bad fucking luck, but she was fine, she'd hurt herself worse that time she'd slipped in the tub, also because Ashley wasn't watching her…which he'd been forced to point out once she'd started accusing him of things. She'd taken the baby and gone to her mother's, and although he missed them, it was better that they were gone, for now; he needed to be able to think, to listen to the cool voice that told him what was what, that reminded him of his duties. He could hear it best at night, before he slipped into the brief two- or three-hour coma that passed for sleep lately, the cool voice echoing sometimes in the empty house.

"Lucky break," Leary said.

"What?" Vincent blinked at him, frowned.

"Elwes going out of town," Leary said, and chuckled. "This'll keep that asshole busy."

Vincent looked around them, back at Leary. "Shut the fuck up," he said. Of all his boys, Leary had the biggest mouth; he'd want to watch that. Besides, it wasn't luck, it was fucking fate. He had the town's best interests at heart; he would keep it safe.

><

"Did you hear about Jaden? Jaden Berney?"

Tommy shook his head, and Jeff smiled, a weird, excited smile. "I knew him, kind of. He moved here last year. Ninth grader? They think some pervert got him. His mother thought he ran off, like, a week ago? But some other little kid disappeared, day before yesterday, ten years old. Another boy. You think it was that same guy off the pier?"

They were in Tommy's room. Up until five minutes ago, he'd been alone in his room with the door locked, surfing the Net for pictures of naked girls. Not the gross stuff; he didn't want to see all their...their *parts*, but the pretty girls, the smiling ones that weren't wearing much and seemed to be looking at him while they smiled. He'd looked around for stuff every day, lately. Sometimes for way longer than he realized.

Thinking about the guy on the pier in connection to his own jerking off made him feel uncomfortable. Not the same thing at all, except it was the exact same thing. Not in the same way, then. Tommy shrugged. "Maybe, I dunno."

"I bet it was. I read this thing once about a guy who ate little kids, you believe that? Like in the twenties or something, his name was Albert Fish. He molested them and then he *ate* them."

Jeff's inappropriate smile had widened. Tommy had no idea what to say. He'd been looking at a girl named Angel and playing with his second boner of the day, and then there was his mom's voice, calling up that Jeff had come by and he'd had to scramble to put everything away and unlock the door before they came up the stairs. It was weird; Dad had given him "the talk" when he was ten, about how jerking off was normal and sex and stuff, but it was still totally embarrassing. He still felt a sick thrill of something like guilt every single time he did it. He didn't even like to *think* the word *masturbation*; jerking off seemed way less disgusting than masturbating. He couldn't imagine getting caught by his mother, how terrible that would be. Especially now, with what she'd been doing.

"Maybe that guy is like that; maybe that's where Jaden and that ten-year-old ended up. Like, boiled, on his stove."

"That's gross," Tommy said, with a measure of real disgust.

Jeff nodded happily and abruptly changed the subject, catching him off guard. "Yeah. Hey, you weren't at the raid this morning. I didn't see you last night, either. Where you been?"

Tommy felt himself flush. "Here. I've been busy, is all."

"Doing what?"

Tommy opened his mouth, not sure what would come out. "What the fuck do you care? You taking a survey?"

"Jeez, lighten up," Jeff said. "You know the carnival's coming in next week? They've got a Zipper and an Octopus and this giant slide, you go down on a little mat. They've got a bunch of baby shit, too, but it's mostly pretty cool. Everybody goes."

Tommy wanted to ask if Jenny Todd was going, but he already knew it didn't matter. He wasn't even an actual teenager yet, and she was perfect. "What's a Zipper?"

"You know, one of those cage-spinner Ferris wheel things, only it's like more tall instead of round?"

Tommy nodded. There was something like that at the fairgrounds outside Tacoma, only they called it the Terminator. He'd stood in line for it twice, but chickened out before he got to the front. Not like he'd tell Jeff, who'd call him a pussy.

I'd go on with Jenny, though, he thought, and that was exciting, but then he thought about the man on the pier again, and then his mom's voice not five minutes ago, calling up the stairs, her voice all sweet and motherly while he was jerking off, *masturbating*. The swoops between sexual excitement and total disgust with himself were dizzying, which made him feel angrier for some reason. Why should he care if Jeff thought he was a pussy? Fuck him.

"Two years ago, this guy Clark, he was a senior? He was shit-faced on beer, right? Him and his girlfriend started spinning, up at the top? And he threw up and puke went *everywhere*; it was like this watery beer-puke, and they couldn't stop spinning for some reason, so they got soaked, and so did like six other people in the cages all around theirs. Some of them threw up, too."

"Nice," Tommy said, smiling in spite of himself. "Think I'll skip that one."

Jeff nodded. "No shit, those cages are gross. Hey, there's these guys up there every year, though, the carnies? There's a couple of them that'll sell you drinks. There's this one guy, he carries a big flask around full of tequila, for a buck you can take a drink."

Tommy grimaced. "You know how many diseases carnies must have?"

Jeff laughed, but that creeping smile was behind it. "Yeah, but they could buy us beer, though. And my mom's got some stuff she wouldn't miss."

Tommy didn't say anything. He'd had a sip of beer a couple of times; it tasted like soda made out of moldy bread. Nasty. Ditto with the tiny glass of rotten-grape juice his mom let him drink last Christmas. Having the option, though…that was interesting.

"And there's this other guy, he's like the manager or something? He's always trying to get guys to go in his trailer. He says he's got a bunch of porno, and all kinds of liquor. And pot."

Tommy made a face. "That's—nobody ever does it, do they? That's freaky."

"No, it's not like *that*. It's mostly older guys, like sixteen, seventeen. I know some guys who did it, and they said he just wanted to brag about all these women he fucked and how he ran a nightclub about a million years ago, and all these people he beat up. He says fuck like every other word, they said, and he says he killed people for money, twice. He's old, though."

"Oh." Tommy wasn't sure what to say to that. That didn't sound so safe, but they were too young, anyway.

"We should go up there, when they're setting up," Jeff said, as though he was just thinking of it, but Tommy could tell they'd gotten to the reason for Jeff's visit. "It takes them like two days; there's always kids going up there after dark, running around in the woods, drinking. It's like an unofficial party." He leered. "Jenny Todd will definitely be there, with her equally hot cousin, Allison. They hang out with a bunch of girls."

Alcohol, parties, girls, after dark. Jenny. Even thinking about going, he felt scared and excited…and the fear was losing ground fast. He was practically a teenager already. And everyone was always saying how much older he seemed, because he was smart. He could handle himself, and it wasn't like he was going anywhere *alone*. Still, there was no way in hell his mother would let him go, even if she hadn't heard anything about kids disappearing. Which she probably had, by now.

The lure was too great. He'd find a way. "Yeah, whatever. Sounds good."

Jeff raised his eyebrows. "Seriously?"

"Yeah, seriously."

"You gonna get permission?"

"Are you?"

Jeff's grin was wicked, and Tommy thought his probably looked the same. That was how it felt, anyway.

><

Amanda sat on John's back porch alone and smoked and drank iced coffee. John was at work and Bob was in the study, still on the phone to one of his so-far-useless reporter friends, trying to drum up interest in the plight of Port Isley. There were news vans scurrying back into town, but Bob only knew newspaper people, it seemed, mostly in Seattle, and almost everyone he'd talked to had blown him off as cracked or drunk or both.

It was day three of living at John's, and she felt restless—but strangely, not so bad. Her life had just gotten too fucked up, she figured; she maybe wasn't capable of freaking out anymore. At least not with any real enthusiasm. She felt daydreamy all the time, distant from herself, wandering around John's house, randomly jotting down images and ideas, reading his books, napping. Maybe she was in shock, but since John had first led her up the stairs to the guest room, she'd felt...it wasn't like anything had really clarified, but she felt *better*, like she was taking a step in the right direction. She couldn't describe it exactly. It was like...like waking up afraid because you can't remember if the test is today, and then realizing that you studied for it already, that there is nothing to worry about; she felt like *that*, that warm, sleepy relief like she'd done the right thing and could feel good about it. That was stupid, probably, but there it was. She was still afraid when she thought about Eric, but compared to her freak-fest on poetry night, she was, like, relaxed, practically.

Sid had been great about everything, even Eric showing up and shouting for her on their doorstep the night after the poetry reading, the same day she'd sneaked out. John had talked to him, explained how it was—leaving out the psychic stuff, obviously—and Devon's uncle had promptly volunteered to file a police report and take turns "sitting" with Amanda, although so far it hadn't come to that. Sid had put dead bolts in, too, which made her feel better. She didn't know if Devon knew what had happened, but she supposed he'd find out. She didn't spend much time thinking about it, actually, which she recognized as unlike her. Normally, her reality kind of revolved around Devon, but he, too, seemed distant, too far away to worry about, to wonder if he would call, to wonder what she would say. As for the police report, the cops were all busy organizing and running a search for that little kid; Bob had been giving her updates. Following up on a teenage summer kid yelling his girlfriend's name wasn't going to be topping any lists anytime soon. She felt bad for the trouble everyone had to go through, apologetic as hell, but she also recognized that guilt wasn't going to help anything. She kept her self-torture to a minimum where she could.

On Eric, there was no word. He hadn't popped up anywhere since making a scene at Sid's. John had been to his house twice in two days, and his father had been as clueless as he'd seemed when she'd met him, insisting that Eric was being a typical teenage boy. When John had continued to push the idea that Eric might need help, Mr. Hess had finally taken offense and ordered John to leave his family alone. Both times that John had been there, Eric had conveniently been "out." Lurking in the basement, probably. Working himself into stalker mode. It was bizarre that all her feelings for Eric had turned bad so fast, the change so seemingly complete. She didn't miss him or moon over happier times; they'd fucked a bunch and he'd turned out to be a creep; the rest of it was just...just her believing what she'd wanted to believe, and that was all.

She tilted her head back, heard the sound of the wind crashing high up in the trees, but there was only the barest of breezes across the deck. It was nice here, and for some reason she thought she wouldn't be staying very long, so she wanted to enjoy it. She'd been having the oddest daydreams, some of which bled into her sleep, becoming images as she dozed out. Flying over a vast forest of dark trees in a tiny plane; walking through a desert at night. They were interesting...although if her daydreams were mild, she still saw most of the same repeating images as before in her deeper dreams, which made sleep not so restful. Some of them getting brighter, the details changing, some fading. They were all still frightening to her—she thought that they all meant *death*, but she didn't know for certain. The big fire she kept seeing, maybe there were people inside the building, maybe not. The vignette with the sobbing mother and the small baby in the tub, she hated that one, there was no way around whose life was in peril, and she felt helpless and terrible when she heard the high-pitched wails of the baby and became the slumped, pale mother with tears of total abject misery coursing down her cheeks, her heart a dead black hole of exhaustion. She tried not to think of that one if she didn't have to. The kid in the darkened hall of mirrors, he was scared, he thought someone was after him...and she was now certain that he was right. She sensed a sick longing somewhere in the dark, a rapid heartbeat, sweating hands. With that kid—those kids—disappearing, the distressing nature of the image had taken a definitely ominous tone.

There'd been other changes. At one time there had been a clear image of a woman with blood in her hair, smiling, but that one had stopped broadcasting or whatever; she hadn't seen it in nearly two weeks. John had suggested that perhaps circumstances had changed, that the incident may have been bypassed somehow, but Amanda didn't think so. She'd have bet on the woman having already had her bloody, smiling night, and it sucked, not knowing what had happened, how things had turned out. It was disappointing, like watching a season finale cliff-hanger for a show that didn't exist anymore, and she was thinking that she was going to have to get used to that if her newfound abilities stayed with her. She thought that they would, she *hoped* they would, because in spite of all the trouble, the fear, all the promise of future disappointment, she was already deeply attached to having superpowers. Not just because it was cool, but because she felt like big things would have to happen for her now: no waitress job, no average life. Maybe that was selfish, but she couldn't help it.

Her psychic ability hadn't grown, exactly, but it seemed to be sharpening, picking up subtleties of feeling since she'd moved into John's guest room. There was this new thing when she was awake sometimes, these brushes of...of *something* that didn't come from her, and she didn't think they felt like anything from Bob or John, either, pretty much the only people she'd seen in three days. It was like this fluttering of chaos that edged around her wandering thoughts, something about numbers or mirrors... prisoners. Shadows. Lines of numbers. She couldn't explain, nor could she quite catch hold of the threads to follow them anywhere. She didn't think it was Eric...it didn't feel like anything she'd ever felt before.

John seemed to be stuck in a kind of purgatory of inaction, frozen by too many considerations, by his romance with Sarah. He rarely said her name, but he thought it all the time, Sarah, Sarah. He'd told Amanda three or four times now that things would work out, but she could see that he didn't have any real faith in that himself, let alone a plan on how to get from here to there. He spent his nights away. Even without being able to pick up his feelings and thoughts (which she could now, sometimes; it took only the smallest effort), Amanda could tell that his mind was elsewhere. It was in the way he couldn't seem to concentrate, didn't seem to be listening.

Bob was drinking less, she could tell, but he actually looked older since the paper had been canceled. His obsessive interest in reading old newspaper articles online took up most of his time. They *had* come up with the idea of calling his old cronies and telling them about the sharp rise in violence and general wackiness around town, hinting at a chemical spill, but the only people who had even been willing to listen had been other retirees, no one still on the job. She was starting to think that they were all just spinning their wheels, killing time until everything changed… which she felt would happen soon, but she didn't know why she felt that way, if it was psychic or just some worst-case-scenario feeling. Everything was going to change, though, suddenly and completely. Like, maybe she was going to die. She didn't know, but thought that panic was at least as useless as guilt.

Amanda took a sip of the coffee and adjusted her shades. Most of John's back deck was shadowed by the park's trees, but it was near noon; the sun laid a bright strip over the bleached and weathered wood. She leaned back against the heat of the chair. Every exposed part of her was positively greasy with SPF thirty—in shorts and a tank, that was a lot of sunblock, but she still wouldn't stay out long. Too much direct sunlight made her feel dizzy, like her brain had turned to bleached mush, and it usually gave her a headache. Still, sunlight was supposed to be good for brain hormones or something, and she could chain smoke, and compared to Grace's apartment, being up against the trees was nice, it was so quiet...

"Amanda."

She sat up, her heart freezing in her chest—and there he was, Eric Hess, leaning against the porch rail on the wooded side. His face—his expression was angry, but his voice was tight with pain.

"What the fuck, huh? You tell me to make coffee, then fucking disappear?"

Amanda could yell for Bob; he'd come running. Or she could probably make it inside and shut the door; he'd have to jump the rail *that'll take him a few seconds, go go—*

"Why are you looking at me like that? What did I *do*?" Eric's voice was plaintive. "What did I do, can you at least tell me that?"

"You scared me," Amanda said, carefully getting out of the chair, edging behind it. "I got scared. I have to go now, OK?"

His fingers tightened on the railing. "No! I'm losing my fuckin' mind here, don't leave!"

"You're scaring me now," she said, as evenly as she could. She continued to back toward the sliding glass doors. "I'm sorry I ran away. I'm crazy. Totally nuts. Decide that I'm a crazy bitch and drop it, please, OK?"

"Drop what? What are you doing?" Eric leaned forward and heaved himself up on one lean arm, swinging his legs easily over the rail, the movement taking about a second, and he was on the deck, he was close enough that she could see his cracked lips and bloodshot eyes and feel his need, pouring out of him like the heat of the day.

"I'm—we're broken up now," Amanda said. "I'm sorry, but it's over."

"What did you see? What scared you?"

"What don't you get about *it's over*?" She took another sliding step back, and he held up both of his hands.

"Don't leave," he said. "I won't come near you, OK? Just—don't do this. It's not over. I love you."

"Oh, shit," she said.

"I love you, and I know you love me," he said.

He hadn't come any closer, and she was drawn in despite her fear. She wanted him to understand, to leave her alone without being angry about it. "No, listen, you think you do, but it's whatever's happening here; it's the same thing that makes me see things about people—it's making people feel things too much. We talked about this, I know we did. Think about it. Have you ever been like this before?"

"I love you," he said again. "I don't just think it, I feel it. We feel it, when we're together, when I'm fucking you, and the way you look into my eyes…we belong together."

He stared at her, his gaze strangely flat—and then he had closed the distance between them, faster than she could think, and his arms were around her, and he was holding her, trying to kiss her.

Amanda turned her head, drew a breath, and screamed, loud and long. Eric's arms loosened, and she tripped over her own feet trying to get away and shouted again as she fell, thumping heavily to the deck, whacking the shit out of her right elbow. Behind her, the glass door was shoved open.

"Hey! Get away from her!" She couldn't see Bob, but he sounded mean and strong. She felt the vibrations of his shoes on the hot wood beneath her legs and her butt. Her sunglasses had gotten knocked off when she fell, so Eric seemed overexposed, like in a picture, as he turned to confront Bob, a snarl of rage contorting his white features. Whatever he saw changed his mind. He backed away, looking at Amanda, his expression going tortured, sick, lost…furious. He turned and ran, off the deck and into the park.

A few running steps against dirt and then nothing, a wind in the trees. Amanda fell onto her back, cradling her funny bone, looking up at her savior—who was holding a handgun, still pointed the way Eric had run. It was a revolver, had the cylinder thing in the middle, and Bob's finger was on the trigger.

"Jesus, Bob, where'd you get that?"

Bob pointed the weapon straight up and looked down at Amanda. "Are you hurt?"

"No, I'm fine," she said, and sat up. "Didn't know I had Cowboy Gunpants as my babysitter."

He held out his hand and helped her pull herself to her feet. "Yup. I get a senior discount on the ammo. You might want to sit down for a minute."

"I'm fine," she said again, and then felt her legs go wobbly all at once, like her muscles decided to lie back down. Bob caught her, supporting her against his body. He was strong and smelled like whiskey and soap, and it occurred to her for the first time that he was a man, not just an old person. The realization was surprisingly unsettling.

"Did I not just tell you to sit down?"

"You *suggested* it," she mumbled, and took a breath, and willed her legs to be legs again. The mental command worked well enough for her to be able to step away from him a second later, as soon as she could. "I'm OK, thanks."

"What happened? Did he attack you?" He tucked the gun into his belt.

Amanda shook her head. "No, he was confused. I tried to talk to him, but he was—he's already down…"

In Crazy-town, she'd been about to say, one of Devon's quips, but the thought ran deeper. The feeling. She chased it, suddenly sure that it was important. From the beginning, she'd felt a sense of inevitability about the things she saw, like they were supposed to happen. She felt that now, stronger than ever.

What if they really are? What if no matter what they tried or did, all of it was supposed to happen, so it would happen anyway, like Devon had once proposed about a billion years ago? She'd run from Eric in the first place to avoid the scenario she'd created by running. Even thinking it hurt her brain a little, it was like one of those Escher drawings, but did that *mean* anything?

No, no, it can *be changed.* She'd seen Devon dead, and he wasn't, he wasn't going to be, that image was gone because he'd left town, he'd put himself out of the picture.

Does it have to be an all or nothing deal? Isn't it possible that only some things are fated to be?

She blinked and felt that flutter of chaos she'd been picking up for the last few days, of numbers, lines, mirrors, grow stronger, become like a color she could almost see, shadow, balance, *shell sea…*

"For every darkness, there is light," she said.

"Right," Bob said, looking at her with some concern. "We should go inside."

Amanda blinked again and felt some concern herself as the weird intensity faded. She was getting a headache, and she was suddenly quite sure that she was fated to see Eric again, that there was nothing she could do to avoid another confrontation…and she'd just made things way worse with him.

"Yeah, OK."

Whatever limbo she'd been in, she felt like things were going to start happening, fast, and she'd better wake the fuck up if she wanted to make any difference. She followed Bob inside feeling scared and alone.

✦✦

He ran through the woods until his hurting lungs finally slowed him down, his heart torn in two, his throat stuffed with horrible hard stones that he couldn't swallow. He finally doubled over, hands on his knees, regretting every cigarette he'd ever smoked. He felt like shit, like dog shit scraped on a curb, and what the fuck game was she playing, anyway? He'd known she was a freak, but she was *his* freak; he loved her, he took care of her; what was she trying to do? She'd been touchy all day before the piss fiasco at that theater, she'd avoided him on the way home—then she'd climbed out a fucking *window* to get away from him. And fucking *moved*, and sent that shrink to talk to his *father*, for fuck's sake. He'd had to play it all wounded-teen-runs-to-father-for-advice or risk being sent back to Boston to stay with his batty Aunt Marla until his mother came home, and what the fuck had *happened*?

He drew in great painful gasps of air, seeing her on the deck, her skin glowing white in the sun. She was so beautiful, so amazing and beautiful, there was no way she was going to leave him, no way in hell. She couldn't just fuck him and make him love her and then tell him it was over; that was bullshit, fucking bullshit, and she didn't even mean it. She loved him. She couldn't have done the things they'd done together if she didn't.

He needed to get her alone so they could talk. If he could just talk to her, show her how he felt, he'd make her see. He *would* talk to her. He told himself that they'd laugh about this someday, but there was a very hurt, very angry part of him that would never, ever laugh about what she'd done, how she'd run away from him like he was that fuckhole who was doing her mother, like he was dog shit. What the fuck, she was *scared*, what did that mean?

"Fucking bitch," he panted, and he didn't mean that, not really; she was his soul mate, and she had freaked out because she was a freak, but that was just part of her. He could accept that, he *would*, and they'd get past this. He just needed to talk to her, alone, that was all, a measly fucking few minutes without having a fucking gun shoved in his face, and everything would be fine.

There was still almost three weeks of his "family" vacation left, before he went home, but his father had been making noise about going back to California early; the new missus was getting bored. Eric had already planned to have Amanda come with him, at least long enough for him to pack up his shit and move wherever she wanted to go—Seattle, California, Africa, he didn't care. He hadn't been prepared to take no for an answer, let alone *fuck off.*

She doesn't mean it.

His breath caught for just a second. He thought about the way her face had changed when she'd been trying to convince him that he wasn't totally in love with her. He'd seen the compassion, the pain in her face, for him. And when he'd touched her, the hesitation, the heat of her skin against his...she still loved him, and wanted him. Maybe those two numbfuck grown men she was playing detective with, maybe they'd been filling her head with shit. She didn't know them, didn't know what their motivations were. They were probably hot for her ass too, even the oldster, Mr. Lone Ranger.

He stood up, still breathing deeply, the idea catching hold, confirming what he suddenly firmly believed—she was being brainwashed; those fuckers were brainwashing her. It was like that Stockhold syndrome or whatever it was called, where the hostage identified with the kidnapper or terrorist or whatever. *That* was why she was scared; that was why she'd screamed.

They're probably with her all the time, working on her, fucking with her mind...watching her. He felt a physical revulsion, thinking of either of those old men touching her, putting their hands on her smooth, soft skin...

He saw a tree he could lean against and did so, closing his eyes, thinking of her little sounds and sighs when he had his hands on her, in her, that first time on the floor, when she'd parted her legs for him. He remembered the tremble of her creamy white thighs, the crimp of hair against his lips, the smell of her sex against his mouth…

Eric's poor, thrashed dick stirred to life. He'd jerked it for better than an hour last night and then again this morning, tortured by these sudden memories, only days old. He'd kept losing his erection, wondering where she was, why she wasn't with him, but then kept pressing and pulling anyway, kind of liking the unpleasant, electric feel of fraying nerves, and now he felt like he'd fucked a pinecone. He couldn't help himself, thinking of her. The magic of the two of them, flesh to flesh, that was way too good to give up on so easily. He could remind her…and maybe break whatever spell the reporter and the doctor had cast over her. She was psychic, he believed that, and he'd let her look inside him, see how pure his love for her was. He didn't like the psychic thing; he'd felt that she was too distracted from him, which made him feel so desperately unhappy that he could only think to pick a fight with her to get her focus back to what was important. He'd use it, though, to convince her of his feelings. He just had to get past her self-appointed guardians…

Dad had a gun. He kept it on the boat, wrapped in a piece of oily leather, under the back bench. A .22 semiautomatic.

Eric straightened his shoulders and started to walk, his breathing finally calming. The shade of the trees was cool, the path speckled with floating shafts of bright sunlight, like some cheesy postcard. It smelled like summer camp to him—the only time as a kid that he'd ever bothered with nature, when he'd been stuck there by his parents for two months every year—like green things and mold and dirt, a smell he associated with loneliness.

He felt ravaged; running away, believing that she really wanted him to never see her again, that had been like running through hell, but the devastation was slipping away, becoming a call to action. He got it now. She put up a hard front, but she was a damaged little thing, hiding behind the armor of shit childhood, trying to survive. Kicked out, desperate, her future uncertain…how hard would it be for a couple of unscrupulous fuckers to start convincing her of things?

It wasn't over. He hadn't lost her, only parted from her for a moment, and realistically, all the great lovers went through turmoil; their dynamic was too powerful, the forces around them too great even to be overcome in some cases. The sophomore English final had been on Romeo and Juliet; he'd written an essay about how they'd had to die so that their love would remain perfect…

No one was going to die; he didn't even know why he'd thought that. No one was going to die because if *he* was holding the gun, he'd be in control. He'd make them promise him an hour with her, that was all, away from their influence, and then he'd make her fucking listen to him, and he would listen to her, and she'd see that there was nothing to be scared of, that he would take care of her. He'd give her the gun; he could see him handing it over to her, see her drop it on the floor so she could lean in to kiss him. They could make love and then decide where they would go, start dreaming the life they wanted together, and maybe John and Bob would come back with the cops or whatever, but once she was with him again, once they'd reconnected, none of that shit would matter. He would be happy.

Still, better to avoid confrontation…he'd hang around, wait for an opportunity. He'd finally convinced the old man that he'd needed some alone time, and his father had been only too happy to comply, letting up on the let's-pal-around scenario after Eric had tearfully, angrily confessed that his girlfriend was breaking his heart, could they please stay, he had to talk to her. Dad had hugged him in a stiff, movie-like way and promised to give him his space. As though he wanted to do anything else; he and Jeannie didn't even leave a note most days anymore, they were just gone, shopping down the coast or out on the boat or just locked in their bedroom, humping. Being rich, bored assholes, pretending that he didn't exist. He could wait for a long time. And she'd go out, eventually, or both of *them* would leave, and maybe the gun didn't have to come out at all.

He smiled, thinking of their reunion, of watching her doubts fall away, of being trusted again, and was still smiling when he passed an elderly couple a few moments later, and he heard one of them say something about young love.

His smile widened. That would be them, someday. They would be together for as long as they both lived.

CHAPTER

26

The police came and took a statement about Eric coming to the house, though Bob left out the part about pointing a gun at the kid. A flinty-eyed, round-faced officer, Kyle Leary—Bob remembered not liking him at some point in the past, and the feeling was confirmed as reasonable—with a semiautomatic and a condescending attitude asked a few questions and then bothered John with a few more when he came home, asking if John was Amanda's doctor, asking if her mother knew where she was spending her nights. Grace Young did, actually. John had called her and explained that Eric might be a danger, assured her that Amanda was all right—and Grace had asked bluntly, drunkenly, if he was fucking her daughter yet, and then said she'd call the cops if he did, and then hung up on him. He'd told Bob about it the day before, while Amanda had been watching a movie in the other room; just hearing it made Bob want to go over there and give that barfly a piece of his mind and a boot in the ass. In spite of his denial, John felt pretty much the same. Bob could hear it in his voice, see it in the way he cut his eyes toward the living room, toward their persecuted, smart-ass little friend. Except for her taste in boyfriends, Amanda had turned out awfully decent, considering her life up until lately. Grace Young was a vampire.

"You had lunch?" Bob asked, still rummaging as John walked into the kitchen. He found a box of biscuit mix in the pantry. Biscuits and eggs, coffee...he had some vague idea of getting them all fed and clear-headed to talk about what Mo had told him.

"No, I was just going out when you called," John said. "You cook?"

"Only when necessary," he said, and found he couldn't wait another second. "Listen, I think I found something. I talked to a friend of mine, and he gave me a name. A place, actually. Where, four years ago, they had a run of very bad luck. Big increase in impulse crimes, basically, including murder. There was some serious shit, in the same neighborhood of weird as what's been going on here."

John leaned against the counter. "You're kidding."

"Jenkin's Creek, in California," Bob said. "My friend got into it because he used to write a column for one of those super-market alien conspiracy–type rags. He kept the post office box when the paper sank, and says he still gets these random letters from people about strange goings-on. Government conspiracies, UFOs, like that.

"He said he got several letters from a woman in northern California, an ex-hippie fan of his, documenting a 'change' in the air that she believed lasted from June until early in September in 2008. He said the letters seemed paranoid at first, and the woman had suggested that while she didn't believe in aliens, she wasn't ready to *disbelieve* in them, either, considering what was happening. Standard crank, right? Thing was, her letters were accompanied by articles. Not photocopies or printouts; they were cut from real newspapers. My friend, Mo, he checked. Articles about violent crime. There was some occult-influenced thrill murder… and a guy wiped out his entire family and disappeared."

"Jesus."

"Yeah, but here's the thing. Mo dropped her a line, asked him to keep her updated, and she wrote a few more times. Her initial fears, that perhaps there were aliens involved, disappeared; in the last letter, she talked about how good she was feeling, and how her close friends had become closer, and she was really feeling connected to her family, to her husband and children…Mo said that the letters were about everything changing, relationships, sense of self, sense of community…"

John was nodding. "Right, not just violence. Impulse control, sure, but that doesn't necessarily lead to total chaos, not for everyone. Not even for most people."

He rubbed at his eyes and looked at Bob. "So what happened?"

"Ah, Mo said she wrote a short letter sometime later that fall, to tell him that she believed the event, or series of events, was over. The tragedies of the summer were still being mourned, but the town was putting itself back together. She called it a summer of evolution and said that she hoped he'd file it with his 'serious' casework, because she—and several of her dear friends, according to her—firmly believed that something paranormal had been at play. He hasn't heard from her since."

John frowned and folded his arms. He seemed to forget that Bob was in the room, his gaze looking inward. Bob let him think a moment, found a bowl, and preheated the oven.

"What are you thinking?"

John blinked at him, still frowning. "She thought that some people gave in to positive influences, some to negative, is that the idea?"

"Obviously," Bob said. "Maybe she was a kook about why, but it seems to me—"

"No, wait," John said. "I don't want to lose my way here. Before you consider the details, consider the whole. The same thing that's happening in Port Isley, it happened somewhere else. Four years ago, in California. Also in the summer."

"OK."

"There's a precedent," John said. "I'd say our own activity started up in June, wouldn't you? We can base the next search on clusters of events within the last five *summers*. Maybe it won't mean anything, but it's a starting point."

"It's a man," Amanda said.

Both of them looked toward the open arch of the kitchen. Amanda stood there, her expression thunderstruck.

"That's what I've been hearing and picking up," she said, and looked at John, at Bob. Her short hair was still wet, slicked back from her face. She looked about twelve. "It's him, the guy, the *he's here* guy. He's causing this. That's totally it."

"Since when?" Bob asked. "What are you picking up? How do you know?"

"Last couple of days," she said. "I've been getting this…like, a different channel. I don't know, but the way he thinks, what I'm thinking…I don't know how to explain."

"You're sure about this?" John asked.

"Fuck no," she said. "Are you making coffee?"

John did so, while Bob filled Amanda in on what she'd missed…and Amanda filled them in on her new feeling from this person, this man who she insisted was responsible for the changes in Port Isley, only able to describe him in single words. Words about him, or from him, or because of him. Prisoners. Mirrors. Lines of numbers, maybe. Shadow, movement, something about seashells…Bob listened, trying to let the information become part of his understanding, realizing how much he trusted Amanda's psychic perceptions—he didn't question her assertion. A man, a human being, was responsible for those people dying. For people changing.

"Why do you think you're picking it up now?" John asked. Bob had the biscuits in and was cracking eggs into a bowl. *Hope you like 'em scrambled…*

"Yeah, that's fine," Amanda said, as though he'd said something aloud. She didn't seem to notice, though Bob and John exchanged a look, Bob raising his eyebrows.

"I dunno," she continued, back to John's question. "Maybe… maybe he's getting stronger? His influence, I mean?" She shrugged. "Or maybe he's closer."

"Is he doing it on purpose?" Bob asked.

"No. I don't think so."

"A man," John said. "You're certain."

"I keep saying I'm not, don't I? I'm *pretty* sure." Amanda accepted a cup of black coffee. "It's got to be a tourist, right? He was in Jenkin's Creek four years ago, and now he's here for the summer."

Bob and John looked at one another. "That makes sense," Bob said.

"If it *is* a man," John said. "And there are thousands of them here for the season, or some part of it."

"Yeah, but we can track down a man." Bob grinned. "If she can read his mind—"

"I didn't say that," Amanda said. She lowered her coffee mug, looking alarmed. "I can't. I mean, I'm getting these impressions, but nothing specific, I told you. No way I can track him."

"We shouldn't assume anything yet," John said. "This is a lot of information, a lot to consider."

Bob felt a surge of frustration with both of them. He poured the eggs into an overheated skillet, the crackle loud enough to kill the conversation for a second or two. These things Amanda kept seeing, that she was sure were going to happen if no one intervened—how long did they have? There were officially missing children, at least two boys. A building had already burned down, and not the one Amanda thought she was seeing, which suggested a budding arsonist in their midst, no joke in an old, dry town like Port Isley, swept by constant winds. No joke anywhere. The traveling carnival was due to open on Friday, which meant they'd be pulling into town in the next day or two, presumably with their hall of mirrors in tow. Amanda had heard gunfire and screams, she'd seen a possible infanticide, a probable killer—why couldn't she get any names or times? Why didn't she recognize anyone? He'd been digging, hard; and true, Mo's story had provided a possible picture, that was a lucky break, but he was sure they were finally getting somewhere, and John's initial reaction was, naturally, to stop and think things over. Amanda's was to backpedal.

Yeah, well, yours was to drink, he reminded himself, and kept his mouth shut. He served up the eggs, and they went to their respective silences as they ate, both of them clearing their plates with enthusiasm. Bob felt like he had an appetite for the first time in a week. Amanda started to talk about Eric, saying that she thought she should call her mother, to warn her—then looked at John sharply. Considering that she'd answered his thought about scrambled eggs, Bob had it figured before she spoke.

"Oh," she muttered, her face flushing. "I'm sorry. She's got issues."

"You don't have anything to apologize for," John said, glancing in slight amazement at Bob.

"She's getting stronger, too," Bob said, and John nodded.

"*She*'s right here," Amanda said. "And she knows."

She took a sip of her coffee, her expression turning bleak. "Don't ask me why I think this, I don't know, but I keep thinking that it's all going to be over before we even know anything has happened."

"What is?" Bob asked.

She shook her head, her wise eyes in her child's face troubled. "Everything."

CHAPTER

27

Jeff called early on Tuesday afternoon, and Tommy's mother called him down to the kitchen. Tommy picked up the phone to hear an open dare in Jeff's voice. The carnival had come, they were setting up even now, and people would be going up starting tonight—when did Tommy want to go?

Tommy had worked everything out a hundred ways since Jeff had first mentioned the carnival, and his heart started thumping, loudly, but he was ready. He jumped before he could think twice.

"Cool, I saw the ad for that," Tommy said, then hesitated. As though Jeff were asking him something.

"What the fuck?" Jeff snapped. "You deaf?"

Tommy glanced at his mother, obviously lingering near the sink. "I'll have to ask."

He didn't quite cover the mouthpiece. "Can I stay over at Jeff's? He got a new game."

His mother smiled, but she was frowning, too. "So you'd be staying in?"

"Yeah."

"What's the game?"

He'd thought of that, too. She didn't like war games or the hardcore vice stuff, but she didn't care about anything she considered age appropriate.

"One of those band ones, with guitars," he said. "*Rockstar Reality.*"

Her brow smoothed. Maybe she was thinking about the free time she'd have for fucking John Hanover, which she was still doing in spite of Tommy's very obvious feelings on the matter. He refused to talk to her about it, furious that she didn't know what to do. She was his *mother*; she was supposed to do what was best for *him*.

"Sure, I don't see why not."

Tommy turned his back to her, sure she'd catch the anger or the lie in his face if she looked. He thought he was getting better at hiding things, but she'd been watching him so closely lately, he didn't want to risk this triumph of deception. "Yeah," he said. "I can stay over."

Jeff wasn't a total idiot. "Gotcha. Go log, I'll be there in a minute."

"Yeah, OK." Tommy hung up and started immediately for the stairs, through the open arch next to the refrigerator.

"Hey, hang on a second."

Shit. He turned back, making himself look irritated. "Jeff's sending me some stuff. Important stuff."

"That can wait," she said. "You're about to go hang out with him until midnight, aren't you?" She was wearing sweats and a T-shirt and looked frumpy as she leaned against the sink, her hair tied back in a straggling tail. "I need to ask you something."

Why don't you ask, then, he thought. He hated feeling like she made plans to talk to him, like he was going to freak out or something if she didn't *plan*. He felt unprepared. Worried. He'd been on the computer a lot, and not playing *Warcraft*...

"What?"

"Do you want to leave here?"

He wasn't expecting that. "What? Why?"

"I'm concerned...I'm worried that it's not safe anymore," she said. "Those poor boys, disappearing. And what happened at the beach that day."

She shook her head, her expression strange, twisted. "Maybe it was never safe. I'm just…I…"

She gave him her most loving, pleading, motherly look. "I love you, Tommy. You're my baby. If anything ever happened to you, I don't know what I'd do."

He couldn't tolerate that. "I'm not a baby."

"No, of course not," she said. "I didn't mean it like that."

"What about Aunt Karen?"

"I don't know, honey. I guess I'd ask her to come with us."

"To where? To our new apartment?" It was tiny. He heard the sneer in his voice and felt slightly out of control. "What about Doctor John?"

"I—I don't know." She faltered, turning those pleading eyes at him again, which made him feel seriously pissed. What right did she have to make him feel so guilty? *She* was the one having sex; she was the one who'd dragged them to this stupid, dangerous place and taken up with a stranger. *No wonder they got divorced.* She wasn't supposed to ask him for anything.

"Whatever," he said, and his heart was pounding even louder than when he'd lied about his reason for going to Jeff's, hot in his ears, he was leaving, turning away from her and going up the stairs, amazed that he was walking away from her, that he was angry enough to do it. That she was letting him.

Jeff was waiting for him when he sat down.

Smooth mufu.

what about u?

If Jeff didn't have a plan, Tommy would be able to back out. He wanted to go, but he was afraid of getting caught, he was afraid something would go wrong.

Momll be out til midnite at least. Come over 6. we raid cabnet 1st, go up, b home by 11.

Tommy hesitated, felt a scramble of butterflies in his gut, of excitement, of daring, of fear, then sealed his fate with two letters: *ok*.

→←

Jeff's mother was just leaving when Tommy came over. She was dressed in too-tight clothes and wore too much makeup. Jeff's stepdad was a trucker, out of town for weeks at a time, and Jeff had mentioned a couple of times that she liked to go out with her girlfriends and drink too much, that she'd been doing it a lot this summer. She made Jeff promise to lock the doors and actually patted Tommy on the head while he was putting his stuff down, giving him a clear view of her cleavage. Jeff was obviously embarrassed, practically pushing her out of the house, and when the door had closed behind her he shook his head.

"She better watch it," he said, cryptically, and led Tommy straight to the kitchen. Everything was green—the counters, the linoleum—and there was kind of a garbagey smell, like coffee grounds and garlic and frying. Big Blue was way nicer than Jeff's house, but Jeff's had better stuff to eat: Twinkies and frozen pizzas, white bread, shit like that. Jeff opened the fridge and took out two sodas, some store brand. Generic lemon-lime.

"Did you eat dinner?" Jeff asked.

"Not really…"

"Good. Me either. You get more drunk if you don't eat first."

Jeff listened for a minute, cocking his head toward the door, then heaved himself onto the counter, onto his knees. From the cabinet high over the stove he pulled down a bottle of something, handing it down to Tommy, then climbed down holding another.

Tommy looked at his, a bottle half full of what looked like water but was, of course, vodka.

"You mix it with something, you can't even taste it," Jeff said. He held up the other bottle, a small, rounded one labeled Peppermint Schnapps, mostly full. "This one's clear, too. I figure we take some out and add water back so they look the same."

Tommy nodded. That seemed reasonable. He watched as Jeff pulled down two water glasses and poured out alcohol from both bottles—only half-filling each glass—then carefully funneled water from the tap back into each bottle before returning them to the cabinet.

Tommy had no idea how to mix a drink, so he followed Jeff's lead, pouring some of the soda into the glass Jeff handed him.

"Here's to Jenny Todd," Jeff said, holding up his foaming glass.

"Gotta drink to that." He tapped his noxious-smelling concoction to Jeff's.

Both boys drank, one big gulp each—and Tommy was immediately a hair away from throwing up, the thick, minty soda like fire going down his throat, like the worst cough syrup ever. He grabbed for the half-empty soda can and upended it, letting the carbonation wash the terrible mint out of his mouth. It was a close thing for a minute as the taste lingered.

Jeff made a tremendously funny face, his teeth bared, his eyelids fluttering. "*Yahh*," he said loudly. For a second, he looked like he was going to throw up too, but then shook it off.

"Definitely more soda," he said, his voice strange and raspy.

"And ice," Tommy said.

They doctored the drinks, Tommy already feeling a kind of heavy heat in his stomach and in his knees, like he'd drunk nighttime cold medicine. As bad as the taste was, the second swallow wasn't as god-awful as the first...his throat was going numb, maybe. Jeff was saying something about something at school, and Tommy tried to listen, but he was getting more and more preoccupied with what his body was doing.

"You feeling it?" Jeff asked. He wore a big, dopey smile.

Tommy nodded, his head rolling heavily on his neck. He felt good. A little off balance.

They drank more and carried their drinks to Jeff's room and watched YouTube movies for a while, this one of a guy getting hit in the nuts over and over again, and they both laughed for a long time. Maybe it was the alcohol, but Tommy felt really good about Jeff, like they had a lot in common. They watched a bunch of stuff, but somehow Tommy didn't realize that time was passing until Jeff said they could probably head up, it'd be dark soon. Magically, two hours had passed.

Jeff grabbed a flashlight, and Tommy went to pee, and totally peed on the ring in Jeff's bathroom, then used like half a roll of toilet paper to wipe it off. He felt clumsy and strange, but he liked the feeling, liked that everything in his mind was a funny joke, that Jeff was his best friend and they were doing something exciting.

They stopped in the kitchen long enough to finish their drinks and for Jeff to carefully rinse the glasses and put them away—a complicated activity that Tommy could only watch, swaying, like his body was listening to music that he couldn't hear—then headed outside into a hot, late day, the sunset brilliant orange and pink down on the bay.

"You're walking funny," Jeff said, as they started up the hill, through long shadows lying across the street. There were cars and people around, but not many and Tommy didn't really notice, working too hard to not walk funny, and he saw that Jeff was practically tripping over his toes, his own walk a kind of controlled fall. Their shadows staggered in front of them, monstrously distorted.

"Not as funny as you," he said, and they both cracked up, leaning on each other for a moment. Tommy was glad it was

S . D . P E R R Y

getting dark; they probably *looked* drunk—he was pretty sure he was, anyway—and he thought that if he saw Jenny Todd tonight he might have to kiss her. Being drunk was awesome; he felt like he could say or do anything he wanted.

They staggered onward, Jeff telling some story about some guy, Tommy wishing they had more to drink—he was thirsty, and he didn't want to lose the wonderful drunkenness—and neither of them noticed the man in the little blue car who drove past them three separate times on their way to the fairgrounds, a man with sandy, receding hair and a careful consideration in his gaze as he watched them through the gathering dark.

><

John continued to have a backlog of calls and clients, but it was official: as many people were canceling as showing up. He'd spent a free hour before lunch considering what Bob had found about Jenkin's Creek, refining his interpretation of what was happening in Port Isley. The woman who'd written the letters to Bob's friend, who'd called it a summer of evolution…he'd looked through his recent case notes and felt that her case affirmed what he'd already been thinking.

His three o'clock had canceled, and he had spent most of the hour trying to get someone at the police station to confirm that Eric's assault had been pursued, that someone had been to speak with Eric's father, but he'd been put on hold both times he'd called, the first time for nearly fifteen minutes, then been disconnected. An agitated woman finally took his number on try number three, but no one had called back. He'd considered walking over to the station but doubted he'd do much better, not before his four o'clock. No one answered the phone at the Hess household. Amanda had insisted that she didn't want to leave town, but he was starting to think he should push harder. If Eric was dangerous—and it seemed he was leapfrogging over the lengthy stalker build-up, going straight for the scary stuff— and the cops weren't going to be available, it would be best for her to get away from him. John couldn't see sending her away alone, she wasn't legally an adult, but she wasn't a child, either; he couldn't see making her leave if she didn't want to go, and he wasn't about to kick her out; she'd had enough of that for one lifetime. And in truth, they needed her. For whatever good had been done, was still being done, people had died, and Amanda believed there would be more; considering her ability to sense the cause of everything, to pick up "his" feelings, she might actually be instrumental in stopping further bloodshed.

He still hadn't settled on any clear course of action when Sarah called, late in the day. Tommy was spending the night at a friend's and would he care to join her for dinner...John hated asking Bob to stay again, but the idea of a whole night with her, especially with their future so uncertain...he spent the drive home trying to think of the best way to ask. He would have begged if Bob had declined, or taken Sid Shupe up on his offer to have Amanda over to his house, but Bob said he was happy to stay; he'd spent most of the day fact-checking on Jenkin's Creek, on the phone or at the computer, and said that Amanda had stayed inside and read or watched TV, except for excursions to the garage to smoke cigarettes. They'd already made a plan to order in Chinese, barricade the doors, and watch movies, Amanda's choice. Amanda wandered into the kitchen while they were talking and made a few jokes about making Bob sit through a zombie movie marathon, but she was distant, all wry surface, as she'd been since her revelation about the influence being a man, just after Eric's attack the day before. She didn't want to talk about Eric, her dreams, her tenuous connection with the summer man, her mother…she had an amazing talent for making her face an expressionless mask when John tried to lead their conversation anywhere she didn't want it to go.

John brought up the idea that she leave town again, and she promptly changed the subject, pointing out that as of today, the carnival was at the fairgrounds. She had an idea that they could find some way to close the fun house down. Bob was as enthused about the idea as she was, and they promptly fell to planning. John left them to it, heading upstairs to pack a few toiletries.

He waved good-bye to Amanda and Bob on his way out, reminding them that he had his cell; they barely glanced up from their perusal of the delivery menu for Uncle Chan's, only open in the summer.

The sun was setting as he drove to Big Blue, the streets deserted compared to only the day before. He'd heard from his final client of the day, and again on the radio on his way home from work: the alleged child-snatcher, a Port Isley local with an apparent history of exposing himself to children, had been apprehended in Oregon. The media had packed up and run after him. John shook the thought before it took hold. The idea of some sick man working his will on a child, an innocent, creating such horrific emotional damage, assuming the child was even lucky enough to be found alive…it made him feel cold with disgust, with horror and rage. If the guy had been caught in Port Isley, he would have faced a lynching. One John felt he would gladly attend…

But all this was only thinking, only his day before this moment, as he parked around the corner from the Victorian and walked back, feeling the stir of excitement in his belly, of anticipation as he jogged up the front steps, as he knocked and waited.

She opened the door and reality shifted, became the brightest and clearest it had been all day. Here was his life, her smile an open book, an invitation, a promise, and the fog he'd lived through from the last time until now was gone. He was complete.

><

It appeared that Amanda was serious about the zombie marathon. John had a setup so his television could show movies off the Net, and Amanda's first pick was the remake of *Dawn of the Dead*. Having seen the original in the theater, Bob didn't expect to be impressed, but the movie was actually pretty good. If incredibly gruesome.

Amanda seemed to enjoy his reaction, initially, but she began to fidget after a few moments. She seemed restless.

"You doing all right?"

"Food's here," she muttered.

He listened, hearing nothing over the sound of the movie— and then a car door slamming at the side of the house.

"Pause it if I'm going to miss anything good," he said, and stood up.

The .38 was in the back office, but the timing was right for it to be dinner. He walked toward the front door. Amanda paused the movie, and when he looked back she was watching him, her face suddenly paler than usual.

"Wait," she said, as he stepped to the door. She half rose from her seat.

Cautiously, Bob looked through the peephole. The young man on John's front step held up two laden plastic bags, knotted at the top. He was the regular delivery guy, a townie in his early twenties.

"Uncle Chan's," the guy said.

"Yeah, hang on," Bob said. He raised his eyebrows at Amanda. "It's fine, I recognize him."

She didn't respond, only stood all the way up as he opened the door, reaching for his wallet. The kid smiled. "Hey, Mr. Sweet and Sour Chicken!"

"Great, that's great," Bob said. "Hear that, Amanda? I've got a reputation."

She looked relieved. Bob had paid for the food over the phone, but he always kept a couple of fives in his wallet. He fished one out now after signing the receipt, and the kid's face lit up.

"Hey, thanks."

Amanda had come to the door, and she took one of the bags of food, Bob the other. He closed the door, locked it, and nodded toward the kitchen.

"You get the plates and forks, I'll get drinks. What'll you have?"

"Whiskey, neat," she said, and grinned back at him as they walked. "Or Snapple, whatever."

A knock on the door. John handed the food to Amanda.

"He must've given me the wrong copy or something," he said. At her worried expression, he chuckled, shooing her toward the kitchen.

"What are the chances," he said, unlocking the dead bolt, opening the door even as he heard delivery kid's car door slam at the house's far side.

Eric was holding a gun, a small semiautomatic, pointing it at Bob's face.

"Ah, *shit*," Bob said, rearing back—and before he could consider the action, lunging forward, pushing the gun up and away as Eric's face registered surprise. Eric wheeled back, jerking the gun down, and it seemed to explode in his hand, and a burning fist slammed into Bob's left side accompanied by a deafening roar.

Bob fell down.

➤◄

Amanda had just stepped into the kitchen when she heard the gun, so loud that her ears rang immediately. She heard her own shriek, though, and dropped the takeout. The bags split open, an order of fried noodles spilling across the floor in a pea-specked, greasy mass.

Eric.

For what seemed like an hour she froze, so terrified that she didn't know if she could move; he was here, he'd shot Bob, he was going to come in and kill her, put a bullet through her skull, and she'd be dead. She was still staring down at the spilled noodles, and they were still spilling, settling to the floor, and she realized only a breath had passed, there was still time, and she ran.

Through the kitchen to the back door that let out next to the porch, fumbled with the dead bolt, got it, outside, the shot still echoing in her head, she could feel her heartbeat in every part of her body and adrenaline charging her muscles, *delivery guy!* Plan, she had a plan.

She tore left, around to the front of the house, bare feet thumping on the warm ground. The delivery guy was stopped halfway down the block, brake lights shining, a pickup of some light color. In the last of the day's light, she could see the driver craning to look back, his eyes wide.

She took a single running step toward him, and then the truck screeched away, blowing the stop sign at the corner. She turned and saw Eric on the front steps, saw that he was pointing a gun at the retreating truck.

"Call the cops!" she screamed after him, screamed to anyone listening. Her plan hadn't gone past *escape with delivery guy*. She was at sea. "Call nine one one! Rape! Fire! *Fire!*"

Her next words were muffled as he clasped a hand over her mouth, his body pressing into hers from behind. He used his gun arm to pin her arms to her body. She struggled for a second, felt his strength, and went still.

"Shhh," he hissed, his voice hot in her ear. "Stop it. I didn't *mean* to shoot; he grabbed the gun. It was an accident. He'll be fine. Come inside with me, I'll show you."

She shook her head violently, trying to get her mouth free from his fingers. They tasted like salt, like dirty sweat. *Some fucking psychic.*

"Just come inside. You'll understand, I can explain everything."

Amanda caught hold of her stuttering thoughts, focused on keeping her body still. She took a deep breath and understood what was happening because she'd known that they would meet again, and she knew how to play it from a hundred movies about girls being terrorized by estranged boyfriends. The best, the *only* option was to convince him that she wasn't going to run or fight, that they were pals, still an "us," and she wasn't going to blow it too fucking soon like the stupid chicks in the movies, she was going to use her head.

She sighed, leaning her head against his arm, and he hesitated, his breathing rough, and he totally had a hard-on, she could feel it against the small of her back. He took his hand away and relaxed his grip.

Do what you have to do.

"We have to take care of Bob," she said. Firmly. "Right now. First."

He hesitated again. Then stepped back, letting her go. She turned and walked past him, making her face blank, letting him read whatever he wanted. She'd had years of practice, and it often calmed her mother down. She had to focus; Bob, first priority, and she knew that Eric wanted her, wanted to be with her, and she would play it as hard as she could, as *real* as she could until the police came, the delivery guy would call them, *someone* would call.

Bob, then stall. Bob. The front door was standing open, but she didn't see him, only saw—

"Oh," she said, and realized she saw Bob's feet, that was all, he was down. She hurried, her body desperate to move anyway, to run, and she had a horrible fear that he was dead—and knew that he wasn't, even before she ran up the front steps, the welcome mat scraping her feet, and dropped to her knees, to his side. She could feel him, fighting against the pain. He was lying flat on the floor. He held his right hand to his chest, just under his left armpit—his left arm wasn't moving at all—and was pale and breathing shallowly. His shirt was dark, but she could also see that the fabric was wet all around his fingers, and of course there was blood on them, there was *that*, but his eyes were also open, and he was looking at her.

"Hold still," she said, trying to think; stop the bleeding, that was first—

Bandages, fucking move!

She stood and ran to the kitchen; there were clean dishtowels in the drawer under the silverware. She stepped over the greasy fried noodles, she remembered seeing them ooze out like the Blob, already that was, like, ten years ago, but really only two minutes, three, maybe. Her hearing was still mostly just a high-pitched whine from the gunshot that had started this nightmare.

She grabbed all of the towels and stumbled back to Bob. Eric was standing in the open doorway, a look of misery and anger on his face as he stared down at Bob. At least he wasn't pointing the gun; his arm was lax at his side, but she was aware of it, she couldn't help being aware of it, the control that he was wielding.

*Don't fuck this up, don't let him see you afraid, don't look him in the eye...*no, that was dogs. She felt a little dizzy. She'd thought that things were coming to a head, and she'd known that she would see Eric again, and that it was going to be a bad thing. But she hadn't expected anything to happen so soon, or involve Bob being shot.

Everything's going to happen, she thought from nowhere. *No more waiting.*

"I'm going to press a cloth over it," Amanda said. She folded the dishtowel and folded it again. "Stop the bleeding. Can you move your hand? When I count to three."

Bob nodded, then winced at the movement.

"One—two—*three*."

He pulled his hand away, and she could see the hole in his shirt and bright blood underneath. She promptly pushed the makeshift bandage over it, pressing down...he let out a groan through clenched teeth, but then started taking deep breaths, ragged, careful. Eric stood there.

"It was an accident," Amanda said, catching his gaze. "He just wants to talk, that's all. I can talk to him, OK? While we're waiting for the ambulance. We'll be fine. Eric doesn't want to hurt me."

"OK," Bob said, although the look he shot at Eric was an extremely black one.

"I didn't mean to shoot him," Eric said. His tone was defensive. "I was going to make him leave us alone for a few minutes."

She ignored him. "How bad is it? What hurts?"

"My left arm," Bob said. "It hurts like hell to move it at all. Tore a muscle, maybe. Maybe one of my ribs, too."

"Can you hold this one on, tight?" Amanda asked. "I have to see if—if there's another place. Uh, exit wound. Underneath."

Bob took another breath and was careful not to move his head again. His right hand crept to cover hers.

"Yeah. Go ahead."

She slipped her hand out from beneath his, his fingers were cold, and he pushed down on the dishtowel.

"I need to talk to you," Eric said. He stepped over Bob's feet, moving around him until he was at Amanda's side. He crouched next to her.

"Kind of busy at the moment," Amanda said.

"You know what? *Fuck* him. He's trying to make you crazy. You think you got scared, but it's *him*, him and that fucking pervert doctor, they're trying to make you crazy. He grabbed for the gun. I didn't pull the trigger, even."

He looked hard at Bob. "Maybe he meant to get shot."

"Oh, that's brilliant," Bob said, panting. "What a great plan."

"You shut the fuck up, or next time won't *be* an accident. And if you hurt her, if I find out you hurt her, you're *dead...*"

Amanda pulled gently on Bob's skinny hip and leaned down to look, saw fresh blood on the other side.

"Shit," she said, because there was more bleeding to stop, but that was good, too, that meant there wasn't a bullet inside him, and there weren't any major organs right at the surface there, were there?

She folded and pressed a second cloth to where the new blood seemed to be coming from, pushing up, and quickly stuffed the other cloths underneath, holding it in place, feeling more freaked by the second.

"You're going to be OK if you hold still," she said, meeting Bob's eyes again. "Seriously. Don't move. I have to go talk to Eric now."

"Stay in here," Bob said. He looked dazed but coherent.

"Hey, fuck you," Eric said. "You caused enough fucking trouble, you know that?"

Amanda stood up, drawing his attention away from Bob, and Eric rose with her. "We'll be in the kitchen," she said. "We call an ambulance, then we can talk. Bob, don't fucking move."

Before either could respond, she turned and walked into the kitchen, walked away from Bob. She'd told him clearly that she could handle it, and why she thought she could; she hoped he'd been able to read her, she hoped she'd be able to pull off acting like she knew what she was doing. Eric was upset and confused, and she thought that if she took the lead, he'd follow.

Eric walked in behind her. There was a little fifties-style Formica table tucked at the end of the sink's counter, where the kitchen window overlooked the side yard, and there was a phone on the cabinet over it, a landline. She went straight for it, picked it up, dialed 911.

"We don't need any interruptions," Eric started, half raising the gun, and she glared at him.

"Could you wait one minute? *God!*" She let a measure of her anger out, enough that he could see it was real. Enough to make him forget that he was holding a gun. "It was an accident, fine, I got it. You want to talk, OK, great, we'll talk. But first I'm going to call an ambulance so you don't go to jail for fucking *murder*, and *then* I will talk to you, do you—hello?"

Medical, she said, in answer to the query stated by a woman with a mechanical voice, maybe a million miles away for all she knew, and she made up a story, fast. Her uncle accidentally shot himself, they were at—shit, she didn't know the address, the very last house on Eleanor, before the park. West? West of the park? She didn't know, the side facing the bay, top of the hill, please hurry, he was in a lot of pain. She punched one of the numbers as though she was turning the phone off and set it the counter, leaving the line open.

"Don't shoot me," she said. If the robot woman was listening, she'd advise the police accordingly.

"No, never," Eric said, oblivious to the phone. He tucked the gun in his belt. "Where's your bedroom?"

"Upstairs."

"Show me."

He stepped aside, let her walk past, and she turned left, climbed the stairs, still feeling the pump of adrenaline through her body. He wanted privacy because he wanted *her*; the lust coming off him was even stronger than his anger, and she couldn't imagine having sex with him but thought she might have to. Fucking was what was driving his obsession, and that was her fault; she'd been all over him for weeks…if she had to put out now so that no one else died, she'd do it; she felt like she deserved as much. A few minutes of acting, of invasion, and it would be over, and the cops would be right behind the paramedics, wouldn't they? They'd bust his ass for shooting Bob, and he'd go off to jail, and his rich father would see to it that he got help, finally. The hoped-for outcome was in direct contrast to how she felt, to what she suspected was going to happen, but she was afraid to think any further in that direction, afraid that her growing dread meant the very worst thing.

They walked to the bedroom she'd been using, which had a nice double bed with a fluffy duvet thing on it and two overflowing bags of her clothes and stuff on the floor. There were no chairs in the room, just the bed to sit on, and she didn't bother trying to evade the inevitable. She sat down at the head of the bed, and he at the foot, facing her. He held the gun in his lap.

"I want you to look at me," he said. He stood up, moving closer so that their knees were touching, so she could smell his breath. "I want you to look inside, so you can see that I would never hurt you, *ever*…like you did with that *doctor.*"

He made the word sound insulting. "Are you kidding? You think I can concentrate? You just shot Bob."

"You have to see. Take some deep breaths, calm yourself down. I love you. Just let yourself be still and feel how much I love you."

He was serious. She was deeply embarrassed for both of them.

"If I do that, will you put the gun down? Like, away?"

He nodded solemnly.

She closed her eyes, humoring him, taking a deep breath, blowing it out…and then found herself reaching for him with her thoughts as he put his free hand on her leg. She covered his fingers with her own, breathing deeper, Bob was going to be OK, this was recon, she should be welcoming the chance to find out how to manipulate him into doing no further harm, keeping him out of her pants, his fingers were as cold as Bob's had been and she didn't see anything but she heard—

—drop your weapon—

Stop

freeze I'm gonna shoot if you don't drop it now drop it now

She didn't recognize the voices, but that didn't matter. She opened her eyes, slightly astounded at what she'd just done. "You have to get out of here. Seriously. Cops are coming; if they see you with a gun, they're going to shoot you."

Shit, and they'll be expecting a hostage situation. She'd thought she'd been so clever with the whole don't-shoot-me bit, wanting to make sure no one got hurt.

Maybe this wasn't something that could be changed.

His hand slid farther up her leg. "I'll put the gun down. Tell me that you want me, I'll put the gun down."

Oh Jesus. "Would you listen to me?" She enunciated each word clearly. "They—are—going—to—fucking—shoot—you."

His breathing had gone husky. She made her legs relax, and his cold hand slipped between her thighs.

"I thought you wanted to talk."

"I do," he said. "I just, I ache, looking at you and not touching, you know?"

"Uh-huh," she agreed. "You really want to be caught by the cops while you're fucking?"

"At least I wouldn't be holding a gun," he said, and then his hand was pushing against her. She was wearing pajama bottoms and a tee, not the slightest bit sexy, but he thought she was beautiful, she could feel him, *hot heavy tits pressing against my chest and her dilated eyes open mouth tongue—*

She felt a flush travel through her, a shadow of his want, and pulled away, disturbed by the sensation. Bob was still bleeding on the floor downstairs.

"You say you love me, stop trying to fuck me for like two seconds," she said. "What is it you want me to see?"

"I *do* love you," he said. He met her gaze, and she saw the flat, self-absorbed shine of mania in his; he looked like he hadn't slept in days. "I know how I feel, and I know what makes you feel good. What do *they* want, have you asked yourself that? A divorced shrink and a guy old enough to be your grandfather? All this shit they're telling you—I don't know why they'd want to fuck with your head, but that's what they're doing. I'm here, I'm *real*...we're real, together, all the rest of this, whatever they told you, it's not reality."

Amanda nodded. "Right; no *way* I'd be scared of you. You have a gun, you shoot my friend, you flip out totally like we're star-crossed lovers or some shit, and now you're my reality. Not the slightest bit nuts."

She thought for one terrible second that she might have pushed too hard; he only stared at her, but he decided to forget what she was saying, to not even hear it. She could feel him do it. He was so firmly committed to his version of things that nothing else was going to edge in.

"You have to get away from those fuckers," he said. "Come with me. We'll get out of here, just go."

How old was he, ten? "Go where? You have a car, a destination…?"

"I don't know. Down the coast, somewhere nice. Wherever you want. California. Mexico. Just get away from all this bullshit, someplace we can be together. We can take my father's car."

He closed the small distance she'd managed between them. He leaned forward, slipping the gun behind him, leaving it on the bedspread. She felt her heart hold for a beat. He wasn't touching the gun. His arms went around her, pulled her close, and he wrapped a hand beneath her ass, bringing her up and into his lap.

"I love you," he said again. "I want you so bad."

She closed her eyes, let herself be kissed. There was no siren, but she thought she heard an engine out on the street. The front door was still open; Eric hadn't closed it before following her, she was sure. They'd find Bob first, get him help, and come upstairs with weapons drawn.

"Get rid of the gun first," she said.

He leaned back, cupping her breasts through her shirt, keeping up the eye contact, which was getting ludicrous and creepy. "You don't trust me yet. You're holding back. I want you to feel what I'm feeling. I want you to know what you're doing to me, right now."

"You're…" She focused on his face, let the sensations come… and felt her stomach knot, her defenses slamming down. Beyond a height of arousal she'd never personally felt, disorienting all on its own, his thoughts were desperate, screaming billboards proclaiming his love. Beneath that, everything was dark and sexual, threaded with feelings of brokenness and a driving desire to have what he wanted, to persevere until she gave up and was sorry and they lived happily ever after. There was nothing resembling reality in his thoughts, not even a little. Maybe most frightening of all, he'd already forgotten that he'd just shot someone. Bob was nowhere in his mind.

"Eric, listen to me," she said, grasping for reasons that he might believe, stilling his hands with hers. "I saw you getting killed by the police, that's why I freaked out, that's why I took off, you are holding a gun and they shoot you down. It's going to happen here, tonight, now. Hide it under the bed, put it in a drawer, just get rid of it. *Please*."

Eric looked into her eyes. "Then will you come with me?"

She had to resist an urge to scream. "Yes. Hurry."

He smiled, and in spite of her fear, her disgust, she felt like crying suddenly, he looked so much younger, like a little kid. Tears welled in his eyes.

"I'll do whatever you want," he said. He shifted her onto the bed and picked up the gun. He ejected the magazine, a clumsy, unpracticed move, and pulled the top part back, popping a bullet out. He tossed the gun and the magazine and the bullet onto the floor, and she felt a huge surge of relief. He was fucked-up and a selfish dick, and he'd hurt Bob, but he didn't deserve to die.

He surged forward like a wave, was all over her, his hands on her breasts, his tongue in her mouth. She thought of Bob and heard the creak of the stairs, and Eric was pulling her comfy pants down and off, and her underwear, and she was going to endure the sex, she didn't see that she could get out of it, except he was still fumbling at his belt, kneeling between her legs when the door was kicked open.

It was that fuck-knob Kyle Leary, posing like a cop in an action flick, holding a gun much bigger than Eric's, something heavy and black. He took in the scene, saw the gun on the floor, shot a look over his shoulder. He turned back to where Eric and Amanda had frozen.

"Drop your weapon!" he shouted.

Amanda looked at Eric. They both looked at the empty handgun on the floor.

She looked at Leary again, sweating, his face red—and felt the poisonous immensity of his presence, the poison defining itself to her in a surge of sick realization. Leary was going to shoot Eric. He wanted to kill someone, he wanted to shoot a bad guy, a *rapist*. What she felt was wasn't heat and excitement, it was deliberate murder.

"Stop!" Amanda screamed, and no wonder she hadn't recognized her voice, it was shrill and mad, she was fucking Cassandra, doomed to tell people the truth and have it make no fucking difference.

Eric instantly held his hands up, still holding his belt. It fell from his hand, landed on the bed, slid to the floor.

"Freeze! I'm gonna shoot if you don't drop it now, drop it now! Don't do it, buddy!"

Leary still sounded frantic, his voice high and strained, but he took a second to aim carefully for Eric's stunned expression, his own fixed with a sudden wide grin. Amanda could hear footsteps crashing up the stairs behind him, but they weren't going to be there in time—

Leary fired three times in a row, the gun bouncing in his hand, and Eric was blown back and over to the side, crumpling over her left leg, trapping it, she had the briefest sense of jetting blood and that the shape of his face had changed, that it was crooked where his right eye had been, and then she was screaming, kicking desperately to get away from him, her naked legs spattered with his hot blood.

She screamed and screamed and when she ran out of breath, she stopped. Leary pointed his gun at the floor, his lips moving but she couldn't hear him, her ears were ringing so badly. Another cop, a pinch-faced red-headed woman, Cam Trent's mother, came in behind Leary. Leary said something she couldn't hear; Trent looked at the gun on the floor, nodded, said something back.

"What the *fuck*," Amanda gasped, looking at the fat-faced cop, Leary; she wouldn't look at Eric, she couldn't. She could barely hear her voice. "You *killed* him."

He leaned forward slightly and spoke, his lips outlining his words as much as his voice. "You're safe now." The mask of compassion he wore couldn't entirely cover his excitement. *Blew him away*, he thought, again and again. *He was going to rape her and he had a gun, armed and dangerous, he shot that guy and I blew him away, blew him away, honest-to-God 10-55 right here!*

"Motherfucker," Amanda whispered, and rolled on her side and curled into a ball.

Everything was cool, at first. The walk had been hilarious, and by the time they got to the turnoff to the fairgrounds, it was almost full dark. They passed a group of older kids, a couple of girls and a guy, and Tommy heard someone laugh farther ahead and felt a real excitement, shuffling along with Jeff and smelling the trees and seeing a gibbous moon in the dark-blue sky; this was the best night of his life.

They lurched their way over a ditch, and then they were in the woods, the shadows thickening to night. Walking through the fringe of trees, they could see lights flickering off and on through the screen of branches and as they got closer, a couple of trailers strung with Christmas lights and a bunch of massive, shadowed heaps of folded metal, and buildings shading off into darkness. There were some people moving around, putting up lights, moving things; there was a radio on, and some ancient arena-rock ballad was playing, the sound far across the wide field. They stopped in the trees, hanging back.

Tommy looked around. He had to pee. "Where is everybody?"

Jeff shrugged. "They'll be here. 'S early. Or they might come up tomorrow. It's not an everyday thing."

Tommy blinked, trying to think of why that might be important. No good. He returned to something he knew.

"I gotta piss. Where can I take a piss?"

Jeff looked around. "Uh, not here. Back of the park. Come on."

They skirted the open fairgrounds, staying to the trees. Tommy could see a parking lot off to their left, empty but for a handful of cars and a lone figure walking toward them, toward the trail to the fairgrounds.

They went another half dozen stumbling steps on the near-black trail before Jeff said, "Ah, shit, I forgot about the flashlight."

"Dumbshit," Tommy said, although he'd forgotten about it too, and they both laughed, the sound too loud in the still of the trees. There was no one around. The carnies were mostly on the other side of the field, and the low-hanging branches made everything seem very quiet.

Jeff fumbled around, and a beam snapped on, throwing the woods all around into deeper night as it illuminated the beaten dirt of the trail they were on, the brown and green washed out by the flat, yellowing light. Something small crashed through the underbrush ahead, and the light swooped toward the movement, back and forth through a wall of dark, layered washes, the night stretching out behind the many trees.

Tommy noted the possibility of nausea, but his need to urinate outweighed all other sensory considerations. "Come on, I gotta go."

"Little further."

Tommy thought he was going to piss his pants, but then Jeff stopped near a kind of tall hedge that ran across the path and shone the light down its length, and Tommy saw they were at the back of the massive field, the rough, rounded hedge separating the woods from the open grounds.

"Anywhere behind the bushesh," Jeff said, and laughed, but Tommy was already hurrying around the far end, forgetting he couldn't see without the flashlight, tripping over something the second he stepped out of the beam.

He fell down, hit knees hitting the dirt, hard, but it didn't hurt at all. His body felt startled, like he'd been hit with a giant pillow. Jeff caught up as he was crawling back to a standing position.

"You OK?"

"Fuck, no, I'm seriously going to pee my pants," Tommy said, and that set them both off, and Tommy turned away and whipped it out of his shorts before he really did, his stream of piss shaking because he was laughing so hard. He almost fell over again, and that made him laugh harder.

Jeff dropped the flashlight and joined him, the light illuminating nothing as he turned the other way, also laughing and pissing. As their laughter tapered off, Tommy realized that the music had changed, more rock but something heavy and driving. He heard a grown man laugh and shout out something incomprehensible in a coarse, rough voice. The sound made Tommy remember that they were out here alone, drunk and alone, and he had a sudden sincere urge to be back at Jeff's, watching more dumb movies on his computer. With food and water and a place to lie down.

Safe.

Tommy finished first and bent down to pick up the flashlight, almost falling again in his effort to keep his balance. He turned the light back toward the carnival. The bigger building attractions were back here, a fun house, an arcade; he couldn't tell what was past that. There was no one in sight.

"Shine the light over here," Jeff said. "'S fuckin' dark."

Tommy turned, the light turning with him, and out of the dark was a face suddenly, a man's face only a few steps away, blinking at the bright beam.

Tommy stepped back. "Hey," he said, in a high, strangled voice.

"I'm sorry, I didn't mean to scare you," the man said, and he sounded friendly, but his face was made indistinct by the brightness of the light. Tommy couldn't tell if he looked friendly. "You guys OK out here?"

"What the fuck," Jeff said. "Who the fuck're you?" He sounded scared.

Tommy lowered the light slightly, the better to see the friendly stranger's face. Rounded, full cheeks and a double chin, sunburned; thinning, light hair—

He didn't want to realize who it was, standing there in the dark woods with them, but the realization came anyway, a slow burn of mounting terror that threatened to freeze him solid. It was the fisherman from the pier. He hadn't been able to describe him that well to the police, but he could see him perfectly in his mind's eye, remembered the way his tongue had stuck out a little, when he'd, when he'd—

"You guys like to drink?" the man said. He sounded casual and nice, a favorite uncle, maybe, a likable coach. He was big, too. Tommy's father was six two and this guy was that tall and much broader. "I've got some beers in my car."

Tommy started to back up, running into Jeff, the light bobbing across the stranger's face. He felt supremely unprepared for this to be happening; even understanding it was taking too much effort, too much time.

Tommy grabbed Jeff's arm and turned the light back toward the fairgrounds, toward life and people, but the man was in their way; they'd have to run past him.

Fuck that. Tommy wheeled Jeff around. They'd go through the woods, cut back across the hedge farther along. Jeff seemed to understand that they were in trouble; he didn't ask any questions, just fell in right behind Tommy. They crashed through the litter of brush behind the tall hedge, Tommy fighting the drink, trying to make himself think better, be more coordinated.

He heard the man on the other side of the thick bushes, a few feet away. "Why are you running?" The voice wasn't friendly anymore, but mocking, and it occurred to Tommy that the stranger wasn't having to break trail, he was just walking along the fairgrounds side of the hedge, waiting for them to come out. "Are you afraid?"

"We'll kick your fuckin' ass," Jeff said loudly, but the man didn't answer, and Tommy couldn't imagine that he'd been scared away. He crashed forward again, shining the distinctly dying flashlight at the hedge, looking for breaks, looking to see if there was something, anything they could use.

There, a gap in the thick bush, past that a wall, the back wall of something taller than the hedge. The arcade or the fun house. He couldn't hear the guy on the other side; he'd probably stopped at the corner of the building. *We'll run around to the front, someone'll be there—*

"Here," he said to Jeff, his voice low, as if the man didn't know where they were, as if he couldn't just look over and see the flashlight's beam. No time to mourn his stupidity; Tommy snapped the light off, took a shaking breath, and then tore through the dark-green leaves, sharpened twigs poking his bare arms and legs, and then he was clear, between the wall and the bushes. He didn't wait for Jeff; he turned away from the direction they'd come and booked, steadying himself against the wall, painted wood whipping beneath his hand.

"Wait!"

The man's voice was way closer than Tommy had expected, and he ran faster, his legs carrying him over the black, pitted ground. He grabbed the corner of the building as he reached it, letting it pull his body in a different direction, not sure if Jeff was behind him, too afraid to look back.

He didn't see anyone, saw nothing but the building itself, edged in moonlight, and the building next to it, both dark and still. He reached the next corner and took it as he'd taken the first, letting himself pivot to the front of the structure, the fun house, he could see the giant clown face even in the dark.

He heard running steps from where he'd just been and didn't know who was coming. He saw the opening at the front of the ride, up two steps, and there was a padlock on the gate, but it was hanging open, and he jumped the second step and was inside, dizzy with terror and the beat of a dawning headache, his mouth as dry as a desert, his eyes wide and unseeing in the pitch black of the fun house.

><

Cameron Trent was at the fairgrounds with her best girlfriend, Brittany, and they were high, high, high, passing the pipe with this kid from school, Clay Russel, a little rocker shithead, but he had awesome shit, and any port in a storm; they'd seen a couple of little kids go by but no one else was around, it was positively dead, and when Clay had run into them coming off Bayside and asked if they wanted to smoke out, the girls had exchanged a shrug and then followed. Clay was trying to get something going with Britt, it was obvious, but talk about nonstarter. Brittany had said that these guys from Port Angeles might be up at the carnival tonight, and they'd dressed accordingly, but so far it was barely worth the trip; smoking out with Clay Russel was only saved by the quality of his pot.

"Those jeans are way too tight," she said, interrupting whatever Clay was talking about, which was probably his car or death metal or something. God, he was short.

"Shut *up*," Britt said, her eyes round. "Whattup, whore?"

Cam smiled. "Slut. You'd totally blow Clay here for his pot, wouldn't you?"

Brittany laughed, her mouth hanging open. "Shut *up*. I would *not*."

Clay looked back and forth between them, his eyes shining, a look Cam had come to know and expect from the boys she met.

"You would if I dared you," Cam said.

"I have a full fucking eighth at my house," he said, his voice so sincere that Cam couldn't hold a straight face. She and Britt both laughed, and Clay joined in after a minute, his sounding forced and embarrassed. Poor Clay.

There were running footsteps, coming from behind them. As one they rose and turned toward the sound, Clay grabbing the pipe from Brittany and stuffing it in his pants pocket. He stepped forward a little, his stance wide, his shoulders back.

It was too dark to see anything, and the footsteps were getting close fast, coming at them out of the shadows and moonlit alleys that ran between the trailers and platforms at the back of the carnival, coming at them from out of the woods. Cam's hand rose to her throat, and she felt a chill of sincere dread that her best friend obviously wasn't feeling.

"Maybe it's your *mom*," she said, and Clay started laughing, and Cam didn't have time to be offended before a kid came running at them out of the dark. Cam recognized him. Seana Halliway's little brother, Jeff. He looked terrified.

He saw them and shifted course. The way he ran made Cam think that he'd been drinking, the way his head bobbed up and down, but what the fuck did she know, she was totally high. He stopped in front of Clay and gasped something, swallowed, said it again.

"*Help.*"

"What the fuck, little man?" Clay said, not unkindly.

"There's a sex pervert up here," the kid gasped, and he was piss *drunk*, the way he blinked all slow and slurred his words, but he also looked awful, like he'd seen a fucking ghost.

"What?"

The kid, Jeff, nodded, still catching his breath. "He went after my friend. We gotta get someone."

"You're shitting us," Clay said, and Jeff shook his head. Clay was still all puffed up, all manly.

"Where'd they go?"

Jeff shook his head again, the action pulling him to one side. It was like watching a slow-motion crash as he stumbled, turned away—and fell to his knees and puked, a flood of liquid jetting out of his mouth, the sound a kind of massive *huh-gluh* that would have been funny except for the idea that there was some kiddie freak running around in the woods. Jenny Todd had told Cam all about last week at the pier when she'd been watching Valerie and Jay Luther; that shit was fucked-*up*. It had already been such a strange, strange summer; sometimes Cam felt like she was outside herself, watching herself, doing things that she wasn't really doing. Sometimes people said things to her and she heard their words and saw their mouths moving and still didn't understand what they were saying, not at all...and then later, she wasn't able to remember if those conversations were real or something she'd dreamed. Sometimes she wondered if she was going insane.

"Call the cops," Britt said.

"No way," Clay said, backing away. "It'll take 'em like twenty minutes to get here."

"Where the fuck are you going?" Cam snapped as he turned away from them, suddenly certain that he was a total chicken-shit fucker, leaving two girls and a drunk kid to deal with a sex predator—

"My cousin works here," Clay said. "Kevin. Remember?"

Cam had no memory of that whatsoever but nodded as Clay turned and ran, thinking that maybe she and Britt should take off, it maybe wasn't a good idea to be superhigh and wearing what she was wearing with Clay running off to rile a bunch of carnies into a mob.

"Let's blow," Brittany said, reading her mind.

Cam nodded but looked at Seana's little brother and felt bad about it, him still kneeling and throwing his guts up with some molester running around.

"Hey, Jeff, right? You should come with us," Cam said, but Jeff wasn't hearing her; he was connected to the ground by long strings of spitty puke, and he wasn't hearing *anything*. Little dude was on his first drunk, maybe.

"Leave him. They'll be here in like two minutes; they'll protect him," Brittany said. "Seriously, Cam, you know what my dad will do to me if he finds out we're up here?"

Cam couldn't argue; her own mother, Miss Piggy, would shit a brick if she knew even a tenth of what Cam did, and she was on duty tonight. Cam could play straight with no trouble, but there was no way she could explain the tank top; if the cops were going to be up here, she should definitely be somewhere else.

"Peace out, bro," Britt said to Jeff Halliway, who yurked again, and then they were hustling it back to the safety of the trees, the shine taken off the night for Cam, who would dream that night that a giant black wave crashed over the kid after they left him and he was gone, forever, and no one ever talked about him ever again.

><

Tommy turned the flashlight on and found himself in a round tunnel painted with bright stripes. The power was off, which he silently thanked God for; just looking at the spiraling stripes made him feel like he was spinning, like everything was spinning, but he had to get away from the door, find somewhere to hide or find another exit, whatever came first. He hurried through, keeping the beam low, sick with fear and guilt. What if the guy had gone after Jeff? Tommy had the flashlight; he hadn't even told Jeff what his plan was, just run off and left Jeff alone in the woods. Bad, this was all so bad.

The next room was a little graveyard, wooden tombstones painted in colors of dirt. Tommy could see the cutout creatures and ghouls behind the gravestones, ready to pop up when the fun house was open, when someone took your ticket and you went through with your friends and you all shrieked and laughed at the lame ghosts, the recorded howls, the sudden gusts of air shot out of wheezing vents. The next doorway was to the left, near the back wall of the fun house, painted to match the graveyard, and Tommy reeled toward it, realizing with dismay that there were only stairs going up—this place had a second floor—and he heard the front gate open behind him.

He snapped the light off, the adrenaline on top of the drinking making him sweat, making his stomach roll. He held on desperately to the hope that Jeff would call out, but he couldn't hold on long— and then he thought he heard someone coming through the tunnel, moving almost silently in the dark, and he knew it wasn't Jeff.

Tommy grabbed the rail and went up the stairs, tears leaking from his eyes, his mouth filling with the slick spit that was a precursor to throwing up, he was so sick and stupid and afraid. He swallowed, and swallowed again, the taste of his mouth sour and terrible.

At the top of the stairs he turned and edged away into the next room; there was a rail he could hold, and he hurried in spite of the dark until the rail ended. He put the light end of the flashlight against his leg and turned it on, lifting it a tiny bit so that he could see where to go next, and saw a half dozen circles of light, a half dozen sets of his half-tied sneakers snapping into sight.

Hall of mirrors, stupid baby shit...when it wasn't dark, when you weren't drunk, when you maybe weren't alone. He had to ignore his misery, his self-pity, he had to go on; he couldn't just stop and wait for whatever was coming, and the fundamental unfairness of it all was as terrible as the fear. Why was this happening, why was it being allowed to happen?

Tommy turned off the light and walked straight ahead, his hand extended in front of him. Light wouldn't help, anyway. These things were laid out like mazes; he just had to turn when he ran into something. One step, two—and there was a panel, cool to the touch, and he had to turn left again, and did he hear footsteps on the stairs, or was he only hearing his pulse hammering through his ears? He had to pee again.

Step, step, turn. Turn again. Two more steps. He breathed shallowly, through his mouth, trying not to make noise. At every pause, he strained to hear, his eyes wide in the dark. Was he alone? Had he even heard the door open behind him, or was he just imagining everything, his messed-up brain crying wolf? Step. Turn. Turn again. *If I get out of this, I swear to God I'll stop looking at stuff and be nice to my mom and never drink ever again, I swear—*

Somewhere else in the mirrored halls, a sound. Tommy froze and held his breath—and heard breathing, a clear intake of air that wasn't an echo, it was a man, it was *him.*

Tommy tried to hurry and jammed his reaching fingers into another panel of mirrored glass or whatever they were made out of, which hurt. He pulled his hand back and decided he would risk the flashlight for just a second, surely he had been in this place forever, he had to be near the end, there'd be a slide or a backward escalator or something, and he'd be out, he'd scream for help and run for the lights and be safe.

As before, he pressed the light against his leg before turning it on, then raised it a fraction—

And there were his high-tops, and there were the legs and feet of his pursuer, moving toward him and away from him as the beam of light spun through the chamber of mirrors, and he couldn't tell what was happening or how close they were to one another. He reined in the sudden frantic urge to run, sure he'd knock himself out, and aimed the light at the floor instead, following the mirror panels where they met in corners at his feet, where they opened next. Left, right, right, left. He thought he saw the exit and shone the light up, into the mirrors, but kept his gaze on his shoes, on navigating his way out, hoping that the reflecting light would confuse the predator while he made his escape—

"Gotcha," the man breathed, and Tommy looked up and saw a hand reaching for him, but Tommy was a reflection away; the man was close but wrong.

Tommy used the second of confusion. He raised the flashlight and threw it at the man's sneering face, as hard as he could, then turned and ran the maze, left, right, right, left—

—and he slammed into a panel he couldn't see. There was no light at all, but there was open air around it, and he felt a hand brush his shoulder. He threw himself forward, into a room that had an inflatable trampoline floor, but the air mattress or whatever it was wasn't inflated; he fell three feet down as he hurtled through the door, but like outside, before, he didn't crash and burn or even feel hurt, he just sprawled with his limbs all loose and stupid and then was getting to his feet again, stumbling on the thick, loose rubbery floor for the next floating gray door-shaped hole, across from where he'd fallen in.

Behind him came a startled cry, and the floor vibrated with a heavy thump; the man had gone down hard right behind him, and Tommy sincerely hoped that he'd broken both of his legs or at least twisted his ankle, but he wasn't stopping to see. He scrambled up through the entry to the next terrible stupid thing, only another spinning tunnel, this as dead as the first, and there was the end, a platform with an opening at the end for what had to be a big slide. Tommy didn't know if the slide was set up or if the latched gate at the platform's exit would open into empty space, but he had to get away or he was going to be taken, maybe just killed outright because the pervert recognized him, saw that he'd been recognized.

Tommy unlatched the gate, swinging it outward, the cool air rushing over him like good music, cooling his sweat, clearing his mind. By the faint lights from the front of the carnival, by the fainter light of the moon and stars, he could see that there was no slide, or not yet—but there were rungs going down the side, and there were people down below, two, three men reaching up as he swung himself around and started to descend, supporting his way down with words of encouragement and then with strong hands, holding his legs, grabbing his waist, plucking him away from the ladder.

"We got the kid!" one of his rescuers screamed, and Tommy jumped.

"Where is he?" another one asked, his breath sour and hot in Tommy's face. "Is he in there?"

"Yeah," Tommy said, and the abrupt transition from terror to salvation was too much; he shook his head and pushed them away, staggering toward what he thought were bushes. He didn't know where he was anymore in relation to anything else. He leaned over, feeling a burn all the way up his throat and then out, hot, slick mint and sugar and bile, and he took a heaving breath and did it again, and the burning liquid came out of his nose, too, and he fell to his knees and tried to breathe. Behind him, men shouted and other men ran but he was too ensconced in his body's misery to make sense of anything, not until he heard a voice behind him, heard his good buddy Jeff say his name.

Tommy wiped his mouth with his hand, as sick as he'd ever felt, and turned to look at Jeff. He thought he'd have something to say, but he couldn't think of anything. He just wanted to go home and drink water and lie down; he wanted this terrible night to be over.

The men's voices had grown louder. There was a scream, and Jeff and Tommy looked to the dozen or so figures gathered near the front of the fun house, four or five of them beating another man down, kicking him, stomping on him, and the man screamed again, a gurgling plea for mercy, and the dark, moving shadows closed around him while others laughed and called out encouragement, their voices cracked and brutal.

One of the figures detached from the watching men and came their way. Tommy had backed away from his puddle of vomit and with Jeff's help, got to his feet. He wiped his mouth and tried to stand up straight.

"You kids get outta here," the dark shape snapped, not close enough to see—a crooked nose, bushy eyebrows, a slash of a mouth; he could have looked like anyone. "You didn't see nothin', right? Now get the fuck outta here and don't come back or I'll beat your asses."

They were already backing away. Jeff looked terrible and smelled like puke but Tommy leaned on him anyway, too dizzy to do otherwise. One staggering step led to another, and somehow the ground passed beneath their feet, the men yelling, bloodlust falling behind them, no sound at all from their victim anymore unless you counted breaking bones and wet boots stomping into flesh.

Tommy didn't think anything and let Jeff lead him away.

>‹

John's cell phone rang just after they'd eaten. Sarah had grilled steaks and made a salad, and there was fresh French bread from the bakery and a blueberry pie. Karen hadn't put in an appearance, although Sarah had invited her—but when Sarah took a plate to her room, her sister had been gracefully thankful, smiling sincerely at her. Maybe she was getting past the very worst of it; Sarah could hope.

She'd just met John back in the living room—they would talk and drink wine until their food digested, until they were ready to make love, and she was anticipating every moment—when his phone went off. He smiled, stepping forward and slipping his arm around her as he answered.

"Hello?" John's smile faded; he frowned. "Amanda, slow down. Where are you?"

Sarah felt a rush of disappointment, a flicker of jealousy. John's body went stiff as he listened.

"How bad?"

The tone of his voice killed her hopes for the rest of their evening.

"And you said the cops—yeah, of course, I'll be right there. You stay where you are, OK? I'll find you."

He hung up, automatically embracing Sarah tightly.

"I have to go, I'm so sorry," he said, and then stepped away, already gone. "Eric Hess broke into my house. He shot Bob and then the police killed him. Amanda's OK but Bob's in the hospital."

"Oh my God," Sarah breathed. "I'll come with you. Maybe I can help."

"You don't have to do that."

"I want to," she said, vaguely aware that her motives were less than altruistic; it was just after nine, and there was still a possibility of salvaging some part of their night together, even if it was just giving him support at a bad time. "Let me tell Karen. She can listen for the phone if Tommy calls."

Karen said she would, and Sarah grabbed her purse and shoes and they left in John's car, Sarah's hand on his knee as he drove down the hill to the small hospital and parked. He came around to her door, and they embraced, kissed in the parking lot, hungrily, as if they might never have another moment alone together, and Sarah was glad she'd come; she was glad that she was in love.

At the entrance, a young doctor or intern was smoking a cigarette, a policeman standing nearby with a firmly blank expression, his arms folded.

The doctor turned and saw them and hurried in their direction, flicking her cigarette into the driveway that ran past the front door.

"Hey," the cop snapped, but the young woman ignored him, and Sarah noticed that the girl's scrubs fit poorly, the overlong pants legs flopping to cover hospital socks. Her dyed hair looked like it had been cut by a lawnmower.

Amanda. Wearing borrowed hospital scrubs.

"He's going to be OK," the girl said, and John opened his arms. Sarah saw that her hair was wet as she pressed her head against John's shirt as he embraced her. She looked like she'd been crying, but her eyes were dry when she finally stepped back.

"Amanda, this is Sarah Reed," John said. "She was with me when you called."

The girl nodded in her direction, then turned her attention back to John. "They said the bullet went right through the pad of fat under his arm, the axilla or something, I didn't catch that, and it nicked one of his ribs, and because his arm was up it also took a chip out of his scapula, which is why his arm hurts so bad. But they said nothing was broken and he didn't lose too much blood; they said he could probably go home soon."

"Thank God," John said. "What about you? Are you OK?"

Amanda glanced at Sarah then back at him. "Yeah, I'm OK. Eric and I were in the bedroom when the cops came. Eric had put the gun down. That fucking cop, Leary, he shot him anyway."

The policeman who'd been lingering near them spoke up. "Saving you from getting killed, most likely. Maybe you should be a little more appreciative. Kyle Leary's a hero."

"Oh, right, I forgot, you were there when the empty gun was on the *floor* and he shot Eric because he just really, really wanted to, and doused me in his fucking *blood*, that's right," Amanda said. "Excuse *me*."

The sarcasm verged on hysteria. Her hands were shaking.

"Take it easy," John said. "Let's go in, we'll see Bob, then I'll take you home, OK?"

The cop—his badge read Miller—shook his head, speaking to John. "She's not leaving until the chief gets here. He wants to get her statement tonight. And you can't go home. Sorry."

"Why the hell not?"

"Crime scene," Miller said. "Gotta wait for a CSU to get here from Port Angeles to process the site. The chief says no one goes in till they're done."

"And where's Vincent now?" John asked. "Come on, Dave. Cut us a break."

Officer Miller shook his head and turned his back on them, went back to staring out at the half-empty parking lot.

"You don't want to go back there, anyway," Amanda said. She swallowed. "I'm so sorry, your guest room is ruined. We were on the bed, and the cop shot him three times in the head, and there was so much blood…"

She trailed off, letting out a soft, hitching sigh. "There's a mess in the front hallway, too. And I, I spilled takeout in the kitchen and didn't clean it uh-up…"

"It's OK," John said, as the girl's face worked, as she struggled to hold herself together. "You're OK."

"You can both stay at Big Blue, as long as you need," Sarah said. Tommy wouldn't like it, but it was ridiculous to send them to a hotel. Karen's house had eight empty rooms.

"You're OK," John repeated, looking into Amanda's face as if Sarah hadn't spoken. "You've survived a terrible ordeal, you've seen terrible things, but it's over now. Already in the past. And Bob's going to be OK. I'm just so, so sorry about Eric."

Amanda's features contorted, and then she was sobbing, leaning into John again. "I never wanted this to happen," she wailed.

"Of course you didn't," John said. "No one thinks that."

"It's my fault; if I hadn't been with him in the first place, this never would have happened."

"Don't think like that," Sarah said, automatically. She'd told herself the same thing a thousand times after Jack had left. "You couldn't have known how it was going to turn out."

Amanda blinked at her, her cheeks streaked with tears, a runner of snot falling over her lip. "Maybe I could have. Maybe I just didn't want to."

Sarah didn't have a response for that.

"It's only some things," Amanda said, looking at John, wiping her nose with the back of her hand. "What I'm seeing. Some of it *is* fated, inevitable, and some is still, like, variable. Open for discussion. It's not one or the other, like everyone thinks. We have to find him, the tourist, the summer man; we have to tell him. Or maybe he already knows…I have to meet him. I'm going to meet him."

Sarah didn't know what the girl was talking about. She didn't seem too clear herself.

"We should go inside," John said. "I'd like to see Bob, talk to the doctor. And you should be sitting down. Have you been treated by anyone?"

Officer Miller cleared his throat. "She came out here to smoke AMA. Doc said shock, maybe. I would have kept an eye on her, anyway."

"Thanks, Dad," Amanda snapped. She glared at him a beat but couldn't seem to sustain her attitude; she mostly looked young and extremely tired. "Whatever. Hey, what's a ten-fifty-five?"

Miller frowned. "Where'd you hear that?"

"Never mind, I'll look it up," she said.

He kept frowning, but he sounded slightly less hostile. "It's code for coroner's case."

Amanda nodded as though that was what she'd expected. They went inside, Sarah trailing behind John and the teenage girl, feeling possessive and guarded and irritable, telling herself that was a silly, immature reaction to the situation, telling herself that she needed to grow up or go home, already aware that she wouldn't leave him, not tonight, not as long as she could be with him.

>‹‹

Bob felt bad that the kid was dead, he really did, although he couldn't deny that his initial reaction had been a sense of relief—he'd still been struggling to sit up when Eric and Amanda went upstairs, presumably to her bedroom. He'd start to get up and then the pain would take him down, every nerve and muscle in his left arm spasming, and he'd curse himself to cowboy up and take the pain, but he kept almost passing out, he couldn't seem to get up no matter what, and he kept thinking of what Eric was doing to her and feeling minutes slip past and feeling useless. When the cops had come—that prick Leary, unfortunately, but he had a gun and Amanda was in danger, no matter what she believed—Bob had filled them in quick. Teenage boy with a gun and a hostage, very fucking dangerous.

He'd heard the gunshots a moment later, and Amanda's scream, her loud, living scream. Bob had been unable to help a burning, self-righteous satisfaction along with that initial relief, the feeling one has when vengeance has been fulfilled or justice served, depending on one's point of view. Amanda was alive, Eric—who'd *shot* him, the little bastard—probably wasn't. He was in too much goddamn pain to think about much of anything else as the Keystone paramedics went to work. Everything after that was a blur of pain and movement.

"...think he's sleeping. We should come back tomorrow."

"Not sleeping," Bob said, opening his eyes. Amanda was next to his right side, John at the foot of the bed. Bob tried to push himself up a bit and felt a burning slice of hell shimmer through his left shoulder and along his side. That woke him up.

"Somebody prop me up a little more, would you?"

John found the controller, and the hospital mattress slowly tilted him forward. When he finally faced them, he felt something in his chest loosen.

"You're OK?" he asked Amanda.

She nodded. "Yeah. You?"

Bob smiled. His lips felt rubbery. "Hospital meds," he said. "I'm pretty close to useless, actually. But I'll be up and around by tomorrow, I guess."

Amanda nodded. "We'll need you," she said. "I think we're close to the end. The things I've been seeing, they're here, now, I'm pretty sure."

"Now, like—" John gestured, a helpless, hands-to-the-ceiling, "now? Tonight?"

She nodded, looked to John, back to him. "It might already be too late to do anything. Or maybe...what I'm feeling is like everything's going to stop suddenly. I don't know; everything seemed so clear when I was at John's, I had this really clear understanding for a minute…but I can't get it back."

Bob made a sincere effort to concentrate. Something she said, it was important.

When I was at John's.

Bob closed his eyes, the better to think. Another conversation surfaced, from John's kitchen.

Why do you think you're picking it up now?

Maybe he's getting stronger…or maybe he's closer.

"Do you know everyone on your street?" Bob asked, looking at John. "Who lives next door to you?"

John shook his head. "I don't know. A man, ah…*Mallon*, name's Mallon. I ran into him the day that…that Mr. Calvin died. Why?"

"Because being at your house is different," Amanda said. She looked at Bob. "The way I've been feeling, since I've been there. You think…"

"Mallon," Bob said, and felt a great rush of certainty, so strong and right that the drug haze seemed to burn away. "Mallon. That was Typhoid Mary's last name. I ran across it a couple of times recently, when I was looking at articles about contagion. It's him; it's got to be him."

"Not so fast," John said, but he also looked fully connected, hearing what Bob was saying. "Next door? You think he's been next door to me, all this time?"

Amanda's eyes were wide. "What do we do?"

"We go talk to him, I guess," Bob said. "If you met him, you think you could tell if he's the one?"

"Yeah, I think so," she said. "I'm already pretty sure, though."

"How?" John asked. "Why?"

"I don't know how to explain it…"

"Try."

Amanda shook her head. "Everything is changing, every-thing is in motion, moving, ah...like, pivotal moments are occurring, maybe that's what I'm seeing, maybe I'm seeing choices being made...I feel like...I feel like the movie's almost over. I thought maybe that meant I was going to die, but Eric died, not me..."

She trailed off, her chin trembling. "I don't know what I mean."

"It can't hurt to go talk to the man," Bob said, looking at John. "We're not accusing him of anything, just stopping by to chat."

John finally nodded. "OK, but not tonight." He glanced toward the hall and looked at his watch, back at Bob. "You're in no shape, old man."

Bob wasn't about to argue. His sudden excitement appeared to have exhausted him; he was back to struggling to stay awake.

We'll want to get the gun first, too. Still tucked in John's back office. "Tomorrow, as soon as they let me go. I want to be there."

Amanda and John both agreed, and John put his arm around Amanda, and Bob said he was sorry, and Amanda said that *she* was sorry, and then he blinked once, twice, and they were gone, and then he slept.

><

Three separate times on the way home Jeff had just lain down, picked a clear spot on the side of the road and sat and then top-pled over, and three times, Tommy had urged him back to his feet, sure that it was past midnight by now and his mother had called the cops when Jeff's mother had called *her* to see if they were at Big Blue. Jeff had wet his pants a little the last time he'd lain down, and Tommy had kicked him in the shin, really hard, desperate to be home and safe.

Jeff's, he told himself. If God was merciful, Jeff's mom wouldn't be home yet and they could go inside and hide in Jeff's room and this monstrous night would be over. No one would ever know that they'd been drunk or at the carnival by themselves or that they'd seen a bunch of men beat another man to death. Tommy knew he was still fucked-up, but he also knew what he'd seen and heard. The guy who'd whacked off to little boys, who'd followed them through the woods and chased him through the dark, he was history.

The closer they got to Jeff's, the more Jeff seemed to recognize where they were and where they were going, and he stopped trying to lie down. There was no car in the drive. Jeff led them around to the back door. Tommy tried to straighten up, thinking that if he had to pretend to be OK they were fucked, he couldn't remember ever being so tired, and there was puke on his shirt and dirt on his knees. They stepped inside and looked around—and Jeff laughed.

"It's ten o'clock," he said, pointing at the digital green readout on the microwave. "She won't be home for like two *hours.*"

Tommy wanted to cry; that was the best news he'd ever heard. He was so thankful, so grateful to be somewhere, a house, a friend's house. "I gotta lay down."

"Yeah," Jeff said, and Tommy closed the back door, and Jeff led him down the hall to his room.

For Aaron Reese, the summer had started off shitty, as usual. He was still two classes short of his diploma, which his mother wouldn't let up about, even though he was going to fucking summer school. His stepdad said if he couldn't do better than hanging around with his dumbshit friends at retard school, he better get his GED and get a fucking job. Aaron hated his stepdad, Michael; he was always saying how Aaron was lazy because he was a year-plus behind and that his friends were stupid, and he'd never even met any of Aaron's friends. Not that Aaron had any, unless he counted Calvin, who was even more of an outcast than Aaron. Calvin was heavy into porno and was superugly. Aaron wasn't ugly, at least; a little plain but not deformed or anything. He maybe wasn't as smart as some, but if anybody ever bothered to try to get to know him, if anyone gave him a chance, ever, he figured he'd do OK. He just didn't talk so great; words got stuck in his head sometimes, and he'd stand there and stare at whoever had spoken to him, and they'd act like he was retarded.

Aaron had spent nineteen years being lonely, feeling frustrated, becoming angry, seeing how poorly he fit into the world. The things that came so easily to other people were a struggle for him, and that wasn't his fault, it was just the way things were, and that was somehow the worst of all; that made him burn inside.

In late June, he'd lit his first fire, a neighbor's unlocked garden shed. It had pretty much been a dud in terms of damage, but the smoke, the alarm, the excitement…watching all those people scramble, that had been awesome. He'd gotten away with it, too. Mr. Winters kept a gas can in the shed, and everyone thought it was an accident, brought on by rising temperatures. The incredible ease with which he'd gained such bone-deep satisfaction…a next time was inevitable.

In July, there had been the barn on the empty lot outside town. Aaron didn't know who owned the land or why they'd allowed their sagging wood barn to slowly decay over the years, although it had become kind of a landmark. The abandoned barn was the first thing you saw as you turned off the highway to come to Port Isley, standing in an overgrown field backed by evergreens, the roof hanging like an old horse's back, the paint weathered away. There was even a postcard of it in one of the stores downtown. The rush he'd gotten from burning Mr. Winters's shed had set him daydreaming, imagining places where he could do it again, where no one would catch him…and then he'd just done it, said he was going out to a movie one evening last week and he went to the barn and went inside, parking in a ditch farther along and coming back through the woods so no one would see him or his mother's car. The place was empty except for a lot of trash and broken shit that had been dumped there over the years, plus about a hundred giant bales of rotting newspaper. It stank. There was rat shit and mold everywhere, although it hadn't rained in so long, everything was dry. There were a few signs of occasional human habitation—cans and bottles and wrappers, what looked like a girl's panties crumpled and faded pink beneath his flashlight's beam, stuffed in a convenience store big cup. There were a lot of birds in the rafters; after he started building his fire against one corner of the dried-out wall, once the smoke started rising, he heard panicked fluttering and cries. Too bad for them if they couldn't get out. Not everyone was a winner.

He'd stayed until he'd started coughing and then watched from the woods as his small fire grew, as it swept up the walls and the smoke glowed and the firemen came. He'd wanted to stay, very much, but hadn't wanted to be caught, not after he'd seen what he was capable of doing.

There was no local paper for some reason, but there was a report on TV and there was some footage of the smoking wreckage in the early morning and firemen gathering up their equipment. The lady reporter looked so serious when she said that the beloved landmark would be missed and that arson was suspected. Aaron went to the library the next day and watched it again online. After some hesitation he looked up *fire*, and by clicking from link to link he found a lot of useful information about accelerants. He'd never had much use for computers past video game/porno capacity, but the ease with which he navigated the sites for articles and videos made him feel smart and capable. He wanted to do something bigger than the barn, something fantastic, and after watching a clip of a kid throwing a propane tank on a fire, he thought he knew just the thing.

There was no end of targets but he picked the community theater because it was all wood inside, and it would burn well. Also, no one was using it for anything, so far as he knew; he walked past two days in a row and everything was locked and shaded.

He spent endless stuffy hours of remedial geometry survey dreaming of the fire, imagining the thrill of seeing it devour a beloved landmark that wasn't an empty, stinking barn. He fell asleep thinking of that computer video, how it had taken a full minute at least for the tiny, hand-size propane tank to explode after the guy threw it in the fire. The tank strapped to Michael's expensive, rarely used barbecue was way bigger; it would blow the burning walls to pieces, spreading the fire everywhere; he could throw it in once the fire got going really good and be all the way back to his car before it exploded.

He parked a block behind the theater on a silent street. It was very late and very dark, the very dead of night, a few minutes before four. He shouldered the backpack of accelerants—stuff he'd found in the garage or in the bathroom, turpentine, motor oil, some kind of degreaser made with alcohol, a bottle of nail polish remover, and most of a bottle of rubbing alcohol—and took the propane tank under his arm. The tank weighed about twenty pounds, and he thought it was mostly full, the little gauge thing said so, anyway, and except for one forced, unpleasant family picnic on the Fourth, Aaron couldn't remember the last time the barbecue had been used.

He cut through an open backyard and around a fenced one, and then he was at the rear of the theater. There was a narrow back alley and then some hedges, and there were a couple of places where he would be hidden from everybody, where he'd have time to build something substantial. He had the perfect place in mind, too, a wooden door to the theater's basement. It was down a half dozen steps—cement—but he thought if he could block the drain hole at the bottom of the stairwell, he could build a fire that practically covered the whole door. Plus the stairwell would be ideal for dropping the tank into, once he was sure it was hot enough. If the door hadn't burned by then, the blast of the tank would blow it open and the fire would be sucked inside. Of course, the explosion might just blow everything out, but the backpack was heavy with cans and bottles; he thought he could make something that would spread.

He'd only brought some newspapers, thinking that he'd find something else he could use; there'd been a ton of shit in the barn. He figured at least old bark dust or dried branches from around the theater, but everything was well watered, the hedges trimmed, the wood and dirt moist from an automatic watering system, one that obviously had been at work only recently; some of the low branches on the hedge he pushed past still dripped. Whatever. He was committed; he'd figure something out.

Aaron set the tank at the top of the stairs and lowered himself to the dark bottom, crouching, opening his backpack. By the light of a tiny keychain LED flashlight he slid the newspapers out and started twisting some of them into tight little logs, crumpling other sheets into balls, building a varied pile. After a moment's consideration, he crammed the storm drain with some of the heavy twists, sticking as many in the metal holes as would fit, and poured a quart of motor oil—10-30, whatever that meant—over them, clogging the drain. He spread his crumpled paper all around the drooping, oil-drenched wicks and stacked more paper on top, then upended the can of turpentine over everything, splashing the door liberally.

He climbed to the top of the stairwell with the backpack and carefully moved the propane tank around the corner, maybe ten feet away. He returned to the stairs and crouched, the sharp tang of the turpentine searing his nose. He struck a wooden match with shaking fingers and threw it at the sodden pile of paper, throwing himself back at the same time.

Nothing. After an eternity of waiting, afraid that he'd stand up and look down and then there'd be a big movie explosion and he'd be thrown twenty feet, outlined in fire, he carefully crept forward and aimed his tiny flashlight down the stairwell. It wasn't bright enough to show him anything; he couldn't see the match, and there wasn't any fire.

He lit a second match, held it until half its length was ablaze, and threw it into the pit, quickly stepping away. Counting, slowly, to ten, and…nothing.

Shitballs. It was just one of those little boxes; there were only a dozen matches left in it. He sat down and spent a moment arranging the matches so that all their heads stuck out one end of the box, the wash of fumes alerting him to the possibility of a fireball. He would throw it and dive, throw it and dive...

He lit the box, the sudden hiss and flare of the multiple match heads catching like a promise, a chemical reaction that would flare all the way down to the soaked paper, and he threw it and dived, crashing into the wall of the theater with one shoulder in his hurry to get away.

There was no fireball, but there was a sound like *whooof*, and the flames came up right away, orange and yellow and blue, the air heating quickly, and he leaned against the wall and felt himself swell with joy.

He waited a moment, then risked a look down the stairs— and was disappointed. The flames were licking at the door, and the pool at the bottom of the stairs was afire, but the brightness was already fading. The fire seemed content to burn itself, a guttering candle against the treated wood. It would get through the door eventually, but that wasn't what he wanted.

He looked around. The night was still; there were no windows lighting up, no doors opening, no dogs barking. He stepped to the side of the building again and opened the backpack, selecting something plastic, nail polish remover, and threw it down the stairs.

Aaron waited, grinning, pressed against the wall, and seconds ticked past, and there was a brief flare of light accompanied by a furious crackling...and then nothing again.

Before he could reconsider, he picked up the entire backpack and threw it down the stairs, knowing at once that he was being stupid but unable to stop himself. He wanted something to happen so badly; he needed to see the thing he'd been dreaming, the great fire, the explosion.

Grabbing the propane tank, he stumbled away, leaning against the damp hedges as behind him, there *were* explosions, but muffled and flat, nothing like in the movies, more like aluminum cans stuffed with firecrackers, but then there was a big *crack* and a bright rattle of thin metal hitting concrete, and he was sure the door had blown open, was sure that his liquid fire was pouring into the basement even now, finding the ancient wooden support pillars, the storage racks of nylon and polyester costumes wrapped in plastic, acetate, old wooden props, and everywhere layer upon layer of thick, dry paint...

He found a safe spot on the other side of the theater, between a hedge and a Dumpster, and he waited.

A few lights had come on, and two or three dogs barked. Someone had opened their front door, and Aaron didn't hear it close, but a minute, two went by, and he didn't hear anything, so they'd probably closed it again. He knew he wouldn't have long once the call went out, but it seemed that God was watching over him, granting him another chance at happiness; the night went silent again.

Time passed, eternal moments, and he reveled in each one. Aaron could feel the fire working, could smell it and hear its gasping breath, even if no one else could. There were no cars, no lights or sirens. The world was deaf and stupid and blind, and only *he* knew the huge thing that he had done, that was happening right now.

He had to see it. He wanted to drop the tank into the stairwell and run, but first he wanted to see for himself. He'd waited as long as he dared.

He lifted the tank and crept back around the theater, between the hedges and the back wall, the smell of smoke thickening, the blaze finally catching on, he could see by the orange light coming from the far side of the building, shining against the hedges around the corner, fogged by gathering smoke. Aaron could hear the sizzle of frying heat, and he couldn't remember ever being happier. Holding the tank in nerveless fingers, he stepped around to the side of the building where he'd set the fire...and was transfixed.

Bright flames swept up from the cellar door, over the wall, spreading up to the antique raftered ceiling inside in sheets of brilliant, wavering copper and white. He could hear glass breaking somewhere inside. The heat was intense, blasting his face, reddening his exposed skin, but he didn't feel it, his wondering gaze fixed to the thing he'd made. Sparks cracked and popped into the troubled air, lifting into the sky, and the smoke was hovering over it all like a shifting, flickering mass of darkness, of hate, and he felt excited and peaceful all at once; he felt *vindicated*. The fire wasn't just beautiful, it was a force of fucking nature, and he'd unleashed it, fuck you all very much, wouldn't everyone just shit if they knew that ol' Starin' Aaron had given birth to such a magnificent creature.

Now he heard doors and people; now he heard a neighbor shouting. It was time to leave. He lifted the propane tank and edged for the fiery pit, the metal warm in his hands, the heat from the burning theater like a wall, like a slap. He had to get rid of the tank and go; it was past time. He aimed for the burning, blackening concrete well and threw, and the tank went right in, a perfect shot, and he turned to run. From the video, he knew that he probably had at least a minute before it blew, but to be safe he—

The tank gauge snapped off when it hit ground, ejecting a liquid jet of propane into the burning soup that Aaron had created. Traveling at better than seventy-five feet per second—a fairly low velocity, he might have remembered from his reading at the library—fist-size chunks of concrete and three separate twists of metal from the propane tank gauge and a substantial piece of the burning door slammed into Aaron's back, taking him down. He had time to feel his body burning, but he was, in fact, dead before he hit the ground. Considering how far he was thrown, that was no great mercy, but then, not everyone can be a winner.

><

Officer Trey Ellis was doing his turn on night shift. They were all pulling it at least twice a week to deal with what the chief called "serious" stuff. He wanted one of his best people watching, all the time, and though the other guys crabbed about it, Trey was proud as all shit to be getting so much responsibility so fast. Vincent trusted him; he'd already shown how much by having Trey fix up that guy's house, to get that fucking cock-blocker Dean out of the port. A lot of things had changed since Annie Thomas had gotten herself killed. The way things were now, it was so much better. He and Leary had accidentally dropped a wife-beater on his face when they were taking him into custody last week. Five or six times, they'd accidentally dropped him, and that was fucking job satisfaction, right there. The chief was all about justice since Annie'd died, and Trey was a hundred and ten on that shit. He had been pumped up all summer, seemed like, and Trey liked the rush; he liked being able to do the right thing because he *said* it was the right thing, he was the *man*, and Stan Vincent was one big-dick cop; he was walking the walk. Trey was ready to take a bullet for him, he just respected him all to shit, more than he could even say.

It was just about four when the chief came into the station, to the back room where Trey was keeping an eye on the roads, waiting for something to happen. When he saw Vincent's pale, sweaty face, Trey was on his feet in a second.

"They're coming," Vincent said. He looked angry and...and afraid? No, no way.

"Who is?"

Vincent was wearing jeans and a T-shirt, and his hair was sticking up, like he'd been sleeping. "Dean called me at home. Said he felt like it was professional courtesy to let me know. Smug fucker. Him and one of his top IA people, they'll be here first thing. By eight, he says."

Trey clenched his fists. "What for?"

Vincent had a tic under one eye; the thin skin there spasmed as he spoke. Tic. Tic. "He said they've got some questions about how we're running things out here. He says there's been some complaints. He wants to talk about Elwes, too." The chief smiled thinly. "Guy says he was set up, apparently, and some kiddie freak's word is enough for a man like Dean."

"What are we gonna do?" Trey asked.

Vincent shook his head slightly. Tic. Tic. His eyes were haunted by the shadows beneath them. "I think we should stop them," he said. "What do you think? You think you might be able to help me with something like that?"

Trey clenched and unclenched his fingers, excited and a little freaked. He was all for banging some asshole's face on the pavement, but Vincent was talking about other cops.

Deputies, though, he told himself. *And he's asking me, not Henderson, not LaVeau.* Wes Dean and someone off the rat squad, no great loss for law enforcement in the state of Washington, but it was some serious shit nonetheless, and Vincent had picked *him*.

"You bet, Chief," Trey said, and that was when the explosion thundered down the street, and the phone started ringing out in the squad room.

><

The explosion woke Poppy up a few minutes after four. He told himself he'd dreamed the sound and got up and shuffled to the bathroom and shuffled back and sat on the edge of the bed. He heard the fire engine heading south on the waterfront. He heard his next-door neighbors, a young couple with a baby, outside on their porch, talking, and heard a car start up down the street and wondered what had happened.

He lay down on his bed, pulling the soft, aging comforter up to his chest, and thought about what Bob Sayers had said to him about helping people. He'd fallen asleep earlier thinking about it; no reason to think it wouldn't work a second time. After a few minutes he closed his eyes, and a few minutes after that he was up and pulling his pants on over his boxers, looking for his shoes, wishing he'd been able to go back to sleep.

CHAPTER

30

Ian Henderson pulled the patrol car into one of the designated slots at the back of the station, noting with some dismay that there were at least two news vans in the lot. Maybe because of the community theater…and what the fuck was that about, anyway? The theater was a good ten blocks away, he couldn't see it from the lot, but the air smelled like smoke, like burned trash. Was the fire out? Had anything else burned? He half ran to the back door, wishing to *fuck* he'd had a cup of coffee at least, feeling like a little caffeine would at least prep him to face whatever was coming. He'd been snug and deep asleep in bed less than twenty minutes ago; it just wasn't fucking fair.

Through the back room, where the battered coffee pot was always gurgling, where the lockers branched out on either side. Margot Trent was talking to Dave Miller near the cafeteria table, and they both shut up when he came through, conspicuously looking away. Miller had a smear of what looked like ash on his forehead. Henderson considered stopping to tell them what might happen but still thought there might be time to avert the disaster, and he didn't want to waste it talking to those two. Margot took herself way too seriously, and the only reason Miller wasn't wearing jackboots with the rest of them was because he was a pussy.

He settled on saying, "Heads up," and patted his Glock.

There were a couple of cops milling around in the squad room, part-timers. The press liaison from the council, a retired lawyer named Dawes, was talking to a trio of reporters in the waiting area plus a handful of summer people, some kind of impromptu press conference at the very front of the building, but Henderson ignored all of them. The man he wanted was where he'd expected, in his glass box of an office at the grand, old building's northwest corner. LaVeau, Leary, and Trey Ellis were with him. Vincent's team. All armed, including Vincent.

Henderson didn't bother knocking. Leary and LaVeau both looked anxious, but Trey was bouncing on the balls of his feet; he looked wired, like he was going to jump out of his skin. The naked gratitude in Vincent's eyes made Henderson feel sick. He closed the door behind him.

"You're here," Vincent said. "Good, that's good. They'll be here anytime."

"You said Wes Dean was coming, with county IA?" Henderson asked.

"A fuck and his rat," Trey said, and barked laughter. Henderson and Vincent both ignored him.

"They have questions," Vincent said.

"Are you going to answer them?"

"Whatever I do, Dean's going to nail me. Us." The chief drew himself tall, his chin up. "We going to let that happen, Ian?"

Henderson answered carefully. "I don't want to die, Stan."

"Anyone dies, it'll be that fuck and his fuckin' rat," Trey said.

"Shut up," Henderson said. He kept his gaze on Vincent's, but the chief's kept darting away. He *looked* crazy, his face twitching, his attention all over the place.

"No one's going to die," he said.

"Yeah, I might think that, except all of us are carrying, and you know they will be…and none of us are exercising much self-control lately; you know that, right? You gotta know something's weird."

"Weird?" That from Frank LaVeau, who'd watched the exchange with some interest. Frank had taken it upon himself in the last six weeks to roust anyone with a seedy look, to convince them that Port Isley was not a good place for them, and he'd used his fists to do it. One of the drifters he'd beat up had traveled on and died at a shelter in Port Angeles from injuries sustained during his run-in with the cop. Upon being informed of the death, LaVeau had said, "Well, that's one less coming back, right?"

"The way things are, the way everyone is this summer, since June," Henderson said, still looking at Vincent. "Think about it. You know what it's been like. Like what those people were saying, the reporter and that doctor, how violence is up, how we're all…" Henderson trailed off, grasping at the concept, applying it to himself for the first time.

"We're all what?" Leary sneered. "Seems to me, you're either on the team or you're not, Ian. You've been here, haven't you? Man up. That fuck is coming in here to bust us for running things the way they should be run, and you know it."

Trey laughed, a high, whinnying sound. "Straight up."

Frank LaVeau looked to Vincent, who wasn't looking at any of them. His attention was fixed on the squad room outside the glass box of his office, on Wes Dean and a pretty woman with a decidedly unhappy face at his side, at the pair of uniforms that accompanied them. Debra had stalled them for a moment at the front desk, but they were about to go around her. Henderson recognized one of them, his counterpart on the county, Dean's right-hand guy, Brett Rusch.

Early. He might have gotten somewhere with Vincent, but he had been counting on another five minutes, at least.

"Don't do it," Henderson said, giving it all he had. "Surrender your weapons, lay them down now, we can get out of this, whatever it is. Don't let it get out of hand. Think about Ashley, Stan. Ashley and Lily. You want her to grow up without her daddy?"

"Get out," Vincent said.

Trey Ellis had his hand on his weapon; so did Leary. Henderson had no doubt he could outdraw them, but Vincent was letting him go; he should get out and be fucking thankful. Vincent had gone Brando from whatchama, that awesome flick; Henderson had tried to read the book it was based on like four times and couldn't get past the flowery descriptions, *guy's name was...*

Get out! Go!

He half turned and walked sideways to the door, not wanting to turn his back on Trey, who wanted to draw down. The dumbshit was looking forward to the confrontation; that was written on his face and in his stance. Henderson backed out of the office watching Vincent's face, a brave commander witnessing an act of cowardice. Henderson respected war veterans all to hell; his family had always had someone in the military, a cousin, an uncle. When he was a kid, he hadn't understood how people could put themselves on the line for an ideal, for a principle...but after some time as a cop, he'd started to get it. Soldiers fought for the guys standing next to them, because they'd all been stuck with a shit deal, because they didn't want to die...but this wasn't a war, and these weren't his brothers because they all wore badges for the fucking PIPD. He had been sincere and honest with Vincent; he did not want to die, and if that meant a dipshit rookie or a fat shit like Leary or some closet Nazi thought he was chickenshit, so be it. Vincent's reproach didn't hurt nearly as much as the idea of being dead, of no more fucking or watching movies or eating fresh fish he'd caught himself. And all because they'd been infected with something, maybe. That was like eating a bullet because you caught the flu.

He backed into Wes Dean, but it was his guy who stepped up, Rusch.

"You want to watch it, Ian," Rusch said, working to get in his face, but Henderson couldn't think of anything more ridiculous, more useless at the moment.

"Vincent's crazy," he said, speaking as he backed past the posse. "Get out of here."

The unhappy-looking woman spoke. "Officer Henderson? Perhaps you could make yourself available to us for—"

"Shut the fuck up, he's 5150, you get it?" The name from the movie and the book suddenly came to him. "Kurtz, he's gone Kurtz. Back out or you're looking at a situation, you copy? Anyone?"

Debra, at the front desk, gave him a wide-eyed look and then hurried for the back room, pulling one of the rookies with her.

Dean spoke up, his voice naturally commanding. "Someone get those civilians out of here."

"All over it," Henderson said. He stepped around the front desk, grabbed Henry Dawes, and whispered in his saggy ear that everyone needed to be evacuated ASAP, that there was an emergency. The press liaison barely skipped a beat, turning a calm, solemn face to his group of listeners.

"Excuse me, I'm told that we need to clear this area immediately," Dawes said. "If you'll come with me—"

Two of the three reporters started snapping questions at him—the third was apparently involved in an important cell conversation, one he just couldn't walk away from—but Henderson was still really feeling the whole not-wanting-to-die vibe. He was tempted to keep moving in spite of the sudden blockage, to just push his way through…but he also wasn't such a selfish dick that he would leave without trying. He turned to the nearest person, a summer man with a cane, his fat wife at his side, and spoke low and clear, so that everyone around might hear.

"Bomb threat," he said loudly, making eye contact with the surprised tourist. "Everyone get out, now."

A half dozen shocked expressions, and then they were all turning, heading for the door, quickly, Henderson right in the middle. The third reporter had finally snapped his cell phone closed.

"What? What did I miss?" he asked, and the guy with the cane called him a dumbshit, and his fat wife agreed, her frightened face bobbing on a couple of chins. Henderson didn't disagree. He pressed with them at the doors. There weren't enough people for anyone to get squashed so long as they kept walking, and he found himself ducking a little; he was a tall man, and he wondered if all those myths were true about not hearing the shot that killed you.

He was outside then, all of them were, and he headed for the parking lot at the side of the building. At least it was a wall between whatever was going to happen and—

The shots were sudden and terrible. Henderson automatically counted, and lost count before he'd gone two steps; there were at least four or five weapons firing: 9 mm rounds punctuated by heavier thunder, had to be the .357 Smith and Wesson revolver Rusch liked to carry. Around him, the herd of civilians ducked, shouted, ran faster for the possible safety of anywhere else.

Henderson headed for his patrol car in the lot. More shots were fired. Nothing more from the .357.

"Get down! Get down!" Dawes screamed from the front of the building, his courtroom voice carrying. "Keep low!"

Henderson didn't duck now that he was out of the direct line of fire. He'd been too late, after all. He was going to go home, pack a bag, and he was going to get out of town for a while, until this shit was resolved. He was officially on vacation until further notice.

In the low, ugly square hedge that separated the parking lot from the station, a woman crouched, her eyes rolling in her head like a rearing horse's. She was so terrified that she'd frozen in an unlovely squat, clutching her purse with both hands, nothing about her moving but her eyes, her teeth gritted in a weird parody of a smile.

Henderson sighed.

"Ma'am? Come with me, please," he said, and reached down and helped her to her feet. She let herself be pulled, a middle-aged woman who might have looked nice, it was impossible to tell through her rictus of fright. She clutched her purse tighter, and Henderson looked back and saw that at least four of the people from inside had followed him.

"This way," he said, steering away from his car. He'd at least have to get them out of harm's way, establish a safe perimeter. Inside, three shots from a Beretta 92FS, the M9, weapon of choice for most of the county sheriff's office—Henderson had one himself—and then there was nothing. In front of the station, people were shouting.

"I haven't even had coffee yet," the middle-aged woman said. He still held her arm and thought that if he let go, she might fall. She'd fixed on him with her stunned expression, but he was noting the time on his watch. Last shots fired at 7:48. Maybe. Henderson finally heard what she'd said, and nodded.

"Tell me about it," he said, passionately.

CHAPTER

31

Amanda didn't sleep well, was half-awake when the explosion rolled up the hill in the very early morning. In her half sleep she was sure that she was hearing the effects of her young-man-at-fire dream, but when she woke up a little, she wasn't so sure. She also thought that if she was still at John's, closer to their tourist, she might be certain; she was way more calm and focused around *him*, she thought, although maybe she was just freaking because she'd seen Eric Hess blown to shit; Eric, poor, lost Eric, murdered, and she knew she was supposed to be afraid of their tourist but the more she thought about him, the more she wasn't.

She and John had stayed at Big Blue, which had been every bit as lacey and self-conscious as she'd expected, and Sarah had lent her some clothes, and she'd finally passed out for a couple of hours before she heard someone get up and start a shower. She had dreamed that she was very small in a land of screaming giants, where every time she tried to move, she was kicked down into the mud. When she finally ventured out and saw Karen Haley for just a moment, heading down the hall, she thought she knew who'd influenced her sleep...but maybe not; maybe the dream was her subconscious reaction to seeing Eric gunned down practically on top of her or knowing that for the rest of her life, she'd remember clearly that split second when she realized what Leary was going to do; she'd remember screaming at him to stop and knowing what was going to happen, anyway. That had been far more traumatizing than the actual bloodbath, and that had been fucking horrible. Amanda felt like she was an old woman already, the things she would have to think about and talk about and know for the rest of her life, whatever else she did.

She spent better than an hour lying in the clean, comfortable bed with her eyes closed, thinking, half dozing, seeing things. By the time she finally got up to go downstairs, she thought she had some idea of what was coming. Maybe. She wasn't sure if she was ready.

Bob arrived just before eight, pale and wrapped snugly in an uncomfortable-looking sling. He insisted that they go to John's house first for his gun, over John's protests that the gun had surely been found and confiscated, and that the police might not let him inside, anyway. The two ducked off into another room to discuss the matter, as if there was any doubt where they were going or what they were going to do.

Amanda drank two cups of coffee with straight heavy whipping cream and ate a plain roll that Sarah gave her, to keep herself from monster acid indigestion. And to fortify herself a little, anyway. She didn't know what was going to happen when they knocked on their tourist's door—

Prisoner, shadows, shell...sea?

—but she thought it would be important, a very important day in her life, and she didn't want to throw up because she'd been living on coffee and nothing for two days. Plus, she'd thrown up already in the shower at the hospital—when they'd finally let her wash Eric's blood off her after swabbing her thoroughly in embarrassing places—when she'd watched the pink water swirl down the drain. She'd cried and puked and cried some more.

The thing was, since shortly after Eric's death, when they'd taken her to the hospital, she'd had this very strange feeling of...of having choices. There were paths that lay in front of her, unexplored…not just paths, but an infinite array of steps in every direction, and she had only to take a first to understand how absolutely free she was. She *could* see herself, fairly clearly, the person she was, if she could let go of the things that had sheltered her from the casual brutality of her life until now…her defenses, her beliefs, her selfishness; her right to bemoan her fate. There was a higher ground, and lying in bed this morning she had actually *seen* it, had seen that if she wanted to be, she was strong enough to face her life without attaching herself to its drama.

This is so fucking out there, she told herself, stuffing the tasteless roll down her throat, waiting for John and Bob to come back and act like they knew what they were doing, like they were in charge. She was like a grown-up or some shit, the things she was thinking, the way she was thinking them…but she also suspected that most adults didn't think like this, or not much. Not that she'd ever noticed. It was frightening, but only a little because she could decide whether to run from the fear or let it pass, whether to follow the emotional rules she'd invented for herself or try something new. The world was shifting from the black and white she'd always known and counted on, to know how to act and what to think, to a continuum of endless gray consideration, and she was also scared because she didn't know if she was ready to be something else.

It's a perspective shift, that's all, she told herself. Sarah decided to stay at Big Blue, which seemed appropriate for some reason. Amanda realized, as John's girlfriend started talking about wanting to be home when her son returned, that if Sarah had wanted to go, Amanda would have had to tell her *no*. It was only supposed to be her and John and Bob, that was just the right thing. She was glad it didn't come up.

Amanda felt herself looking for their tourist's influence as John drove Bob and her back to his house, to park in his drive, which had been cordoned off with police tape…and finding it, finding his gentle, tortured thread of energy easily. He was there, in the gray house next to John's. There'd been enough shock in her life this summer for the wow factor of the coincidence to be a little thin; she'd already accepted that some things were fated to be, which meant that of *course* John lived next door to the guy, it just figured. She was a little surprised she hadn't pinned it down already, but it made sense to her that Bob and John had been necessary to put all the pieces together. Fuck if she knew why.

"Leave the gun," she said, as they got out of the car. There were no police in front of John's house, but there was a county van parked at the side and a government-issue sedan. Amanda couldn't imagine why there weren't reporters standing around…although maybe they'd been distracted by one of her dream images come to life. The fire that had exploded, killing the young arsonist, perhaps. Her thoughtful, dozing half sleep this morning had been laced with conclusions, of knowing things that might be true, but she hadn't said anything to them yet, not sure if it was important anymore. It was crazy; the shit she'd been tripping on all summer suddenly didn't even seem relevant. Important, but not the way they thought. Being here, so close to him, she felt like…like her channels were expanding, receiving things more clearly.

"Seriously," she added, off Bob's expression. "We just need to meet him. He's not armed."

"How do you know? Do you know that?" Bob looked like death. The bright, hazy sun made him look like a vampire. Amanda wore her shades, her arms folded tightly although it was already warm, and the car had been warm.

She nodded. "Yeah."

"Any other useful tidbits?" Bob snapped. "Like what's going to happen? Like who this guy is? Like how we're going to get him to come to the door?"

"Chelsea," Amanda said. She looked at the small, gray house, so quiet and still. He was thinking about the girl even now, the little girl in the pink dress from the picture she'd seen in her dreams, when she'd first thought the words *shell-sea*. But she wasn't a little girl anymore, and it wasn't shell-sea; it was *Chelsea*. "We tell him it's Chelsea. He thinks about her name. She's important to him."

John was looking at her with a careful eye. He and Sarah had made love after they'd thought everyone was asleep, long and slow, and he was trying not to think about it, he was trying extremely hard, and so it kept coming back; she could hear him.

"Amanda," he began. He was going to question her further, try to find out what she knew about everything forever, but she didn't want to *talk* about it anymore, she wanted to meet him. She wanted to see his face; she wanted to explore the mysterious chaos that cloaked his thoughts; she wanted to know what he knew, just for a moment. She wanted to know his real name.

"Seriously, John, enough," she said. "Bob should be in bed. We need to see him to get this over with. *I* need to see him. Bob's right; things are clearer here. Or less clear, depending on who you are, I guess."

"What do you mean? Why are you in such a rush?"

"Because I want to know how it turns out," she said. "Because I saw some things this morning, and I feel…I feel like this is part of it, what we're doing right now. Maybe even the whole point. Probably the whole point, at least for me. Let's just please go, OK?"

She turned and started for the rental, and they fell in behind her, Bob walking slowly. He wasn't as doped as he needed to be to feel no pain, and John was still trying to ask questions. She went to the back door, sure that he was closer to the kitchen, that there was a basement, and started knocking, and saying that it was Chelsea, would he please open the door, and after a minute she was banging at the door with the heel of her hand, her voice breaking as she called herself by a stranger's name. She could feel light burst inside his head each time she said it; she felt him walk up the stairs on numb legs, and the expectation she was generating made her cry, it was so sad and lonely and, and *hopeful*. When he opened the door and saw her he thought she was the girl, older and taller than he'd expected but still her, his niece, and when he gathered her up, she let him, wishing she *was* the girl, he was so happy, his relief like a cool, sweeping wave.

"Hey there," Bob said, alarmed, but Amanda was feeling his heartbeat against her face beneath his thin tee—

—and she made her decision, accepting what was going to happen. *I can do this*, she thought. *I'm supposed to do this.*

She slipped her arms around him and pulled him close. Held him. And knew him intimately in their embrace, her understanding of another human being so far past friendship or sex or the few sad family ties she'd experienced in her short life that she was engulfed, filled to overflowing. She heard what he'd heard, saw what he'd seen. The feelings were those from a dream, intense and raw, bigger than life. His mind was unguarded and full and incredible and sad, and he couldn't see himself anymore; he was a knot of self-doubt and inconceivable, stretching loneliness. The shapes of his thoughts as he held her were enchanting in their starkness, in their honesty…and they were not for her.

"Let her go," John said, from light-years away. "Amanda?"

"I'm sorry, I'm so sorry," she said. "It's not me. I'm sorry."

She felt him pull back from her, the sudden intimacy cut off a second before he managed to extricate himself physically, stepping away, confused. She knew that he had to pull back, just as she had to tell him who she was; she couldn't know him like that and lie for one more second.

He felt it, too, part of it. Something between them. She saw that he was younger than she'd imagined, pale, his eyes dark with doubt and fear. She'd seen him before…drinking coffee by himself, that day in the restaurant. Outside the theater, for poetry night. Always alone.

Again, she could see a hundred ways this could go, ways she could choose to handle this unprecedented meeting…but she already had a sense of the outcome and didn't feel any urge to rebel against what she now believed would happen, what she mostly understood. Chelsea was his niece, by his brother who was dead, who'd killed himself.

"You're David Abbey," she said. "Invite us in, please."

He gazed out at them, his face closed, his heart aching. "Who are you?" he asked, looking at her.

What a fucking trip. She was aware of all of them, Bob's aches and John's fears and David Abbey's need for her, for what she could provide, and there was no hesitation, no fucking fear at all. She didn't have to be coy or manipulate, she didn't have to be what anyone expected. What she expected. There was nothing to win here, just what would eventually be acknowledged, by all of them.

"Fate, if you can believe it," she said.

>←

John was hopelessly adrift. He'd felt the chemistry between Amanda and David Mallon—Abbey?—when they'd embraced, not sexual but electric nonetheless, and now Amanda was talk-ing about fate, and they were walking through the kitchen of the bland, gray rental. His neighbor, all this time. His goddamn neighbor.

Their host led them to the living room where he awkwardly offered them seats before sitting in the room's one nice piece, a wing-backed chair. He nodded acknowledgment at John as they sat.

"Doctor," he said, his voice low and even. He looked composed, but barely. Whoever Chelsea was—and how well could he know her, if he'd mistaken Amanda for her?—she was extremely important to him.

"Right," Amanda said. "Excuse me. I'm Amanda. Young. You've met John; this is Bob Sayers, he's a reporter. This is David Abbey."

Abbey nodded. "So you say. And you know this because…"

"Because when you came to town, I went psychic," she said. "Like, see the future, feel people's feelings psychic. You came in mid-June, right? Like a week and a half in? I started seeing things. And Bob knew something was going on in town, and he found some things, and John's our brains guy who happens to live next door, and we figured it out."

Abbey's expression was as carefully noncommittal as he could make it, a blank, but anyone looking at him would have seen his eyes. He was mortified.

She looked back at John. "He can't help it," she said. "He knows, but he can't help it."

"You knew this would happen," Bob asked, not really a question. "You came here knowing that people would die."

Abbey shifted in his chair. He held his head up. "Yes. I'm sorry. I'm leaving, tonight."

"Maybe that's not good enough," Bob said.

"Different angle, Bob," Amanda said. "Did you not hear me? He can't help what he does."

"He can sure as hell help where he *goes*." He shot a look at Abbey. "Why here? Why did you come here?"

Abbey only stared at him, his gaze unreadable but infinitely sad.

John cleared his throat. "What *is* it you do? Do you know?"

Abbey's voice was soft and careful. "I don't, not exactly. People around me change. I don't know the cause, but it propagates genetically; my brother had it, too. This influence. There's a history in our line. What exists in the people around me is magnified and reflected. Things they might normally hide, I believe. Jung's Shadow. I'm a...catalyst. A random element, or a deliberate design. Arguments could be made either way."

He looked at Amanda. "Is there something about Chelsea? Is she all right? Did you see her?"

Amanda shook her head. "Not yet. But you're going to see her, and I'm coming with you."

They all stared at her. The look she wore was patient and ready.

"Hang on a second," John said.

"Over my dead body," Bob said.

Abbey's cheeks had flushed. "I—that's not going to happen."

Amanda sighed, looking at Abbey. "Listen to me," she said. "Look at me. I know about your brother, about Matthew."

"What?" Abbey was transfixed, the word a dumb whisper.

"Before Chelsea was born, before he even knew about her, he killed himself. Before he knew that you had it, too. And you're afraid she might be a carrier, and you're afraid...you're just afraid. But I can tell you what you need to know."

Abbey shook his head, his eyes still, his attention entirely on Amanda. "Impossible."

She leaned forward and spoke in a kind, careful voice. "I'm the balance, David. For you. For now. In my dreams, I think I see the things that are fated, because of what you do."

She swallowed, her smile a nervous tic. "Not all of it; I can't promise that. There's a lot I don't see. But there are other things, when I'm awake. Some things *can* be changed. I'm sure of it. My

friend Devon did it; he's alive because he changed the circumstances, because of what I told him. And I know what people are
thinking. Where they might go, in their minds."

Abbey was shaking his head again. "You wouldn't be safe."

"I already am," she said. "I'm twice as strong here, with you,
and not just in a psychic sense. I've been through an amazing
amount of shit since you got here, and everything that happened
it's like I got older, I got smarter…I got closer to you. To this."

She dropped her voice to a whisper and said something
John didn't catch. He thought she said *to love.* Whatever it was,
Abbey's expression flickered. He studied her face.

"Amanda, how 'bout you get this batshit idea out of your
head, right now," Bob said. "You don't know this man—"

"Yes, I do—"

"—and there's no way in hell you're going anywhere with
him, not based on five seconds of contact, I don't care what you
think you see."

Amanda looked at him calmly, at him and then John, ignoring Abbey for the moment. "OK, listen up," she said. "You've
both been great. Really, really great. I think both of you are
good guys, and you want to do the right thing. Granted, I'm
a teenager so therefore an idiot about some things, but even
with you two watching out for me, there is nothing for me in
Port Isley, no future at all; I was leaving anyway. And I just met
someone who needs me, who absolutely *needs* me, and this is
why everything happened at once, this is why everything ends
here, now, not because I'm going to die. Because I'm leaving.
We both are."

She glanced back to Abbey. "I dreamed it."

Bob looked at John, his expression a twist of frustration.
"Would you speak up, Doctor? Explain to her about stranger
danger, maybe?"

He turned and shot silent daggers at Abbey. "And you, don't get your pecker up. She's not legal."

Amanda's tone was calm, so calm and reasonable. "I can make this decision, Bob. It's fast, but not impulsive. I want this. For a lot of reasons."

Abbey seemed slightly awed by Amanda. "I haven't said what I want."

Amanda reached out and tried to take his hand, but he pulled away, avoiding her touch.

"You want to see Chelsea," she said. "I can meet her first. I can tell you what will happen. What might happen."

Abbey fisted his hands in his lap, the picture of anxiety. "And then what?"

Her expression said nothing. "Then we decide if we keep being useful to one another or if we part ways."

"Do you know?" he asked. His voice trembled. "Can you see…"

"I see *you*," she said, and that electricity from before passed through the room. John felt as though he were witnessing a private moment between old friends, a first kiss, a power surge, a mother and son talking; he couldn't relate it to any one thing. It was all those things; it was a palpable feeling of energy.

"I think we should talk about this," he said, finally. "No one has slept well, and there's nothing saying a decision has to be made right this second, is there?"

Amanda rolled her eyes at him. "Ah, the voice of reason. You were planning on taking me in permanently, John? Your plate's full enough."

"What do you mean?"

She looked at him with an unlikely kindness. "Whether you're meant to be with her, that's not set in stone. People change all the time; people decide things because of who they are and what they want. You can make it happen or let it go…and it will work or it won't. What guarantee is there that it all won't end tomorrow? For anyone, ever?"

To have his silent fears so neatly laid out and inspected… John couldn't say he cared for the feeling. He couldn't fault her honesty, but as a therapist, she lacked finesse.

"Little contradictory there, aren't you?" he asked. "You're arguing both sides, determinism and free will. Is it fate or choice?"

"Both. Or neither."

"That doesn't make sense."

Amanda nodded. "You got me there. Everything else has been so clear for all of us, up till now."

"He's a grown man," Bob said. "You're seventeen. You think he's not going to find that *useful*?"

"You have no idea what I know," Amanda said.

"Why don't you tell me, then?"

"You're going to give up the paper, turn it over to Nancy," Amanda said. "You're going to start writing a book about what happened in—"

"Stop it," Bob said. He looked ill. "Stop. I don't want to hear that."

"Right. He does, though," she said, and tilted her head at Abbey. "For him, it means being able to have a life. To know where he can go and how long he can stay."

"I don't like being treated like I'm not here," Abbey said.

"Yeah, it sucks, doesn't it?" Amanda said, turning back to him. Her tone was affectionate, as though she'd known him forever, but her expression was dark. "I think everything had to happen the way it did for me to get here, to where my head is. For us to meet and have it be the right thing at the right time for both of us."

John looked at Abbey, the man he'd dismissed as an introvert not so long ago when they'd crossed paths in the park, the man responsible for the depth of his connection to Sarah, if all this madness was true, if Amanda knew what she was talking about. The man responsible for everything.

If, if. He knew better. He believed.

"How long will the effect continue?" he asked. "After you go."

Abbey shook his head. His eyes were cool and clear, if perhaps dazed from their meeting. From meeting Amanda, certainly, who was as calm and implacable as the tide, who already treated him as though their future was a certainty. Abbey was responding to it, too, leaning toward her slightly, as a plant leans toward the sun. "Varies. A week, maybe? Two at the outside. I could look it up."

"The lines of numbers," Amanda said. "He writes everything down. Since Matthew died, since he realized he's like his brother, he's been trying to document the effect."

Off the young man's shocked expression, she added, "I'm sorry, David. Mr. Abbey. I wish you knew what I do, that's all, about yourself. About what kind of person you are."

She addressed all of them. "If you need more time to adjust to this concept, this unexpected turn, that's fine. And I guess if one of you wanted to be an ass about this, *Bob*, you could, but please don't. Just think about it before you say anything. I can see things now that I couldn't see before. This is what's supposed to happen."

She looked almost fondly at the man who'd taken the last name of a disease carrier to come to their town, to move in next door to him. He wished Sarah had come, that she was standing here with him so that he could see her face, so that he could see her thoughts.

Annie. Karen, Rick Truman, Ed Billings, the fire that had burned four houses close to the theater before the fire department had brought it under control…how many hurt, how many killed?

How many could be prevented if she went with him?

"What happens with the fun house?" Bob asked abruptly. "With the mother and the baby? Do you know?"

Amanda frowned. "I...I don't know what happened, exactly, but either way, it's over. The carnival, I mean. It's already gone. The baby...I don't know about him, either. That one I haven't seen."

Her expression said that she hoped she wouldn't.

"The explosion this morning, though, that *was* the fire I saw," she said. "The kid blew himself up, I'm pretty sure. You know, I think it might have been Aaron Reese? He was a senior, second time. Just this guy. Remedial."

John scrambled for the other images she'd dreamed, ignoring, for the moment, that she hadn't told them this before coming here, that she'd chosen to do this in front of a stranger.

"The gunfire?" Bob asked.

Amanda shook her head. "I don't know. I didn't see that, but it will happen today, before we leave. If it hasn't already. I mean, if my theory is correct."

"So we could still stop it," Bob said.

She gazed at him a moment, then shook her head again. "No. That one can't be stopped, I don't think."

"Pretty sure. You think. You don't know." Bob shot a meaningful look at John.

"Bob, stop protecting me," she said.

"What if I don't want to write a book? What if I decide not to because you just told me I would?" Bob asked.

"That's OK, too," Amanda said. "Whatever. What are you fighting? Are you trying to argue with *shit happens*? Is it so impossible to believe that there are some things you can change and some you can't? Or that I'm just seeing one possibility of many?"

"I need time to think," Abbey said. "And you want to talk about this, obviously. I'm sorry, if you'll excuse me…"

He stood up, and so did they. Amanda reached out and touched him again, his arm, and he started as though she had burned him.

"Right," she said. "I'm sorry. I can see why that'd be…we'll set down some ground rules on the drive. What time do you want to leave?"

Abbey shook his head. "Today. Tonight. I thought I'd pack and then try to get some sleep first…"

"Good luck with that," she said. "I'll be here by dark with a few essentials. If you want to keep being alone, you can tell me then…though you can at least drop me in Seattle, right?"

"I…"

"Good, OK," she said. "It's going to be OK. You're right in the middle. You can't see it, but you can trust me. I know that's a crazy thing to say after how I got you to come to the door, but I didn't know what else to do. I really am sorry. You will see her. You can, if you want to. If you'll let me help you."

Abbey didn't answer, only waited for them to walk ahead, back the way they'd come. He was still flushed and obviously disturbed, his face boyish although he had to have a decade on Amanda. He wore his social ineloquence like a much younger man, like an open book. John wondered why Abbey might jerk away from someone touching him and didn't like any implication he could imagine. He wondered what happened to the people who touched him or what he was afraid might happen. Did Amanda know? Or care?

They left by the door to the kitchen. Abbey stared after them, after Amanda, with a look that John couldn't quite define, finally closing the door.

They automatically started walking toward John's house.

"You really think this is a good idea?" John asked her.

"I know it is."

"How do you know so much about him?"

"How did I know so much about you?"

"We're going to talk you out of this," Bob said.

"You'll try, for reasons that are sound," Amanda said. "And very sweet, which is why I won't be a jerk about it if I don't have to be, but you gotta give it up. Unless you want to hogtie me, you sort of have to let me go."

"He won't take you," Bob said.

"He will. He has to." John thought she looked like she might cry, suddenly. "He doesn't have a choice."

When they reached John's back door—not crossed with crime tape—John used his key, and the door opened. There was no one in the kitchen or living room, though they could hear footsteps upstairs. In the guest room, John figured. By silent consensus, they sat at the small table, the breakfast nook table that Lauren had ordered special for their fifth anniversary, when the kitchen had finally been deemed complete.

"Think they'll kick us out?" Amanda asked quietly.

"Fuck if they will," Bob said. He looked sullen, like he wanted to yell at someone but had no decent target. The old reporter really did look awful.

"No one should be in the study," John said. "Go lay down, Bob."

Bob slumped in his chair. "Yeah, OK. But just for a while. This is not decided."

Amanda stood up. "It is, and you're being stubborn. Is that, like, some old guy thing, your sense of entitlement? Your feeling that things are the way you think they are because that's what you've decided despite any evidence to the contrary?"

Bob slumped lower. "You said you weren't going to be a jerk."

"Come on, you look like shit," Amanda said, and reached down to assist Bob to his feet, careful not to touch the arm in the sling. "Little help here, John?"

John helped. Awkwardly flanking him, they shuffled down the hall toward John's office, Bob leaning on them, his expression sour.

"Amanda," he said finally, as they maneuvered him to the sofa, "you're going to be surprised, someday, how much you thought you knew. How wrong you were."

"Yay, Bob supports my decision," Amanda said. She got the pillow off the chair and set it at her end of the couch. "What's your take, John? You've been awfully quiet. Swing his feet up on your side...careful..."

Bob winced and gritted his teeth, but they got him lying down. John covered his legs with one of the blankets stacked on the desk chair. "I don't know," he said. "I'm...I really don't know. I thought we were going to have to stake him through the heart, or sic the government scientists on him, something...something else." What he thought was, *A week. Maybe two.*

Amanda pulled the chair next to Bob, dropped the rest of the linens on the floor, and sat down. Her voice was calm and clear.

"I'm going, with or without your support. But I'd like it. I'd like to know that someone gives a shit what happens to me after I'm gone. Maybe somewhere I could come for Christmas, or some shit."

"Well, of course you have our support," Bob mumbled, closing his eyes.

"Count on it," John said, and the door, partly open, was suddenly kicked all the way in. A startled-looking chubby guy in a white hairnet and wearing gloves stood out in the hall, wearing a CSU jumpsuit.

"Who are you? Where'd the cops go? This is a closed crime scene, the whole house."

"It's my house," John said.

"It's OK," Amanda said. "Ah, that guy said we could be in this room."

"Who?"

Amanda studied his face a moment. "The old man. Whelan."

The guy looked surprised. "Is he here?"

Amanda hesitated. Reading him.

These aren't the droids you're looking for, John thought. Amanda had gone Jedi.

"No, why would he be here?" she asked. "But something came up and the cops had to run, and they called him. He said finish what you're working on and pack it home."

The tech looked at John, then back at her. "You're supposed to have badges."

John nodded at Bob. "Our friend is ill. That's his blood you're swabbing up out there."

He seemed to realize that he was alone in his battle…and Amanda had used the magic name, the one he'd thought of, that she'd plucked from his thoughts like some theatrical trick. John wondered if the old man, Whelan, also said *pack it home*, and suspected that he did.

"Stay out of the taped rooms, OK? And no smoking."

The guy disappeared as quickly as he'd come, a set of footsteps moving up the stairs.

"You could open in Vegas," Bob croaked.

Amanda looked at him, all seriousness. "This is what I want to do. What I want to be."

"You like the power," John said. "You like knowing things."

"Wouldn't you?" Amanda reached over and smoothed Bob's hair away from his forehead, the gesture more unselfconscious and kind than John would have given her credit for, which made him feel like he didn't know her at all. She had changed.

And she's leaving, either way. She was right; Bob was being stubborn.

"Don't go without me," Bob said, already halfway to sleep.

"I'll say good-bye, don't worry," she said. "Rest easy, codger."

"Fuckin' kids," he mumbled, and was asleep.

They watched him for a moment, neither speaking.

"You got work today?" Amanda asked.

"Yeah, I do," he said, and sighed. "But I'm going to have to call in, considering. Even without all this"—He gestured vaguely toward the ceiling, to the footsteps overhead—"I'd cancel. To be with her as much as I can, if there's only a week or two left."

"It doesn't have to be like that, you know."

"No, you're right, of course. It will be what it is. And forcing it would be the antithesis of...never mind. There's just...I still can't believe any of this. The idea of some genetic disorder carrying a psychological influence...that's paranormal, that's like science fiction. What would that do to a man, to understand that he was responsible for so much chaos?"

"Anyone ever tell you that you think too much?"

"Don't you care why he is the way he is?" John asked.

"He doesn't know, and he's been researching it since I was in grade school," Amanda said, and John felt a chill, wondering what she'd seen, exactly, when she'd touched Abbey.

"I feel like there's so much that hasn't been answered," John said. "Who is this guy, really? Why doesn't he want people to touch him? Why didn't he know that you weren't Chelsea?"

"Some of that is personal," Amanda said. "But I'll ask him to send you copies of his records, if you like. What he knows. I'm sure he will, if I ask."

John nodded. "I would insist."

"I'll miss you," she said. "Both of you." Her eyes welled, but she blinked back her tears.

John felt helpless before her open admission. "It's weird, everything ending like this."

Amanda smiled. "It's beginning, actually."

>‹

Bob slept most of the day and woke in dizziness and pain just after dusk on John's couch. He staggered out to the living room, where John and Amanda were watching TV, her bags packed and sitting by the front door. The CSU guys had apparently packed up and left shortly after Bob had passed out, in a great hurry, the reason already played to death over the cable news by the time he finally woke up. Six cops had been seriously injured in a shootout…about the time, in fact, that Bob had been climbing in his truck to drive over to Big Blue this morning. Stan Vincent and the county sheriff, Western Dean, were both dead. Four others wounded, one still in critical.

Bob looked at Amanda. "That's everyone you dreamed about, isn't it? Except—"

"Yeah," Amanda said. "Except for the baby. Well, and that woman with blood in her hair, but that one happened weeks ago."

"Maybe if you stayed…" Bob started, but she waved her hand at him.

"Walk me out," she said. "It's time."

David Abbey was standing next to his car, a green BMW lightly covered with late pollen from the park's trees. When they stepped outside, he popped the trunk, making room for Amanda's things.

"So this is it?" Bob asked. "The two of you leave, and everything goes back to normal? The end?"

Amanda tilted her head. "You could see it that way, I guess."

"Did any of it mean anything?" Bob asked, not sure what he was asking.

"It will," she said. He thought about asking her to elaborate, but then thought of her telling him about the paper, about writing a book; it was the only time all summer long that he'd been utterly terrified. He didn't want to know if there was a fate at all, let alone what it had in store for him.

They said good-bye beneath a waxing moon, the sky clear, the night warm. David Abbey kept his distance, which Bob thought just as well. Amanda promised to be in touch, and Abbey gave John a card with a law firm's name on the front and a personal cell number written on the back and avoided looking at Bob. Bob had no problem with that. It didn't seem right to him, her running off with someone who made joke names for himself and sat around feeling bad that he was a goddamn killer, oh the torture; he knew that appealed to some girls. He didn't think Amanda was one of 'em, but she was so young, so idealistic in spite of herself.

She hugged both of them, Bob got a kiss, and they were gone, too quickly, the car's lights sweeping over them and driving away. John rested a hand on Bob's good shoulder, and they watched her disappear, taken away by the man she felt was her destiny, the man who'd wrought death and destruction on their little town.

"It doesn't seem right," Bob said.

"No."

"You going to Sarah's tonight?"

John shook his head. "She called earlier, said Tommy came home feeling like he was catching a cold." He smiled a little. "She's been hanging out with him all day, bringing him juice, watching movies with him. She's happy."

Bob nodded. "Mind if I go back to sleep on your couch for the next week? I'm feeling like dodging my phone. Killing a couple of houseplants, too."

John shook his head. "Be my guest. You'll have to fend for yourself, though."

"Perfect."

They went inside, Bob thinking that he would sleep and recover, that they all would, and get back to who they were before Abbey had come. He was gone. Whatever else happened, it was the end.

➤⬥

Chrissy Fine had thought she knew what tired was, before the baby. She lay down on the floor next to the couch and thought about how she wouldn't get enough sleep, she never got enough sleep, ever. She used to say how tired she was, but that was bullshit, that was nothing. Since Carter had torn his way through her long, dreamy pregnancy, the self-centered moodiness of that whole thing, she hadn't slept more than four hours in a row. For *weeks*, for almost two *months*. Now there was only the baby, feeding the baby, changing the baby, walking in circles with the baby slung across her shoulder, howling into her ear, barfing down her back. Days of slow torture, of getting just enough sleep to keep from screaming all the time and there was no payoff. She only wanted to sleep, and it was the one thing she couldn't have. She did everything with desperate, exhausted intensity, feeding him, rocking him, trying to get him to shut up and sleep, just sleep, he was so, so tired, but he didn't care about her, he didn't know anything, he was a baby. And it got to where she started crying when he woke up, even when he wasn't immediately squalling. Sometimes he just looked at her and she wept, unable to understand how other people did it. There were assloads of single parents, and how did they *do* it, what was she doing wrong? Because most of the time he just cried, his flat face turning red, his tongue quivering, his fists balled by his ears, one tiny arm hitting outward and around in an endless cycle, hit, hit, hit, and she was starting to fear that she'd made a mistake, a bad, bad mistake, the kind you couldn't take back.

She lay on the floor and rocked herself, wondering how she could have wasted so much time, and just as she started to drift, to imagine that the bottle under the couch wasn't more than a day old and that it was actually a sleeping bird, Carter woke up with a long, snuffling grunt and immediately started to bawl.

Chrissy closed her eyes, aching inside. She was scared of Carter; she wanted him to stay asleep, to not wake up and need things from her all the time, every time. She dreaded him.

Carter wailed to wake the dead and choked, a wet, strangling sound. Chrissy sat up immediately and saw by the light of the television that Carter had puked up the bottle he'd fallen asleep with, and it had run down his face and into his mouth, down around his squashed little neck, all over the couch. He was only wearing a cheap onesie, and it was soaked.

"Shit," she said, and sat him up, patting his back with one hand, holding his tiny chest with the other. Warm, reeking formula coursed over her wrist, and then he was just shrieking; she'd blown her only chance for real sleep, maybe for another whole day, because he wouldn't settle down for hours. He was furious, and she'd been so stupid, wanting a single moment for herself.

She picked him up and walked into the bathroom, holding him as far away from her as she could manage as he screamed, beating at the air, kicking wildly with his still-bowed legs, and she nearly tripped over a towel on the floor but then didn't. She caught sight of herself in the mirror, the look of despair on her own face, her bad complexion, her paralyzed eyes. She saw the leaking, howling bundle of need that she'd invited into her life reflected, his cyclic cries beating at her, echoing in the miniscule bathroom that only had a shower that wasn't even sealed properly; Carter's face was crooked and unknown in the mirror, a changeling baby. She saw the roll of her stomach and her flat hair. She was twenty-three but looked forty and felt worse, and this was her life now; this was what she'd chosen for herself.

"It's OK, baby, it's OK," she said, and knelt in front of the shower stall, trying to hold him with one hand while she flipped the plastic tub over. She managed, only getting a little puke on her arm, and got him into the tub.

Carter kicked and squalled, and she reached up to turn on the shower; the head hung down on a long, metal hose, and it was aimed away from Carter, but the water pressure spun it around, spraying both of them with cold water.

"Shh, shh," she said, grabbing the showerhead, holding it, waiting for the water to get warm, while he screamed, the sound her mother had referred to fondly as the newborn cry, a kind of toneless, undulating wail that went on and on. She adjusted the water, leaning against the stall's moldy plastic floor, aiming the pulse of warm water onto Carter's belly, up to his sticky neck. He screamed and screamed.

The tub, a cheap, angled bin shaped like a frog with a foam mat glued to the bottom, was filling up. She reached up and turned off the water once it was to his chest, his flailing legs submerged up to their chubby knees. Sometimes warm water did the trick, but tonight this wasn't the trick, he wasn't having any of it.

She unbuttoned his stained suit and pulled it off him, and he screamed, and she used the wet suit to mop the spit up from around his neck, and he screamed, and she took off his diaper, and he screamed, and she saw that he had a nasty diaper rash in spite of all those changes, the skin around his tiny penis red and raised. She hadn't changed his diaper since…since after lunch, could that be right?

"Carter, baby," she said, and felt tears coming, she was so, so tired, so stupid and tired, and she was doing a shit job, anyway.

He didn't deserve this. She leaned against the thin metal that held the shower door and watched him wail and circle his arm around in the pukey water, and her tears were for both of them. She just wanted to sleep, that was all, just to sleep. She couldn't do this.

The days stretched on forever now that the baby was here. He was exactly eight and a half weeks old, and she couldn't imagine doing this for another day, another second, and there was no choice. She was trapped because she'd gotten pregnant and she'd been twenty-two and full of stupid ideas about raising a baby on her own, because she'd had no real responsibilities and it had sounded like something solid, a goal, something to do.

Carter cried, *aaa, aaa, aaa.* Chrissy cried, hating the sound of him, hating herself for wishing that he hadn't been born, wishing that she would wake up from the dream she'd been living since the day she'd given birth to this screeching stranger, the nightmare of her life.

I should go get the baking soda, she thought. The rash was ugly, but the baking soda was in the kitchen; she couldn't leave him in the tub, even angled like it was. Little babies drowned when they were left alone, even for a second. She'd read it in one of Cindy's old magazines, how people turned their backs for a second and their babies inhaled water and died, just like that, no suffering, no nightmares ahead of them. They were just gone.

I could go with him. Even if she got away with it, she'd never be able to live with the guilt. She wouldn't want to. She could go get the baking soda and the bottle of aspirin, too, and come back and keep the water warm and eat pills until the unthinkable happened and everyone would be better off. Maybe he wouldn't drown. Maybe he'd scream until the neighbors came up, but she'd be gone, she'd be sleeping, and maybe—

Carter peed suddenly, an arc of urine that splashed up and out of the slanted tub, splattering across his tiny nose, droplets landing in his open, gummy mouth. He gagged, startled, and looked at her, his dark-blue eyes seeming to seek hers, his expression comically shocked.

Chrissy stared back at him, and then he started to scream again, outraged, and Chrissy laughed, feeling her wave of hopeless despair give way before a sense of sudden excitement. It was the first time she could remember him actually looking at her, *seeing* her. And it was the first time in a month she hadn't felt alone, totally alone.

I'm his mother, she thought. *I'm Carter's mother.*

"It's OK," she said, and pulled the plug on the little tub. "I'm sorry, baby, I'm so, so sorry."

Water gurgled down the shower drain. She grabbed the towel from behind her and lifted him out of the water, wrapping him snugly, putting him against her shoulder. He leaned into her, resting against her, his cries finally dying down, his tiny fists curled against her shoulder, and she walked him back into the living room and threw a baby blanket over the puke spot on the couch. She bobbed as she walked, speaking softly, letting him hear her voice, and he was calming down, he was actually yawning against her neck, his body a helpless, warm weight.

She decided suddenly she would fess up to her mother about how she was feeling, and how sorry she was about everything, and maybe her mother would help her figure out what to do, to make actual plans. If not, she could call one of her old girlfriends. Leslie would help her. So would Tamara.

I could do that, she thought, marveling at the awareness.

Chrissy doubled the towel up under Carter's bottom and laid him down, curling herself around him at the couch's edge, and she fell asleep watching her son study her face, watching him clutch at her fingers. After a while, Carter fell asleep, too.

CHAPTER

32

A few days after the tragedies, Port Isley's mayor called an impromptu town meeting at the community center. He welcomed representatives from churches and other places of worship and several business owners to his panel of speakers, scheduling the meeting for six o'clock. When it became obvious that the community center, which could easily seat a town basketball game, wasn't going to hold half of the people who'd turned out, Poppy moved everyone to the fairgrounds, suggesting that they all grab some food and reconvene at eight somewhere big enough to accommodate them. No one objected, and word spread.

Better than a thousand people were there by eight, and more continued to arrive. Someone had thought to bring candles, boxes of them, and when Poppy spoke to them about their losses, flickers of light spread across the open field, mostly lost in the gold of the setting sun. People wanted to talk. Dozens of men and women from those who'd gathered stepped up to the stage to ask for help, to say a few words, to share information. A man was missing: Herb Winchell, middle-aged, receding light hair; a slightly hysterical wife held up his picture. Neither Jaden Berney nor Max Reeder had been found, but searches were starting up again, independent of the PIPD or the county. Someone had started a fund for Georgia Duray, a young, pregnant widow whose husband had died in a fall down the stairs; the bank was accepting donations in her name, and there were similar funds set up for the families of the officers and deputies who'd died. The line of people seemed to keep growing, and Poppy stood back and watched, occasionally speaking to his assistant, having him write down reminders of things that needed to be done.

Henry Dawes had stopped by to talk earlier that afternoon, and they'd made some decisions. The council needed to be reformed, a new police chief elected—the remnant of the PIPD was limping along with help from a similarly traumatized county sheriff's office and some mediators from the state, but they weren't prepared for any more emergencies, not as things stood.

Poppy saw and spoke to a lot of people that night. He didn't know if Bob Sayers was among those gathered—he wasn't, in fact—but he thought of the old reporter often as the daylight faded, as the candles re-created the fairgrounds in curving lines of light and more people came, joining a community that they hadn't known they'd needed. What Bob had said, about doing something instead of talking about it. It was nearly fall, the hot weather having peaked, and the summer people were drifting away, many of those who promised to be back not meaning it, afraid of how they'd felt there, afraid of the things they'd done or thought of doing, but Poppy wasn't worried. Port Isley would take a hit, but the seasons would change, as always, and summer would come around again.

The meeting lasted until well after midnight. Poppy stayed until the end.

><

Tommy was on Hemet Nesingwary's latest hunting quest when his mother called up the stairs. The tone of her voice told him that it was time for the talk, which he'd been expecting. School was due to start in a couple of weeks, and his mother had been conspicuously silent about when they were going to leave. Tommy, who'd been extremely good since that night he and Jeff had gone to the carnival, wasn't sure what to expect.

He left *Warcraft* running and headed down the stairs, to where his mother and Aunt Karen and John Hanover all waited in the living room, John's presence hinting at the direction things were going to take. He thought of Jeff, who'd been as frightened and sick as he had after what had happened at the fun house. Tommy thought that he wouldn't mind staying, maybe. Karen wanted it, no doubt, and John had been around a lot lately and had been cool, not really a dick at all. Tommy had been so freaked after the carnival that John's gentle, steadying presence was kind of nice. He was always polite, and super nice to his mother, not in a fakey way. Jeff was a year older than Tommy, but that wasn't a big deal, here; they hung out almost every day now, and he could go here or go to a school where he didn't know anyone, just to be an hour closer to his father and Vanessa.

Maybe they want my opinion, he thought, but looked at their faces and saw that it was already decided, one way or the other. They all looked so serious, afraid at how he would react to whatever they wanted to say.

"Tommy," his mother said, and glanced at John, who looked nervous, and Tommy waited, thinking of what he'd promised so that he could survive in the fun house, about being good to his mother. No matter what she said, he would try to accept it with grace and good humor. He would try to make her proud.

EPILOGUE

They decided to drive to California, to where Chelsea lived with her mother; Amanda suggested it. She thought they could get to know each other a little on the way. The first night, he'd driven and she'd slept, stars passing overhead, their headlights eating the dark, spitting out dotted lines and the hum of the engine. She woke when he pulled into a hotel parking lot, a nice place. He rented a single room with two beds, but after he'd crashed on one of them, she'd curled next to him, sleeping deeply and without dreams in the silent, semisterile quiet of the dark room, pressed against his back. She woke a few hours later and showered and changed, going for breakfast and cigarettes while he slept on.

She sat in the restaurant across the parking lot from the hotel, a chain diner, and ordered pancakes and coffee. The waitress had three kids and a mother with cancer, but she was OK, worried and stressed out but basically OK. Her name tag said "Wendy," but she thought of herself as Dee. Amanda smiled sincerely at her, feeling brave and alive, feeling like the world was different, like she was different in it. She thought of David, asleep, and remembered his arms around her in the early morning, and thought that things might go that way, someday, if she wanted. She might go to school, she thought; he had money, although for the first time in forever, that seemed unimportant. For now, the possibility was one among a billion, and there was nothing to decide, not today.

They were somewhere in Oregon. Maybe they could stop in Portland and she would see Devon...or maybe that was a trip for another day. It was somehow wonderful, not knowing for sure.

Amanda gazed out at the parking lot, the midday sun glinting off car mirrors and into the blue sky. She watched the people go by and listened to her heartbeat and waited for her order to arrive.

ACKNOWLEDGMENTS

This book would not have been possible without the support of my friends and family and the occasional very helpful helper. They are, in no particular order:

The entire Perry clan—Steve, Dianne (love you, Mom!), Dal, Rachel, and all the boys. Special thanks to my father and brother for reading the first draft—as did my good friend (and renowned teacher of kids with ASD, by the way) Sara Vanzee. I'd also like to thank my occasional collaborator Britta Dennison, on general principles.

Big shout-out to my previous editor and all-around awesome dude, Marco Palmieri, for giving me so much work through the years; to my swim friend Karen Berning and her granddaughter, Ashley, and Ashley's friend Brittney, for letting me ask them questions (I hope I spelled your names correctly, girls!); to Jennifer Weltz for agreeing to read my first non-tie-in book; thanks, too, to her editorial advisers, Wes Miller and Laura Biagi, for their excellent suggestions. Thanks to David Pomerico for buying and Christopher Cerasi for editing and the whole Amazon team for listening to me stutter through my first conference call. Also a howdy-ho for supercool Quinn Kaylor-Gaunt for standing by and to Tamara and Leslie for existing...and to my own boys for making me feel things more deeply than I thought a person could stand: Cyrus Jay and Dexter Alexander.

I would like to thank a few of my favorite writers for the inspiration: Stephen King, Dan Simmons, Neil Gaiman, Joe Hill, and Ramsey Campbell. And thanks to my father, Steve Perry, for teaching me how to make a sentence work.

Last but most, I'd like to thank my honey-bunny, Myk Olsen, for watching the boys so I could work and for being my first reader and greatest support. We got together when we were still cool, and we'll be together still when we're old and fat (OK, older and fatter). I love you, Kabuki.

ABOUT THE AUTHOR

S. D. Perry was born in California and grew up in Louisiana and Oregon. The child of a best-selling science-fiction writer, she is the author of more than two dozen movie tie-in novels, her imagination fed by her love of horror movies, zombies, and Victorian ghost stories. She lives in Portland with her husband, children, and two dogs.

Made in the USA
Charleston, SC
06 June 2013